From
Tova + Noso

To

Mom

Sheila Schor

GIVE ME THE MOON

LIBBY LAZEWNIK

GIVE ME THE MOON

A Novel

TARGUM/FELDHEIM

This is a work of fiction. The characters are imaginary; any resemblance to actual people, living or dead, is unintentional.

First published 1996
Copyright © 1996 by Libby Lazewnik
ISBN 1-56871-102-6

Published by:
Targum Press, Inc.
22700 W. Eleven Mile Rd.
Southfield, Mich. 48034

Distributed by:
Feldheim Publishers
200 Airport Executive Park
Nanuet, N.Y. 10954

Distributed in Israel by:
Targum Press Ltd.
POB 43170
Jerusalem 91430

Printed in Israel

DEDICATED

To the memory of my beloved father,

Rabbi Eli Shapiro, zt"l

May his example be a shining light always.

Father: What shall I give you, my child? Chests
of gold, or barrels of silver;
Baskets of jewels for your pleasure?
Child: One single thing is all I ask.
Father, would you grant it?
Father: A humble request! Ask, and it is yours.
What do you wish for, my child?
Child: Only the moon.

Anonymous

PROLOGUE

Avraham Weisner, known to his friends as "Avi" and to his adoring congregants merely as "Rabbi," leaned his elbows on the lectern and gazed out over the throng.

He made an imposing picture up there and knew it — and was annoyed that he knew it. He would have preferred the dignity of unawareness: of his charisma, of his talents, of his power over this expectant audience. But part of Avi Weisner's charm — and perhaps also his flaw — was a certain wry self-consciousness that made a mockery of even his most towering moments. Even now, as he stood before a host of hundreds, everyone agog to drink in his words of wisdom, he was acutely aware of the impression he was making.

What the audience saw, and what Avi Weisner saw in his mind's eye, was a man of medium height and broad shoulders in a good black suit; dark brown hair, newly minted with silver at the edges and mostly hidden beneath a stylish black hat; neatly trimmed beard, two or three shades lighter than the hair; penetrating brown eyes behind gold-rimmed glasses; and a mouth that could be merry but was solemn at the moment, taking itself seriously.

Even as he tried to review in his mind the various points he would be making tonight, he found himself thinking things like, *There's Feinziger in the front row — tape recorder all set to go, as usual. Hope I remember to pitch my voice low.* Recently, he'd been taking elocution lessons from a former operatic tenor-turned-voice teacher. Avi had a tendency to hoarseness, the result of pitching his voice too high when emphasizing a point. Aiming for soaring drama, he would, on occasion, achieve an embarrassing shrillness instead. Mr. Metucci was helping to change all that.

In the big shul, a subdued murmur rose, swelling like the muted roar of an incoming tide. The back rows were filling fast. Each man who entered paused at the wide double doors to stamp the snow off his feet and brush the feathery stuff off his hat brim. The doors stood directly opposite the podium; each time they opened, Avi caught a glimpse of soft-falling white against black velvet. Occasional gusts made the snow dance, but for the most part, it fell slowly, gracefully, hypnotically.

Watching it, the rest of the world fell away. How unearthly the snow looked; how untouched by the pull of the sordid, by the fear and pain that inhabited so much of what the rabbi witnessed daily. Hope seemed to flutter there among the flakes, just as weightless and equally white. How beautiful were the wonders of His creation!

Then the doors swung shut again, locking out the cold, white magic. Avi looked away but found the tall windows framing the same beauty. Irresistibly, the sight brought to mind another winter, long ago, and endless snowy walks together with (though he hadn't known it then, not for several more weeks) his future *kallah*, Malka Chaimowitz. How many years ago now? And how much had happened to them since those first sweet, shy strolls...

He caught himself. There was a time for ambling down memory lane, and this was definitely not it. He couldn't afford the distraction. Tearing his eyes away from the treacherous windows, he looked down instead at the bland, smooth-grained lectern, seeing on its surface, as if in print, the words he would soon be speaking.

His remarkable memory scorned the prop of written notes. Quotes, sources, interesting turns of phrase were at his fingertips after a bare minimum of review. It was a talent that had stymied many a former rebbe in his yeshivah days. As the teachers had soon learned — sometimes to their chagrin, more often with respect — it is a risky business to scold a student for inattention when that student is liable to casually replay the entire lesson, word for word! That same memory was a gold mine when it came to taking tests and, later, conquering the Talmud. From his earliest youth, and without really trying, Avi Weisner had dazzled.

The thing was habit-forming. By his teen years he would not have known how to cope with anything less than the robust homage of his teachers and peers. Admiration became his second shadow. To his credit, he did apply himself, with good result. Hard work honed a natural intelligence into something that bordered on brilliance. The day, nearly twenty years ago now, when he had earned his *semichah*, his rabbinical ordination, had been a fulfillment — and a promise. On one point all who knew him had agreed: Avi Weisner was a young man with a future.

The rabbi smiled out over his people. The future was now.

When there were no more than ten or twenty unoccupied seats in the generous *beis medrash*, the rabbi cleared his throat and smiled. There fell an instant hush. A ripple of anticipation, almost visible, travelled along the rows of dark-suited men. Above, in the balcony, the women shifted in their seats and were still. Pens hovered near notebooks. Fingers poised over record buttons. Rabbi Weisner focused on an anonymous ginger-bearded face in the third row and smiled.

"*Shalom aleichem*, everyone. Good evening. Nice weather we've been having..."

Laughter rose from the rows; it had been snowing and storming more or less steadily all winter long. Avi smiled again, waited a beat, then continued quietly. "If you remember, last week we were talking about..."

There was a clicking of tape recorders and a happy, if muted, shuffling of feet. The *shiur* had begun.

His words rang out in the big room. Each was like the pure note of a bell, beckoning the listener: *Come with me. Share my journey.* It was an intellectual journey, and a spiritual one, and the rabbi knew even without the testimony of their intent faces that they were with him, step for step.

Elation, no less powerful for being familiar, swept through him. It was the euphoria of fine wine, the exaltation of high places. Surveying the sea of faces raised so fixedly to his own, this vibrant oceanful of people — *his* people — Avi had the sensation of being above the world. He might have been straddling a mountain with his head among the clouds. The feeling filled his chest and brought a sparkle to his eyes. Sometimes some of us are lucky enough to recognize, at a particular moment in time, exactly what it is we were born to do. Avi Weisner knew it every week.

The thrill came, not so much from the sense of holding the rapt multitude in the hollow of his hand — though that was part of it — but from the knowledge that he was reaching them with his words of Torah. Avi was a teacher at heart. His greatest satisfaction came from winning wisdom and then sharing the prize with his fellows. But the life of the classroom was not enough. A simple educator's existence would not have satisfied his need for largeness, for breadth, for sheer *scope*. Avi liked doing things on a grand scale. Here, every Thursday night in this vast shul hall (not his own), he had the chance to educate and elevate and inspire en masse.

No wonder he felt as though he were flying like one of the snowflakes on the wind, when, in fact, he was leaning over the lectern and posing a series of incisive questions that made his audience frown and nod their heads and try to think. This, more than any other aspect of his rabbinical calling, was what he most loved to do.

He did it very well. And his people — not only his own congregation, but the many neighborhood *shiur*-goers seeking a weekly talk that would both instruct and challenge — loved him for doing it.

Their love lapped over him as he patiently postulated and explained. This was one of Avi's medium-difficult *shiurim*; not as complex as those he could, and did, offer on occasion, but one, nevertheless, that demanded the listener's close and persistent attention. Now, having set up the building blocks of tonight's thesis, he proceeded — slowly in places, in others with a startling intuitive jump, like the leap of the mountain lion across unknowable chasms — to climb them to their logical conclusion. He pulled his audience up after him. With practiced skill the rabbi brought them to the brink of understanding, felt the exquisite intellectual tension before he coaxed them over the edge. Currents ran their course, from rabbi to students and back again, as if some invisible switch had been pulled: a high-voltage closed system of spiritual electricity. The audience was charged, and they, in turn, charged the teacher.

They were learning something, seeing old familiar facts in entirely new ways. He watched them absorb his essence and be nourished by it. They were enthralled. He was uplifted, a man above himself. His people lent him wings.

One person in that audience, in particular, shared that sense of joyous flight. He was a young boy, no older than fifteen or sixteen, with a head of curly brown hair, thickly lashed brown eyes, and a well-formed nose liberally sprinkled with golden freckles. Yehuda Moses hadn't been in this neighborhood long, but he'd heard enough of this fascinating weekly *shiur* to make him want to see for himself. He'd made sure to come early this evening and had had his pick of empty seats, but with sudden diffidence had chosen to sit near the back of the vast room. His view of the rabbi was consequently a little vague — a figure seen more in outline than actual detail. But vision seemed almost redundant at the moment. Every other sense was submerged in a single one tonight: his capacity to hear.

With all the intensity of his youth and the passion of a newly questing mind, young Yudy listened. He stumbled after each concept that the rabbi threw out like markers on some mysterious trail, sometimes losing his way, at others seizing an idea triumphantly by the tail just before it disappeared from view. Slowly, as the pattern of the speaker's thoughts began to emerge, Yudy began unconsciously to smile. He was caught fast in the talons of intellectual excitement — a new feeling for him.

When had it happened, this change of focus from absorption in the physical to delight in the endless possibilities of the mind? Until just a few months ago, the boy had asked for nothing better from life than a good, solid baseball in one hand and the friendly leather of his mitt snug on the other. Then he'd moved to Brooklyn, changed yeshivos, and discovered — or, rather, rediscovered — the wonder of learning Torah.

As pleased with himself as any new-taught swimmer, Yudy swam the sweet tide of the *shiur*, of thesis and counterthesis, of question and discovery. He strained after the rabbi's words and revelled in the rabbi's presence. If there was a touch of hero worship in his reaction, well, that was only natural. Yudy was young; and Avi Weisner, up on his podium, was certainly, in his way, a heroic figure.

The lives of the two were about to be intertwined in the most unexpected way, like the sudden hurling of a rock into a still pool. Very soon a ripple effect would form, drawing in the lives of those closest and dearest to them. Danger waited to reach out with a clammy finger, as well as its loyal attendants, heartbreak and fear. There was great joy in the wings, too, waiting in its patient way for the cue to step out under the lights.

But that time was not yet come. Right now it was the rabbi who stood in the spotlight, and the boy was still just another face in the crowd.

Avi Weisner had reached his ringing peroration — modulating his voice and inserting frequent pauses between words, as his voice teacher had taught him, for minimum strain on the vocal cords — when his eye chanced to fall on a figure seated in the second row. The young man had brown hair, lighter than the rabbi's, and was still clean-shaven. He was both slimmer and shorter than the speaker at the podium, and his eyes, though the same deep brown, held a more wistful quality. But the greatest difference between them lay not so much in looks as in manner: where the rabbi was confident, with large, expressive gestures — a man at the height of his powers — the younger man was more diffident, less secure. He looked at once hopeful and haunted. He was Mordechai "Mutty" Weisner, the rabbi's son.

Acknowledging the look, Mutty smiled slightly — but only slightly, as if afraid to distract his father in his moment of glory. Avi returned an almost imperceptible nod without breaking the rhythm of his speech. There was something at the back of his mind...something he was trying to grasp in connection with his son.

He remembered. Today was Mutty's twenty-first birthday. Right after the *shiur*, Malka was serving a special, "adults only" dinner for the three of them. It was a momentous point in a young man's life, and there would be much to talk about, away from the curious ears and questions of the younger Weisners.

As he drove home his final point (a part of his mind registering automatically its impact on the intent and admiring host), the rabbi stole another glance at his son. Mutty was listening abstractedly now. He looked miles away, sunk in his own thoughts. It was a familiar look, and one that never failed to exasperate the father. He had hoped that, with maturity, the boy would become more alert. More practical. More down-to-earth...

At this intrusion of human frailty, the wings of inspiration faltered, and the rabbi walked for a moment on two trembling legs. No man is invulnerable; reading his son's face, Avi felt the Achilles' heel of his own anxious tenderness plunge him earthward in a sudden painful swoop.

The next moment, frowning, the rabbi pulled himself back up. He looked away from his son, banishing that train of thought firmly and completely. It was his capacity for compartmentalizing the different portions of his life that was responsible, perhaps more than anything else, for his success. Avi Weisner was nothing if not disciplined.

The rabbi brought his attention back to the thirsty hordes. He said pleasantly, "That's it for tonight. Any questions?"

Arms shot up into the air, waving like stalks in a breeze. This was going to take some time.

Beyond the generous windows, the snow winked and beckoned. Rebelliously, discipline wavered. His momentary surrender to weakness earlier had subtly undermined Avi, robbing him of the tiniest fraction of utter dedication to those he taught. He was tired and hungry, and his own human self clamored for attention.

For just an instant, as he pointed at the first urgent hand, Avi allowed himself to wonder what Malka was serving for dinner.

Part I
HIGH CLOUD

ONE

1

Malka Weisner wiped her hands on the front of her apron, in the same spot that was stained a permanent gray from countless other such hand-wipings, and resisted the desire to taste the soup again.

With some trepidation, the rabbi's wife held the lid aloft and peered inside. Long simmering had melded the vegetables and meat into a thick, almost solid mass. Too long — she'd forgotten to turn off the flame. Though she couldn't remember precisely when she'd set the pot on the stove, she had an uneasy feeling it had been more hours ago than she'd care to think about.

Well, she wouldn't think about it. And she definitely wouldn't tell Avi. What he didn't know wouldn't hurt him. With this comforting thought, she gave in to temptation and ladled out a bit to taste for the fourth time. Yes, it *was* good. Surprisingly so, in fact. Once again, through no merit of her own, the situation had been salvaged. The good old Malka Weisner luck was holding.

The thought, instead of soothing her, put her on edge as she bustled around her big, old-fashioned kitchen, concentrating on putting the last-minute touches to tonight's special dinner. The heavy, wooden cabinets, usually so comforting and maternal, loomed over her now in rebuke, reminding her of the lack of order inside. If the soup had survived her manhandling, it was through no merit of hers. Homemaking, she brooded, should be more than just an exercise in endurance. Why did she have to depend on luck — or rather, as she well knew, God's good will — just to walk the minefield of her own daily life?

Even her children laughed at her domestic ineptness. Or at least one of them did. And perhaps "laughed" was not precisely the word...

"Ma," Hindy had said only that afternoon, in the aggrieved tone that had become dismally familiar ever since the girl had turned thirteen or so, "why can't you be like other *rebbetzins?* I mean, look at Chaya Gitty's mother." Chaya Gitty Rudman was the eldest of a neighboring rabbi's thriving brood and a close school friend of Hindy's. "Rebbetzin Rudman never overstarches her husband's shirts so that they're stiff as a board. She never oversalts the soup and has to throw in potatoes to salvage it. When she says 'jump,' her kids jump! She has at least ten guests at every Shabbos meal, and always —"

"Well, we have lots of guests, too," the mother had interrupted in a desperate bid to break the unflattering flow. "And you'll notice they keep coming back. Hmm...I wonder why that is?"

She didn't really expect an answer, and she didn't get one — unless you counted Hindy's long-suffering sigh. But Malka knew exactly what her daughter meant. She might prepare and hostess lavish Shabbos and holiday feasts, but never with the effortless grace of a Rebbetzin Rudman. Rather, it was with a mixture of eager good intentions and slapdash energy that she threw herself at her domestic duties — and then spent nearly as much time extricating herself from the debris. So far, in a broad, general way, her luck had more or less held. But was this really the way she wanted to spend the rest of her life?

Actually, she thought as she began to virtuously sprinkle Ajax into the sink preparatory to scrubbing it, she knew why Hindy had chosen that particular afternoon to lodge her complaint. The girl was affronted because she hadn't been invited to Mutty's birthday dinner tonight. At nearly sixteen, she considered herself adult enough to be privy to the family's inner council.

"Shani's not going to be there, either," Malka had pointed out.

"Oh, Shani." Hindy's tone dismissed her sister. "She's only twelve. What do you expect?"

"Well, neither will Shmulie."

That argument was weak, as Malka well knew. Hindy treated that observation with the scorn it deserved.

"Shmulie's away at yeshivah, Ma. I'm right here."

Yes, the mother agreed silently; there she was, and all aquiver with righteous indignation. Malka felt tired.

"I'm sorry," she sighed. "Tatty said this should be private."

"Then I'll ask *him*." Hindy was smiling again, sure of her ground when it came to beguiling her father into saying yes.

"No," Malka said firmly. "Tatty's giving the *Shiur* tonight." (The other classes he taught during the week were just classes. In the Weisner home, Thursday night was "the *Shiur*.") "He'll be coming home tired and hungry."

"But Ma —"

"No."

Things don't really change, Malka thought, watching her oldest daughter flounce from the kitchen. It had been "I'll ask Tatty" when Hindy was four, and it was the same today. Always it was Malka who had to be the bad one, the naysayer. It was almost funny: in bald fact, she was much softer-hearted than her husband. Her no's were really his, the mother only acting as the father's mouthpiece. But Hindy didn't know that, or didn't want to believe it.

Fifteen. It was a tender age, a difficult age. Hindy was confident one moment, insecure the next; beautiful in her good moods, hideous when roused to anger. She could discuss world events with an insightfulness that took her mother's breath away, and the next minute stamp her foot like an irate four-year-old. The description was one that fit many teenagers, but Malka felt (with some justice, despite motherly pride) that Hindy had something extra. She combined the best that was in each of her parents, and some of the worst as well. But Malka believed — wanted very much to believe — that the latter traits would disappear in time, or at least diminish in their intensity. Those things weren't the "real" Hindy.

The real Hindy was a witch's brew of moods, an all-knowing seer, and a magnet for experience — the newer, the better. The real Hindy aggravated her, perplexed her, drove her to the brink of madness. The real Hindy was wonderful.

"Don't worry about her, Ma," Mutty would soothe her when Malka confided her Hindy troubles. "She'll grow out of it. Look at me." Remembering, Malka smiled. Yes, Mutty had grown up very nicely.

She paused with her hands in the sink, suddenly struck by the implications of tonight's dinner. Perhaps all her musings, these idle wanderings into the past, had been no more than a device with which to distract herself from the fact that Mutty, her firstborn, had turned twenty-one years old today.

The fact bordered on the incredible. Years ago, when the children would ask her how old she was, she'd lightly reply, as a matter of course, "I'm over twenty-one." It was an age that spelled maturity. It defined the irrevocable end of childhood. Malka had no illusions about her own claims to youth, but her children were another matter entirely. They might grow older, but they were children still!

Something had happened, though — an amazing thing. Somehow, at some sinister but unnoticed point in the hectic stream of her life, a red line had been crossed. Her Mutty could no longer, by any definition, be called a child.

But Malka still felt very much the mother.

Abandoning the sink with a pang that was part guilt, part relief, she stooped to observe her reflection in the toaster's gleaming surface. It was gleaming because Anna, her new Russian cleaning woman, had been there only yesterday morning. In a whisper, Malka confided to the toaster, "I turned forty this year."

The machine was indifferent. Perhaps it was the distorting effect of the metal, but her face seemed rounder than usual tonight. Malka's soft brown wig had ridden up slightly on her forehead, giving her the look of a small girl with short bangs. Her eyes were light brown, too, and arresting, if she could only have known it: rich, warm, full of life and love and laughter. When she was happy, the eyes shone with appealing, golden lights. Just now, though, they were clouded with dissatisfaction.

Disconsolately she murmured to her reflection, "Meet Malka Weisner: incompetent, overweight, and basically over the hill." She straightened with a sad little jerk. "The Rebbetzin. Hah!"

There was a clatter at the door. Her two youngest came into the room, drawn by the aroma of soup and baking chicken. The boys were barefoot, clad in matching, blue-striped pajamas. Chaim, at six, was some three inches taller than Tzvi, a year and a half younger. Both had the fair Weisner coloring, their mother's big brown eyes, and winsome smiles. The smiles were in evidence now. "Ma, we're hungry."

"Chaim, Tzviki, you had your dinner hours ago. Why aren't you in bed?"

But even as she spoke, she was enfolding the little boys in her large, warm embrace. They submitted for a moment, then wriggled out to sniff at the stove like a pair of puppies.

"That's right," said Chaim. "It was hours ago. We got hungry again, see?"

"I'm so hungry, I can't sleep," Tzvi moaned, pathetically clutching his stomach.

"Oh, you boys give me no peace. Here." Quickly, guiltily, she sliced a chunk of the chocolate cake that was sitting uncovered on the counter. "Don't show anyone."

"Thanks, Ma!" The cake was crammed into their mouths even before they were out the door. With chocolatey smiles, the boys scampered out again, trailing dark crumbs over her almost-clean floor.

Malka smiled, too. The encounter had lifted her spirits. She cut a third slice of cake for herself and, with a glance at the kitchen clock, decided she just had time for a quick cup of tea to go with it before Avi and Mutty came home.

2

The crowd around the rabbi had noticeably thinned. It was the diehards, the core group of Weisner devotees, who remained, milling around the speaker at the podium like moths around a source of light. They raised difficult points in connection with the talk he had just given, basking in the focused attention as he answered them. Rabbi Weisner had only to look at you and you felt you were the most important person in the world — for the moment, at least. It was part of the charisma that had led to his immense popularity.

But these were no fools to be swayed by a charming smile, a gregarious manner. It was his mind they respected — that still-brilliant memory and the intelligence that could slice like a knife through the most complex subject. People had said it when he was a young man, and they were saying it now of Rabbi Weisner at forty-two: The man had a *head!*

When he had his father's ear for a discreet moment between questions, Mutty whispered, "Ta, Ma's waiting for us."

The rabbi looked blank. Then, quickly, he recovered himself.

"Sorry, everyone, it's getting late. Let's discuss this some more next week, all right?"

There was a murmur of disappointment, of assent. The knot of people slowly dispersed. Mutty found his father's coat and trailed him to the big double doors with their intricate patterns carved in wood. On either side of the rabbi walked a couple of wealthy *balebatim*, businessmen who worshipped in his shul and supported it generously. Snippets of their conversation drifted back to Mutty:

"...continue our discussion... new shul building. It's time we got started on that already, no?"

"...a dinner, or maybe a major mailing...at least half a million..."

They reached the doors. At the threshold, a gust of cold air skirmished with the overheated room. Mutty shivered. The men stepped out and paused on the broad doorstep, taking their leave, fast-chilling fingers plunged deep in the pockets of their overcoats. Mutty lingered to one side, waiting for his father.

With startling abruptness, a figure materialized out of the snowy darkness and stepped up to the rabbi.

It was a moment before Mutty placed the man: Yankel Bruin, a member of his father's congregation. He was a short, graying man of indeterminate age, with narrow shoulders and an incongruous paunch. Close-set eyes gleamed nervously in the yellow light from the street lamp. A long, bluish shadow hovered grotesquely over the snow behind.

"Excuse me, Rabbi." The short dash from his car at the curb had left Bruin breathless. "I missed the beginning of the *shiur* and didn't want to come late and disturb everyone."

"You've been waiting out here all this time?" The rabbi was astonished.

Bruin nodded. "I have something I need to speak to you about, Rabbi. Something important. I need your advice."

In all the years of their association — nearly eight, since Avi had taken on the congregation — this was the first time Bruin had ever approached him about anything more personal than a question of shul procedure. Smiling, the rabbi said, "Of course, Yankel. I'll be glad to help. I have to check my book at home. Why don't you call me for an appointment?"

For a moment, Bruin seemed disappointed. Had he really, Mutty wondered, expected the rabbi to sit down with him that very minute?

Then, "Thank you," Bruin said. "I'll call you later tonight, if that's all right. Or is it too late?"

"No, no, you can call. I'll be home."

Mutty, standing in the shadows behind, wondered if his father had forgotten about his birthday. A small part of him wished that were so. A pleasant dinner at home was something to look forward to; tonight's special event loomed ominously. Just the thought of what lay ahead of him in the next hour or two caused his heart to sink like one of his mother's sponge cakes.

There was a good reason for his distress. On the table tonight, along with

Malka's loving but uneven cooking, would be his, Mutty's, future.

Such discussions, he uneasily suspected, lend themselves all too readily to comparisons with the past. When his father turned twenty-one, he was nearing completion of his *semichah* program and earning a dazzling name for himself at the world-famous Lakewood Yeshivah.

Mutty also learned in Lakewood, and now he, too, was twenty-one — but there, he was afraid, the resemblance ended.

The rabbi's son, poised on the glorious threshold of life, hunched more deeply into his overcoat and sighed like an old, old man.

≈ও

"Well!" Avi said, reaching for the ignition. He was in the expansive mood that always enveloped him after one of his public addresses. "That's that. I thought it went pretty well tonight, hm? I wonder what your mother has for dinner. I'm starved! What about you?"

Mutty roused himself. "Sure am. I could eat a house. Even that gargoyle on the corner." The big, ostentatious corner house was a standing joke with the Weisners, being the antithesis of their own home and, in their minority opinion, something of an eyesore.

The father chuckled. "You must really be in a bad way."

Avi had already brushed most of the snow off the windshield from the outside. Now he switched on the wipers to keep it clear. The snow had strengthened. Avi concentrated on driving; it was no easy task steering the aging machine through the ever-dropping curtain of white. The sky beyond the snow was an eerie orangey gray. Beneath its pale, lowering expanse, the city streets — with their endless capacity for discovery, for adventure, for violence — seemed to constrict. The world ended three feet beyond his windshield. It was a disconcerting feeling, like moving about on a stage and knowing that one step too many would bring him hurtling over the edge into a different reality. The illusion made him curiously nervous.

When a red light allowed him to relax, he flexed his fingers. "Miserable night for driving. Well, we're nearly there now."

"Home," Mutty said inconsequentially, "sweet home."

"Hm." Avi glanced at his son out of the corner of his eye. "Oh, and Mutty?"

"Yes, Ta?"

"Happy birthday."

Soon Avi was gratefully easing the car into a parking space directly across the street from the broad, unassuming, stucco-and-brick, two-story house the Weisners called home. A square of gravel and some scraggly, clipped hedges took the place of the garden Malka had always wanted but never had the time to tend. Right now, both gravel and hedges were thinly but solidly white. The wind had dropped, leaving the snow-muffled street very still. The noise of their slamming car doors seemed overly loud in the hush, like the crack of rifles. Mutty took a deep swallow of air, exhilarating as champagne. At that moment, he would have given anything, paid any price, to be able to get into his own decrepit Chevy and drive away, back to Lakewood, to his yeshivah and his room and the comfort of his dreams.

Avi hurried across the street, head down against the bite of the wind. Mutty was cold, too, but his step lagged behind his father's. The *rebbetzin* had the front door open the instant they reached it, as though she'd been waiting for them — as, indeed, she had.

From the depths of the house came the smell of baked chicken, slightly burnt potatoes, and something — some sort of soup, Avi thought — that had been left to cook just a little too long.

"Welcome home," beamed Malka. "Dinner's all ready."

"Can't wait." The rabbi smiled, too. "We're in a bad way. Mutty here was talking about eating houses." Still on the doorstep, he brushed some snow off his coat and bent to remove his galoshes.

He had just stepped inside when the phone in the kitchen started to ring.

3

"Oh, let's not answer it," Malka said impulsively. "You're hungry."

The rabbi's conscience wasn't so easygoing.

"That could be Yankel Bruin. Quick work."

He began crossing the room, galoshes in hand, but his wife shooed him back. "Oh, take off your coat and hat, Avi. They're dripping all over the hall. I'll get it." She scurried to the kitchen.

"Ta, look. Here's a letter from Aunt Esther." Mutty held out an airmail envelope with an Israeli stamp in the corner. It was unopened. Avi took it, wondering why Malka hadn't read his sister's letter yet. She was usually eager to rip into such mail and catch up on all the family news from across the world. Divesting himself of coat and hat, he strolled into the kitchen, a thoughtful forefinger inserted into the envelope to slit it open. Malka was still on the phone, chattering with more than ordinary animation. Discarding the letter, Avi planted himself in front of the phone and mouthed, "Is it him? Yankel Bruin?"

Smiling, she shook her head and continued talking.

"Really? That's amazing. It's snowing again over here... Oh, we're all fine, just fine, *baruch Hashem*. Did you know that today's Mutty's birthday? He's twenty-one. Can you believe it?... Yes, I'll put him on in a minute. I'm sure you want to say hello to Avi first."

Curiosity made Avi impatient. "Who —?"

She covered the receiver and held it out, her smile broadening. "See if you can recognize the voice."

"I gather," he said drily, "that's it's not Bruin." Into the receiver, he spoke a cautious, "Hello?"

"Well, well, the illustrious rabbi himself. *Shalom aleichem*, Avi! How've you been?" When Avi didn't answer immediately, the voice continued. "You do know who this is, don't you?"

Avi tried to speak, swallowed, then tried again. "Sure. Sorry, I'm a bit hoarse — just finished giving a *shiur*." Conscious of his wife listening, he continued quietly, "Hello, Binyomin. It's been a long time."

"Yes," said the other, quiet now, too. "Too long. How are the kids?"

The question was perfunctory; he had already covered that with Malka. Avi dispatched his six children with a quick, *"Baruch Hashem."* He waited.

"Well, Avi, I've got some news."

"Yes?"

"I've been kicking this around for a while now, and I've finally decided." His wide courtroom experience had made Binyomin a master at prolonging suspense.

"Decided what?"

"What I should have done, probably, years ago. Well, that's water under the bridge now. The important thing is that the die has been cast. I'm going to do it."

"What do you mean?"

"Avi, I'm coming back."

The rabbi closed his eyes. His first cowardly reaction was to feign incomprehension. "What — another vacation?"

"No, not this time. I've been offered a job in New York, with a very good law firm. I guess you could say they made me an offer I couldn't refuse."

Avi forced himself to breathe again. When he spoke, he was amazed at how natural he sounded. "Good enough to tear you away from sunny California?"

A chuckle. "You're forgetting the other side of the picture. Earthquakes aren't exactly my cup of tea."

"What? Don't tell me big, bad Binyomin is actually afraid."

"Big, bad Binyomin is sometimes afraid of his own shadow."

"Are you thinking of this as a...permanent move?"

"As permanent as anything can be in this impermanent world of ours."

There was a short, awkward silence. Binyomin broke it.

"There are other considerations, Avi."

"Other —?"

"There's more going on in New York...for me."

"Oh." Avi collected himself. Heartily, he said, "You could be right about that. Malka and I will certainly do our best to help. Hey, this will be great! So when are you flying in?"

The conversation took a practical turn. Presently Mutty was summoned to the phone to accept birthday wishes from his father's old friend. Malka was eyeing Avi curiously as he took back the receiver to say goodbye. Her canny instinct for human drama had picked up a scent. His long familiarity with her made him aware of it.

He hung up, thinking, *I can't tell her now. Not after keeping it to myself this long.*

Without ever analyzing it, some part of Avi Weisner was aware that he depended a great deal on his wife's full and unwavering respect. He couldn't risk losing that.

No, he wouldn't tell her.

છ•✑

The first part of Mutty's birthday dinner, then, revolved around his father's longtime friend, Binyomin Hirsch, and Binyomin's startling news. As they spooned up the thick, viscous, surprisingly tasty soup, the three speculated on Binyomin's planned move back to the city that had birthed him, raised him, seen him grow to man's stature — and then spewed him out on the wings of heartbreak.

Binyomin had moved as far away as he could get from New York, eventually settling in Los Angeles and into a rocketing career as a criminal trial lawyer. His visits back East had been sporadic and infrequent, but the Weisner children looked forward to them eagerly: "Uncle" Binyomin was a family favorite.

As for Avi, Binyomin was a constant thorn in his side, a painful reminder of one of the few — very few — times when he had been found lacking.

Avi's work in the rabbinate had been touched with the golden wand of success; so much so that failures, however small, rankled all out of proportion. It made his heart ache — and, to be honest, also galled his pride — that his oldest and closest friend must be counted, despite the spectacular career, among the rank of his nonsuccesses. To the extent that Binyomin Hirsch's life had failed, Avi Weisner considered himself responsible.

It was a secret responsibility. No one but Binyomin himself had any idea of the part Avi had played in the old drama, and it was an open question whether even Binyomin really remembered it any longer. The secrecy provided a balm to the rabbi's pride while heaping hot coals on the flames of a very private shame.

It wasn't until the soup had been cleared away and Malka was dishing out the chicken and potatoes that the evening's real agenda was called to the table.

"So, Mutty," his father began, "you're twenty-one. *Mazel tov.*"

"Thanks, Ta."

In a burst of sentimentality, Malka had produced a pair of candlesticks and switched off the bright, cold ceiling lights. During the course of the meal, the wax had melted in strange, knobbly shapes all down the candles. The mellow golden light, Mutty thought, lent an air of unreality to the scene. Under cover of the dimness, he nervously twisted his napkin.

"Twenty-one," continued Avi, "hardly means anything these days. After all, you kids get to vote at the infantile age of eighteen. But once upon a time it was a milestone. In my mind, it still is one."

Mutty reached over to fork a chicken leg onto his plate. He had not the smallest desire to eat it. "Funny, I don't feel much different from yesterday."

"Birthdays are like that, aren't they?" bubbled Malka in a valiant attempt to ease her son's obvious discomfiture. "I mean, look at me. I was so psyched up for my fortieth birthday that I actually lost ten pounds just worrying about it! And then it was over, and I was the same old me. Notice the stress on the *old*, ha ha. I even managed to gain back those ten pounds! If that doesn't say something, what does?"

"It might say something about your long addiction to chocolate," her husband remarked mildly. "But let's get back to Mutty, okay?"

Mother and son exchanged a look that was almost conspiratorial. The look said, without words, *It's got to be faced.* While the mother didn't really know what was putting that strained look on Mutty's face, her heart went out in sympathy to him. She gave a tiny shrug and subsided.

"It's time we began thinking about *shidduchim*," Avi said briskly.

Mutty jumped. "Er, I guess so."

"Are you interested? Do you feel ready?" Malka asked.

"Of course I'm interested. Who wouldn't be? As for feeling ready..." Mutty suddenly broke out in the boyish grin that transformed his serious face and lit it with a ray of his father's charm. "I don't know if I ever will be. But I guess the only way to find out is to take the plunge."

"Fine!" Avi leaned back in his chair, smiling. "Your mother and I will get the word out. We're not exactly experienced at this sort of thing, but we're fast learners. Eh, Malka?" There was a trace of uncertainty mixed in with the bravado, a vulnerability that was strangely endearing because it was so unexpected.

She beamed. "I've got a whole list of people to call. Don't worry, Mutty. We'll find Miss Right for you."

The son took a deep breath. "I'm not worried." *Not about that.*

"Okay. Next." Avi was on firmer ground now and businesslike. He might have been heading one of his shul committee meetings instead of enjoying an intimate dinner with his family. "It says that a father is obligated, not only to find his son a wife, but also to teach him a trade. You're doing well at Lakewood, Mutty. There's no reason why you shouldn't continue to learn full-time for a few more years. But what do you have in mind for afterwards? Do you want to get your *semichah*?" Without waiting for a reply, he hurried on enthusiastically. "The way I see it, you could probably find a good *shteller* out of town somewhere to begin with. I've got the connections to help you start looking when the time is ripe. Eventually you could come back to New York, with some solid experience behind you, to make a name for yourself here." He laughed. The laughter held some embarrassment under the gaiety. "Want to hear my fantasy? One day I retire, and you take over the *shteller* here. Father to son — the Weisner dynasty, eh?" He laughed again.

Mutty was unnerved. Despite the laughter, it was painfully obvious that his father was in deadly earnest. This was no fantasy, lightly tossed off and as lightly forgotten, but a long-cherished master plan for Mutty's future, encompassing all the dreams his rabbi father held most dear.

"Well, I don't know," he said slowly. His voice, in his own ears, sounded thick and remote, as if coming through a fog.

"Hm? What do you mean? Tell me, Mutty."

"You want me to do...what you did." The words were like syrup, slow and clogged.

"What?" Avi was startled. "I didn't say that. Of course, you're free to be, to do, whatever you want. And the part about taking over the shul one day — well, you don't have to take that seriously right now. It's a long way off." He paused, eyeing his son. "Let's start at the beginning. Are you interested in learning for *semichah*?"

"I guess so." Mutty realized he was shredding his napkin into confetti all over the chicken leg and shards of potato congealing on his plate. Carefully, as if his life depended on it, he placed the remaining fragment of napkin on the side of his plate and looked up.

"I wouldn't mind having *semichah*, Ta, but not necessarily in order to get a *shteller*."

"What? Why not?"

"I don't think I'm cut out to be a rabbi."

It was on the tip of Avi's tongue to snap, "Nonsense!" but something — the misery in his son's face, perhaps — stopped him. Instead, he said quietly, "Actually, I think you'd make a pretty good rabbi. You're a good learner and a good listener. You've got brains and, more important, common sense."

"I'm just not a leader."

"Not everyone can be like Tatty," his mother said, imploring him with her eyes to understand, to give in. "And you don't have to be. You can be fine rabbi anyway, Mutty. I really believe that."

He smiled his thanks, but his eyes were on his father. "I'm no public speaker, Ta. I don't pretend to be. I'm okay at learning, but let's face it — a mover and shaker I'm not!" He continued smiling as he said it, as if the fact did not distress him much. Strangely, Avi believed that. But there was definitely something preying on Mutty's mind.

"What is it?" Avi asked urgently, leaning forward so that the candlelight captured his glasses and burnished them. "What's on your mind, Mutty?"

The younger man was silent.

Malka asked, "Do you have any ideas of your own about what you want to do?"

The son turned to her. "As a matter of fact, Ma, I do."

"Suppose you tell us." The command, insistent for all its gentleness, came from the father.

Gathering his courage by the armfuls, Mutty told them.

"A *carpenter*? That's my son's lofty ambition — to make bookcases and cabinets?"

Avi tore off one of his shoes and flung it down in disgust on the living-room carpet. A moment later, the other followed. Absently, Malka kicked off her own shoes and perched on the arm of the couch. Behind them, in the kitchen, the candles guttered and died. Mutty had already risen from the table and gone up to his room.

Malka said, "Well, you have to admit, he's always been clever with his hands."

"And I'm good at the *Times* crossword puzzle," Avi snapped. "But I don't try to do them for a living!"

As if unable to sit still under the weight of his own emotions, he shot up again and began pacing the room. This was no mean feat, as a goodly portion of the floor space was swallowed up by furniture. Overstuffed armchairs, the large, sectional couch — comfortable but threadbare, like most of the rambling house — and a coffee table piled high with fat books and children's toys in various states of disrepair.

"Where's the boy's ambition? Where's his dignity? He's the son of a rabbi, grandson of another. Doesn't he want to use his mind instead of earning his living as a common laborer?" He flapped his arms as he stalked around, so that he resembled nothing so much as some species of gigantic, exotic, and highly outraged bird. Malka stifled the urge to giggle. She always got that way when things became difficult.

Avi turned. The peculiar light in her husband's eye rapidly did away with any compulsion toward mirth. She stood up, clasping her hands like a supplicant.

"He wants to learn, Avi. That will always be his main focus. He only said he has no interest in a *shteller*, that's all. When the time comes for him to support a family, he said he'd like to do it by designing and building bookcases and things. He said —"

"I heard what he said!"

She bit her lip.

He softened. "I'm sorry, Malka. I'm letting it out on you. But I'm just so...disappointed." His shoulders sagged. The youthful rabbi looked suddenly every day his age. He sank wearily onto the couch and brought a hand to his eyes. "You raise a kid, give him everything that's in your power to give, and then, just when you might expect to start *shepping* a little *nachas*, what do you find? That the boy you raised has no more sense of self-worth than a baby!" He shook his head and amended bitterly, "Less."

"Avi, please..."

Avi lowered his hand. The face he showed Malka bore such a fever of raw pain that she had to force herself not to shrink back, as if from a scorching flame. "To think of my son — *my son* — pounding a hammer for a living!"

"Avi," she whispered. "Why does it matter so much? He's still our Mutty. Nothing has changed."

"That's where you're mistaken." His tone was suddenly very dry and very hard. "Everything has changed."

"Avi —"

He shook his head, despair and a kind of wonder intermingled. "I was ready to give him the moon...and he wants a pebble instead." He struggled to his feet. "I'm sorry," he repeated softly. "It's been a long day."

She watched him walk, slowly but with a firm, unyielding tread, to the stairs. Before he was halfway there, tears had blurred the image, so that she could no longer tell whether it was her husband of twenty-two years who was climbing, or a total stranger.

TWO

1

The letter Esther Markovich of Jerusalem had written to her brother and sister-in-law in New York lay unread for nearly a week.

This came about through no fault of Malka Weisner's — and yet, in a way, it was very much her fault. Her husband, it will be remembered, had carried the letter into the kitchen on the night of Mutty's ill-fated birthday dinner to answer the summons of the phone. In the course of his conversation with Binyomin Hirsch, he'd let the letter fall onto the cluttered counter. There it lay peacefully for six days. The *rebbetzin*'s housekeeping skills being what they were, it was nothing short of a miracle that the letter was unearthed even then.

Malka typically waited until her cleaning woman's arrival each week to exert herself to the much-delayed chores that awaited her. Today, in advance of Anna's onslaught, she'd decided to tackle the kitchen. She paused at the threshold, surveying the battleground. She didn't much like what she saw.

The table was decorated with all sorts of flotsam that had nothing in the world to do with dining, and the color of the cluttered countertops had long ago become a well-kept secret. Her method of clearing surfaces between the sporadic major campaigns was to sweep up great armfuls of *things* and shove them all into a corner, to be sorted through "when I have the chance." Her chance, after that disastrous dinner, had not come about until today, Wednesday of the following week.

The *rebbetzin* strode purposefully into the room, determined to set at least this one modest corner of her life in order.

Assuming the martyred expression with which she was in the habit of attacking her household chores, Malka transferred a messy stack of papers and envelopes from the counter to the kitchen table (ruthlessly shoving aside the odds and ends on the table in order to do so), prepared coffee, and sat down to try and impose — or, at the very least, to decipher — some sort of method in the madness. Almost at once, with a guilty start, she recognized the pale blue airmail envelope with "Family Weisner" emblazoned in the center in her sister-in-law's handwriting.

The envelope had been partially slit open, but the letter was still folded neatly inside, clearly undisturbed. She wrinkled her brow. When had it arrived? And how had it come to be buried on her kitchen counter, unread?

Slowly, like weary divers emerging from the deep, the memories dragged themselves up into the light: the letter's arrival the week before and the reason Malka had left it unread. All too vividly, she recalled the malaise that had gripped her that Thursday (to be honest, it had not quite departed even now) and which had left her feeling old, overweight, and underequipped to cope with the monumental trivia of her life. She remembered the *swish-clump* of the day's mail falling through the slot in the front door, and the way she'd eagerly abandoned her desultory Shabbos preparations in her hurry to retrieve it. The mail was an interesting bright spot in her day. It was a breath of the greater world beyond her doors, bearing the scent of mystery and possibility and the unexpected. The mail might bring — oh, anything.

But that day, it had not brought what she needed. A note from some affectionate and equally hopeless friend would have cheered her to no end; a letter from a perfect sister-in-law could only deepen her depression. So she'd put it aside — not without a qualm — to be read "later."

She gazed now at the envelope, until the familiar, tidy writing held her mesmerized. Esther's face rose before her, a handsome one, if molded along prim, rather disapproving lines. Avi's sister was, superficially at least, opposite his wife in every way. Where Malka was openhearted, eager to please, and (generally) cheerful, Esther presented a no-nonsense front, all straight, hard edges. To her, life was black and white; the fuzzy areas that Malka found so intriguing only made her sister-in-law impatient. There was some of the same quality in her Avi, Malka knew, but somehow, in a woman, she found it more intimidating.

To be sure, Esther's businesslike approach to life was a boon in her work. She administered a small but thriving vocational school for religious young women. Girls who finished high school were able to enroll in courses calculated to give them a source of livelihood that would stand them in good stead when they became *kollel* wives. Her extraordinary energy and clearsightedness, unwatered by undue sentimentality, had earned her — though American-born — a respected place in the tight-knit circle of religious Jerusalem women who made a difference in education.

You'd think, Malka sometimes reflected, that her outside work would loosen Esther's ever-firm grip on her household. This was not the case. With less time in which to do her work, Esther merely worked harder. Malka's Flatbush house, like her nondemanding philosophy of life (if you could call something so strikingly under-formulated a philosophy), was mostly gray, fuzzy matter. Dust, chores, hobbies, and people were permitted to accumulate throughout its three sprawling floors in haphazard, and mostly happy, fashion. Esther's Jerusalem apartment, in stark contrast — though probably no less contented a setting — was a model of order and efficiency.

Esther had married young and was already living in Israel when Avi and Malka became engaged. Malka still cringed at the memory of her sister-in-law's forceful correspondence during the engagement period: an airborne instruction manual for the beginning homemaker. While Malka dreamed away the enchanted days, thinking of her Avi and the blissful future they would share, Esther sent along such vital tidbits as the *balebusta*'s need to have no less than two brooms in a home, one for indoors and one for the porch. The virtues of Farberware stainless-steel pots over enamelware were gone into just as thoroughly. Common ground between the two future "sisters" seemed sparse indeed.

Malka had been secretly thankful when Avi's sister, already then a mother of two, could only manage a flying visit to attend the wedding and *sheva berachos* celebrations. But even in those few days, she'd succeeded (though admittedly without intent) in giving Malka a thumping inferiority complex in all matters domestic. The fact that the ensuing years demonstrated only too plainly how much Malka had really needed the advice of those first letters did nothing to endear her sister-in-law to her.

It wasn't really Esther's fault, of course. Still, Malka — who, as a rule, loved having people around her, who embraced one and all with the same uncritical warmth — was not sorry that the Markoviches lived so far away...

She was brought back to the present abruptly by a distant roar: the vacuum cleaner switching on upstairs. Anna was getting on with her work; so must she. With a wry smile, she shook herself free of her trance and turned the envelope over.

A sip of coffee fortified her enough to finish slitting open the flap with a clumsy forefinger. She was too comfortably ensconced to get up for a knife; and the special letter opener Avi had given her had long since gone the way of most small objects in the Weisner household that were not nailed down. The opening words sprang out at her: *Dear Avrumi and Malka.* Esther was the only person, in the family or outside it, who persisted in calling her brother by his old family name, "Avrumi." The letter continued in a friendly, if rather formal, vein.

I hope this letter finds you all well, as we are, b"h.

Dutifully, Esther called the roster of her eight children. Beginning with the youngest, Yoni had just cut his first triumphant tooth; Batya was a star first-grader; Eli had begun to learn *mishnayos*, at which he excelled; Aryeh Leib was beginning to settle down; Tzippy had a solo in the school choir. Next on the list came the twins, Shoshana — known as Shoshie — and Bracha. The news here was more interesting:

Can you believe the twins are eighteen already? They finish seminar (that's the Israeli term for the Bais Yaakov high school) in June, and then the shidduch *game begins. In fact, there's a certain family in Bnei Brak who've*

been putting out "feelers" about the girls (one of them, anyway!) for their son.
He's supposed to be a very good boy... Well, no more on that now. It's still the
dead of winter; time enough to go into details when the time gets closer.

As for our bechor, Moshe Dovid's very happy at the new yeshivah and
learning well, b"h. I hope we marry off the girls before it's time to start with
him!

Zalman is, as ever, hard at work and at his learning. He was recently
asked to check the mezuzos of his former rosh yeshivah — *a signal honor! He*
sends his love.

So how's the winter treating all of you?

Malka reread the letter while absently drinking her cooling coffee. The
Markovich Success Story, she thought irreverently, though not with any real
rancor. She had nothing but respect for Zalman, though she couldn't claim
to know her *sofer stam* brother-in-law very well, and she adored her nephews
and nieces. It wasn't their fault that their mother, with a single word, could
reduce the *rebbetzin* to the status of a naughty seven-year-old. Did everyone,
she wondered, feel that way about their husband's older sisters?

Anna clumped into the room, dragging a bucket and mop. "I clean floor
now, yes?"

Malka hesitated, then struggled to her feet. "Yes." Suppressing a sigh,
she gathered the slipping, sliding mass of papers and returned them,
unsorted, to their countertop nest. Well, she'd tried...

As she left the room to Anna's far from gentle ministrations, she
entertained a quick, painful vision of her sister-in-law's kitchen, as seen
when she and Avi had visited Israel four years before. Immaculate marble
counters, shining stone floors, well-scrubbed table, and superbly gleaming
sinks. Towels stacked in their cabinets in perfect (she'd peeked), even rows.
A pantry in which you could actually find what you needed without emptying
half the thing. Malka had no doubt in the world that Esther, in the middle
of the night or in the heart of an electrical blackout, would have no trouble
laying her hand, not only on the sewing box that sat on an upper shelf of her
closet, but on a specific needle in that sewing box.

Pretending a nonchalance she didn't really feel, Malka shrugged. You didn't judge a person by the state of her closets, after all, *or* her towels. Defiantly she went up to her room to phone her new friend, Adela. Esther's letter went into a pile of paperwork she'd put aside on her bedroom dresser, to be dealt with...later.

2

S ome hours after Malka Weisner forcibly thrust her sister-in-law's perfect household from her mind, Esther Markovich was seated at her own considerably smaller but indubitably spotless kitchen table in faraway Jerusalem, busily taking stock of that household.

Scotch-brite, she wrote in her neat, firm hand. *Ritzpaz floor cleaner. Tomato paste. Flour. Baking powder.*

Her thoughts trotted off on a wayward scent. What kind of cake to bake for Shabbos? The children loved chocolate, but Savta couldn't tolerate the caffeine. Apple cake would suit Savta, but the kids turned up their noses at that. She thought for a minute, then decided: it would have to be both.

Apples, she wrote. *Cocoa.*

Briefly, she played with the idea of concocting a frosting whose recipe had caught her eye the other day. Almost immediately she discarded the notion. Too much trouble for too little dividend: the kids would eat the cake perfectly happily without the frosting. Besides, she'd just remembered that there should be a chocolate cake already in place in the back of her freezer, baked a month ago and just waiting to be thawed and served. One more thing to cross off her endless list. Yes, she'd definitely skip the frosting. No need to give herself extra work.

Esther's approach to her housekeeping was predicated on a simple motto: "More is less" (in contrast to her sister-in-law Malka's time-honored slogan: "Whatever works"). In Esther's view, the more you put into the thing early on in the game, the less work you had to contend with later.

Thus, she never cooked or baked by halves; she did it by doubles, or even triples. Her freezer was filled to bursting with the foil-wrapped parcels she stuffed into it at regular intervals. Soups, cakes, and hearty casseroles marched from freezer to microwave to table with lightning dispatch. General Esther maneuvered her armies well.

Expediency did have its drawbacks. For one thing, it had meant a fairly large investment in kitchen gadgets and appliances when she'd first set up house — not to mention the duplicate brooms, hampers, and garbage receptacles, strategically placed around the apartment to minimize unnecessary trotting back and forth. Her husband, Zalman, watching Esther's domestic maneuvers in the weeks after their wedding, had laughingly called her a one-woman efficiency team, even as he'd privately cringed at the price tag of that efficiency.

Once she had her system in place, however, he stopped laughing. There was no question that the price had been worth it. Every penny returned rich dividends in terms of domestic order. Esther's household ran with the smoothness of a conveyer belt. Theoretically, with a few well-calculated strokes, she could demolish the twin enemies of dirt and clutter and subdue the daily demands of ten hungry stomachs.

What she hadn't calculated on was the enormous gap between theory and practice.

The weak link in this awesome chain of efficiency was the human element, namely, the kids. Esther had not yet found the means, beyond nagging and criticizing and the occasional, well-placed *potch*, to integrate this uncertain human factor into the Eden of efficiency she so longingly envisioned — and which, for a single year until the coming of her first child, she had actually lived.

That paradise was unquestionably a thing of the past. Today there were the twins, nearly eighteen now and in their final year of high school, who with all the good will in the world had little time to help out at home. Moshe was away at yeshivah, and the younger boys, Aryeh Leib and Eli, seemed to regard neatness as the Enemy. Aryeh Leib, in particular, seemed to go almost out of his way to upset Esther's sense of order. Batya, six years old and going on sixty, was aloof from the whole thing, operating, it sometimes seemed, according to some private rule book of her own.

There were exceptions. Tzippy, Esther's third daughter, desired nothing more in life than to be like her mother. With her wavy auburn ponytail and omnipresent smile, she looked much more like her father, and, indeed, she resembled him in temperament as well. But it was Esther she strove to emulate. She cleaned and diapered, swept and baked, all the time casting anxious looks in her mother's direction, hoping to win a smile. But for all Tzippy's good intentions, she was by nature too easygoing to meet her mother's demanding standards. Tzippy would never be more than a lowly lieutenant in Esther's army.

Interestingly, it was Yoni, the baby, who showed the real promise of following in the mother's footsteps. Already, at the age of a year, he had shown himself meticulous in his habits, compulsive in his demands, high-handed when thwarted. When things went according to plan — his plan — he could be sweet as honey. Despite his insistence on having his way, the baby had captivated the hearts of his family — just as Esther herself had captured Zalman's, all those years ago. The other kids had learned about Yoni what Zalman had come to understand about his wife: things went more smoothly if you just did things their way. And, really, was that so hard?

Esther's appearance, like her domestic methods, was a triumph of efficiency over sentimentality. Her clothes were simple, neat, tucked-in, and then forgotten. Her shoes were no-nonsense allies that would carry her anywhere with a minimum of fuss. Her very bones seemed inspired by the same ideal: she was tall and straight-backed, and her brows, like the nose and mouth, were neat, straight lines.

In the quiet, tidy kitchen the mental inventory continued. *Milk*, she wrote. *Margarine*. Did she have enough potatoes? Onions? Dishwashing soap? *Cream cheese*.

Her concentration was shattered by what sounded like an explosion but was actually nothing more dangerous than Eli and Aryeh Leib coming through the front door. In a flash, as if some invisible barometer had plunged to its lower limit, the atmosphere in the apartment went from peaceful to frenetic. Eli's backpack thudded to the floor, closely followed by his older brother's. A vigorous *thwack!* was Aryeh Leib kicking his new soccer ball across the living room. Esther was on her feet in an instant.

"Aryeh Leib, how many times have I told you not to kick that thing indoors? Go outside and play."

"Okay, Ima. In a minute." *Thwack!*

"Aryeh Leib!"

"What?" Bounce, bounce, bounce...*clunk.* "Oops, sorry about that. I'll pick it up."

Esther reached the overturned flowerpot at the same time as her son. "Picking it up is just the first step. What about the dirt all over the floor?"

"Oh, I'll sweep it up, Ima. Soon." He gave the ball another tentative shove with his foot. It hit the lower rim of the couch with a discreet bump.

"Oh, go outside already. I'll clean it up."

A flash of a wide, charming grin, a smattering of freckles on a snub nose, a resounding slam, and he was gone. His mother's belated, "Wash your hands first!" was lost in the noise of his departure.

"Esther?" The querulous voice came from the closed-in balcony, converted three years before into a tiny bedroom. "What was all that noise? It woke me up."

"I'm sorry, it was Aryeh Leib. Try to go back to sleep, Ima." It was a vain hope. Zalman's mother was a notoriously light sleeper. She'd be creaking and shuffling around the apartment half the night now, despite the curtailed nap. The only time she seemed to be able to drop off into a really sound sleep was in the early afternoon, after her lunch — just when the boys came bursting in from school, rippling with surplus energy.

Sighing, Esther went for the broom and dustpan. But two events occurred simultaneously before she could return with them to the scene of the crime: Eli asked for a snack, and the baby, Yoni, woke up wailing.

These days he always seemed to be furious upon facing the world again. It was his teeth, poor thing; they were probably killing him. She'd have to run back to the pharmacist for some more of that ointment. It had seemed to work pretty well the last —

"Esther, can you help me? I want to get up now." Savta was still mobile, *baruch Hashem*, but needed a hand in getting into and out of bed. Depositing the broom and dustpan in the approximate area of the spilled dirt, Esther scooted into the small boxlike space her mother-in-law called home.

"Here you go. Just a little bit more... There."

The elderly woman wobbled on her matchstick-thin legs, clutching her daughter-in-law's arm. Esther gave her a moment to steady herself, handed her the metal cane with an encouraging smile, and slipped away. Yoni was still howling. A new note of panic had joined the sound of generalized misery.

"Here I am. Here I come. Ssshhhh..." She hurried to the back bedroom, the one the boys shared. She just managed to scoop up the baby and change his diaper before the phone rang. Carrying Yoni in her arms — he was very clingy these days, doubtless from the pain, poor dear — she hurried to the kitchen to answer it. Eli, eating his fruit-flavored *leben* at the table, seemed serenely oblivious to the instrument shrilling just inches from his head.

"Hello? Is that Mrs. Markovich? This is Rebbetzin Sandler calling from Bnei Brak."

The ensuing conversation removed Esther, for a few heady minutes, from the world of housework and shopping lists. When she hung up, her expression was bemused and excited. She glanced at the clock. The twins should be home in about an hour. Abandoning the list on her table, she dandled the fretful baby on her knee while drifting into the luxury of an unusual — for her — pastime: daydreaming...

෧•ඏ

The sound of the opening front door told her that Tzippy and Batya had returned from school.

Tzippy sang out, "Hi, Ima, we're home!" The coat closet creaked as her schoolbag was deposited neatly inside.

Then, from the first-grader: "Hey, Ima. What's all this dirt in the middle of the floor?"

Sighing, Esther abandoned her rosy visions and returned to the fray. The time is short, and the work is plentiful... "Batya, put your schoolbag away. Eli, you, too. How many times have I told you it belongs in the closet? And did you put your cup and spoon in the sink? How many times do I have to remind you there are no servants in this house?"

"I'll sweep up the dirt, Ima," Tzippy said quickly.

"Thanks, Tzip. I appreciate it."

Though Tzippy tackled the spilled earth with a will, her work did not pass muster with her mother: the girl had neglected to check under the rug and sofa for stray bits of soil. For the next quarter of an hour Esther industriously pushed dirt, dishes, and kids into their appropriate places. Yoni, a little more contented now, was deposited in a corner with a pile of plastic Duplo blocks, while Eli and Batya had to be coaxed and bullied into taking their places at the dining-room table with their homework. "Try to start it yourself," Esther ordered. "I'll help you if you need it." Twelve-year-old Tzippy, hoping, perhaps, to win the praise her sweeping had not earned, was already hard at work on her own assignments. The mother sank into a chair and gazed sightlessly out the window.

There was supper to think about, and she had to get the shopping done so she could start Shabbos. But before she could shop, she had to finish the list she'd begun — when? Hours ago.

The mornings were peaceful affairs compared to these hectic afternoons with the kids home. Sometimes it felt as if she were running in place. Esther hated when the clock — when Time itself — seemed to conspire against her. And how hard she'd tried, was always trying, to make it her ally! The rigid timetables, the hopeful schedules, the endless lists of "What to Do When"...

She reached for the pile of sewing she'd had to put aside earlier when

Yoni had quite vocally let her know it was time for his nap. The phone call from Bnei Brak swam into her consciousness like a recurring tide. Shoshie and Bracha would be sailing through the door any minute. How to handle this? She felt out of breath, though she'd been sitting still. If only there was time to talk it over with Zalman — a little time to think...

"Esther?" First the cane came into view, then the birdlike figure, very slowly. Savta wore a faded, checked housedress and a white kerchief, slightly askew, on her head. "Don't get up, just tell me — is there any hot water for tea?"

Esther's hands automatically put aside the sewing once more. Her lips curved into an automatic smile as, jack-in-the-box-like, she popped up again. "I'll get it, Ima."

Esther whizzed back into the kitchen. Her feet hurt, but she couldn't let herself stop to feel them. She couldn't stop. There was too much to do. Always too much to do.

The time is short...

3

The twins were late coming home that day. By dint of putting Tzippy in charge of the rest of the gang for a few minutes, Esther managed to squeeze in a lightning visit to the workroom where her husband spent half the hours of the day bent over his parchment and quills.

The converted *machsan*, or storage room, where Zalman worked was located on the subterranean level of the building directly beneath the main lobby. It was a cramped space, airless despite a small window high up in one corner, hot in summer and icy in winter. But it was rent-free, it was conveniently located in the neighborhood — and it was all he could afford.

To say that Zalman Markovich's livelihood as a *sofer stam* (scribe) was precarious was to say a mouthful. Like many struggling *kollelniks*, he was all too familiar with the names and addresses of the city's *gemachs*, or free-loan associations. Each month was a wrestling match between income and expenses, with the latter holding the firm title for years now. His overdraft at the bank was the most impressive figure of his career.

But Zalman wasn't bitter. He had chosen his life and — except for those excruciating few hours each month when the money had to be found to defray the most pressing bills — he revelled in it.

Half of each day he spent in the *beis medrash*, swaying over an enormous Talmud with brain afire and heart utterly at peace. The second half was spent here, in his cluttered, friendly workroom, among his quills and parchments and ancient holy lettering. If one had to put aside Torah learning to make a living, what better way than in writing and checking the sacred scrolls and mezuzos? Zalman was happy.

And Esther, his wife, was content. She was, if anything, even more idealistic than her husband. Curiously, despite her undisputed hold on the practical realities of life, it was the call of the abstract that really drew her. Even as she cooked and baked and laundered and swept, her whole being was caught up in the transcendental value inherent in these mundane acts. She had nothing but pity for the rich and idle, those birds in gilded cages. Forever constrained by her duties, her responsibilities, and financial insecurity, Esther was nevertheless unshackled. She was free — as a maidservant who truly loves her Master is free.

She emerged at the lobby from the scarred, old elevator. It was cold down here. Shivering in her thin cardigan, she hurried down another flight of stairs to the *machsan* level. Time itself seemed to speed her along, propelling her to the door she wanted, guiding her hand in a rapid rat-a-tat on its surface. Soft voices, indistinguishable through the heavy door, broke off at her knock. She called, "Zalman? It's me. Open already."

The door was opened, not by Zalman, but by a young girl in the blue-checked blouse of a Bais Yaakov high-school student. Another girl, similarly attired and identical of face, sat on a stool by the worktable, her lingering smile evidence of the quiet laughter Esther had overheard. The girls had Zalman's handsome, even features and Esther's tall, slim carriage. Both girls wore their thick auburn hair pulled back from their faces in neat half-ponytails over brown eyes that were merry just now.

Esther stared. "Shoshie? Bracha? You're back already? Why didn't you come upstairs?"

They shrugged, a little embarrassed. It was their father who explained mildly, "The girls often stop in for a few minutes on their way home. It's the only time we get to chat a little."

The mother's eyes went round the cozy threesome. Her ears caught the echoes of their laughter, still hanging in the air like an elusive scent. While she had been upstairs, waiting for them, trying to keep up with the million-and-one things that needed to be done, the girls had been down here, chattering away with Zalman! Esther felt a pang of uncharacteristic resentment.

Then, recognizing the absurdity of the feeling, she put it firmly aside. The girls had a right to see their own father once in a while! It was just that they looked, the three of them, so...happy and lively together. Zalman seemed more relaxed than he ever seemed upstairs, and the girls looked — well, the way they looked when they chattered with their own friends. They never appeared quite this lighthearted when they spoke to her...

This thought, too, she put away. The twins were watching her. Shoshie said slowly, a little uncomfortably, "We're sorry, Ima. We just didn't think it would make a difference if we came in a little later than usual. Were you waiting for us?"

"It's okay." The mother waved this, like her own feelings, firmly aside. "It just so happens that I wanted to talk something over with your father. Tzippy's keeping an eye on things upstairs. I can only stay a minute..."

The girls jumped to their feet. "We'll go," Bracha said, beginning to gather her things.

"No, no, stay," Esther commanded, sinking onto the stool Shoshie had vacated. "This concerns you, too. In fact," a slow smile spread over her face, "it concerns you most of all."

"Me?" Bracha was surprised.

"Both of you."

The twins glanced at each other, then at their mother. "What?" they asked in unison.

Esther addressed her husband. "Rebbetzin Sandler called before. From Bnei Brak."

Zalman looked alert. "About...?"

"Yes."

"Ima, Abba, what is it? What's going on?" Shoshie's voice had risen in frustration. Bracha touched her arm and made a wait-and-see gesture. Bracha was always the more patient one.

"She's a *shadchanit*, girls — a matchmaker."

A breathless silence met her words. It seemed to vibrate in the tiny space, forming questions without words. Naturally, the next big step in any Bais Yaakov girl's life — *shidduchim* and marriage — had been discussed before. It was a fascinating topic at the best of times, and with twins to launch simultaneously, the scope of the talks had expanded. Who would be first to go out, and how would the parents decide which boy met which girl?

Shoshie was the elder, by all of five minutes, but Bracha was, perhaps, slightly the more stable. Mirror images of each other physically, they were miles away in temperament. Shoshie was the impetuous one, moody and talented, with large, dark eyes that could flash a thousand messages to the one who knew how to read them. Bracha was like a lake compared to Shoshie's river. Calmer, with unsuspected depths, her eyes — so exactly like her sister's — reflected the watcher and gave him back to himself. The mother looked from one to the other and smiled.

"Rebbetzin Sandler and I first spoke some time ago. She's friendly with a family in Bnei Brak — the Koenigs. A fine family, the father's a *rosh yeshivah*; the mother's been teaching at the Bais Yaakov there for years; and the aunt knew Savta from before the war..."

"Ima," Shoshie squealed. "I'm going crazy! Would you please *tell* us?"

"Okay. I'll tell you. They have a son. His name is Benzion — Benzy, they call him. A fine boy. A good boy. Wonderful *middos*. A real *talmid chacham...*"

"And?" Bracha couldn't wait any longer. She had gone very pale.

"And they want to arrange a *shidduch*."

The girls let out their breaths in a long, synchronized sigh.

"I thought we were waiting till we graduate," murmured Bracha.

Their mother said briskly, "You're eighteen already, and there's no point in waiting for June if a good *shidduch* has been suggested right now. Is there?"

Zalman had already heard the first installment of this drama; in fact, he had been the one to investigate the prospective suitor after the initial phone call from the matchmaker some weeks before. He opened his mouth to say something, but the twins forestalled him.

"Ima, Abba," Shoshie said, clasping her hands together and turning shining eyes on each of her parents in turn, "does this mean...me?" She was, after all, the older twin. She swallowed hard. "Maybe it'd be better to just flip a coin or something."

"Not a very logical way to do things," her father said. He considered. A slow smile spread over his bearded face. "Esther, didn't you mention that the boy plays some sort of instrument?"

"Yes, the clarinet. Not professionally, of course. But he's talented in music. That's for sure."

"Well, then, you've got your answer." Zalman sat back, smiling.

"Me!" Shoshie gasped. She was the musical one in the family, the one who could lose herself at the keyboard of the old, upright piano for hours at a stretch. After graduation, she hoped to enroll in the psychology portion of her mother's school program and eventually become a music therapist.

"Well, why not?" Esther said, suddenly in the grip of a new gaiety, a lighthearted relief at having the decision made. "Why not you?"

"Bracha, you're next," Zalman said quickly. "Don't worry."

"I'm not worried." The color had returned to Bracha's face. "To be honest, I'm glad Shoshie's first. I'd be scared stiff. Aren't you scared, Shosh?"

But her twin didn't hear her. She had the same look she wore when playing her favorite études: rapt, soaring, as if seeing — or hearing — something that none of the others could see or hear. Watching her, Bracha smiled wryly. She didn't ask again.

4

H ey, Mutty," said Fish. "What do you say we go to Israel?"

They were strolling around the perimeter of the big, placid lake that had given Lakewood its name. A half-moon cast its silvery spell over the black waters. Walking mindlessly, as it were, Mutty felt more at peace than he had in a long time. When thoughts turned treacherous, it was best not to think. Hadn't he learned that from Fish himself?

He turned to peer at his friend, trying to judge in the uncertain light whether he'd been serious. "Israel?" he tried. "You're kidding."

"No, I'm not. I've got the midwinter blues, that's all. I need to get up, make a change. Why shouldn't we go learn in Israel?"

"Just for a *zeman*?" Mutty asked doubtfully.

"Just for a *zeman*."

They strolled in silence, while Mutty considered the idea. Thinking out loud, he said, "We could leave after Pesach, in time for the next *zeman*."

"No, we could come back *for* Pesach," Fish corrected him. "Did you think I was talking about waiting around here another two, three months? When I said I wanted to get up and go, I meant now."

"Now."

"Or as close to it as possible. Any problem with that?"

Money would be a problem, but trust Fish not to think of that. Fischel Mann was one of the wealthiest young men at a yeshivah that boasted its share of the monied elite. As a boy, he'd cheerfully and almost systematically flunked nearly every subject in a succession of high schools, but none of those schools, surprisingly, had held a grudge.

"Fischel's no scholar," they told his parents frankly. "Set him up in the business. He's got a good enough head on his shoulders for that — street smarts he's got plenty of. But book learning?" A dismissive gesture, a negative shake of the head, disposed of that option.

Perversely, upon graduation, Fish had turned his back on his father's thriving import-expert business and chose instead — now that he no longer had to — to pursue the "book learning" he'd avoided, more or less successfully, for twelve years. Over his father's protests, he enrolled in a *yeshivah gedolah* in Boro Park and later in Lakewood, at both of which places Fish proceeded to prove that all his former teachers had been absolutely correct.

He had neither the "head" nor the patience for intensive Torah study. He was restless, frivolous, hopeless — and determined. For a year and a half now he'd appeared every morning at his *shtender*, plowing or muddling his way through the day and its portion of learning. Mutty had to admire his persistence.

Others, more cynical, whispered that Fish was only marking time, waiting for the right *shidduch* to come along so he could end this farce. Mutty was one of the few — the very few — who was privileged to know otherwise. Daily he witnessed the depth of his friend's desire to learn how to learn, the dogged drive to snare what had so long eluded him. And only Mutty, in all the world, had seen the tears streaming down Fish's cheeks and heard the broken words, so soft they were almost lost in the crickets' song one Lakewood summer's night: "I can't do it. I'll never do it. They were all right. I'm stupid. Just a stupid, no-good *failure!*"

Socially, Fish was fine. His open, rugged face welcomed companionship. He played a mean basketball game and delivered an excellent joke. He was a good raconteur and a better listener. The circle of Fischel Mann's acquaintances was wide; of his intimate friends, very narrow, indeed. Of these, Mutty Weisner was the closest.

They made an interesting study in contrasts. Where Fish was

lighthearted, Mutty was serious. Where Fish was sturdy, dark, and pleasantly homely, Mutty was slight, fair, and delicately handsome. They were an ill-assorted — and strangely suited — David and Jonathan.

"Israel," Mutty said thoughtfully, as they rounded a curve of the shimmering lake. "It's far enough, anyhow."

"Far enough for what?"

Mutty hesitated. "From my father. My stock's not very high with him these days."

Fish didn't ask for details. That wasn't his way. They walked on in silence, Fish warm in his thick overcoat with the fur collar tickling his chin. Beside him, in his less expensive though perfectly adequate coat, Mutty dragged his feet through a powdering of snow. To distract his companion, Fish asked brightly, "So, Mutty, build anything interesting lately?"

He saw at once, from the expression on the other's face, that he'd said the wrong thing. Unabashed, he grinned. "Oops. What'd I say?"

"Oh, nothing." Mutty felt perversely heartened. Fish had the gift of being able to raise his spirits without even trying. He glanced at Fish sideways, wearing a wicked grin of his own. "I have relatives in Yerushalayim, you know. And Aunt Esther's a great cook."

"That settles it!" Fish yelped. "We're going."

"I'll have to talk to my parents."

Fish said quietly, "Right. I've already got the okay from mine." Then, even more quietly, he added, "Good luck."

Mutty said nothing. He was concentrating on fighting the depression that the mere mention of his parents had brought surging back. All his life he'd tried to be what his father wanted. By and large, he'd succeeded. Now, through an ironic twist of circumstance — or maybe the twist was only the belated recognition of his own personality — he found himself in a no-win situation.

If he followed his own desires and thereby disappointed his father, he'd hate himself. And if he gave in and accepted his father's map for his life, if he followed the dotted line of the route his father had drawn for him, he'd despise himself.

The darkness hid the bitter shrug of his shoulders (he hoped) from Fish. Mutty gazed bleakly out over the lake. He couldn't stand much more of these roller-coaster emotions. Somehow, somewhere, he'd have to locate his center again. Find serenity. He would pray harder, redouble his efforts at communicating his despair to the only One Who could guide him at this impasse.

In the meantime, it helped, he found, to stare at the broad, black expanse of water and switch off his mind completely. The feeling was like the closing of a door.

5

A vi grunted with the effort of heaving the laden shovel over his shoulder. He stood and watched the clumps of flying snow settle into the grayish heap near the curb before turning to stoop again. "A rabbi's work is never done," he muttered. If he expected a sympathetic response, he was disappointed. The snow showed him only its dirty, indifferent cheek.

The snow that had enchanted him on the night of his big *shiur* and continued to fall in fits and starts during most of the ensuing week had, by this Thursday morning, definitely lost its charm. That first smooth, white coat had turned lumpy and bedraggled, like poor-quality wool. Amazing how quickly time — with a little help from the sooty New York air — could wreak its havoc. With a final heave, he disposed of the last mound blocking his front steps and straightened up.

A path lay cleared from his front door to his car. Good enough. Shouldering the shovel, Avi stomped triumphantly up the steps to the house. *Shacharis* had ended nearly an hour before, and the hard, physical work had made him ravenous for his breakfast.

"Malka, I'm home!"

His voice echoed hollowly. She must be in the basement, up to her neck in laundry. Little Tzvi, home from kindergarten with the sniffles, sat at the dining-room table, swinging his legs as he colored a vast purple rhinoceros on the back of an old computer printout.

"Hi, Tzviki."

The boy mumbled, "Hi, Ta," without looking up. A large, nasty-looking horn sprouted on the rhinoceros's nose.

Avi continued in a chatty vein, divesting himself of coat and galoshes. "Had your breakfast yet?"

"Hm?"

"Breakfast. Have you eaten?"

"Yup."

"What'd you have?"

The rhinoceros sprouted a second horn.

"Tzvi."

The tousled, fair head reluctantly rose. "Yes, Ta?"

"I was talking to you."

"Um. What'd you say?"

"I said, what'd you have?"

"Have?"

"For breakfast."

"Oh. Cheerios." The head sprang back down again. Avi watched the rhinoceros grow, under the influence of the purple crayon, to ferocious proportions. So much for meaningful conversation with his offspring.

Stifling a pang of regret — and the image of the other, older son whom he refused to think about — Avi made his way to the kitchen to fix himself some breakfast. Something substantial to fill up the empty spaces.

⧫

Malka joined her husband at the kitchen table. Though she'd already had her breakfast, she nibbled companionably at some toast while they chatted. This was her favorite part of the day. The next hours — often lasting

far into the night — would be devoted to their separate routines. Like racing
cars speeding strictly along their own lanes, in a few minutes their ways
would diverge. She had learned early in the marriage to seize upon their time
together when it came. Gradually, breakfast had become that time. With the
school-age kids out of the house and the little ones sated and content — for
the moment — it was a peaceful hiatus before whatever the day threw at them
next.

Both treasured the simple routines of that meal and the inconsequential
talk that went with it: like a tiny exchange of gifts that meant nothing to
anyone in the world but the two of them.

"Schoenbrunner and Dickstein are coming by the office today," he
remarked, reaching for the marmalade. "About the building fund."

"What building fund?"

"Their question exactly. In their opinion, it's high time to start putting
one together. We have our eye on a lot, if only we can scrape together the
money for the construction."

Malka held up the coffee pot, gesturing silently, "More?" He shook his
head. "When does the drive start, and how long will it last?" she asked.
"Maybe the women can do something."

"All those details need to be worked out. The first thing, I think, will be
to tap some of the old *chevrah*." He was referring to the various figures who
supported him, with varying degrees of anonymity, from behind the scenes.
Men who had initially organized and still ran the Thursday-night *shiur*;
another couple who had dedicated a book he'd written dealing with Torah
perspectives on marriage and parenting; wealthy congregants who helped
out with the present shul's upkeep.

She nodded. "Sounds good. Are you excited?" Before he could answer,
she added, "Pass the butter."

He scraped the container over and turned his attention simultaneously
to Malka's question and to the eggs on his plate. He'd scrambled them
himself: given his wife's haphazard cooking skills, he'd long ago learned the
only sure method of having his breakfast eggs the way he liked them. A

forkful hovered, cooling in the air, while he tried to unravel his feelings. "I do want a building of my own, but sometimes I think about all the really important things we could do with that money. The *hachnasas kallah* fund, the Shabbos packages... Think of how many people we could help with what it'll cost to put up a building!" He looked troubled.

"Avi, lots of people will be helped through the shul, too. Especially the *shiurim*. You know that."

"I know." She had said what he needed to hear, but the troubled expression remained.

Malka leaned forward. "Avi, you're always taking too much responsibility on your shoulders. You do plenty for the community — enough for three men! Leave something over for someone else, eh?"

He had to laugh. Some of the doubt rolled off his shoulders. "I guess you're right."

"The kids would not mind seeing you a little more in the evenings," she said wistfully.

"I'll try to make it back for supper tonight. After the meeting with Dickstein and Schoenbrunner."

"Keep me posted."

"Sure." He reached for a *bentcher* to say the Grace after Meals, while Malka shuffled around, clearing the table. Presently, Avi retrieved his hat and coat, exchanged a smile with his wife, and stepped out through the front door. It was a frigid morning. At the top of the short flight of stairs, he paused abruptly.

Below, the sun raised glassy lights on the sheet of ice that lay on the sidewalk like some weird, upscale linoleum. The glitter was everywhere, hurtful to the eyes. He weighed the benefits of taking out the car again, then decided that the advantages of warmth and relative speed were outweighed by the dangers of skidding on that treacherous ice. Regarding the sheathed walk dubiously, he took the steps with care, one at a time.

The rabbi's wife, his children, and even his ambitions, passed out of his knowledge the moment he turned his back on the house and set off —

cautiously, step by slippery step — to shul. Avi smiled, his heart fully in the day ahead.

He smiled again some twenty minutes later, this time at the four walls of his small office. It was entered through a door leading off the main office, which was itself situated to the right of the main shul hall. He was grateful, after the difficult walk, to accept the warm welcome of his sanctum. This, more than any other, was his place, the physical symbol of his achievement.

Here he conducted shul business, dealing with the myriad problems, great and small, that cropped up from one Shabbos to the next. Here, too, he met with those members of his congregation who were troubled, in need of sound Torah guidance, a bit of caring advice. Lining the walls on either side of the desk were the *sefarim* he used in preparing his classes and talks, their gilt-lettered covers familiar to him as the faces of his own children.

This morning, he went over some accounts with his longtime bookkeeper, Mrs. Gerber, before his first appointment. At 9:55 she gathered her ledgers and made her stiff-backed exit to the outer office, her own domain. At precisely 10 A.M., the rabbi greeted a pair of newlyweds who, stammering in embarrassed confusion, pleaded for his help in resolving a problem of *shalom bayis*.

The difficulty that weighed so heavily on the young couple's shoulders seemed to Avi — longtime husband and experienced counselor — a trivial, almost laughable, matter. But he didn't laugh.

"Sima, you have to understand something. Men are not like women. And, more specifically, Leib is not like you nor you like him."

The young wife looked startled, even dismayed. Hesitantly, she smiled. "I know that. But —"

"Do you?" Avi's voice was solemn, but the twinkle in his eye put her at ease. "Let me ask you a question. If it was time to cook dinner, and there was a fascinating book on the weekly *sidrah* waiting to be read, which would you do first?"

"Uh, I guess cook dinner. I wouldn't want Leib to come home hungry and find nothing ready..."

"Exactly! The intellectual stimulation of the *sefer* would take a back seat. You want to please your husband, to feed him and to take care of him. Right?"

Sima nodded. Leib looked interested, if slightly embarrassed. The rabbi turned to him next.

"Now, then, let's move to Leib. If *you* had the choice of learning a new *sugya* or, say, eating in a new kosher Chinese place, which would you choose?"

Leib thought. "I like Chinese food, but I guess I'd want to go after I finished learning. It...it would feel more satisfying that way." He lifted his eyes to the rabbi's, half-defiant, half-puppylike, yearning for approval. Avi rewarded him with a smile. "You're an intellectual, Leib, and intellectuals rarely take notice of external distractions. You'd be the type that could enjoy some good music on the radio even if there were terrible static coming over the air. You just wouldn't notice the extraneous noise."

"While I," Sima said drily, "would go bananas from it. And I *do*."

The rabbi nodded, pleased. "Do you see where I'm headed?"

Slowly, not without much frustrated backing and filing, the couple groped toward a different view of themselves, of their marriage.

"When Leib leaves a trail of dirty laundry on the bedroom floor, it's not because he doesn't care about you, Sima," Avi said as they neared the end of their time together. "He's just so excited about something he just learned, or something he's going to learn, or something he's thinking about, that the laundry just doesn't register. See?" He turned to the husband. "And if Sima doesn't get as absorbed in hearing your *chidushim* as you'd like, it's not because she doesn't respect your mind. It's not because she doesn't love you. Just the opposite: She may be thinking about some wonderful new dish she'd like to cook for you tomorrow. That's how *she* shows she cares."

A shy look passed between the young husband and wife — hopeful, but suspicious of leaning too hard, too soon, on that hope. The couple left after an intense hour, effusive with gratitude, radiant with their newborn understanding. Seeing them so, Avi was nearly as radiant himself.

Not that all the problems brought before him were so easily resolved. In the case of Leib and Sima, the couple had been essentially compatible, both were earnest and well-intentioned, and they were travelling the same road with a similar luggage of values and beliefs. The difficulty came when the worldviews differed too substantially, or when one or both lacked the maturity, stability, and plain old mule-headedness to see a marriage through. In a society where people were increasingly on the move, where individuals switched jobs and homes and spouses with ever-growing ease, Avi sometimes felt as if he — and all of traditional Judaism — were waging a kind of war. The prize: that special, indefinable glue that holds a family — and through them, a people — together. It seemed the most valuable gift he could possibly give, yet the hardest, sometimes, to transmit.

The young pair had overstayed their time. Not five minutes passed before his second appointment arrived. This couple was older: well-dressed, thirtyish, clearly success-oriented. They had come to the rabbi in desperation, seeking guidance in coping with a difficult teenage son. This was a somewhat more complex matter, demanding all of Avi's tact and insight.

After long, intense discussion, the pair left, if not exactly happy, then at least a little more thoughtful than before. When they were gone, Avi wrote the boy's name down on a private list he kept in his desk. A little timely prayer couldn't hurt.

વ્°

By dint of a monumental effort, Malka had a grilled-cheese sandwich piping hot and waiting for him when he walked through the door for lunch. She was nervy and distracted, halfway through a list of phone calls to the women on one of her *chesed* committees. His well-attuned ear assessed the situation as "painful but not life-threatening." In other words, something had gone wrong, perhaps even badly wrong, with the committee; but the women would see it through. There was an enormous reservoir of competence in such women, as the rabbi knew from his personal dealings with the shul's sisterhood. It would not be going too far to say that many of them actually throve on crisis. Avi chewed his sandwich while listening absently to his wife's frantic communications, then left again as quietly as he'd come in. He returned to his office, where he spent the early part of the afternoon preparing his *shiurim* for the week.

There was the twice-daily *daf yomi* class in the shul, once in the early morning and the other after the last *ma'ariv* service at night; a weekly class for women on the laws of Sabbath; and, of course, the *Shiur* tonight in the huge shul around the corner. He spent a busy and enjoyable few hours researching, thinking, jotting notes. If anything suffered from Avi's full to bursting schedule as shepherd to his people, it was the amount of time he was able to devote to his personal Torah study. It never seemed enough. He was always thirsty. These precious hours each week, though devoted to the specific goal of preparing his classes, brought him the pleasure and the gift he most desired: extra time at his Talmud.

At four, he rose to lead the afternoon *minchah* service. He greeted his regulars and had a smile and a handshake for the one or two strangers who'd dropped in to daven. For a lingering moment, the rabbi deliberately cleansed his mind of the myriad fascinating and half-formulated thoughts that had been chasing each other through these last few hours of study. Then he bowed his head and began the prayers.

Afterwards, in his little office, he continued working steadily, to the soothing background accompaniment of the ongoing round of prayers in the shul beyond. It was nearing five when Mrs. Gerber brought him a cup of tea. He put down his pen and flexed his arms gratefully behind his back.

"Thank you, Mrs. Gerber. That's very kind." He glanced past her to the uncurtained window, remarking, "Look, it's almost completely dark already. Doesn't it sometimes feel like the winter'll never end?"

"We haven't seen the worst of it yet. February is always the worst month," she responded with a certain grim satisfaction. Gray-haired, gray-spirited Mrs. Gerber was a chronic doomsayer. Show her a silver lining, and she'd pounce on the cloud. Avi's wife didn't know how he could stand working with such a negative personality, day in and day out.

Avi didn't mind. His own inner resources were generally determined and fueled by his own moods, making external factors, however unpleasant, more or less irrelevant. Besides, Mrs. Gerber was an excellent bookkeeper.

She'd scarcely closed the door behind her when a new thought struck him for tonight's *shiur*. He seized his pen again and began writing while the coffee cooled at his elbow. It wasn't until five-thirty that he lifted his head from his *sefarim*, the heavy, holy tomes sprawled like casualties of some violent cerebral war over every available inch of desk. He only lifted it then because there was a knock on his office door.

Like a man jolted from a deep sleep, he consulted his watch. Five-thirty. Memory came flooding back. Of course — he'd made an appointment. An important matter.

The knock was repeated, louder this time.

The rabbi called, "Come in!" The outer office was awash in silence. He had a vague sense of having heard Mrs. Gerber say goodbye sometime in the past half-hour or so — or maybe that had taken place solely in his imagination. He was about to stand and go to the door himself, when, in a brisk and not at all hesitant fashion, it was pushed open.

6

The pair who entered his office this time sought, not to take advice, but to dispense it. They were Schoenbrunner and Dickstein, two prosperous *balebatim*, members of good standing in his shul, and they wanted the rabbi to commit himself to a fund-raising drive for a new shul building.

As Avi greeted them, he consciously switched gears. He was no longer the rabbi/counselor or rabbi/teacher. Now he was Rabbi Weisner, shul founder, and a businessman among other businessmen. They shook hands all around and got down to their business without preamble.

"We're talking at least half a million here," Dickstein said in his gruff, though not unkind, way. Shoenbrunner's voice was even deeper, gravelly, the result of too much smoking for too many years. He claimed recently to have quit, but then he'd made that claim many times before, mostly in the hearing of his sharp-eyed and sharper-tongued wife. Avi made a mental note to find an opportunity to speak to the man seriously about the perils of tobacco. Schoenbrunner owed that to himself — not to mention his wife, his four grown-up children, and a slew of grandchildren. It was a responsibility, no less imperative than that which he bore toward his employees or his community. It was time he realized... "Rabbi, are you listening? What do you think?"

Avi gathered his thoughts, annoyed at the momentary lack of discipline that had allowed them to wander. "Half a million. Yes. Well, what do you suggest? A dinner?"

"I have a different idea." Dickstein leaned forward, clasping his pudgy, meticulously manicured hands together. "Let's spearhead a drive. A big drive. Hit everyone who's ever contributed a penny to the shul, and then some. Gather some big bucks, some big names. *After* that," he leaned back in his seat, unclasped his hands, "we have the dinner."

Avi frowned. "What's the point? Why the dinner if we've already collected everything we need?"

"Rabbi, a shul *never* has everything it needs." It was Schoenbrunner who answered, his voice like an over-aged cement mixer. "Dickstein's onto something. Get people excited about the big figures you've already collected. Make them feel the dinner'll be just the thing to clinch it. Tell them there's only a little way to go — the icing on the cake, so to speak."

"A few more steps to the top of Everest," Dickstein rumbled, unexpectedly lyrical.

"Right. You'll generate a lot of interest that way. Hopefully a lot of money, too. You deserve a big place, Rabbi." He paused, watching Avi's face, gauging the effect of his words. "A place of your own, where your people can come to daven, to hear you speak."

Avi looked down at his desk. Schoenbrunner had hit on his weak spot, his secret craving for just such a setting. "Your people..." The rented shul was fine for a young, aspiring rabbi just beginning to attract a following. But he was approaching his forty-third birthday. He was well-established; let's face it, he was very popular. He did deserve a bigger place, a showcase, as it were. Not for himself, but for his Torah.

He looked up to find both men gazing directly at him. His own gaze was steady.

"Okay, gentlemen. The building campaign has, as of this moment" — smiling, he glanced at his wristwatch and held it up for them to see — "been officially launched. So what's our first step?"

Almost tangibly, the atmosphere in the room changed. The air, tentative until now, became charged with purpose. An undercurrent of excitement ran strongly between the three men. The preliminaries had been put out of the way. Consent had been won. An ignition had been switched on, and forward momentum became, not just a possibility, but a necessity.

Schoenbrunner said, "We'll need to find honorees."

"The first step," Dickstein overrode him crisply, "is to find someone to run the campaign. No, not you, Rabbi. Excuse me, but you've got better things to do with your time."

"Not us, either." Schoenbrunner had divined Avi's next words. "No, not us. You need a younger man, Rabbi. Experience at fund-raising would be a big plus, but the main thing is to find a fella with drive. With energy. Get-up-and-go."

"A little chutzpah wouldn't hurt either," Dickstein grunted.

"Exactly," Schoenbrunner agreed. "We're talking big time here, Rabbi."

"I see." Avi thought a moment. "I don't have anyone to suggest right at this minute, but I'll get to work on it. There must be some young, er, go-getter who'd like the job." He paused. "For a cut, of course, I suppose."

"Of course," Dickstein said promptly. "Why should anyone work for free?"

"Well, naturally I'd pay him a salary —"

"Salary shmalary. Excuse me, Rabbi. There's nothing that motivates a fella more than a piece of the action." Schoenbrunner spoke with the finality of an oracle. His deep voice and heavy delivery gave his words a kind of profundity that impressed Avi. Dickstein nodded his heavy head emphatically, as if to underscore the point.

Slowly, Avi nodded. "You're right, gentlemen. No question about that." He stood, extending a hand. "Well, let's stay in touch. We're off the ground now."

Dickstein beamed with rare approval. "Rabbi, we're finally going places!"

Schoenbrunner said, "You bet we are."

The three parted with handshakes all around and expressions of mutual goodwill. Avi promised to keep them informed of his decisions and progress. As he saw the visitors out — two graying, slightly rumpled, more-than-slightly-overweight men in good business suits — Avi found himself in the grip of an overwhelming excitement. He'd committed himself at last. The building drive was on!

Now, in the privacy of his little room, he gave free reign to his imagination. In his mind's eye he saw the shul — though not its precise outlines; that would be the architect's domain — as it would someday stand. *His* shul. *Avi Weisner, rabbi.* Even more than his present, temporary location, it would be a center, a base from which to operate — more, to expand his operations. He'd thought himself content, but his ambition had only been lying dormant, a seed in fallow earth, waiting for the signal to rise again.

Energy and purpose surged through him until his very fingertips tingled. The shul building represented much more than plaster and brick and a fancy frontage on the street. For Avi Weisner, it went beyond even the profound and ancient meanings inherent in all houses of worship and study. For him, it had a personal meaning that could not fail to thrill. In the new edifice, he would find the final accolade of his people and his ultimate acceptance as their leader. He would scratch his own modest, unique mark in the soil of history.

He felt as if a curtain had just dropped on a portion of his life and another had risen on a brand-new stage. True, the setting was not yet built, but it soon would be. If Avi had anything to do with it, it would be!

The outer door had scarcely clicked shut behind his visitors when the office phone rang. Euphorically, he lifted it. "Hello! Weisner here."

The flat voice at the other end of the line made a curious contrast to the rabbi's exuberance. "Yes, hello, Rabbi. It's Bruin, Yankel Bruin. I...I never got a chance to call this week..."

"Oh, that's all right, Yankel. I wasn't worried. How are you?"

"Actually, not so good." Then, in a rush, "Do you think I could come right over? I've got a problem. I need to see you right away."

Avi glanced out the window. Outside, full night had descended, and a wind had risen, howling angrily through the glass. He felt tired but exhilarated. The building drive filled his mind. He wanted to take off his shoes, eat dinner, talk to Malka.

But of all this there was no sign as he answered cordially, "Come right over, then. I'll be waiting in my office."

"Thank you. Rabbi?"

"Yes?"

"I'm bringing someone along."

Avi hung up the phone. As he prepared to wait for Bruin and his mysterious companion, dimming the lights to ease the strain on his eyes, he began turning over in his mind, in a probing, preliminary way, the names of young men who might be approached about heading the drive. No one sprang to mind who was both talented in that area and immediately available.

When the car drove up some ten minutes later, Avi was ready for it. In his customary, self-disciplined way he'd cleared his mind of everything that did not have to do with Yankel Bruin and his impending visit. He felt alert and pleasantly relaxed, ready to meet the challenge of whatever problem

Bruin lay before him. It was this ability to give himself over to his congregants, fully and without restraint, that had endeared him to them from the start. If he would lead, he must take the burdens of his followers onto his own shoulders. This he was, and had always been, prepared to do.

At this moment, in his little office, Avi Weisner was every inch the rabbi he'd set out, all those years ago, to create of himself. Personal ambition nestled within a great and abiding love of his fellow Jew; the service to which he'd been trained was fine-honed. This willing acceptance of Bruin's unknown burden, despite his own weariness and on the heels of his decision to move up a rung, as it were, on the ladder of his career, was in its own small way a moment of triumph: a tiny pinnacle, insignificant in itself, and yet encompassing all that was significant in his life. *Avi Weisner, rabbi.*

The car slid into a parking space on the side of the shul nearest the rabbi's office, so that the headlights momentarily lit the room before they were extinguished, plunging the room back into darkness. Avi switched on his desk lamp, then sat back to wait for the rap on the door that would herald the new arrivals.

But at the last minute, as if he could not bear to sit still and wait passively for events — for the future — to come to him, he sprang up from his chair and rounded his desk with a vigorous stride to meet them. He had the door open for the visitors even before they reached it.

THREE

1

The two men — one middle-aged, the other young — sat before the rabbi's desk, avoiding each other's eyes.

Avi's own eyes were irresistibly drawn to the younger man. Perhaps it was the contrast to Yankel Bruin's tired face and defeated shoulders that made the other so striking. The young man, whom Bruin had quietly, almost sullenly, introduced as his nephew, held himself casually erect in his chair. Good humor and intelligence shone from his blue eyes, and an engaging smile played about his lips. He seemed a man at ease with the world, ready to raise a cup of friendship with anyone who happened to pass his way. "I like you," his manner seemed to say to the world and everything in it. "Please, like me back!" It seemed a hard thing to disappoint him.

"Well, what can I do for you gentlemen?" Avi asked amiably. "Yankel?"

Bruin pushed back the brim of his gray hat and scratched his head. With a nervous glance at his nephew, he cleared his throat and said, "I...we... Well." He rubbed a bristly chin, then tried again. "Well, we've got a problem, Rabbi." His accent was broadly Brooklyn, faintly Eastern Europe.

Avi waited. When Bruin didn't continue, he prompted, "Yes?" He was intrigued. Though he didn't know Yankel well, this behavior seemed out of character for the man — a tough old bird, by all accounts.

At length, Bruin repeated, "A problem. I didn't like to bother you with it, Rabbi. I like handling my troubles by myself. That's the way I've always done things, and that's the way I would have done it this time." His voice sharpened. "But it's gone too far. I don't want to hurt my sister. Chayke's got enough on her plate as it is. But I don't want to suffer any more losses, either! My wife said —"

Avi held up a hand. "Please, Yankel. I'm afraid I'm not following you. How about starting at the beginning?"

"Suppose I tell you?" the younger man interposed suddenly.

At the rabbi's questioning look, pink crept into the smooth-shaven cheeks. "What I mean is, I wouldn't mind filling in some of the details. Uncle Yankel's obviously..." He cast around for the right word, ending finally with a delicate, "upset."

Bruin exploded, "You bet I'm upset!" Beside the nephew, his manner was excessive and overblunt, like a sledgehammer smashing china. "You tell me, Sammy — don't I have a right to be?" He waved an outraged arm in the air. "Upset, he says!"

Sammy sat back and said softly, "Well, why don't you tell him then, Uncle?"

"You bet I will. I'll tell him. I'll tell him what's been happening to my business ever since I took you on. As a favor to my little sister," he added parenthetically, for the rabbi's benefit. Avi nodded to signal comprehension. Bruin plowed on.

"From the goodness of my heart I took the boy in. A diploma he didn't have. Experience he didn't have. Talent — maybe. Charm, luck — oh, plenty of those. He charmed everyone at first, including me. Got them all eating out of his hand. I thought to myself: 'Yankel, maybe this is gonna work out. You might make a salesman out of that kid yet.' "

"Is that your job?" Avi asked swiftly of the younger man. "Salesman?"

The nephew nodded. "We — er, my uncle — manufactures plastic bags. My job is to cultivate new clients. There's a whole team of us, actually. I'm the last one Uncle Yankel's hired — the fifth. But not," he added modestly, "the worst."

"No," the uncle admitted, "not the worst. You did bring in business, I'll grant you that."

"Then what's the problem?" Avi was puzzled.

Bruin sat silently, chewing his lip.

"It's a hard thing, accusing your own nephew," he sighed finally. "But waiting's no good, either. Believe me, I wouldn't have come if I hadn't tried to wait a while, to see it through, hoping I was wrong."

Avi watched the older man's struggle with himself. He witnessed the way, almost visibly, the iron will that had been so invaluable to Bruin in building his private plastics empire came to his aid now, stiffening his resolve. Leaning closer to the desk and carefully not looking at his nephew, Bruin said, "Well, this is the story, Rabbi. I've been going over Sammy's expense accounts for the past few months. There's some funny business going on, or my name's not Yankel Bruin."

The rabbi asked carefully, "What sort of funny business?"

"Inflated expenses. Duplicate items. Trips and hotels in places where we have no accounts."

"My job is to drum up new business, Uncle Yankel," the nephew said. "Not just visit old customers."

"Then where's all the new business?"

"I'm a good salesman; I'm no miracle worker." Sammy spread his hands. "I try."

The uncle snorted. To Avi, he said, "He sets a bad example to the other salesmen. Following his lead, they become more slipshod in listing their own expenses. He's completely charmed my accounting department — has them eating out of his hand. They pretend not to notice the discrepancies. I tried not to notice, too. For a long time. But I can't let anyone — not even my sister's boy — drain my business!"

The rabbi glanced in an assessing way from the older man to the younger. Sammy, with an inscrutable smile, met his eyes directly. Bruin glared at the desktop.

Avi made up his mind.

"Yankel, would you mind if I have a few words alone with Sammy? I think it would be useful."

"Have as many words as you want." Bruin heaved himself out of his chair. His navy suit was creased, his tie askew. "He's a master of pretty words, that one." Grumbling under his breath, he went to the door and passed through it into the outer office.

Left to themselves, the two men sized each other up. In the light from the desk lamp Sammy seemed relaxed; at any rate, he sat perfectly still, his eyes never leaving the rabbi's. Avi read respect there, and more — liking, comradeship. The message of the young man's steady gaze was sincere, serious, flattering.

Avi tapped a pencil thoughtfully against the papers on his desk. "What's your last name, Sammy?"

"Mirsky. From Boro Park. My father has a jewelry store in the city."

Avi shook his head. "Sorry, don't know him." He paused, measuring the other man, trying to make up his mind about him. "Why the plastics factory? Why didn't you join your father's business?"

"It's strictly a mom-and-pop place, Rabbi. Unless I want to spell one of my parents behind the counter, there's really no room for me. I wanted a job with potential for growth. A place with a future." His cheeks were pink, the blue eyes earnest. A lock of curly brown hair had fallen onto his brow. He looked very young and idealistic.

"I see." Avi leaned forward, impaling the younger man with his stern gaze. "So what's been happening here, Sammy?"

"I'm glad you asked me that. I don't want to say a word against my uncle, G-d forbid. He was good enough to take me into the business, like he said, without any experience. But I've paid him back, ten times over. I brought in lots of business. Ask him if that's not true!"

"He admitted that much freely. But what about the expense items?"

Sammy hesitated. "Rabbi, can I tell you something? Honestly?"

"Go ahead."

"This factory — it's like Uncle Yankel's baby. He never had any kids of his own, you know. He poured himself, heart and soul, into those plastic bags of his. To give him credit, he's built the place up tremendously. He has a lot of people working for him, turns a nice profit. But when it comes to his precious business, Uncle Yankel can be a little...overprotective, you know?"

Avi nodded slowly, pressing the fingers of one hand against those of the other. He knew the type — hard-working, independent, fiercely and narrowly protective of his interests. And suspicious of possible usurpers.

Avi asked, "Do you think your uncle is afraid of you? Afraid you'll try to take too much power into your own hands?"

"I don't know." Sammy was frankly nonplussed. "Heaven knows I was only doing my job. Uncle Yankel's from another generation, Rabbi. I guess he doesn't understand modern business methods very well. Clients take a lot of cultivating — wining, dining, all that stuff. I've even taken potential customers out to ballgames!"

"But he doesn't like to see all that on your expense account."

"No." Sammy straightened, turned harder, more businesslike. "Look, I want to get ahead, Rabbi. I've worked like a dog to bring in business. And done pretty well, if I do say so myself!"

"But he's not happy with you."

Sammy spread his hands again. "I tried to explain. I've put up with his endless questions and...the suspicions." Sammy bent his head, so that his next words came oddly muffled to Avi's ears. "I just don't know. I don't know if it's worth it anymore."

Avi thought this over. He pictured the scenario as Sammy had painted it. He saw a young, ambitious salesman with a flair for his work, a knack for winning friends. Sammy was doubtless very good at what he did. Yet his uncle, bound by the customs and constraints of an earlier era, shackled him at every turn, questioned the nephew's methods, demanded explanations for what he considered outsized expenses. Maybe they would have been, once. These days, the economy being what it was, different techniques were called for. Different — and more expensive.

The young man chose that moment to raise his head. There was misery in his face, and worry, and hope. The blue eyes were wide open, guileless as they waited trustingly for the rabbi's verdict. Avi decided he liked the young man very much.

"I understand, Sammy." He steepled his fingers again. "I'll have to give this a little thought. We don't want to offend your uncle or show ingratitude for what he's done for you."

"Of course not."

Avi considered him. "You could just quit."

Sammy looked startled. "I've considered that, of course. I don't know if I'll find another job like this one."

"Oh, I don't know about that." The rabbi began to smile. "Sometimes what seems like the worst luck can actually be a blessing in disguise."

"What do you mean, Rabbi?"

It took Avi fifteen minutes to tell Sammy just what he meant.

As he described to the young man what he had in mind, the rabbi's love for his calling flowed over him like a newly risen tide and shone from his eyes. How wonderful it was when the ways of the *Ribbono shel olam*, the Creator of heaven and earth, became visible for an instant to the humble man struggling through the murk of his daily affairs. For Avi, the inspiration he'd just had was such a moment. Hashem had sent Sammy to him at this time, not only so Avi could solve Sammy's problem, but also to give Sammy the chance to help Avi with his own. His gratitude swelled upward in a silent, joyous wave.

When he judged that they'd covered enough ground in this initial talk, the rabbi summoned Yankel Bruin back into his office. Sammy, with a quick, nervous glance at the rabbi, offered a prettily worded apology to his uncle for any pain he might have caused him. Bruin listened with arms folded, then said mulishly, "That's all fine and good. But what about the future? What about those expense accounts of yours?"

"The problem," Sammy said with an airy wave of the hand, "no longer exists, Uncle. I'm resigning."

Surprise overtook Bruin's stony expression and melted it into something else — a different look, one which Avi could not read. For a moment it appeared as though Bruin would speak; then he apparently thought better of it.

Staring at the desktop he muttered, "What'll I tell Chayke?"

"I'll tell my mother myself," Sammy said, flushing. "That's no concern of yours anymore, Uncle."

The rabbi said quietly, "I think you owe your uncle a big *yasher ko'ach*, Sammy — a 'thank you' for the wonderful opportunity he gave you. Naturally he still cares about you and your parents. What kind of uncle would he be if he didn't? Eh?"

"You're right. I'm sorry." Sammy was instantly contrite. "I'm sorry, Uncle. And yes, thanks for everything. Don't worry about a thing. It's going to be all right now."

Some five minutes later, Sammy and his uncle said their goodbyes to the rabbi, got into Bruin's car, and drove off. Presently Avi, in his decrepit station wagon, drove away in another direction, toward home.

What Bruin or his nephew might have been feeling at that moment was a matter of conjecture to the rabbi.

He himself was feeling absolutely wonderful.

2

It being a Thursday night, Avi found himself, after conducting the *ma'ariv* service, a little pressed for time.

He had prepared his notes for the *shiur*, but his unexpected visitors had undercut the time he would have taken to review them. This was one evening he would have enjoyed spending quietly at home, unwinding after the various tensions and complexities of the day and, most of all, discussing his decision — no, *decisions* — with Malka. He glanced at his dashboard clock. As things stood now, he'd have time to snatch only a quick meal before closeting himself with his notes. The talk with his wife would have to wait.

But when he arrived at his house and parked in front of the morning's arduously etched path through the snow, he saw something that changed his mind. Mutty was home.

Only now, face to face with his son's ancient Chevrolet, did he allow himself to recognize the thought — the fear — that had lurked in the back of his mind all week. Last Thursday night had represented a break of sorts. Avi hadn't been sure just how far, or how deep, the rupture went. In rejecting the father's dream, Mutty had — in the language of the heart, at least — rejected the father, too. All week long, as he thought about and jotted his notes for the big *shiur*, Avi had wondered: would Mutty appear at the shul Thursday night, as he had appeared virtually every week since the *shiur's* debut nearly a year ago? Or would his absence trumpet a message louder and more final than any other possibly could?

He had the answer now. Brows knitted, Avi unlocked his front door. He was uncertain of the form the reunion would take or what sort of welcome to expect: both his for Mutty and his son's for him.

❧❧

Down in the basement, Malka was gasping for breath. "I'm...in... terrible...shape," she wheezed, a hand pressed to her heart.

"Take it easy, Ma," Mutty said, trying without any great degree of success to suppress a smile. "Aren't you supposed to build up to these things gradually?"

His mother replied through her ragged breaths, "I *am*...doing it...(gasp)...gradually. Five minutes...(whoosh)...yesterday. Six today." Malka glared at the stepper at her feet, placed just beyond the washer-dryer that had formerly defined the room's entire purpose, and drew another whooping breath into her starving lungs.

Mutty, lounging comfortably against the dryer, asked, "I think it's a good sign that you're breathing hard. Isn't that supposed to mean you've done something aerobic?"

"More likely...(wheeze)...something masochistic." To the stepper she added balefully, "Okay, okay, you win. I surrender."

"Don't give up, Ma. Just wait till you see yourself slim and trim. You'll be glad you persevered."

"I'm waiting." Moodily, Malka shoved the stepper out of sight in a corner. When her breathing was restored to something approaching normal, she smiled at her son. "Sorry to let it out on you, Mutty. Skinny bones that you are, you wouldn't know what it's like. I was just so determined to do something about these extra pounds." Ruefully, she added, "Only it's a lot harder than it looks, isn't it?"

"So they say." He shot her a sideways look. "Are you combining exercise with a sensible —"

"Diet? Don't, *don't* say that word in my presence. I'm liable to start frothing at the mouth." They began the ascent to the kitchen.

Mutty grinned at her. "That bad, huh?"

Sigh. "And it's been only two days."

Above their heads, the basement door opened. Malka peered up in the near-gloom, trying to make out the figure silhouetted at the top of the stairs. A familiar voice asked, "Anybody home?"

"Oh! Avi, you're back!" Malka increased her pace, taking the last few stairs in truly aerobic fashion. Mutty, suddenly nervous, lagged behind.

Avi looked past his wife's shoulder to where his son cowered in the shadows. An urge to forced heartiness gave way, at the last minute, to a subdued, "Hello, Mutty. How are you?"

Manfully, Mutty stepped up into the kitchen, blinking a little in the bright light. "Fine, *baruch Hashem*, Ta. How are you?"

Just like a couple of strangers, Malka thought despairingly. She hurried through the kitchen with quick, flustered steps, gathering things for Avi's dinner. "You're running late today, aren't you? I'll just stick a plate in the microwave. Why don't you wash up in the meantime?" Malka hesitated, then reached for a second plate. "I'm sure you're ready for some dinner, too, Mutty."

Mutty's own hesitation was more pronounced. He wasn't sure he was ready yet for the intimacy of dinner alone with his father. The rest of the family had, of course, eaten earlier. Shani was, in typical twelve-year-old fashion, alternately attacking her homework assignments and dreaming at her desk. The little boys were already in bed.

Malka, observing — and understanding — her oldest son's difficulty, tried to help.

"I nibbled something before with the kids. But I'll join you two again now — diet or no diet."

Mutty shot her a grateful look, even as he was aware, with a sinking feeling, that the very obviousness of her intercession had only underlined the tension between his father and him. Moving to the sink, he said, "I'll wash, then."

In the end, it was Hindy who provided the much-needed diversion. She breezed into the kitchen with an armful of books, which she immediately dumped on the counter, to roost among the other flotsam there. Her cheeks were flushed from the cold, and her whole face seemed lit with a radiance that derived from nothing more commonplace, or more wonderful, than youth.

At the sight of her father, she brightened even further.

"Hi, Ta! What amazing luck, I actually get to eat with you." She pulled up a chair, adding a casual, "Hi, Mutty, how's life?"

"I thought you were studying at Chaya Gitty's house tonight." Malka, busy at the microwave, threw the words over her shoulder.

"I was. We did. Geometry — ugh." Hindy wrinkled her nose to show what she thought of *that* subject. "Chaya Gitty has to babysit. I guess I'll finish on my own."

"How did you get home?" Avi asked, smiling.

"Her father was going out anyway. He drove me." She reached for the plate Malka deposited in front of her. "Yum, chicken. I'm starved."

For some minutes they ate in a silence rendered unexpectedly companionable by Hindy's presence. Mutty chewed stoically, glad of the defusing role his sister was, willy-nilly, playing at the table. But he was also ill with waiting. Sooner or later he would have to confront his father again, raise the painful topic they'd dropped so acrimoniously the week before. The oven-fried chicken — one of Malka's better efforts — tasted like dust in his mouth.

When Avi had assuaged the first pangs of hunger, he set down knife and fork and reached for a piece of bread. From this he took a bite, then proceeded to crumble the rest in an absent way as he spoke.

"Shoenbrunner and Dickstein came in today," he told his wife. "About the building drive." He paused significantly. "They've convinced me to go ahead with it."

"Avi, no! Really? That's marvelous!" Doubtfully, Malka added, "I think?"

"Sure it is! It's going to take an enormous amount of work, but in the end I think it'll be worth it. My own shul." His eyes grew distant. Malka could almost see the image of the new building stamped on his retina, as it was so indelibly stamped in his imagination.

Hindy raved, "Hey, fabulous! Will the new shul be big enough to fit everyone in for the *shiur?*"

"That," her father said wryly, "depends on the amount of money we manage to raise."

Malka asked, "How do Dickstein and Schoenbrunner plan to go about raising it?"

"They don't. They want me to hire someone. A young man. A 'fella with,' as Schoenbrunner put it, 'some get-up-and-go.' According to Dickstein, a little chutzpah wouldn't hurt, either." Avi chuckled. "And you know something? I think I may have found him."

"What? Already?" Malka was amazed.

"Like a miracle. Just minutes after those two left, I get a call from Yankel Bruin. He asked if he could come over with a nephew of his — a Sammy Mirsky."

"Mirsky?" Malka interrupted, instantly alert. "Related to the Crown

Heights Mirskys? Or maybe the ones in Queens?"

"I don't know."

A sudden, furious rattling at the window — a noise as definite as the first burst of gunfire signalling the onset of war — brought the weather to their attention. "It's storming again," Malka said unnecessarily. She rolled her eyes heavenward. "Please, no more snow this time!"

"What did they come about, Ta?" These were virtually the first words Mutty had spoken during the meal. Avi glanced at him inquiringly. Blushing, Mutty said, "Bruin and his nephew."

"Oh, that. A private matter. That's been taken care of... Anyway, I offered him the job."

Malka said, "The job? Fund-raising, you mean?"

Hindy asked, "Who? Yankel Bruin?"

"No, Sammy. The nephew."

3

An agonized howl: the wind was rising. Avi wondered if the weather would affect the evening's turnout at the *shiur*. Thoughtfully he helped himself to some more mashed potatoes, picking out the lumps in what had become, over the years of his marriage, an automatic reflex.

"Ta, wasn't that kind of sudden?" Hindy wanted to know. She had put down her fork and was studying her father with a wrinkled brow. "You don't even really know the guy, do you?"

"It's a big responsibility," Malka agreed. "Can this Sammy do it?"

"He'll do all right, I think." Avi's tone ordered, *Trust my judgment.* "He's young, ambitious, a little brash but essentially good-natured. A natural salesman. Says he wants to expand his horizons. He wants a future." He shook his head wonderingly. "Did you ever see something so *min haShamayim*? This Sammy could've dropped into my office straight from

Heaven! There I was, in need of a good man to sell me, my shul, to potential contributors. And the door opens, and in walks a terrific salesman who just happens to be free at the moment — ready, willing and able to do the job!"

"There's not much of a future in it, though, is there?" Malka said. "It's a one-time project."

"Right. But it'll give him experience." Avi remembered Sammy's reaction to his offer: surprised, thoughtful, finally pleased. "He's an idealistic fellow. A short stint of *l'sheim Shamayim* — a bit of work for *Yiddishkeit's* sake — seems to attract him just now. And who knows? If he does well, other doors could open for him."

Mutty roused himself. "But can you trust him?"

In his own ears, the question emerged gracelessly, almost rudely. Awkwardly he added, "I mean, a lot of money will be passing through his hands."

Unbidden, the memory of Bruin's grievance intruded. Avi frowned. Astute as Bruin the manufacturer might be, he was also protective as a brood hen over the workings of his personal kingdom. With his blatant charm and modern working philosophy, the nephew stood as a threat to Bruin and every old-fashioned business practice he stood for. Following the train of his thoughts, Avi gave a tiny, negative shake of the head. No, he'd made the right decision. He'd been sent just the man he needed. He would not undermine his gratefulness to Providence by questioning the blessing any further.

The rabbi turned and, for the first time that evening, gave his son a level look. "A lot of money, true. But he's going to work out, I'm sure. At least, as well as others who might be...closer to the center of things." The rabbi turned back to his plate as the wind demanded entry at the windows and the rat-a-tat of rain or hail roared its endless angry counterpoint.

First Mutty's neck, then his face, became stained a deep, dull crimson. There was no question of his father's continuing disappointment in him. This unknown master salesman, this Sammy Mirsky, was being tossed up to Mutty, it seemed to him, as a symbol of everything he himself should have been but wasn't: ambitious, outgoing, practical, successful, ready to speak his father's language and accommodate his father's vision. It took every ounce of courage Mutty possessed to raise his eyes and meet his father's.

"I wish him luck, then," he said quietly. "And good luck to the new shul, too. You deserve it."

Avi was taken aback by something strange in his son's manner. It was as if some inaudible judgment had been pronounced, though upon whom it was being pronounced he wasn't certain. Rapidly he ran through a thousand possible responses. In the end, and in the sincere desire for peace between them, he settled on a simple, if rather stiff, "Thank you."

Mutty transferred his gaze to his mother. "Ma. Ta. there's something I want to tell you."

"Yes?" Malka leaned forward on her elbows, eager for a change of subject.

"I...that is, Fish and I — "

"Is that Fischel Mann?" Avi broke in.

Mutty nodded, then spoke fast. "We're thinking about making a move for the rest of the *zeman*. It would just be for two or three months, until Pesach."

Avi asked, "Where to?"

"Israel."

A dumbfounded silence met his announcement. Hindy, who had been in the act of pouring some orange juice into her glass, set down the carton with a thump. "Israel? Are you serious?"

"Yes. We thought we'd learn in the Mir." When no other reaction came, he repeated a little desperately, "It would only be till Pesach."

"The airfare," Malka said numbly, trying to collect herself. She was reeling as if from a bodily blow. "Expenses..."

"I've got some money saved up, Ma. I'll live frugally."

"What about your...your plans? *Shidduchim?*"

Other interrupted projects thrust themselves at Mutty. There was the *sugya* he was learning with his morning *chavrusa* at Lakewood (he learned with Fish in the afternoons) and the half-finished bookcase he was making for a former roommate who was getting married in June. Inchoate behind these were other, more nebulous aspirations: designs for woodwork projects, certain carpentry techniques he wanted to explore more deeply — and, of course, *shidduchim.*

Mutty shrugged. "All that can be put on hold for a couple of months. This'll be something different. An experience" — he shot a glance at his father — "before I settle down."

"I see." Avi thought he did see. The urge to travel stemmed, obviously, from a desire to put off reality for a few months. And the notion, thought the father, might not be such a bad one. It would give the boy an opportunity to put things in perspective; give him time to think things through instead of merely swimming automaton-like against the tide of his father's wishes. A second chance, as it were, at starting off his adult life on the right foot.

To Malka's surprise, then, and her considerable dismay, Avi smiled at his son in a friendlier way than he had all evening.

"I think that may be a very good idea, Mutty. When were you thinking of leaving?"

Hindy gaped at her father. "Is that it? It's that easy? He says he wants to fly off to Israel, and you say, 'Have a nice trip'?" She folded her arms across her chest. "In that case, I'd like to go to Israel, too."

To her chagrin, all three of them — both of her parents and Mutty — burst into laughter. The laughter seemed to bind them closer and to exclude her, again, from the charmed inner circle. She rose with immense dignity from the table.

"I see how seriously everybody takes me around here." She retrieved her books from the counter and clumped off to her room to seek comfort and guidance from the host of sympathetic friends always to be found at the other end of her telephone wire.

Behind her, in the kitchen, the laughter faded. Though anxious to sit down with his notes, the rabbi lingered a few more minutes to discuss with his son some of the practical details of the trip. Malka listened, occasionally inserting a word, but her heart wasn't in charter flights or travel agents. Lakewood was bad enough, but at least Mutty came home once a week for the *shiur* and every three or four weeks for Shabbos. Now Israel?

She tried to tell herself that this was no different from Lakewood or the months he'd spent in various summer camps over the years. She could talk to herself till she was hoarse, but she knew better: it *was* different. It was so far away, for one thing. And in the ever-simmering cauldron of Middle East politics, possibly dangerous, too. When had this resolve been born, and why hadn't Mutty said a word to her before?

Mutty could not have answered her. His head was awhirl. Just before leaving for New York that very afternoon, when pressed by his friend to make up his mind, he'd told Fish he wanted to think about it a little more. He'd been by no means convinced that the trip to Israel was the right thing for him just then. There were unfinished commitments of all sorts dangling around him right here. Things he needed to see to, to work on, to sort out for himself. Fish had been agreeable, though he urged Mutty not to take too much time. He himself was clearly itching to be gone.

Mutty wasn't quite sure just how it had happened — he'd certainly had no intention of broaching the topic when he'd driven up from Lakewood — but the decision seemed to have made itself. He was going.

A tentative excitement battled with a deeper bitterness. Inside, a small, excruciatingly honest part of him acknowledged that his gesture was akin to a rejected warrior's in trotting off the field, leaving it clear for a competitor to serve the master they both loved. The field would now belong to that unknown and so admirable other — that go-getter, that man of the hour — the remarkable Sammy.

Anyway, Fish would be pleased.

4

If there was anyone in his family whom Fish would have called a real confidante, it was his kid brother.

Gedalia Mann was stocky, red-haired, and just turned eleven. The twelve-year gap in their ages had placed Fish, at times, in the role of surrogate father to the boy, which explained, perhaps, their unusual closeness. It was Gedalia who tapped perfunctorily at the door of Fish's room now and pushed it open.

"Hi, Fish. You sleeping here tonight?"

"Guess so. The storm should hopefully have spent itself by 6 A.M., which is when I hope to head back."

Gedalia perched at the edge of the bed Fish used when in residence. The house, especially now that Fish's older sister had married, was big enough to accommodate two or three empty bedrooms for the use of house guests and returning offspring. Fish could drop in without warning at virtually any time and be sure of finding his bed waiting for him. He did not often avail himself of the privilege.

Eyeing his big brother shrewdly, Gedalia asked, "Mom and Dad have been turning the screws, huh?" When Fish didn't answer, he added, by way of clarification, "Putting on the heat. Laying on the pressure?"

Fish laughed. "I get the message, Gedalia."

"Well?"

"Well, I don't think it's any of your business but — yeah." He made a face. "Pressure."

Gedalia settled himself more comfortably at the foot of the bed on which Fish lay facing the ceiling, head pillowed on his forearms. "The usual story? They want you to join the business?"

"You," said Fish, "know more than is good for you, pint-size."

"Well? Is that it?"

"You'd make a good F.B.I. man. Specializing in interrogation."

"Well?" Gedalia was undeterred. The kid could be stubborn — almost as stubborn as Fish himself.

"Or, on second thought, a broken record. Yes, the same old stuff."

Yechezkel Mann had, in a hard-working quarter-century, built up a thriving factory that was his pride and joy — and Fish's bane. It had been expected from his childhood that he would someday step into his rightful place as his father's right-hand man and heir. Instead, the son had chosen the less lucrative, if infinitely more rewarding, yeshivah life.

The decision had been a bone of contention back when he'd first set off for Lakewood. By now, it had evolved into an open battle of wills. Mr. Mann was firmly convinced that the time had come to end this foolishness. Fish had been set on learning for a few years — fine. The years were behind him. It was time to get started on the real business of earning his way. "Ain't no such thing as a free lunch," his father would remind him in his heavy-handed way. "You work, you eat. You know what I mean?"

Fish knew. Mr. Mann had made that abundantly clear. His father needed him. The business needed him. When was he going to stop wasting everybody's time and settle down?

Rochel Mann, a sweet woman who favored spring-like pastels and a wide circle of friends, only wanted everyone to be happy. The problem was, what her husband needed for his happiness seemed to run directly counter to Fish's needs. Neither blamed her for the constant fluttering, the sidling and backtracking from husband to son and back again. In fact, they didn't regard her as a major player in this tug of war at all. This was between the men.

Fish hesitated, glancing at his brother from beneath lowered lids. "Also, I just sprang a new surprise on them. They were *not* pleased."

Gedalia looked alert. "What kind of surprise?"

"I'm thinking of going to Israel for a couple of months."

"To Israel? To learn?"

Fish nodded.

Gedalia thought about that. "When I was little," he said incon-sequentially, "you would've offered to take me along. In your suitcase."

"Times change." Fish grinned a little sadly. "They don't make suitcases your size."

"I know." Gedalia kicked the edge of the bed with a swinging sneakered foot, then looked up. "They don't want you to go?"

"Does your curiosity know no bounds? No," Fish answered himself. "I guess it doesn't. No, Gedalia, they do not want me to go. They want me to 'settle down.' To leave Lakewood and stop trying to fool myself into thinking I can learn. To go to work and make something of myself." Fish paused, then added, "Also to get myself married already."

"Married!" Gedalia yelped. "You're too young to get married!"

"I turn twenty-three in a couple of months. That's old enough."

It wasn't, though. Not for him. Not yet. His father and mother wondered at his reluctance to attend to the litany of assets of fine girls, sung by the matchmakers over recent months. Wondered — and fretted. Neither of them being the reticent type, their exasperation was, from time to time, given lavish expression. This evening had been no exception.

It was not something Fish could easily have explained to them. He found it hard to explain even to himself. Had he been of a more analytical bent, able to put into words the inchoate feelings that drove him, he might have understood better his reluctance to marry. The reason lay, perhaps, in the same obstinate idealism that had brought him to Lakewood three years ago, and kept him there. He had a great deal of wasted time to make up for. Until he reached a certain level — in his Torah study, in his spiritual development — he would not link his lot to that of any young woman, least of all that one particular, longed-for but still-unmet young woman — whoever and wherever she might be — who would make his life worth living. He was preparing himself for a Jewish marriage as he felt it should be. Surely she deserved no less. If that preparation took time, and if time meant an extension of his loneliness, well, he was willing to spend the first and endure the latter. Feeling himself still only half the man he should be, was it fair to do otherwise?

Fish became aware that his brother was speaking — most likely asking another slew of questions. The questions ricocheted off the thin air and bounced back to the increasingly frustrated boy.

"So what's the story?" Gedalia persisted. "What'd you all agree on in the end?"

"We agreed," Fish said slowly — if the uneasy compromise they'd achieved could be flattered by that term — "that I go to Israel until Pesach. After that, I come back to the States, to Lakewood, until the summer break." He drew a deep breath. "By then, Dad'll want my answer. I'll have to make up my mind: to stay in learning, or to join the business."

Gedalia was looking at him with sympathy. "And to start working on getting married?"

"Yes." A wry look settled on Fish's homely, likeable face and lit the dark eyes that were like twin windows opening onto a summer's night. "Yes, that, too."

5

There were, Malka decided as the broken clock on the piano squeaked its twelve strangled chimes, two kinds of people in the world. One kind was the fighter, who contends valiantly with the troubles the world hurls at them —troubles from without. The other was the sensitive one, touched by the finger of melancholy and all the richness of poetry: whose greatest torment comes from within.

Mutty, she further decided — though she'd really figured this out a long time ago — belonged to the latter group.

From the start (which to Malka meant his literal beginning, his babyhood) her son had been, as the expression went, his own worst enemy. The sensitive nature, so gratifying to his mother and pleasing to his good friends, had been a constant irritant to his father. Implicit in their relationship had been the unspoken impatience, the frustration, the "Why

can't you be more like —?" The rest, the name, didn't matter. It was enough
for Mutty to know that he'd been found wanting.

It wasn't, Malka mused as she stared through the front window into the
heart of the storm — which, at midnight, showed no signs of abating — as
though Avi didn't adore Mutty. Love there certainly was, and a certain fierce
pride mixed in with the rest. Maybe it was the very strength of that feeling
that made the father demand so much from his firstborn son. Mutty was, in
a way, Avi's second self — his heir in so much more than just the material
sense. For Mutty to turn his back on his father's expectations now was like
yanking away from Avi's grasp something toward which he'd been straining
for a long, long time. To what purpose had the father labored, after all, if not
for the sake of the legacy he would leave behind?

The legacy was still in the making. Malka, curled up in the big armchair,
wrapped in her thick robe against the downstairs chill, thought about the
years. Which will have seen the greater part of Avi's labor — or, for that
matter, her own: the years behind them, or those still lying in wait?

In the past lay their beginnings. She thought of their first tiny apartment.
Avi, she remembered with a smile, used to call it "a shoebox with a door."
But how delightful a shoebox! Just a small living room and a smaller
bedroom, scarcely large enough to hold the solid bedroom set that had been
her parents' wedding gift to them. In fact, the bulky armoire had found its
place only outside, in the living room, beside the squeaky-new convertible
sofa and the secondhand rug that made up the sum total of that room's
furnishings.

As for the kitchen — well, the kitchen had been almost too small to turn
around in, though that was what Malka had mostly done there in those first
months: turned in circles. Not much edible food had emerged from that cozy,
cluttered space, but a great deal of laughter and warmth was always to be
found there. As the only spot in the apartment that contained chairs, the tiny
kitchen had served as Avi's study, Malka's phoning nook, and headquarters
for the many friends who'd drop in unexpectedly in the evenings for popcorn
and conversation. There was rarely a night when someone did not crunch

the crackly white stuff underfoot, or kick it rolling into a corner under the table. They knew Malka wouldn't care. And she hadn't. She'd been too busy serving up mugs of sweet hot cocoa or frosty orange juice and giggling at someone's home-grown witticism, heard for the dozenth time. To their credit, at evening's end, the visitors had (usually) helped her clean up. Cups and plates would be dumped in the sink, and someone would stand by, chatting companionably while Malka rinsed them. The tablecloth would be shaken out like some huge, indoor flag, while someone else went for the broom. Sweeping up had been especially fun — nothing short of a rollicking popcorn hunt. How happy she'd been in those days!

The happiness had followed the two of them, if in more sedate fashion, to other, larger apartments and ultimately to this big, untidy house, which creaked and groaned like an arthritic knee and gave welcome like a comfortable old friend. It had been here that Shani and the little boys were born. There, on that bottom step, Shmulie had chipped a tooth; and Hindy had cried behind the couch when she lost her charm bracelet. Endless shrieking games of tag and hide-and-seek had been played in and around the obstacle course of this very room, and were still being played... And through it all, like a bright silver thread, ran Avi's rise to greatness.

It had not happened by itself, or overnight. Avi himself had been the mover who taught and advised, who made the necessary impressions, who pulled the obligatory strings. If he was ambitious, Malka thought loyally, it was for the sake of the Torah he loved. From that first shoebox apartment to their present, sprawling splendor, his talents had only grown, and his following along with it. The early, timid phone calls for advice had given way to knocks on the door at all hours of the day and night. Malka, and after her the children, had grown used to seeing him closeted nearly around the clock with those who wished to learn from him or draw on his strength. Their Shabbos table had additional leaves put in to accommodate the flow of guests who came each week, attracted to the rabbi's incisive teachings and fund of homely wisdom. If they came, too, to warm themselves at the *rebbetzin*'s modest blaze, Malka scarcely knew it. She was too busy feeding them and listening to their stories and clucking over their troubles.

When some neighbors had urged him to start a minyan of his own, Avi had responded by throwing open his own living room on Shabbos mornings. Later, the sheer demand for space had led him to the small shul, four blocks away, that was his rented base to this day. His congregation had grown over the years; only a very few of the original group had left. With his installation in the shul, the rabbi's magnetism had seemed to acquire added power, and his personality gained luster. Avi's glamour, for Malka as well as for his congregants, had never faded. He was intellectual where she was prosaic, intense where she was matter-of-fact, spiritual where she was frivolous. Avi was everything she admired and a few things she didn't quite understand, and, without really analyzing it, she thought he made a terrific rabbi and they, the two of them, a terrific team.

The new shul building he was proposing to build was no more than he deserved. The road ahead was brighter than ever...except for this ominous development with Mutty. She was too clear-headed to think for a moment that her husband's complaisance over Mutty's proposed trip to Israel spelled anything like a capitulation. Avi was still doggedly bent on his own agenda, and Mutty on his. For an instant, she nursed a flash of uncharacteristic anger: against her husband for his intransigence, against Mutty for his mule-headedness. Two colliding visions, two contradictory needs, two stubborn men — with one despairing woman in between. Where would it end?

Malka struggled to her feet, exhausted but too high-strung from the two cups of black coffee she'd consumed in the past hour to sleep. Pulling the cord of her warm robe more closely around her, she shuffled away from the window and across the length of the living room in her worn, comfortable slippers. The house breathed quietly around her. The occasional hiss or creak was so familiar as to be unnoticed. Avi had returned some time ago and was presumably sound asleep upstairs, as was Mutty, who was staying the night rather than pitch his old jalopy against the high winds and sleet on the drive back to Lakewood. Even Hindy had finally replaced the receiver of her phone, giving that hard-working instrument a well-deserved rest, and switched off her light. The voices of rain and wind seemed to wrap the house snugly, making those who slept within its walls doubly blessed. But Malka couldn't sleep. She was thinking.

As will happen when we make the mistake of allowing ourselves to think when we're really tired, her thoughts took a depressing turn. Her natural optimism vanished without a trace in the Bermuda Triangle of worry, fatigue, and self-loathing. Gloom and despair ruled the night, with Malka their willing slave. Nothing in her life was going right. Her children were difficult, the house a disaster, her diet impossible. Worst of all, and contributing in greatest measure to the gnawing ache inside, Mutty was going away.

She had the sense of things changing. A chapter in her life, in all their lives, had ended last week, on Mutty's twenty-first birthday. So many new things to think about: Avi's building drive, Binyomin Hirsch's planned move back to New York, her own wishful and probably futile weight-loss campaign, Mutty going away.

The windows rattled. There was a steadily growing measure of snow mixed in with the rain now. Winter, having lulled its weary victims for a day or two, had returned with a vengeance. She looked ready to stay with them a good while yet.

Malka paused in her pacing to glance at the clock on the piano. (She really ought to get that fixed one day.) Twelve-twenty. Too late to phone anyone, probably not even Adela, night bird though she was. Too late...

Not for Israel, though. As though someone had spoken the words aloud, Malka heard them clearly. Israel was a full seven hours ahead of New York. In Jerusalem, where the Markoviches lived, it would be morning. The kids would be home (would Zalman be back from shul yet?), and Esther would doubtless be standing in the kitchen whipping up something nutritious for their breakfast. The scene grew so vivid in Malka's overheated and overtired imagination that it was all she could do not to pick up the phone and call to find out if she was right.

Then she thought, *Why not?* Esther's letter was lying unanswered on Malka's dresser. There was also her guilt at having left it unread on the kitchen counter for so long. Why not make a quick call, to surprise them all in their distant place with an early "good Shabbos"? Some people phoned all the time rather than submit to the chore of letter-writing. Why, this once, couldn't she?

Some women will, when feeling low, splurge on a new dress or hat. Malka's greatest comfort was talk. Without allowing herself another second to think, she hurried to the kitchen phone, feeling lighter and happier with each step. How surprised Esther would be to hear her voice! And how exciting for the kids!

"I'll make it real short," she promised herself aloud. she held her breath as the connection was made. It always seemed improbable, almost miraculous, that the push of a few buttons could span such a chasm of space. A low, intermittent buzzing told her that the Markovich phone was ringing.

"Hello?"

"Hi, who's this?" Without waiting for a reply, she announced triumphantly, "This is Tante Malka!"

"Tante Malka? Ima, it's Tante Malka from America! Tante Malka, are you still there? My mother's coming right away. She's in the room with the baby. Are you really calling from America? Oh, by the way, this is Tzippy!"

Malka started talking to her niece, asking the usual questions about school and family. She was in the middle of a sentence when she realized that the girl was no longer with her. A new voice demanded, "Hello? Hello?"

"Esther? It's me, Malka! How are you?"

"Malka? Is everything all right?"

"Sure, everything's fine. I —"

"Are you sure? Then why are you calling? Did something happen?"

Malka's heart began to sink. "No," she said, less buoyantly. "Everything's really okay, Esther. I just wanted to call, to see how all of you are doing, and to say good Shabbos."

" 'Good Shabbos?' " It was Friday morning there. Almost as if she herself were standing in that Jerusalem kitchen, Malka caught an all-too-vivid glimpse of what her sister-in-law was doubtless seeing at that very moment: the hastily assembled breakfast in various stages of consumption on the table; kids in the throes of eating or packing briefcases or playing or fighting; mops and buckets on hand to attack the floor after they'd gone; vegetables waiting to be chopped and chickens cleaned; the biggest pots and pans standing ready to serve their Friday duty — hours and hours of weekday still to attack and conquer before the luxury of saying "good Shabbos" was won. She sighed. "I know it's a little crazy. I just felt the urge to say hello, that's all."

Esther relaxed. Her voice, slightly shrill earlier, dropped a few notches. "It's not crazy. It's very nice. We're all fine, thank God. And you? How are you and Avrumi and the kids?"

After that, the conversation proceeded along expected lines. When she finally hung up — after hearing, in brief, the exciting news of Shoshie's prospective *shidduch* and passing on the news, thrilling in its own way, of her own Mutty's impending arrival — Malka felt, for the first time that night, tired enough to sleep.

❧

A little later, in pleasant communion with her pillow and blanket, she felt something niggling at the edges of her consciousness. Something she'd meant to tell Avi when he came home from the *shiur*. Tired as she was, she tried to ignore the half-memory. When that didn't work she made a feeble effort to capture it, but it persisted in eluding her. She felt asleep still trying to remember.

It was at six the next morning, as Avi was leaving the room, trying not to awaken his wife, when he was startled by a mutter from the tangled nest of blankets on the far bed.

"What? Malka, are you awake? Did you say something?"

The heap stirred. "Yesh. Phone call...last night. Forgot to tell you."

"A call, for me? Who was it?"

"Binyomin," came the drowsy reply. "He said to tell you...wants us to find him...place to live. Big favor, he said." The mound of bedclothes churned momentarily as she turned onto her other side and burrowed deep, already more than half asleep again. Her last words were buried and indistinct, but Avi just caught them.

"...says he's coming...two weeks." The bundle of bedclothes moved slightly. "Avi? You heard?"

Avi gazed without seeing through the window at the flat gray of a winter's dawn.

"I heard," he said tonelessly. "Two weeks."

With a satisfied sigh, Malka promptly fell back asleep.

Avi remained glued to the window, lost in thoughts of his own, until the dawn had begun to brighten into day. With a start, he woke from his trance and began rushing outside. The early minyan would be waiting.

FOUR

1

Binyomin Hirsch pulled up in front of his rather oddly shaped white house. With a flick of the wrist he switched off his car, his thoughts, and the whole California jurisprudence system in one neat motion.

Another long week in the attorney's life was behind him. Industriously, he'd defended, prosecuted, and billed clients powerful and wealthy and considerably less of both; he'd analyzed and soliloquized and compromised. Many of his colleagues were still to be found where he'd left them, in their offices, with the tall windows overlooking downtown Los Angeles, buzzing around the beehive of their legal affairs on this late Friday afternoon. But for Binyomin, that portion of his existence had been neatly excised the moment he'd stepped into the vast, muggy parking area beneath the commercial complex and hurried to retrieve his car. The mental break had taken a little longer. Stray thoughts of his current cases and their complexities revolved in their habitual way through his lawyer's mind on the drive home; but these, too, dissolved with finality at the sight of his house.

It sat in its square of modest garden, waiting, it seemed to Binyomin, with a reproachful air. He had planned on freeing himself much earlier today. As it was, there was little time now for anything except getting ready: Shabbos was coming.

As he stepped from the cool comfort of his expensive car into a hazy Los Angeles winter's day, his thoughts reverted, as they'd been doing virtually nonstop for the past few weeks, to New York. In a little less than two weeks, he would be trading the West Coast for the East; substituting the new for the routine; exchanging security for uncertainty, and only the hope of better things to come.

It would be a tremendous change in so many different ways. Hadn't Malka Weisner, the last time they'd spoken, mentioned that it was snowing in New York? And also, if he remembered correctly, the time before. They were having some winter back East — one storm after another. Hard to imagine ice-covered streets here, where the date palms waved in the breeze and the yellow acacias bloomed overhead. Winter's cold, cruel face seemed very remote in this place; Californian bad weather was of the suffocating rather than the stinging variety. Thinking of the East Coast and winter storms, Binyomin had the uneasy feeling that he just might be about to plunge into a very personal maelstrom of his own — and one that encompassed much more than just the weather.

Snow. It had been a long time since he'd stepped into the stuff, though he'd loved it as a boy. Snow, and the skyscrapers of Manhattan that dwarfed all else with such magnificent disdain, and Boro Park pizza... Good things, all of them, or at least, not evil. But like a film on a mirror, they were overlaid with the dark sheen of the pain that came after. Strange, how the bad times were so barbarously interwoven with the older, better ones, so that the bad fouled the good with its poison. All the years of his youth before he'd met Pessie, before he'd married her, should have remained, in memory, the sweet, hopeful things they'd been. But it didn't work that way. Looking back, the knowledge of what would come impinged on the innocence, the happiness, of what was before. The mirror of memory had grown black, speckled with something more than just age. It didn't seem fair.

Grinning wryly, Binyomin rummaged in his leather briefcase for the key to the front door. Since when, in all his experience as a man and as an attorney, was life "fair"? If you were a religious Jew — as, thank God, he was — you discarded whining, childish notions of "fair play" and clung instead to the Source of the truth, Creator of *emes*, true activator of events in this world. You stopped expecting to be let in on the big secret behind it all, quit demanding to be privy to the behind-the-scenes workings of the divine plan. You just concentrated on doing your part, on fulfilling your sacred obligations toward man and God, and tried to grow up a bit in the process.

The house was a Spanish-style villa, with a great deal of white stucco surface meant to imitate adobe, terraces flying into the air on three sides to give the place a contrived and lopsided look, and long red shingles over a flat roof. It wasn't a house much to his taste; but then, fleeing New York ten years before, and the agony of disillusionment, he'd had neither the heart nor the energy to prolong the search. This was the first place he'd been shown. It was in the right neighborhood, and the rent wasn't any more outrageous than usual. The housing agent got her finder's fee, and Binyomin got a place to lay down his head and to try, in a blaze of furious activity, to create a new life for himself from the ashes of the old.

There had been moments when the big house echoed with its own emptiness until Binyomin thought he'd go mad. But a new life was what, after a fashion, he had indeed carved out in these L.A. years. In the first aftermath of grief, he'd returned to Torah study with a passion that made his earlier efforts pale by comparison. His professional accomplishments, too, were impressive enough to make his services in constant demand. The attorney's reputation went before him. Now, Binyomin Hirsch could be fairly certain of a warm welcome in whatever city and with whichever firm he chose to practice.

He had yielded at last to the many lures that were cast out at him — but not for the reason his soon-to-be employers thought. Money had little to do with his decision, though his New York earnings promised to be an impressive improvement even over his current one. No, his leaving marked a surrender of an entirely different kind. After ten years of avoiding it, Binyomin had succumbed at last to the logic of his own life. California might be a paradise, and he had gained prestige and real satisfaction from his work here. But this was not where he belonged.

On the level where it really counted, he had reached an impasse. To progress any further, to grow past the place where he'd taken root and happily vegetated during all of this long, lucrative decade — to take up the reins of what truly constituted his life — he must go back to the place that represented its bleakest aspect. In the same dark closet that held the monster memories, he would seek the shining sword that would finally slay them. L.A. had baubles aplenty to amuse and distract him; swords were in pitifully short supply. New York would have to supply that.

The decision had not come easily. Resistance was strong. He was like a child who screws up his face and turns away from a bitter medicine, knowing it necessary but not liking the need. It had taken him literally years to understand that to embrace his future he must find the courage to confront his past.

A long time, longer than necessary, perhaps. Maybe that was because the present was so bearable — at times, much more than merely bearable. Binyomin was not by nature a sufferer. The pain had been imposed upon the man, not fashioned by him. He could dance through life's ballrooms with the best of them. The only problem was, he was dancing in place.

L.A. had treated him kindly; but he had finally come to recognize that she could never be more to him than a traveller met on an alien road and soon parted from, with some affection but little regret. He had pretended hard and pretended well, but he had finally come to recognize the truth that New York had known all along. That ocean-licked city held him fast in her grimy, glorious, violent, vibrant grip. New York owned Binyomin Hirsch.

કર્જ

The phone rang just as he entered. Throwing off his jacket and pulling loose his tie in one fluid motion, Binyomin went to the nearest extension — in the living room — and lifted the receiver.

The voice that greeted him was that of his neighbor and friend, Daniel Fruchter.

"Binyomin? Just calling to confirm that you'll be with us tonight."

"I haven't forgotten, Danny. Tell Miriam I'm expecting a nice big slice of her mocha cream pie. On second thought, make that two."

Danny Fruchter chuckled. "Sorry, it's homemade sherbet tonight. Plus some fabulous brownies."

"Can we change the subject?" Binyomin asked plaintively. "I'm starving."

"So eat something, you big ninny. Or didn't they teach you that in law school?"

"I wouldn't remember that far back. Besides, there's no time for food; I just walked in. Haven't even showered yet. Where are you davening tonight, Danny?"

His friend allowed the conversation to amble along for a few more minutes, before saying in an unexpectedly somber vein, "We're all gonna miss you, boy. Yanky's heart is broken already, just thinking of it."

So is mine... "Seriously, I'll miss you guys, too. You've been good to me."

"I hope your friends back in New York appreciate you the way we do." Fruchter paused. "And take the same care of you."

"Don't worry, Danny. Avi Weisner and his wife are like family. Better, in some ways." Binyomin, as Fruchter well knew, was an only child of parents who had died years before. His nearest relative was an elderly aunt who lived in Cincinnati. He was, in the baldest and most brutal sense, alone in the world.

"What you need —" Fruchter began.

"— is a good wife to take care of me. I know, I know." Binyomin gave a good-humored sigh. "Well, I'm trying. What do you think I'm off to the Big, Bad Apple for?"

Five minutes later he was in the shower, and five minutes after that racing with most unlawyerlike haste to get ready for Shabbos. He thanked God for the need for haste, which banished the unwelcome thoughts — and thanked Him, too, for Shabbos. That holy day, even more than the rigid timetable of his workaday responsibilities and courtroom obligations, bound and gave structure to his life. Shabbos not only lent a physical context to his week, it also reminded him of the higher, broader purpose of his life in which offices and courtrooms had no part.

Whistling under his breath, Binyomin stood before his bedroom mirror. He saw a fortyish man, tall, broad-shouldered, and still fairly trim. His hair was a rich chestnut brown not yet touched with gray. The dark-blue eyes in the mirror met his own with a characteristic directness.

"Well, this is it, buddy," Binyomin told his reflection. "Our last Shabbos in L.A." He knotted his imported silk tie, ran a brush through his still-damp hair, and checked his watch. He had five minutes.

It took four for him to dash across the street and halfway up the block to the Fruchters', another ten seconds to greet them breathlessly and make his way to the white-clothed table bearing its precious weekly burden of Sabbath candlesticks. An overhead halogen fixture filled the room with brilliance and made the silver smile. Miriam Fruchter was just finishing her blessing; she stepped aside for Binyomin to make his over the pair of candles she'd prepared for him.

The beauty of the silver, the bright, warm light, the serenity of the house, uplifted his spirits first — and then hurled them cruelly down. This was, perhaps, the most difficult part of his week. With a tongue grown suddenly thick, he recited the blessing over the Shabbos candles, the archetypical woman's mitzvah. Again he was struck by the almost grotesque inappropriateness of the act. What was he doing here, thousands of miles from the place he'd been born and raised, wifeless and childless and making the blessing that his own father had never, not once in his life, uttered?

As he stared bleakly into the flames, there was an expression in Binyomin's eyes that not even his closest friends would have recognized. It was full of the things he kept hidden from the world. The expression held all his longing, his loneliness, the deep-felt ache for a true companion of his heart. For a man alone, Shabbos, with its emphasis on joyous family togetherness, was a deep, dark well — made deeper and darker by the need to dissimulate before others, and the obligation to drive away the grief that was prohibited on this day. He was like a soldier dealt a fresh wound each week, with scarcely a hope of ever being permitted to stagger off the bitter battlefield. He felt abandoned and alone, cut off from the masses of people who celebrated the day along with him and didn't know, or remember, how lucky they were. Every song, each pleasant, shared ritual, seemed to mock him with the knowledge of his own solitude. Rest he might find on this day, but joy — no. Not yet.

The tiny twin fires he had just lit flickered before him, pure and intense as his own longing. Sometimes, as he worked and laughed and revolved through the busy circle of his days, Binyomin would wonder why being alone should weigh as heavily as a ball of steel on the shoulder — and why that ball should be so utterly invisible to the outsider's eye...

From behind him came the clatter of young feet. The three little Fruchter boys — the precious "second family" born to Danny and Miriam after the youngest of their three older children was already a teenager — were traipsing down the stairs to show off their Shabbos finery. Binyomin squared his shoulders before turning to meet them. Whatever would happen, whatever had already happened, he was trying his best. That was the thought he must cling to.

He greeted the trio of yellow-haired angels with his customary big smile. "Well, who wants a ride?"

"Uncle Binyomin!" squealed the youngest, Yanky, just before catapulting himself into his open arms. He stood and spun the boy around in the air, eliciting further delighted shrieks. He knew Danny was watching him at the door, and doubtless Miriam, too. *A natural with kids, that Binyomin,* he could almost hear them thinking. *Heaven grant that he be blessed with some of his own before too long!*

Well, that was one sentiment he wouldn't argue with.

When the third little boy had had his ride through the air, Binyomin gently disengaged himself from the eager clutching hands. "Well, who's coming to shul tonight?"

Miriam said, "It's too icy out for Yanky. He's going to stay home with Mommy. Right, sweetheart?"

Yanky looked undecided. When his brothers went for their coats, uncertainty turned into incipient rebellion. Binyomin stepped in, tickling him under the pouting chin.

"Say goodbye to Uncle Binyomin now. I'll be back in a little while for the Shabbos meal. Will you help Mommy get the table all ready for us?"

Rebellion died. "Sure!" Yanky assured him, the little face lit by a beautiful smile. "And the angels are coming, too!"

It seemed to "Uncle" Binyomin, walking through the light-filled house to the door, that they had already arrived.

2

Te way I've been running around," Malka told her friend Adela over coffee and croissants, "I ought to have lost twenty pounds this week."

Adela glanced significantly at the three cheese croissants — the specialty of the house — that had found their way to Malka's plate. Tactfully, she murmured only, "No luck, huh?"

"No luck — on any front. I haven't found a place for our friend Binyomin to live yet. I couldn't get Mutty on a direct flight to Tel Aviv; he's going to have to change in London and wait a couple of hours on the ground. And," Malka sighed, biting into the delicious, warm pastry, "I have not yet managed to lose an ounce."

The dairy restaurant/coffee shop was not the best place in the world to contemplate dropping excess cargo. The aromas drifting to their table from the nearby kitchen was enough to make the sternest Spartan abandon discipline. A waiter sailed by at that moment bearing aloft a laden tray featuring whipped-cream-covered crepes. Malka followed the tray with her eyes until it was deposited on another customer's table. It was with some difficulty that she brought them, and her attention, back to her friend.

"You'll do it," Adela was saying cheerfully. "All it takes is some self-control. There's no reason in the world why, with a little will power, you can't lose every one of those extra pounds in no time."

"Goodness," Malka told her croissant. "How I hate skinny people."

Adela laughed.

Malka's new friend — Adela and Yudy Moses had only moved into the neighborhood a little over a month ago — was not only slender, she was *naturally* slender. Malka had never once heard her bemoan her weight or seen her tackle, with wild vows, some promising new diet. Even worse, she insisted on such horrible practices as taking vigorous early-morning walks, attending a twice-weekly aerobic exercise class, and avoiding sugar like the plague. As a result, Adela's skin glowed healthily, and her large hazel eyes were bright, even when burning the midnight oil at her computer. Single-handedly, she had started a small, and modestly successful, business as a computer consultant. Malka could have envied her, if she hadn't liked her so much.

Almost as if she'd read Malka's thoughts, Adela set her coffee cup down in its saucer and said, "Malka, I've just had a brainstorm. A really terrific idea. Why don't you join my aerobics class?" The morning walks, she knew, were out of the question given the size of Malka's family and the nature of her frantic daily rush to get them off to school on time. Even as she voiced the suggestion, Adela was mentally preparing herself for a blunt refusal. She fully expected Malka to gape at her incredulously, then toss back some suitably flippant retort putting both her and her ideas in their place.

"Aerobics?"

"Yes! I know you usually shy away from anything that looks, sounds, or smells like exercise. But it'll help you stick to your diet and give you energy besides — a real boost. Besides, it'll be fun doing it together. What do you say?"

The kitchen doors swung open to reveal another young waiter carefully balancing his load. They were treated to a tantalizing whiff of hot onion soup under a skin of melted cheese. Malka glanced at the passing tray, then looked down again at her mug, slowly rotating it in her thoughtful fingers. Adela waited.

At last Malka looked up. She said, "Okay. I'll do it."

Adela stared. "You," she said solemnly, "must really be serious about this."

"I am. And not just about my weight. I've been thinking about...other things. Getting out more, taking classes, tidying the closets. Generally getting into shape." She hesitated, gazing again into the depths of her mug. "You see, I have this feeling that things are changing, and I need to be at my best to handle them."

"Malka, you sound strange. What is this, some kind of premonition?"

Malka just shrugged. Adela probed, "What sort of things?"

Malka's shoulders rose and fell again, as if she already regretted the confidence. "Just...things. It's a feeling I have. Not very logical, maybe, but there it is."

"You'll miss Mutty." Adela's voice was compassionate.

Malka's eyes filled. "Yes," she whispered, "I will. I know he's not going for long, but it seems like a break anyway. There's something so final about it." She drank again, then set her cup down so hard that the remaining liquid sloshed nearly to the top. "Come on," she said brusquely, rising to her feet. "If I stay here much longer, I'll start eating the tablecloth."

Agreeably, Adela rose along with her. As they sorted out the tip, she remarked, "So what are you going to do about this friend of yours — Binyomin, is it? Where will he live?"

"With us," Malka said, with a return of good cheer. "At least, until we find something better. Binyomin's like family. And we're just about all he has — in New York, anyway." She glanced in sudden speculation at Adela. "You know something?"

"What?"

Whatever it was that had been on Malka's mind, she abruptly dropped it. Starting briskly for the door, she threw back over her shoulder, "Nothing."

Adela raised a quizzical brow. Then she lifted the collar of her wool jacket to her chin and followed Malka out into the cold, bright morning.

3

Shabbos morning, in her husband's shul, was when Malka Weisner came into her own. In that place and that time, she was truly the Rebbetzin.

Flanked by her daughters, she would make her way with an unconscious but becoming dignity to the seat reserved for her: in the center of the front table, closest to the partition. From that position, she had an excellent view of the door and every newcomer who walked through it. Before, after, and between davening she greeted old friends and smiled at strangers, waiting to be introduced. Inevitably, she would be. Everyone wanted to be noticed by the Rebbetzin. Weekly worshippers looked forward to a few words with her, and the odd guest felt privileged to make her acquaintance.

In those two hours, Malka was in her element. It didn't matter that her kitchen sinks overflowed with unwashed dishes and that her closets didn't bear close scrutiny. Her pretty, round face glowed as she held court, secure in the knowledge that the excess pounds were well-hidden beneath the lip of the table. Here, all her natural exuberance and friendliness were given free play. Here, for two hours every week, Malka was most truly herself. And she was happy.

Hindy sat behind her, looking up from her siddur to smile dutifully at those who greeted her. She took her spiritual duties not only seriously but solemnly and considered her mother's chatter in shul — though not actually prohibited — as inappropriate. Malka herself saw it otherwise. Wasn't this a major part of her job as the rabbi's wife, being friendly and warm to the shul's female contingent? Despite the undercurrent of disapproval emanating from her daughter, she enjoyed being in shul with Hindy. She took great pleasure from the whispered compliments of the other women, after they said their "good Shabbos" to Hindy. That is, some of them whispered. Others, turning from the girl to the mother as if they thought the gesture somehow made the girl magically disappear, would announce with very audible rapture, "She's growing up into a beautiful girl, Rebbetzin. A real *kallah meidel* soon. You should have a lot of *nachas* from her!'"

"I do," Malka would return, radiant. "I do."

Hindy's cheeks burned.

Shani, the second daughter, didn't mind what her mother did, except if she introduced her to too many new people. Without a book in her hand Shani was lost. The straight brown bangs hung into her eyes as she bent her head to avoid encountering the glances of the other women. For most of the Shabbos service she could be found staring fixedly into the pages of her siddur, though not for the same reason her sister did. The twelve-year-old was painfully shy.

It was on such a Shabbos morning in shul, exactly one month ago, that Malka Weisner had met Adela Moses.

The *ba'al korei* was just finishing his recitation of the week's Torah portion. As the men, on their side of the partition, busied themselves with the rolling up of the Torah scrolls, Malka looked up from her Chumash. A stranger had walked into the ladies' section. She was on the tall side, but not too tall, and very slender. The hair of her dark brown wig fell naturally to her shoulders; the navy suit well-made but not overly expensive. All this Malka noticed in the few seconds it took the newcomer to walk through the door and look around for an empty place at the tables. The woman's eyes were intriguing, tilted slightly upward at the edges and a vivid hazel color. Just now they were uncertain. Malka smiled and beckoned.

"Good Shabbos. I'm Mrs. Weisner." Malka rarely introduced herself as Rebbetzin. "Are you here in the neighborhood for Shabbos?"

The woman had answered in a low voice, as if afraid of disturbing the others, though by now the ladies' section was softly abuzz. It would remain so until the beginning of the *mussaf* service. "Actually, for a bit longer than Shabbos. I've just moved in."

This interested Malka enormously. "Really? Where do you live?"

The woman gave an address.

"And what's your name?"

"Adela Moses."

Malka beamed. "Good Shabbos, Mrs. Moses! Welcome to the neighborhood. Will your husband be davening here regularly, do you think?"

Adela flushed and pulled herself up in an instinctive gesture of self-protection. "I'm a widow."

"Oh! I'm sorry." Malka had indeed looked so crestfallen, and so genuinely contrite, that Adela had melted. Banishing reserve, she gave the *rebbetzin* a smile that lit her face and transformed it suddenly. Malka smiled back, thinking inconsequentially, *She should do that more often. What a nice person. I hope I'll see more of her.*

She did see more of her. The very next day, Adela had knocked on her door.

"I'm so sorry to disturb you, Rebbetzin, and on a Sunday morning, too. But you see —"

"First of all, I'm Malka. The only people who call me 'Rebbetzin' are people who don't know me very well." The implication was clear. She could see a certain relief in the other's face as she answered, "Okay...Malka. I'm Adela."

"Fine. Now, don't worry about it being Sunday. As far as I'm concerned, Sunday is no more or less hectic than the rest of the week. All right, maybe a little more, with some of the kids home, but believe me, you're not disturbing anything that can't wait." The accumulated mess from Shabbos was certainly not going to run away.

"Well, thanks. I would've called, except that they haven't hooked up my phone yet. The problem is, I work with computers for a living, and my computer's just gone on the blink — probably from the move; you wouldn't believe the way those men handled my things — and I desperately need to find someone to come repair it on a Sunday. I don't know anyone in these parts yet, so I thought —"

"Just a minute, Adela. I'm not really a computer person, but my husband might know."

And before Adela could draw breath to object — she'd had no intention

of bothering the rabbi with her troubles — Malka had gone off to the study
to consult Avi.

Three minutes later, Adela had the name of a reliable computer
repairman (he'd come in more than once, at Mrs. Gerber's behest, to
diagnose and treat the shul's cranky machine). She also had her first friend
in the neighborhood.

Malka had invited the Moseses, mother and son, to join them for a meal
the following Shabbos, but Yudy contracted a mild but enervating case of
the flu that Thursday and Adela, overriding the teenager's assurances that
he'd be fine alone, insisted on staying home to nurse him. The next Shabbos
she and Yudy spent at a cousin's house in Queens. Malka was adamant that
they grace her table on the Shabbos after that but neglected to mention this
to Adela until too late in the week; her friend had already accepted an
invitation from her downstairs neighbors. It was only on the following week
that Malka managed at long last to extract the long-overdue promise from
Adela.

On this frosty Wednesday morning, as she watched her husband put on
his coat to go out to the shul for *shacharis*, Malka said, "I finally got Adela
to agree to come for a meal this Shabbos, and, with Binyomin coming only
on Sunday, we'll be able to give her and Yudy our full attention. I can't wait
for you to meet her, Avi. She's really special. And from what she says, so is
her son, Yudy."

"A good boy," Avi agreed, thrusting his hands into a pair of worn leather
gloves, protection against the frost outside.

"You know him?"

"He's been coming to minyan. In fact, he's davening tomorrow morning.
He has *yahrtzeit*."

"His father?"

"Yes." Avi gave her a goodbye smile, and left. A blast of cold air came
in to take his place. Shivering in her robe, Malka shut the door, her mind
full of the sadness of a fifteen-year-old saying Kaddish for the father he could
hardly remember.

4

R ight from the start, from the very moment of their introduction, Avi realized there was going to be trouble between Mrs. Gerber and Sammy Mirsky.

A spark of mutual animosity was instantly struck as the tinder of Sammy's young, brash charm was brought up hard against the secretary's flinty disapproval. Even in that first meeting, the rabbi felt a noticeable rise in the temperature of his little working kingdom. He wondered uneasily whether and when it would grow too hot for comfort.

At first, the animosity seemed to be all on Mrs. Gerber's side. Sammy greeted her cheerfully enough as he took of his bulky winter coat.

"Hi there, Mrs. Gerber." He threw her a pleasant smile that held just the right touch of diffidence. "Nice to meet you."

"Pleased to meet you," the middle-aged secretary replied in sour greeting, her tone of voice making it crystal clear that the pleasure for her in this meeting was, in fact, slight to nonexistent. Her sharp glance travelled to the rabbi. "A fund-raiser, you said?" She made the word sound somehow discreditable.

"Yes." Avi didn't understand the source of her hostility, except possibly in the very fact that Sammy Mirsky was young, untested, and — perhaps the most important factor — an unknown entity. Mrs. Gerber didn't like changes. "As I told you the other day, we're planning a major campaign to raise money for a new shul building — finally!" He twinkled at Mrs. Gerber, hoping to draw her out of her ill humor. Mrs. Gerber did not oblige him.

"I see."

Avi found himself explaining further, anxious for her approval. Malka sometimes laughed that the secretary was a substitute mother for Avi, who had lost his own at the age of seventeen. If so, she was a dour and hard-to-please mom. "You see, I myself have neither the time nor the expertise to launch such a campaign. Some of the shul's supporters have

urged me to hire somebody with drive, with experience. Well, here he is."
The full power of his smile was turned on the younger man, as if to make up
for his assistant's coolness. "Well, welcome aboard, Sammy."

"Thank you, Rabbi. I'll sure do my very best. Now, if you don't mind,
I'd like to see the lists you have. We have to decide who gets a letter, who
gets a phone call, and who gets a personal visit."

Avi looked faintly alarmed. "Would I have to do the visiting?"

"Only in a few special cases. I'll take care of the rest." Sammy grinned
disarmingly. "That's what you hired me for, isn't it? To take the job off your
hands."

"That's right." Gratitude swept over the rabbi, not so much toward the
new fund-raiser as to the One above, Who had provided this help just when
it was so sorely needed. Sammy, turning abruptly businesslike, took off his
sports jacket and rolled up his sleeves. "The lists, Mrs. Gerber?"

If Mrs. Gerber resented the peremptory tone, she made no sign of it. Her
face, in any case, was already pinched and sour enough this morning. She
moved stiffly but rapidly toward the filing cabinet in a corner of the big outer
office, a blur of gray in her drab dress. Avi watched her anxiously.

"I'm sure the two of you will work just beautifully together," he said with
an optimism that seemed, at the moment, quite baseless.

"Oh, sure." Sammy spoke absently, immersed in the neatly typed lists
Mrs. Gerber had pulled from her meticulous files. Mrs. Gerber sat again at
her desk and set up a clatter at her typewriter; she was staunchly
old-fashioned in her refusal to learn the ways of the more modern word
processor that sat on its stand in lonely splendor. Peace — or a reasonable
facsimile of it — seemed to reign in the outer office. Avi retreated toward
the door of his inner sanctum.

Just as he reached it, Sammy looked up from his lists.

"Oh, excuse me — Rabbi?"

"Yes, Sammy?"

"There's one more thing we need to discuss this morning, if that's okay
with you. Bank accounts."

"The shul has one. The First National City, just around the corner. You'll find it convenient." Avi entertained a brief but enjoyable vision of huge cash deposits borne to their rest within those marble walls, leading, in turn, to meetings with architects and contractors, exciting pages of blueprints, and, finally, the roar of bulldozers breaking ground for his new shul. And one day, an ark of rich, glowing wood to house the shul's Torah scrolls with all the dignity and grandeur he could provide for them...

"We should set up a separate account," Sammy was saying. "A building fund. You want to separate that money from your other income and expenditures."

Avi thought about that, then nodded. "A sound idea. Fix it up for us, will you?"

"Sure." Sammy paused.

The rabbi's mind wandered with increasing urgency toward the *sefarim* in his little office and the sources he'd been meaning to look up this morning before his overfull schedule of counseling appointments. In addition, he had to find time today for a visit to the hospital — old Feinzeiger had been admitted last night with chest pains — and some shopping he'd promised to do for his wife, over her head with last-minute preparations for Mutty's trip to Israel and Binyomin Hirsch's impending arrival. He refrained — barely — from glancing at his wristwatch. "Is there anything else now, Sammy?"

"Just one thing. The bank will probably want two signatures on the new account."

"I'll go, Rabbi," Mrs. Gerber spoke up quickly. "Mr. Mirsky and I can sign. That way, we won't have to bother you every minute for your signature."

Sammy shot the older woman a look of irritation, bordering on pure dislike. "I really think, Rabbi, it would be more appropriate to have *your* signature. Maybe I could save you some time by bringing home a signature card from the bank for you."

Avi recognized the not-so-subtle battle of wills being played out before him, and he wanted no part of it. Trusted secretary though Mrs. Gerber was,

Sammy was the one in charge of this project. It wasn't fair to saddle him with a job of this magnitude and then hobble him hand and foot with doubts, undermining his authority. Without looking at Mrs. Gerber, Avi said, "This is your baby, Sammy. Do whatever you think is best."

"Thank you, sir."

He felt, rather than saw, the smoldering glare his secretary cast first at him, then at Sammy. He didn't see it because he'd already, without a backward look, gratefully escaped to his office and his beloved *sefarim*.

Behind him, the typewriter started up again, fast and furious as machine-gun fire. He closed the door, and the sounds of battle grew comfortably muted. Pulling a thick volume off the shelf, the rabbi sank into his well-padded armchair and lost himself in the most exhilarating pastime he knew: probing the infinite mysteries of the Torah.

5

The boy's voice rose above the deeper, more tired ones of the men, wrapped in their prayer shawls as they'd so recently been wrapped in sleep. Not that Yudy Moses wasn't tired, too. He seemed to have an enormous capacity for sleep these days — and also for the gargantuan appetite for life that drove away sleep. The nights held too many possibilities to make mere sleep enticing. There was his learning, his astronomy books (this past summer, in the mountains, he'd discovered the delights of star-gazing — a delight dimmed, but not destroyed, by the smoggy New York night skies), and his science-fiction adventure books. His mother might bemoan the late hours he kept, but Yudy couldn't bear to close his eyes while there were so many interesting things still left to do. He paid for it in the morning, though.

This morning, he'd risen especially early, yawning repeatedly and so hard that afterwards he was surprised to find his face still in one piece. He had a strange feeling in the pit of his stomach, thinking of the reason for this early-morning rush. It was his father's *yahrtzeit*. Twelve years ago, on this day, the man he'd once known as "Daddy" had died. He'd seen the wedding picture, heard his mother's quiet stories of her good husband, Reuven Moses. But the man had no reality for him.

This was Yudy's guilty secret. He worried about it sometimes. Was it right to feel nothing about one's own deceased father? Was it okay to be just as happy as anyone else, to feel perfectly content with his mother and their own small, comfortable home, even though they were such a tiny, chopped-off sort of family? Once, in a late-night talk over hot chocolate shortly before his bar mitzvah, he'd confided some of these worries to his mother. Adela had told him very firmly that it was all right to be happy. More, it was a big mitzvah. He'd felt better about it since then.

In a sweet singsong not yet marred by the dullness of habit, Yudy recited the Kaddish at the end of davening. From every corner of the shul came a chorus of answering "amens." Slowly he unwrapped his tallis. It had felt right while he'd worn it to lead the minyan; now it felt strange on his shoulders. The rabbi came over to him, smiling.

"Well done, Yudy."

The boy flushed with pleasure. "Thank you, Rabbi."

"You and your mother are due for a meal with us this Shabbos."

"Yeah. We're looking forward to it," Yudy said shyly.

"Good. Well, have a good day." With another smile, Avi half-turned to go.

"Uh, excuse me. Rabbi?"

Avi turned back. "Yes? What is it, Yudy?"

The boy took a deep breath. This was something he hadn't planned on, but now that the rabbi was standing here, right in front of him, why not ask? It was hard to reconcile the man standing before him now with the dynamic speaker he worshipped from afar on Thursday nights. With a shy smile that illuminated his face as if a candle had been lit behind his eyes, Yudy asked, "Maybe, after the meal on Shabbos — if you have a few minutes — we could... Um, I just thought that maybe..."

"Would you like to talk something over?"

Relief shone from Yudy's face. "Yes. Uh, not about something in particular. I mean, I don't have any problems or anything. I just have all sorts of questions...thoughts... Things I'd like to talk about. To, uh, hear your opinion on. You know?"

Avi nodded, while his heart did a queer, little twisting dance. Yes, he knew, or thought he did. Without a father of his own to talk things over with — with whom to share and dissect and discuss the endless wonderment called life — Yudy was searching for a substitute. He needed so much, this teenager. A role model, a confidante, a sounding board. And what made his request so impressive was that he hadn't been afraid to ask.

"Yes," the rabbi said quietly, his eyes and voice warm. "I'll be glad to spare you a few minutes on Shabbos, Yudy. Or more than a few."

"Thanks a lot!" With a duck of his head, the boy mumbled, "Well, see you."

"Goodbye. Have a good day."

"You, too." Yudy grabbed his tefillin bag and all but flew out the door, on the twin wings of elation and embarrassment.

Avi would remember that conversation long afterwards with a curious clarity. It would be the last time he would glimpse that particular grin on the boy's face — a grin of sheer joy in being young, in knowing himself alive to every exciting nuance in the world around him. In fact, it would be quite a while before he saw another smile of any description on Yudy's face. There was a long road to be travelled — by both of them — before then.

But on this windswept morning in late January, Yudy's biggest problem was the snow that kept sneaking into the tops of his shoes and making his sock uncomfortably damp as he sped homeward.

As for Avi, he took his time, folding his tallis and tucking it neatly into its velvet bag. He decided not to think about Mutty, due to depart on Saturday night, or to worry about Binyomin's arrival, until he actually had to drive to the airport to see one off and meet the other. Binyomin was not due in New York until Sunday evening. The days and nights would be full enough until then: there was his usual schedule of rabbinical functions, including the *daf yomi shiur* he gave every morning and evening, his other classes, and the workload of counseling and consulting and writing; a fund-raising meeting on Wednesday with Schoenbrunner, Dickstein, and Sammy; the Thursday night *shiur;* the sweet madness of *erev Shabbos* at the Weisners; and finally Shabbos itself, with the Moseses as their guests. Thinking determinedly of all these things, and very determinedly *not* thinking about the old friend he would soon be welcoming into his home, Avi went home to breakfast.

6

The week passed, as weeks tend to do. Malka saw little of her husband. Avi was busier than ever, with meetings of his fund-raising committee now added to his already substantial schedule. The additional responsibility, rather than weighing him down, seemed to lighten the rest of the burden. He came home whistling at the end of his long day, with a few snippets to share with Malka — progress reports.

"That Sammy's on the ball, Malka! He's mapped out a campaign for us: letters, follow-up calls, a few people I'll have to go see, and a full schedule of personal meetings for himself. Schoenbrunner and Dickstein put together a list of some people with money, people who've been known to help."

Despite his bloodshot eyes and the tired slump of his shoulders, Avi glowed. He broke another piece of bread and used it to mop up the last of his wife's stew — a grayish, indeterminate mess that looked unappetizing in the extreme but was surprisingly tasty. As he ate, he vaguely tried to identify the bits and pieces, then gave it up. The experience of long years had taught him it was better not to ask.

"How long until you have enough to start building with?" Malka asked, elbows propped on the kitchen table as she kept him company at his late supper.

"I haven't asked. That's Sammy's domain."

"Aren't you interested?"

"Interested, yes. But I'm not about to poke around where I'll only get in the way. I'm going to stay in the background as much as possible. Sammy's got things under control, and that's what I hired him for. I don't want to cramp his style."

Avi didn't share with Malka the other, more genuine reason for his reluctance to plunge more deeply into fund-raising strategy. On some private, scarce-acknowledged level, he was a little embarrassed about this ambition of his — this burning desire for a shul of his own. Focusing as he did on affairs of the spirit, he was not as accustomed as other men to reaching out with both fists for material reward. He preferred to leave that end of things to Sammy, with Mrs. Gerber playing a strong — if reluctant — backup position.

That worthy woman might have agreed to take a back seat to Sammy Mirsky with respect to the campaign, but she did it so grudgingly as to skirt the border of churlishness. The tension in the shul office still rose alarmingly whenever Avi's two assistants were there together. But there were, thankfully, two factors that were serving to mitigate the situation. The first was that Sammy was keeping himself busy doing what he'd been brought on board to do. He made many industrious and mysterious trips out of the office — going out "into the field," as he liked to call it. In his frequent absences the office reverted to form, wrapped in its familiar peace.

The second factor was a young, newly married woman by the name of Naomi Brody. She had been hired to assist Avi's assistants in the more menial aspects of the fund-raising campaign. She was no great typist — Mrs. Gerber was twice as fast — but she was a pleasant individual who could stuff envelopes and apply gummed labels with the best of them. Her smiling presence in the shul office defused some of the tension. Whether Naomi was as oblivious to the undercurrents as she seemed to be, Avi didn't know. Nor did he particularly want to. He preferred to remain no more than vaguely aware of the ebb and flow of office politics. The rabbi chafed under the more or less open hostilities of the first few days, blessed the peace when it descended — after a fashion — at last, and put the whole matter out of his mind. He had too much else to think about.

This past Thursday's evening *shiur* had attracted his biggest crowd ever. Just a few weeks earlier, on a frigid, stormy night, the rabbi had stood up before a half-empty shul; this time, the crowd pushing into the enormous room had overflowed the rows of wooden pews and washed up to its very doors, where the late arrivals listened on their feet. Avi had no idea what led to these fluctuations. Right now, he guessed that people were fed up with the vicissitudes of the weather and grimly determined to pursue their lives despite it. Happily, the rabbi flourished under this influx of new students, growing even more eloquent in response to the added stimulus.

Stimulation was not lacking on the home front, either. What with Mutty's imminent departure and Binyomin Hirsch's approaching arrival, the Weisner household was in a frenzy of preparation. Malka hardly knew what to do first. Never at her best when it came to organization, she scurried about the three floors of her home clutching half-formed lists and muttering distractedly to herself. The two little boys were vacated from their room to make way for Binyomin. Malka assigned them to sleeping bags on the floor of their sisters' room. The girls protested the invasion — Shani in an undertone, Hindy at considerably higher volume. Under Malka's supervision they got rid of the unsightly mess of toys and games in the boys' room, then dusted, vacuumed, and polished furniture till it shone. The result was an oasis of order and cleanliness amid the homey clutter of the rest of the house.

Malka was the kind of hostess who believed firmly in the power of the comfortable detail. She spent a fruitless morning combing the house for a vase that was unchipped before finally going out to buy one. There would be fresh flowers on Binyomin's dresser when he arrived, and a selection of reading material by the bed to help him drop off to sleep on his first nights in his temporary, new-old home.

Mutty's departure entailed a massing of forces of a different kind. Malka took to haunting the supermarkets, looking for the little odds and ends that would ease her son's stay in Israel. Daily she returned home with bulging shopping bags; it was Mutty's problem to fit the oddly shaped items into his already groaning luggage. He had hoped to travel light, had even been naive enough to think of getting away with a single suitcase, but he was soon worrying about overweight. His mother was firmly of the Israel-as-wilderness persuasion and could hardly be made to hear Avi's reassurance that soap and shampoo — even American soap and shampoo — could be found in that distant country. This was Malka's labor of love for her son.

The hectic pace of her self-induced frenzy also left her little time for brooding or worrying: a silver lining in all this fog of activity.

Friday caught the Weisners at the height of the frenzy. Mutty was flying out on Saturday night, and Binyomin was due in New York the following evening. It was Avi's job to drive out to JFK Airport both times. Malka would accompany him on *motza'ei Shabbos* to see Mutty off but had elected to remain home on Sunday. "I'm sure you and Binyomin will have a lot to catch up on," she'd told her husband. "The ride back will give the two of you a chance to talk in peace. It'll certainly be quieter in the car than here at home."

Avi stroked his beard and pulled a smile out of it. "That's thoughtful of you."

"Oh, it's nothing. I know what Binyomin means to you."

Do you really? Avi hardly felt he really knew that himself.

But first there was *erev Shabbos* to be survived and Shabbos itself to be enjoyed. The former went by in a blur of motion, countermotion, urgent commands, raised voices, near-hysterical laughter, and, finally, exhausted satisfaction. Malka lit the eight-armed candelabra with fingers that trembled with fatigue as her mind, for the first time all day, ceased its racing. Everything that had to be done had been done. She could rest now.

"Good Shabbos," she called, lowering her hands from her face. She smiled at her second son: placid, blond-haired Shmulie, home from yeshivah this weekend to see his brother off. The table was set with the Shabbos china she and Avi had bought years ago, during their engagement. Though

The quarrels intensified as their bank account grew. What to buy, where to live, how to vacation; the issues were endless and yet monotonously the same. He kept hoping and praying for a child. Maybe a baby would settle Pessie, give her some focus for her life. (He had already, painfully, faced the fact that *he* was not that focus.) But the years crawled past, and the baby didn't come. He buried himself more deeply in his work and in his learning. He donated generously to his favorite causes and earned a name as something of a philanthropist. And Pessie continued to whirl in dizzying circles outside the house, and to fall into royal sulks when she was home.

In all fairness, Binyomin was not an easy person for a woman of Pessie's temperament to live with. When feeling hurt or misunderstood, he tended to withdraw into himself rather than engage in an open, verbal give-and-take. In other words, he refused to fight. This maddened and infuriated his wife. He'd gone into marriage expecting to be understood — in a deep way; no easy task even for a naturally empathetic and introspective helpmate, which Pessie certainly was not. She had married with vague dreams of sweet babies and a husband who would dance attendance on her through a whirl of nonstop gaiety. She was disappointed on both counts.

Disillusion had made life bitter for both of them.

The break, when it finally came, was surprisingly calm. They had spent a Shabbos in the usual way — that is, as separately as possible. At the end of the day, Binyomin sat at the kitchen table and made Havdalah. By the light of the braided candle, he saw his wife's angry, petulant face and realized, with a sense of wonder, that his own expression undoubtedly reflected that same look. He had just recited the blessing to the One Who divides the holy from the profane; and yet he felt as if there were no such divisions in his own life, in his marriage. The weekday misery spilled over into Shabbos, and the alienation of that day only served to further infect the following week.

He dipped the candle in wine, took a deep breath, and spoke his first words of the new week. But instead of the traditional "*a gutte voch*" — a good week — Binyomin turned to his wife and asked if she wanted a divorce.

The speed with which Pessie answered yes showed him plainly, and all too sadly, that she'd only been waiting for him to ask.

☙❧

He opened his eyes. He felt disoriented. By the evidence of his stomach, the plane was making a rapid descent. For a moment he was alarmed. Surely the pilot had, a moment before, said something about climbing?

He glanced at his watch and realized, to his shock, and also a little to his amusement, that he'd been drifting in the land of never-never for three hours. They were approaching Kennedy Airport.

Mechanically Binyomin straightened his seat and buckled his belt. He was obedient to all instructions, whether spoken aloud or flashed at him in lights above his head. He was an automaton, frozen in sudden, blinding fear.

The panic faded almost as fast as it had struck. He was forty-two years old, too old to indulge in such a weakness. If his flight into the past had done one thing for him, it was to negate the magnetism of memory. He no longer felt impelled against his will into the malevolent depths of what had been. He could look forward now — consider and even welcome possibilities. A strange peace washed over him, so that he felt comfortably drowsy and wanted to go back to sleep.

There was a swoop and a rumble, and then the plane touched down on the soil —or, more accurately, the concrete — of New York City.

3

As Avi Weisner paced back and forth before the arrivals window waiting for his first glimpse of Binyomin, he, too, was thinking of his friend's doomed marriage and its final sundering. Those were, after all, the salient features of Binyomin's life. Never mind the glittering and lucrative career; if a instructor, was a strict taskmaster. Tardiness was frowned upon, especially when it caused one of her students to miss any part of the all-important warming-up exercises. Malka was not the only one who found the stretches and sit-ups almost harder than the actual aerobic dance moves. But she didn't dare skip them: so many dire warnings had Mrs. Hellman dinned in their ears about the effects of poorly prepared exercise.

Malka gamely struggled into her sneakers and gym outfit and joined the others beside the gaily hued floor mats. The music blared abruptly from Mrs. Hellman's big sound box. The torture session began.

Some three-quarters of an hour later, panting and perspiring, Malka wriggled gratefully out of her gym shoes. She was not of the ranks of women who wore them for daily comfort. To her, sneakers were too grimly associated with the vicissitudes of exercise. She was glad to shove them into her bag and see the last of them until their reluctant reappearance at the next class.

It was on the drive home that she finally broached the topic she'd been saving up, as a gourmand will save a particularly delectable dessert. For a couple of weeks now she'd been turning the notion over in her mind, picturing it, planning it. For four days, since Shabbos, she had been able to enjoy the knowledge that Avi thought well of the idea, too. And for one whole day she had savored the marvelous taste of anticipation, knowing that she had the green light from Binyomin himself.

"Adela," she began without preamble, "I have a *shidduch* for you."

"Oh?" There was no change in her friend's tone or inflection, but Malka picked up a certain something in Adela's voice that spoke of carefully masked interest. "Want to tell me who he is?"

"Oh, no one special. Just...Prince Charming!" A torrent of giggles followed this pronouncement.

If Malka was giddy with excitement, Adela was granting herself an extra portion of sobriety. Eyes on the road, she inquired, "Does this paragon have a name?"

"His name's Binyomin Hirsch. You remember, our friend who just moved back here from L.A.?"

Adela quirked an eyebrow. "I think you've mentioned his name," she said wryly. "Once or twice."

"So he'll call you this week, okay?"

The car jerked and swerved slightly as Adela's foot eased on the gas pedal. Quickly she regained control. In an equally controlled voice, she said, "Malka, are you serious? Just like that, you expect me to give out my phone number?"

Malka looked suddenly uncomfortable. "Actually, I already gave it to him."

"Malka!"

"Listen, sweetie, he's perfect for you. Wait'll you meet him. He's a very successful lawyer, and a *talmid chacham*, *and* handsome, and rich! He also happens to be a super-nice guy."

"How come Mr. Super-Nice happens not to be married?"

"Well, he was...for five years. Unfortunately, to the wrong woman. He's been divorced for nearly twice that long now. He's Avi's oldest and closest friend, Adela. Avi knows all the details of the divorce and will be glad to answer any other questions. Okay?"

A mischievous smile crinkled the corners of Adela's eyes. She asked with little-girl sweetness, "Please, may I have a little time to think it over?"

"Take all the time you want! Only don't wait too long. The minute word gets around that Binyomin's in town, he's gonna be grabbed right up. Just wait and see if he isn't!"

"Thanks," Adela said drily, "for first grabbing rights."

The irony was lost on Malka. She sat back, absently rubbing her aching legs. This whole aerobics business would have been well worth it, if only she came away with Adela's "yes" in her pocket to bring home and present to Binyomin. She began to wheedle and coax.

"Why don't you just let him call, Adela? One little meeting can't hurt you any, can it? Surely you trust Avi and me enough for just one little date, sweetie."

The car, with nary a skid, swung neatly into place in front of Malka's house. As always, Malka marvelled at her friend's proficiency behind the wheel. Her own Avi had not let her set foot in their car since the beginning of this ice-sheathed week.

Adela turned to her with a smile. Malka beamed back. Softly, but very firmly, Adela said, "I'll just think about it first...sweetie."

And with that Malka had to be satisfied.

She opened the car door. The wind met her there and wrapped her around in its long, chill arms. Malka shivered. She was braced for the leap to the sidewalk and the dash to her house, when, from behind, she heard her friend speak.

"A first date," Adela murmured. She might almost have been talking to herself. "It's been a long time. I'm not sure I remember how."

"You'll be great!" Elated, Malka twisted around to hug her. "So it's all settled. Binyomin will call tomorrow, okay?"

Before Adela could say another word, the *rebbetzin* had left the car and skipped up the treacherous path to the front door. Miraculously, she did not slip.

Equally miraculous, Adela did not phone her up as soon as she arrived home to countermand Malka's blithe assumption. Malka let elapse the full ten minutes she'd promised herself, in fairness, to wait. Then, in the highest of spirits, she ran into the study, where her husband and Binyomin were alternately learning and shmoozing.

"It's on, Binyomin!" she cried. "You can call Adela tomorrow. Oh, wait'll you meet her, she's such a doll!"

Binyomin's first bemused words were a vague echo of Adela's. "*Ribbono shel olam*, another first date? Help!"

"Your first *shidduch* back home. Your first New York date," Avi said encouragingly. "It should go with *mazel*."

"And also," Malka declared triumphantly, "the last. That's a guarantee, Binyomin."

5

If there's one thing that can be said to encapsulate the essence of every young girl's dreams, it is the First Date.

The beautiful strains of Mozart's "Eine Kleine Nachtmusic" wafted through the Jerusalem apartment like the most pleasurable of aromas. Esther, in the kitchen, paused in the act of scrubbing the sink to smile in sudden sentimentality. To hear Shoshie play was to gauge her mood to a nicety. The girl, as much as the notes she played, was floating.

Never mind school assignments and squalling siblings and the winter cold; Shoshie was a princess now, embowered in a place of roses and moonbeams. Esther smiled a moment longer before the sad question intruded: How long would the feeling last?

It seemed such a precious thing to the listening mother, because it was so fleeting. The sweet emotions that inspired the music shimmering now through the small, plain rooms were unrepeatable. The road stretched before the girl today, all unexplored, still utterly unknown. The first, small step — the first tentative venturing onto a new tarmac — would change that. Shoshie would meet this Benzy from Bnei Brak. She would either like him or not like him. In either case, the First Date would be behind her. She would have become, in a small but definite way, a more seasoned traveller than before.

The second prospective suitor would elicit a slightly less rapid heartbeat; the music would be, in some tiny, indefinable way, different. Even if, by the most glorious *mazel*, she became engaged to marry the first one, this Benzy, this one sweet moment of anticipation, of pure, distilled hope, would never come again.

At first Shoshie had babbled. She had discussed the big event with her mother, her twin, her closest friends, her diary. But as the day of the actual meeting drew ever closer, she grew silent, pulled into herself.

It was not that she wanted to exclude Bracha and the others; she was simply incapable of sharing the exquisite blend of hopes and fears with another living soul. The focus of all her thoughts was too elevated, too precious. Her prayers took on a new intensity, as did her music. Shoshie's dreaming fingers seemed to draw a new magic from the ancient piano. The high, pure notes washed over Esther in her kitchen and almost made her cry.

Tomorrow evening, in the spotlessly clean and respectably shabby Markovich living room, Shoshie would be meeting Benzy Koenig for the first time. And nothing, Esther knew, would ever be exactly the same again.

Change *was* lurking, just past the kitchen door and Esther's sparkling sink. Only it was not quite the kind she envisioned. If she had had an inkling of the events about to unfold in the coming days and weeks, she would doubtless have let the threatening tears fall. She probably could not have stopped them falling.

Only they would not have been tears of bliss, born in a delirium of sweet music and tender hopes. No, not those kind at all.

SIX

1

The attack of nerves did not come until the morning of the big day.

Shoshie and Bracha stood side by side at the mirror in their room. They should have been rushing to get dressed and catch the bus to school. Instead, with their usual wordless communion, they had elected to risk tardiness in granting this particular morning the respect that was its due.

In their school uniforms they looked remarkably alike. The mirror reflected identical long ponytails — a lovely auburn color — shining brown eyes, and surprisingly solemn noses. Only a closer study revealed the inner girl. Shoshie's manner was remoter and more intense, her eyes the eyes of a drinker of beauty, a careful sharer. Bracha's features, on the other hand, reflected an approach to life that was both more open and less curious; there was serenity in her look, and an attitude that was essentially down-to-earth.

Shoshie glanced at her sister's reflection and threw up her hands in a sort of despair. "That's it. I give up. I can't go through with it!"

"Silly. You'll be fine. You'll probably have the time of your life."

Shoshie made a face. "And if I don't?"

With a grin, Bracha said, "Then you'll still have a story to tell at school tomorrow."

"As if I'd tell. You know we're not supposed to talk about it to just anyone."

"I know. And I haven't. Now don't worry, Shosh. It'll be great, you'll see."

"If you're so optimistic," Shoshie growled, "why don't you go instead?" She gathered steam. "Who ever talked me into this thing, anyway? Neither Benzy Koenig nor his parents could care less which one of us he sees tonight. Be a pal, Bracha. Take my place!"

"Shoshie — "

"How are we different? Hardly at all. So I play the piano and you don't — big deal. Do you honestly think Benzy will know the difference? Tell you what: If he starts grilling you on Beethoven's sonatas, just tell him you're strictly a Bach woman. Tell him — "

"Shoshie. You're babbling."

Shoshie sighed. "I know. I'm nervous."

"That's clear enough." Bracha faced her sister. "Listen, you do want to meet him, don't you? Seriously."

"Seriously, I can't wait. He sounds wonderful."

"See? Just focus on that, and you'll be fine." Bracha became brisk and businesslike — Esther-like. "Come on, Shosh. You've got enough on your head today without being late for school, too."

Shoshie grumbled, "I don't know why Ima's making me go to school anyway." She turned reluctantly from the mirror to face the reality of her bedroom. Clothes, books, and shoes were tossed helter-skelter across the floor and bed on her side of the room. Bracha's half was noticeably neater.

"What do you need to stay home for?" Bracha asked sensibly, gathering her notebooks into her schoolbag. "To get more nervous?"

"Oh, Bracha. I just wish I were as normal as you."

"We're twins, remember? If I'm normal (and sometimes I have my doubts!), then so are you. Now, come on. Let's get moving."

They moved — Bracha briskly, Shoshie following dreamlike — through the kitchen, where they each downed a hasty breakfast *leben*, and then out the door. Esther, their mother, no less aware of the special nature of this day, had intended to exchange a word or two with Shoshie before the girl left. But Aryeh Leib chose this morning to pick a fight with Eli, and Esther had her hands full separating the two as they rolled and tumbled, half-laughing and half-sobbing, around the living room. The noise of their contretemps roused Savta from a fitful sleep, and she called out drowsily from her cubicle in a high, querulous voice. By the time order was restored, Savta placated, and something like a truce instituted, the twins were long gone.

It had begun to rain. Esther hoped the girls had remembered their umbrellas. It wouldn't do for Shoshie to meet her young man with a case of the sniffles.

The Markovich home that evening was a scene of controlled pandemonium. Esther had managed, by feats of organization hitherto unknown even to her, to serve supper, clear it away, and get the younger children into their pajamas a full hour ahead of their normal schedule. Even Aryeh Leib was induced — not without some difficulty — to abandon his friends and the lively game in progress in the parking lot below and to eat with the others and submit to a hasty bath. With considerable satisfaction, Esther watched the grayish bath water drain away as she shooed her "difficult" one off to his room. The worst was behind her now. Pandemonium, perhaps, but definitely controlled.

All this was accomplished without the helping hands of the twins, who were closeted together in their room, engaged in heavy consultation about Shoshie's wardrobe. As the star of the evening tried on and discarded outfit after outfit, the floor began to sprout a madly colored carpet of clothing. And when, at length, a suitable dress was finally chosen, the accessories called for equally earnest deliberations. Then there was Shoshie's hair to be fixed and her shoes to be shined and her dainty evening bag — bought specially for the occasion — to be crammed full of every necessary and unnecessary thing that could be thought of.

But eventually these decisions, too, were made. By "minus forty-five," the living room had been de-cluttered to Esther's specifications, leaving every highly polished surface utterly bare. The exception was the dining-room table, which bore a selection of tempting cakes. A pitcher of juice waited in the fridge. As for the human half of the equation, Esther had these firmly in hand as well. The little ones were in bed and the middle ones safely ensconced in their bedrooms, with many dire warnings lest they dare poke so much as a nose or a finger out of their doors while Benzy Koenig was in the house. The clock stood at minus forty minutes and counting.

Esther checked on the baby in his crib, then went to her own room to change her dress and see that Zalman's tie was clean. She found her husband there before her, running a brush along the rim of his best black hat. Combing her own *sheitel*, Esther breathed deeply — for the first time in hours, it seemed — and let herself begin to hope that the evening would actually go smoothly.

"Relax," Zalman advised, though he himself looked as though he yearned to be far, far elsewhere — preferably in his crowded little *machsan*, among his beloved quills and parchments.

Esther smiled. "I'll try. You relax, too, Zalman. Benzy's not going to bite."

They laughed comfortably together. The clock ticked on — minus thirty-five minutes...minus thirty and going fast... But Esther didn't mind that now. They were ready, or just about.

ⅎ⅍

It was the baby, Yoni, who formed the instrument of disaster.

In the distractions of the preceding days, an event of otherwise monumental significance had gone virtually overlooked in the Markovich household: little Yoni had learned to climb out of his crib unaided. He did it once, just before bedtime two days earlier, and was rewarded with a surprised, "Yoni! How'd you get out here?" as Tzippy, laughing, scooped him up and put him back in the crib. He tried it again the next night. This time it was Zalman who found him crawling delightedly along the hallway from his room.

"Oh ho, so you're up to that trick, are you?" the father had asked jovially, tickling the little fellow in the ribs. Yoni had giggled and squirmed and finally allowed himself to be put back behind bars.

He decided to give it another whirl tonight.

Quick as lightning, the small, practiced hands grasped the slats. The baby hauled himself to his feet in the crib, swayed for a moment, then stood sturdy. Moving more cautiously now, he lifted one pudgy pajamaed leg up and over the side. The other soon followed. He teetered precariously for a second, then let himself down over the other side and so to the floor.

Clutching the crib for support, Yoni stood still for a moment in the near-dark, savoring his triumph. He was, frankly, delighted with himself. Gurgling quietly, he dropped down on all fours and commenced his victorious crawl toward the light.

There was no one in the narrow passage to see him. From behind various closed and partially-closed doors came the sounds of hectic ready-making, but nobody stepped out to witness the journey of the small figure as he scurried past on hands and well-padded knees. His destination was the living room.

The baby's mind was intent on a particularly enticing image: the Lego castle his brother Eli had finished constructing only that day, and which he'd put up out of reach on the broad windowsill. The sofa stood just under that sill. Yoni, in his new confidence, had decided to attempt the climb up onto the sofa and to his goal.

Of course, there was always the chance that he'd fall off the sofa and get a nasty bump on the head. This had happened once or twice before. But that Lego was worth the risk. His victorious escape from prison had heightened Yoni's confidence. Excitement coursed through his miniature veins. He'd try it!

But when he reached the living room, his attention was diverted by a different, and far more enticing, opportunity. Someone — Aryeh Leib, probably — had left the front door unlatched. It stood slightly open, an invitation that ill became a boy of his caliber to ignore. Just beyond, Yoni knew, lay the stairs, and the unknown. Adventure beckoned! Without a second's hesitation, he changed course.

Ten seconds later, he had reached the heavy door and manhandled it open enough to accept the width of his little body. He wriggled happily through.

Three seconds after that, a howl reverberated up and down the stairwell. Yoni had tumbled down the stairs.

A curious neighbor, one flight down, opened his door and gasped with horror at the sight of the baby sprawled shrieking on the landing. Upstairs, at the Markoviches, it was Shoshie — inspecting herself in the full-length mirror that hung in the hall just outside her door — who heard the noise. She recognized her baby brother's howl immediately, though not the eerie echo that shadowed each syllable. Teetering a little in her new, heeled shoes, so different from the sensible flats she wore to school, she followed the sound to the living room. She saw the open door, heard the shrieks on the other side. She brought her hand to her mouth and emitted a shrill cry of her own. "Yoni!"

A few quick steps brought her to the door. She saw the baby, spreadeagled on the landing. There was a little blood on the floor and on the nearby stairs. A neighbor was clumping quickly up from the landing below. Shoshie started down at a run.

Two steps down, insecure in her high heels, she tripped. In a crazy, slow-motion tumble, she fell in her turn, landing at last, painfully, beside Yoni on the landing. The neighbor stopped in his climb to gape. There was a stab of pain in her ankle and the cheek that lay against the cold stone floor. A wave of dizziness engulfed Shoshie. She closed her eyes.

The clock stood at minus twenty-five.

2

Some seven minutes later, Esther, holding the still whimpering baby in one arm and supporting her shaken daughter with the other, took stock of the situation. What she came up with was, thank God, a relatively mild list of injuries.

Yoni had suffered nothing more dramatic than a nosebleed, which accounted for the spattering of blood on the stairs that had so frightened his older sister. He was bruised, shaken, and badly frightened, but otherwise unharmed.

Shoshie had not fared so well. In falling, she had painfully twisted her ankle. A neighbor doctor, hastily summoned to the scene of the double accident, reassured the anxious parents that there were no fractures.

"Just stay off that foot for a few days," he advised Shoshie. "It should be able to bear your feet by — oh, say, the end of the week."

Shoshie gulped. "Wh...what about my face?" she whispered.

The doctor surveyed the damaged area. A large, ragged, ugly scrape covered most of her right cheek, and her right temple boasted a very respectable bump, already the size of a robin's egg.

"An ice pack ought to keep the swelling down to a reasonable level," he replied cheerfully. "But I've got to warn you, that cheek will soon be turning every color of the rainbow." He dabbed again at the wounded area with disinfectant, then halted, embarrassed and a little impatient, as Shoshie stifled a sob that had nothing to do with the pain he was inflicting.

"Esther, Benzy is due here in less than twenty minutes," Zalman said urgently in his wife's ear. "He's travelled all the way from Bnei Brak for this date. Do you think Shoshie can manage to just sit in the living room with him, maybe?"

Shoshie heard. She jerked up her head, horrified. "Abba! There is no way in the world I can meet him tonight. Not with this face." She tried to stand, then slumped back against her mother's shoulder, wincing. "Not to mention this stupid ankle. It's killing me."

"She's right," Esther said decisively. "What Shoshie needs now is some aspirin and an ice pack and a good night's sleep. We'll just have to explain to Benzy when he shows up, that's all."

Zalman became aware that the doctor was still standing there. "A big *yasher ko'ach*, doctor," he exclaimed, wringing the other's hand.

Esther echoed, "That's right. Thank you so much!"

There was an expectant pause. Then, in a sulky voice like a punished child's, Shoshie mumbled, "Yes. Thanks a lot." She turned to her mother. "I'd like to go to bed now, Ima."

"The baby's still bleeding," Bracha observed anxiously, pressing the damp cloth closer to Yoni's lacerated forehead. "When will it stop, do you think?"

The doctor lifted the cloth to take another look. "It should stop soon. If not, he's going to need a few stitches." Bracha turned pale. The doctor shrugged reassuringly. "Not to worry. He'll be fine. Won't you, Yoni-pony?"

In reply, Yoni whimpered louder. Zalman took the baby from his wife. Esther put her arm around Shoshie's shoulders and helped her to her feet. At the door above, Savta looked down, her pinched features sharp with worry.

"It's okay, Ima," Esther said softly when she reached her mother-in-law. "They're both okay, *baruch Hashem*." As if to give the lie to her words, Shoshie's audible sniff came to the old woman's ears — a split second behind the noise of Yoni's renewed wailing. Savta shook her head.

The entourage turned toward the back of the apartment and began the slow, mournful journey to Shoshie's disordered room.

The mess that had seemed so happy and expectant now looked sordid, unappealing. Shoshie turned her head away. Trying to ignore the pain in her ankle, she suffered herself to be ministered to by her mother.

Bracha, trailing the unhappy group, stood uncertainly at the sidelines while Esther eased Shoshie into bed and Zalman carried the baby off to devise a bandage from an old cloth diaper. When the mother had gone for a hot-water bottle — her inevitable response to trauma, large and small — Bracha took advantage of the temporary quiet to inch over to her sister's bed and perch at the edge. For a moment she twiddled with the bedclothes. Then, hesitantly, she said, "Are you very disappointed, Shoshie?"

Shoshie shrugged. "I guess I should be grateful nothing worse happened to Yoni or me. But what's Benzy's going to think?"

"He'll come back when you're better, I'm sure."

"Not with the same enthusiasm, though."

"Maybe not," Bracha admitted. Her youthful heart, like her twin's, could not bear the agony of postponement. All that buildup, the anticipation, the long drive down to Jerusalem...all for nothing. Postponing the date seemed tantamount, in both their eyes, to eating lukewarm leftovers when you expected a fresh, hot meal. A gloomy silence descended.

Suddenly, Shoshie lifted her head. Her raw cheek was already swollen to twice its normal size and turning blue, green, and pale yellow at the perimeters of the wound. But the expression on her face was unclouded, even eager.

"Bracha," she said with a quick glance over her sister's shoulder to check if their mother was returning, "Listen. Benzy's never met me before. Why don't you take my place, just for tonight?"

"*What?*"

"I mean it. Any description he's had of me applies just as well to you, right? If you meet him tonight, he'll never even have to know what happened." Shoshie spoke rapidly, the words leaping to keep pace with her speeding thoughts. "If things go well, he'll ask for a second date. I'll get Ima and Abba to put him off for a while till I'm all well and can meet him myself." She leaned forward in her bed. "Don't you see, Bracha? It buys me some time! Say you'll do it!"

"Shoshie, that is just the nuttiest idea I've ever — "

To her dismay, Shoshie's eyes filled with tears. They spilled over her lashes and onto the pathetic, swollen cheek. "Please, Bracha. Have I ever asked you to do something this important for me before? I'm begging you."

Bracha stared at her sister.

"I'm begging, Brach." Shoshie repeated, grabbing her sister's limp arm and squeezing, as if the pressure of her fingers could communicate the depths of her wish. "Please?"

Bracha stared a second longer. Slowly she said, "I don't know. Maybe — just maybe — it could actually work."

It might have been the way she said it, or perhaps it was the gleam in her eye that provided the clue. Shoshie lean even closer and tightened her grip on her sister's arm. "Bracha! You thought of it, too! You had the same idea. Admit it."

Bracha shot a cautious glance at the door. "Well, it did cross my mind as a possible solution." She shook her head. "We're both out of our minds!"

Shoshie fell back against the pillow, helpless with laughter. "We're fabulous! Hurry, Bracha. Hurry!" Shoulders heaving, tears of hysterical mirth streaming down the whole cheek and the torn, she made shooing motions with her hands. Bracha, with a single staccato bark of laughter, grabbed a hairbrush, seized something from her closet, and ran like the wind for the bathroom.

᠊᠊᠊᠊᠊᠊᠊᠊᠊᠊᠊᠊᠊᠊᠊᠊᠊᠊᠊᠊᠊

The ring at the doorbell came five minutes after the appointed time. Esther and Zalman were standing ready, the baby — looking like a pathetic little casualty of war with his forehead bound up in the homemade bandage — in the mother's arms. Esther's face was long, Zalman's resigned. The ring, when it finally came, was a relief. Zalman started nervously, glanced at his wife, then strode forward to open the door.

A yeshivah *bachur* stood there, tall and pleasant-faced, his smile one part simple friendliness and two parts terror. At Zalman's "*shalom aleichem*," he gripped the older man's hand fervently and responded, "*Aleichem shalom!*" A bit of the terror left his face. He stepped inside.

"I'm Benzy Koenig," he said, a touch too loud. He cleared his throat and adjusted the volume. "Good evening, Rabbi Markovich." He nodded at Esther. "Mrs. Markovich."

"Did you have a hard time finding the apartment?" Esther asked. "It can be confusing to outsiders. From outside the neighborhood, I mean." She hardly knew what she was saying.

"Oh, no problem at all. I was already slightly familiar with the neighborhood — a former *chavrusa* of mine lives here — and the directions I got were very clear." He smiled again. Esther found herself smiling back. A nice boy.

Zalman cleared his throat. "You must be thirsty after the long trip. Here, have a drink." He poured some juice, offered the cake. Benzy accepted both politely, though he did not relax his alert stance. He was clearly waiting for the Talmudic grilling that the father of the girl customarily initiated at such times, hoping to determine the breadth and depth of the young man's Torah acumen. Instead, Zalman cleared his throat again. "I'm afraid I have some not such good news, Benzy. You see, Shoshie — "

"— is all ready, right on time!" a voice sang out from behind them.

Zalman spun around. There stood Shoshie, but it couldn't be Shoshie. He gaped. It was Bracha, dressed to the nines and smiling for all she was worth. "Surprised you, didn't I?" she continued quickly, as if she hoped to forestall the astonished words trembling on her father's lips.

"Hi," Benzy said, suddenly shy again. "I'm Benzy Koenig."

"Hi. Shoshie Markovich. Abba, I'm sure you want to have a little talk with Benzy before we go. I'll just help Ima in the kitchen." Still smiling valiantly, she ushered a shocked Esther into that room and closed the door. Yoni stopped whimpering and stared at his dressed-up sister interestedly.

Esther found her tongue.

"Bracha!" she hissed. "What's this? Are you crazy?"

Bracha put a finger to her lips. "Sssh, he'll hear you. Ima, I know it's crazy. But Shoshie begged me. She *begged*, Ima! She was crying. She doesn't want Benzy to be put off — oh, it's too hard to explain right now. But I'm going to help her out, just this once. I'm going in her place, Ima."

"No! I'll tell him," Esther declared wildly.

"Please don't!"

"He's such a nice boy. How can we fool him like this?"

"*If* he ever finds out — and I say if, 'cause how could he? — you and Abba can just tell him you had no part in it. It's the truth. I'm doing this myself, for Shoshie. I promised her."

Esther shook her head. "I don't know. It's not right..."

"Ima." Bracha sounded very solemn. "It's for poor Shoshie. I want her to be happy. Please don't give us away."

There was no time to think. The baby started crying softly. Already the improvised bandage was soaked with fresh blood. Peeping through the door, Esther saw that Zalman, with heroic presence of mind, was completing his "little talk in learning" with Benzy. There was a roaring in Esther's ears, like the violent noise of water rushing onto stones. Misgivings assailed her, and longings, and hope. Zalman, glimpsing his wife at the door, raised a desperate eyebrow. He didn't want to embarrass his own daughter by calling her an impostor, but how could he allow the farce to continue?

Esther glanced back at Bracha, and then at Benzy. The discomfort — the shame! — of unraveling the truth at this point would be acute. How could she call her own daughter a liar in front of this nice, young *bachur*? With many an inward qualm, Esther strode into the living room. Her face was very pale. *I'm doing this for Shoshie.*

The men broke off their talk. Esther drew a breath, managed a smile.

"Well, I guess it's time you two got started. Don't bring her back too late, Benzy..."

"Don't worry, Ima," Bracha said, smiling brilliantly at her mother, at her father, and at the youth standing diffidently by the table. "Everything's going to be just fine."

The exhalation of her father's breath was audible.

When, some two minutes later, the young couple sailed through the door, it was hard to tell who looked more bemused: the mother, the father, or the nice young man leaving with the wrong twin.

"We'll have to call the matchmaker," Zalman said.

"How can we?" his wife demanded distractedly. "She'll never make another *shidduch* for either of our girls again! Think what this could do to their reputations!"

With unwonted grimness, Zalman said, "They should have thought about that before."

"Anyway, we can't do anything right now," Esther said. "The baby's still bleeding like crazy. We'll have to take him to the hospital, get him stitched up."

Zalman stroked his little son's shoulder sympathetically. "Okay, Yoni, we're going to take good care of you. The rest of it" — he met his wife's eye — "will wait for the morning." He sounded tired.

With a quick word to Shoshie, another to a groggy Tzippy, plus a heartfelt prayer of thanks that the boys were sound asleep, Esther, her husband, and the baby set out for the hospital.

Shoshie lay awake for a long time after they left. The apartment was very quiet — unnaturally so — but she hardly noticed. For company, she had her frustration, her hope, and a devouring curiosity about the progress of the date she'd sent her sister on in her place.

And, of course, there was her painful, throbbing ankle — most faithful friend of all.

3

The Markovich household was not at all what Fish had been led to expect. Mutty hadn't spoken all that much about his Jerusalem relatives, but his thumbnail sketch had given Fish to understand that the family, if not actually happy-go-lucky, were generally an upbeat bunch, headed by Mutty's warmhearted uncle and his super-efficient aunt. The evidence of his eyes, as he sat at their dinner table one week after the momentous First Date, told a very different story.

There was a distinct and inexplicable aura of strain at that table. The twins, Shoshie and Bracha, sat far apart and exchanged no more words than were strictly necessary. Uncle Zalman (that was how Fish had already, under Mutty's influence, begun to think of Rabbi Markovich) had begun by being friendly enough, greeting his nephew and Fish at the door with every sign of pleasure. But by the time the food was served he was uncommunicative, sunk within himself and his thoughts. Those thoughts did not appear to be particularly pleasant ones.

Nor was there any sign of Aunt Esther's famed organizational prowess. The meal was produced late and produced badly. The soup was scalding, the noodles freezing, the vegetables waterlogged, and the fillets of fried sole overdone to a leatherlike consistency. Fish was hungry enough to do justice even to such fare, but he wondered. From the look on Mutty's face, he was wondering, too.

Apart from all this, the family — or at least certain members of it — looked like refugees from some grisly battlefield. The baby's forearm bore nasty yellowish-blue bruises that perfectly matched the one on his temple; but these paled in comparison with his big sister's scars. In the one time Fish saw her on her feet as she came to the table, Shoshie had limped badly. Also, one entire side of her face was a warring mass of color that would have put a child's fingerpaint masterpiece to shame — a child with no visual sense to speak of, that was. There was nothing beautiful in the welter of purple and green and indigo, delicately framed in mustard yellow, on what had once been a blooming, healthy cheek.

"I fell," Shoshie said shortly, when her cousin Mutty, shocked, questioned her. Her tone discouraged furthering the topic.

Still, Mutty had tried. "And the baby?"

"He fell, too."

"Were you holding him at the time?"

Shoshie had turned slowly to fix him with a cold stare. "Actually, I was in the process of rescuing him when it happened. Okay?"

"Okay!" Mutty had replied quickly, backing off with upraised hands.

There had been no more questions.

Esther Markovich lifted a platter and held it out to her guests. She wore her most determined hostess's smile. It might have been carved in stone.

"Another piece of fish — er, Fish?"

Eli and Aryeh Leib broke into half-muffled snickers, nudging each other under cover of the tablecloth. Fish winked at them, then said to their mother,

"No thank you, Mrs. Markovich. Though it was, er, delicious."

"Mutty?"

"No thanks, Aunt Esther. I couldn't fit in another bite."

"No need to be so polite," Shoshie told her cousin with a slightly sinister smile. "*I* cooked dinner tonight." And, stubbornly, she had, hobbling around the kitchen assembling her ingredients and utensils and taking twice as much time as her mother or sister would have for half the results — just to prove she could. "I know how awful everything turned out."

Mutty and Fish exchanged an uncomfortable glance.

"If you're brave enough to try again," Zalman said, trying for a lighter tone to lift what was threatening to become a totally leaden meal, "you're most welcome back here, boys."

Esther's face softened. "Yes. You'll have to come here often — both of you. Yeshivah food's not enough. I know that from my Moshe Dovid. You need a *heimish* meal now and then."

"It'll be our pleasure, Aunt Esther," Mutty smiled. Fish nodded a trifle uncertainly.

Esther got to her feet. As if a signal had been given, the twins and Tzippy rose to clear the table.

Esther said sharply, "Sit down, Shoshie. The doctor said to stay off that foot as much as possible."

"I'm not a cripple, Ima," she muttered, flushing pink beneath the screen of disfiguring color.

"Heaven forbid!" her mother exclaimed. "Who said anything about cripples? It just makes sense to give your foot a chance to heal. Bracha can take over for you tonight."

"Yes," Shoshie said, slowly resuming her seat. "Yes, Bracha's good at that."

The words were uttered so quietly that Fish might have thought them a figment of his own imagination — except for the reaction they produced. Bracha, her arms full of plates and platters, turned white. Her mother gasped as if in sudden pain. Tzippy set up a great clatter of silverware, as though to drown out the echoes of Shoshie's words. The boys began softly scuffling at the table, the small irritating kicks and nudges that would, if not nipped in the bud, soon turn into full-fledged, boyish mayhem.

It was Zalman who spoke. Fixing his eyes on his daughter, he said softly, "That's enough, Shoshie." There was a world of weariness in his voice and an ache Fish could not identify. His curiosity grew sharper.

Then Bracha hurried into the kitchen and her mother after her. Tzippy plodded resignedly behind them, the reddish-blond braids hanging limply on her thin shoulders, which were bent as if they bore the weight of the world. Eli and Aryeh Leib started on an increasingly obnoxious round of name-calling, which ended in a stinging rebuke from their father and banishment to their room, where the faint sounds of resuming battle could soon be discerned. Zalman either didn't hear or could not muster the energy to deal with it. The baby, Yoni, tried to scramble down from his high chair unassisted, received a bang on the head for his pains, and began howling. Mechanically, his father took him into his lap and murmured soothing words.

And throughout all, Shoshie sat stiff in her chair, spine and shoulders very straight and head held high, like an aloof young princess — or a prisoner condemned to some cruel and drawn-out punishment whose end was nowhere in sight.

An hour later, Fish and Mutty were on their way back to the yeshivah dorm, full, if not exactly satisfied, by the meal they'd just shared, and carefully skirting the subject of the Markoviches.

Mutty was gloomily certain that his friend would never want to set foot in that strained household again, and, frankly, he wouldn't blame him if he didn't. What was going on there anyway? The aunt, uncle, and cousins he'd spent the evening with had nothing in common with the ones he remembered from his last visit, some five or six years earlier, or with the pleasant letters his family received from time to time. There seemed to be some dark vortex spinning out of control in that modest apartment, and its center, it seemed to Mutty, was his cousin Shoshie.

Fish had come to the same conclusion. But, though Mutty didn't know it, he had no intention of avoiding the Markoviches in the two months or so of his sojourn in Jerusalem. On the contrary, there was something there, in that family, that drew him back. His interest had been piqued, though exactly what it was that so excited his curiosity he did not bother to analyze.

In his ears there still rang the stormy strains of the melody Shoshie had been playing as they'd left. She'd disappeared into her room soon after dinner, emerging just as her cousin and his friend were taking their leave. Without so much as a glance in their direction — as if they had already departed and were far away instead of shrugging into their coats and chatting with her parents by the open door — she'd seated herself at the piano and begun to play.

Fish had listened to the passionate chords that seemed to fill the room, the house, with some vast, bottomless rage. Curiously, he turned to Esther and asked, "I know a little about classical music, but that's a piece I'm not familiar with. Do you know what it's called?"

Esther, looking strangely forlorn, told him, "It's Beethoven. 'The Pathetique,' I believe it's called."

"She's good, isn't she?" Mutty said. "She's made a lot of progress since I was last here, Aunt Esther."

"Yes," Uncle Zalman murmured. "Music means a lot to her. Especially now."

On those enigmatic words, and with the crashing fury of Beethoven to accompany them, the young men had left. The music had trailed after them into the street. The cushion of distance lent a haunting quality to the notes, which grew ever fainter with each step Fish took until, at last, they were swallowed by the night.

He quickened his step toward the bus stop. The night was fine. A swath of stars and velvet calm lay over the city like a soft and splendid mantle. He took a deep, contented breath.

"Here comes the bus, I think," Fish said. "Good. Right now, I feel like I could sit down and learn six hours straight. How 'bout you?"

Mutty gaped at his friend. "Right now? Do you realize it's nearly ten o'clock?"

"The night is young. You can go to bed if you want. I'm for my Gemara."

"I'm with you then, I guess. But not for any six hours!"

He waited for Fish to say, "Just kidding about that part." But the words didn't come. Instead, Fish just laughed and bounded up the steps of the waiting bus.

4

S hoshie lay in the dark, willing back the tears. She'd cried every night for a solid week now. Her eyes would soon be as swollen as her cheek, and then she might as well hire herself out to a circus sideshow. Enough was enough.

But logic had no sway with the river of fierce emotion that her own music had unlocked tonight. All this day she'd held herself under rigid control. The yelling at Bracha was over, as were the appeals to her parents and her general venting of rage and frustration. Today she'd been cold, cold as the iceberg that had struck the ill-fated *Titanic* all those years ago... Only it was she, Shoshie, who'd gone under. There were no survivors.

Bracha, she knew, was out in the living room, or perhaps the kitchen, waiting for her to fall asleep so she could sneak into her own bed unobserved. Shoshie would pretend to be sleeping, and Bracha would pretend to believe her. Neither of them would speak. There were no more words to say. They'd said them all on that horrible night, one week ago, and in the furious aftermath.

"Hi, Bracha," Shoshie had whispered when she heard the familiar footstep outside the door of their darkened bedroom. She'd fought to stay awake until her sister returned from the date, but the exhaustion of the day's strong and rapidly changing emotions, and the trauma of the accident, had forced her to succumb. Despite the throbbing pain in her ankle, she'd drifted into a tense, expectant sleep, from which some sixth sense had woken her at the sound of her twin's arrival.

"Oh, are you still up?" Bracha asked, moving more naturally now. She came into the room and crossed it to her bed. A rustle in the dark: she'd divested herself of her handbag and jacket. "I thought only mothers waited up in these situations."

Shoshie heard something strange in her sister's voice. There was some strain she was trying, behind the mask of jocularity, to conceal — an unease. "Ima and Abba aren't back from the hospital yet. Abba called about an hour ago. Yoni got four stitches. I guess they'll be here pretty soon." She peered at her sister in the dark. "So — how'd it go, Bracha?"

Bracha patted back an elaborate yawn. In the wash of silver light that came through the slats of the window blinds, she was easier for Shoshie to make out now. "You know, I'm really falling off my feet. In the morning, okay?"

"Come on, Bracha! I can't believe this! I send you out with my date, and you want me to wait till morning to hear all the details?" Shoshie chuckled softly. "All right, I'll have pity on you. Just answer two little questions, and I'll let you go to sleep."

"Okay." Bracha sounded suddenly a little afraid.

Oblivious, Shoshie pushed on, "First of all, did you have a good time? And second, do you think he'll want a second date? With me this time, of course." She giggled.

There was a long silence. With two soft bumps, Bracha kicked off her shoes. She sat on the bed. Slowly she said, "Well, the answer to the first question is yes. I had a very good time. I think he did, too."

"And the second?"

Bracha hesitated. "Actually..."

"Well?" Shoshie was wide awake now, propped up on one elbow. Her ankle was beginning to send out angry twinges, but she ignored them. "What do you think?"

"I think...he will ask for a second date. In fact, we spoke about it."

"*You did?*" Shoshie hauled herself upright, peering round-eyed at her sister in the gloom. This was not in the program. Usually, the young couple made their wishes known to their parents and, through them, to the matchmaker. Only if both expressed an interest in meeting again, and only through the *shadchan*, was a second date arranged. "Bracha, tell me how it happened!"

"Shoshie, you're not going to like this."

A dread fell on Shoshie's heart. "What do you mean?"

"I...told him."

"You what?"

"Told him that I was me." Bracha giggled nervously. "That sounds funny."

"IT'S NOT FUNNY!"

"Sssh, you'll wake everyone."

Shoshie glared, clutching impotently at her blankets as if she wished it were someone's throat. Now that Bracha had begun, the words came quicker.

"You see, he was just too nice. I couldn't keep on fooling him like that. We were having such a nice talk, and he was being so...sincere. He's a good person, Shoshie, a genuine mensch, I think. And the whole time, I sat there feeling more and more uncomfortable. As if every word I was saying was a lie — which, in a way, it was. It just wasn't fair! Not to him..." Her voice dropped to a whisper. "And not to me."

Shoshie demanded, "Well, how did he react?"

"He was quiet for a long time. Then he started asking me questions — what our relationship is like, yours and mine, and how I felt about doing what I did. And after that... Well, we started talking again, almost as if we were starting over. Only we felt somehow different, you know? Because of what happened, and my confession. And then, at the end, he said he knew it wasn't so usual, but he wanted me to know that he...wanted to see me again."

The final words emerged in a rush.

"Yippee! That's stupendous! But Bracha, did you tell him I won't be up to it for at least another week or two?"

Now it was Bracha's turn to need something to hold on to. She picked up her pillow and cradled it against her chest. "Shoshie, I don't think you heard what I said. He wants to see *me* again."

She put no added inflection on the "me," but this time Shoshie heard it anyway — as she was meant to.

And so the nightmare began.

Betrayal. Her own twin, the closest person to her on earth, had stolen something from her, something too precious to be counted. Her *shidduch.* Maybe her future husband. She'd been walking for a week in a cloud of ever-flowering rage. Black envy washed over in a ceaseless, poisonous tide. And mingled with the envy and the rage was a sense of loss, an overmastering grief that cared little for the fact that she'd never really had Benzy to begin with.

Up until the evening of that first date, he'd been no more than an abstraction to her, a theory of a possible future. But now that she'd actually seen him, heard the litany of his finer qualities, as read by her sister, Benzy Koenig had come to represent riches untold — riches spilled from her own treasure house.

And the worst of it was that her parents, those omnipotent beings whom she had always counted on to see justice done, had failed her, too.

For two hours on that next trembling morning, Esther and Zalman had judged the matter. Shoshie, lying in bed, and Bracha, reprieved from the need to go off to school just this once, had waited with pale, set faces as their parents sat low-voiced in endless conference. The look in their eyes as they came into the twins' bedroom after it was over gave Shoshie the verdict even before a word was spoken.

The judges had come out for the accused! Bracha had been the one to meet Benzy, and it was Bracha whom he wanted to meet again. Moreover, Bracha wanted very much to see *him* again. So the wrong twin became the right twin. Bracha had won. Shoshie turned her face to the wall.

Their weighty decision made, Esther and Zalman had phoned the matchmaker with the story. She, it turned out, had already heard it from the boy's parents. Benzy had not only told them, but had also, apparently, managed to overcome their uneasiness at the bizarre departure from the script to which they clung. For another few hours, fate hung in the balance. Then it became clear that fortune, as well as parental opinion, was prepared to smile on the young couple. In light of the circumstances, the greater crime of the twins' deception, as well as the lesser — Benzy's forwardness in asking Bracha for a second date — were forgiven.

That very evening Benzy had called and, two days after that, appeared again at the Markoviches' door. For this second date, Bracha took considerably longer than ten minutes to get ready. Shoshie had listened with a feeling of indescribable anguish to the murmur of pleasant conversation in the living room before the two of them went off.

There was another date planned for this week.

In those first awful days, Bracha had spoken eloquently and, it seemed, with real pain, of her sense of guilt and her distress for her sister. Since then, she appeared to have made a masterful effort to subdue both the guilt and the pain. A very masterful effort. Bracha was glowing these days, her face as pink and radiant as her twin's was ravaged. It wasn't fair! It wasn't fair! *It wasn't fair!*

Shoshie clenched her teeth and howled silently, painfully, into her sodden pillow.

5

It's only a date, Adela told herself as her fingers fumbled with three pairs of mismatched earrings.

It's only the first date you've had in nearly a year, Honesty reminded her. With tightened lips, she bade Honesty be quiet. She was nervous enough already.

Why was she so haphazard with her jewelry? She wasn't normally this disorganized. Subconsciously, where truths lie hidden in the guise of secrets, she knew the answer. These pieces had been Reuven's gifts to her, doled out in prettily wrapped packages over the four short years of their marriage. For a long time, she'd barely been able to look at the things — let alone wear them — without pain. Even when that first terrible stage had been survived, she'd felt little interest in gold and silver baubles. She'd felt little interest in dressing up, or in meeting the men whom friends and the occasional matchmaker were kind enough to fish out of the modest sea of "eligibles" and throw at her. Some, after a single polite meeting, she'd thrown back. Others she'd declined to meet at all. Mostly, she'd sat home alone — well, not really alone. She'd never be that as long as Yudy was with her.

Yudy. She paused in the act of untangling a length of gold chain to frown into the mirror. He'd been acting so strange lately. She was reminded of long-ago anxieties, when unusual behavior in her baby had signalled the beginning of some illness. But though this particular behavior had been going on for nearly two weeks now, there seemed to be nothing wrong with her son. Nothing physically wrong.

On the other hand, the symptoms had escalated.

Adela hesitated, then abandoned the tangle of jewelry to make her way to the closed door of Yudy's room. Unembarrassed, the mother pressed her ear to the door. The faint strains of some tape came to her ears — someone giving a *shiur*. While this evidence of studiousness or piety would normally have pleased her, she was troubled by one thing: it had never happened before. Yudy loved music and could usually be found plugged into his favorite choirs or wordless medleys. This new fascination with erudition in place of music coincided too closely with the onset of his mysterious malaise for his mother's comfort. She listened for a long moment, then turned away.

When she was dressed — feet squeezed into her Shabbos heels, the touches of unaccustomed gold at her ears and throat — she went down the hall again to her son's door. This time she tapped. She was rewarded with a muffled summons. "Come in." She opened the door cautiously. Though she had known, this time, what to expect, the impact of the room hit her with the force of a physical blow.

The room was plunged in darkness. Not by so much as the glow worm of a night light had Yudy permitted the darkness to be relieved. He lay on his back on his bed, hands locked behind his head, gazing up at the ceiling and listening to the *shiur*. At his mother's entrance, he reached over and switched off the tape recorder.

"Hi, Mom."

"Hi." She lifted her hands, one clutching her evening bag. "Well, I'm all ready. How do I look?"

"Terrific." His ghostly grin was an echo of hers: it was too dark in the room to make out more than her outline.

Adela's grin went first. She took a hesitant step deeper into the blackness. "Yudy?"

"Yes, Mom?"

"I don't want to be a nag, but...is everything all right?"

He rolled over on his side, knees pulled up toward his chest. "Sure, Mom. Everything's fine."

"Don't you believe in light anymore?" She tried to keep her tone light. The strain crept in anyway.

He reached out for the tape recorder again. "Don't worry. I like the dark. It makes me feel..." The last word was nearly lost in the sudden blaring of the tape. Adela thought it was — "safe."

Before she could react, or even begin to wonder why her strapping fifteen-year-old was lying in the dark muttering about safety, the front doorbell rang. Her date had arrived.

With a last, worried look at her son, Adela retreated. She turned at the door to say goodbye to Yudy, but he was already lost in his own world — the dark, snug universe he'd created — ears nourished by the voice from the tape recorder and eyes feeding on the bland ceiling.

" 'Bye, Mom. Have fun," he said vaguely.

"Yeah. Fun."

She went to answer the bell.

6

U nlike many of her friends, the young Adela had not spent much thought on her own future marriage.

Where other girls dreamed and whispered about vague, almost mythical suitors and the promised lands on the other side of the wedding canopy, Adela had been firmly — perhaps too firmly — wedded to the present. It was not that she lacked imagination; the lack lay elsewhere. She was unable, or unwilling, to deal with a thing before it was an actual presence in her life. "Cross your bridges when you come to them" might have summed up her attitude. If a nebulous fear underlay that attitude, it was neatly offset by a wellspring of confidence. When the inevitable bridge loomed, she would rise to the occasion. Yes, she would definitely deal with it — when the time came.

Graduation was the watershed. That over, she arranged her post–high school life with competence and direction. Seminary classes, college classes, and part-time jobs were balanced to a nicety. In the same way, Adela dealt with the strange, new world of *shidduchim* when its time came, as she dealt also — with more grace than she'd have believed possible — with its incredible culmination: the linking of her fate with that of Reuven Moses. For a girl who had refused to envision herself as either bride or wife, her transformation into first one and then the other seemed nothing less than miraculous.

Somewhat to her surprise, marriage suited her. Adela was independent but not a loner. She discovered in her marriage to Reuven a partnership in which she might wield authority and responsibility, yet share the burdens of both with a dear and helpful friend.

Reuven was kind and practical, a doer rather than a deep thinker. Yudy, when he was born, seemed to have inherited these traits and to emphasize them. The vigorous little boy delighted the young father as much as he did the mother. Evenings at home surrounded Yudy and his antics, and even when asleep in his crib the doting parents' conversation often revolved around the son.

Adela was perfectly content, both with her present existence and with the future that lay before her like the placid spread of a cornfield ripening slowly in the sun. Growth and change lay ahead, but they would not be rushed. Each stage would supersede the one before in a gradual process, like the gentle blurring of colors in a landscape painting. Life would be good...

On a freezing February evening when Yudy was three years old, he achieved the high point of his short life. His parents shared his glee as he was moved to a "real bed." He had been ready for the change months earlier, but the bed had not been bought. There had seemed no need to hurry. Vaguely, in the back of Adela's mind, had been the thought that she would effect the transfer when she learned she was expecting her second child; but that day had not yet arrived, though Yudy's third birthday was come and gone. At last, recognizing the folly of her illogic, Adela had gone out and purchased the bed, and it had been an ordinary transaction when stripped of the emotional overtones she'd placed on it. This lesson — to lay bare the difficult things that needed to be done and will herself to see them in a purely technical light — was to serve her well in the nightmare months and years to come.

Yudy had been delighted with his bed, as his parents had known he would be. The parents watched his capering for a while, smiling, and then Reuven had announced in the fond, no-nonsense tone he liked to think of as his Voice of Authority, that it was time to turn out the lights. Yudy had registered the expected protest, and his parents had granted the expected five more minutes. Eventually the boy was tucked in and the lights doused. Adela and Reuven repaired to the living room, the wife to take up her needlepoint, the husband his *sefer*. Peace and security reigned in the little Brooklyn house. For the last time, as it turned out.

In the middle of the night, Reuven made a weird, choking sound, rousing his wife. Adela had watched, first in stupefaction, and then in mounting horror, as her husband suffered a massive coronary. The ambulance was quick, but the Angel of Death even quicker. Reuven was dead on arrival at the hospital.

Overnight — literally — Adela's world disintegrated, as surely as if a bomb had fallen on the roof of her home. The only solid thing left in that world was Yudy. Numbly, she willed herself to go through the necessary motions of seeing Reuven off to his final rest and adjusting to her new widow's existence. And all along, the only emotion she felt, with piercing clarity, was a fierce protectiveness toward her little boy. A granite determination was born in her in those first cataclysmic days. If she did nothing else for the rest of her long, empty life, she would keep her son safe.

The next dozen years had seen a series of changes — predictable, perhaps, to a student of human nature, but each one startling and fresh to the woman experiencing them. The first change, an unpleasant one, was the return of feeling. The numbness wore off, and the ache set in with a vengeance.

No longer did she walk in the dull, anesthetized fog that had characterized the early weeks. The fog dissipated without warning, leaving a daggerlike wind in its place. The knife of memory accompanied her everywhere, twisting and hurting with cruel abandon. Reuven was everywhere — and nowhere. She began to dread the nights, when sleep eluded her and the memories were especially insistent. This phase lasted nearly two years, until Yudy was five and enrolled in kindergarten. Finally, she did the only sensible thing. She sold the house, packed herself and Yudy up, and moved away.

It was a salubrious move.

She didn't go far, only to another neighborhood, but the pulling up of roots had the effect she'd wanted. She was forced to create fresh beginnings, both physically and socially. A new place to live, new furnishings, a new school for Yudy, new friends. But when these friends, and her older ones, urged remarriage on her, she balked. She was afraid of upsetting the fragile equilibrium she'd so carefully forged in her life and her son's. For the moment, this was enough.

It was a long moment: ten years long.

She met some prospective second husbands during that time, but none stirred the faintest chord in her. She was not open to change. Her identity was firmly fixed: She was Reuven's widow and Yudy's mother. The prospect of molding herself to some strange man's expectations held little appeal for her. Her independence, once such an asset, had become her bane, only she didn't see it.

When the loneliness became too oppressive, she cried a little, or phoned a friend, or lost herself in a book. The best antidote of all was her son's company. She was secretly overjoyed when he decided against travelling to an out-of-town yeshivah high school with a dormitory. With no sense of sacrifice, he chose to stay home with her, and she was glad.

After twelve years, she'd become used to her situation. There was much in it that was pleasant and even good — her friends, her home business that left her schedule flexible, and, of course, Yudy. Most of all, Yudy.

Even the painful parts were familiar friends by now. Her aloneness had become a thing apart. It had acquired a life of its own, and it seemed almost a sacrilege to consider ending that life. With her mind, she acknowledged that a better existence was possible, that the right man and a new marriage might, somewhere, exist for her. But her heart would not believe it.

Unexpectedly, in these past few months, another change had happened. It had begun with Yudy and extended to Adela; or perhaps it was the other way around. The fact was, Yudy was growing up. At fifteen, he was beginning to look deeper and further than he had before. His peers and teachers were becoming more important to him than his home life. Adela, for her part, willed herself to let him go gracefully. She was first and foremost a mother — and it was a mother's job to cut the leading strings when the time was right. The pang she felt at the loss of his dependence was balanced and soothed by her pride in his progress. If he had to grow up, it was good to see him making such a success of it!

It was no coincidence that this new turn in Yudy's life found its counterpart in Adela. She experienced an inner shift. Being an independent woman, a woman alone, was not enough anymore. Her heart — though she'd refused to listen for a long time — shouted for something more. She wanted to be more than a Jewish mother; she wanted to be, again, a Jewish wife. Where she'd felt more or less whole before, now she felt almost as fragmented, as incomplete, when she'd said her last goodbye to Reuven. In a word, she was ripe for a change.

Under the impetus of this new restlessness — and in the hope that her desire for change would be satisfied by the gesture — she acted on an idea she'd been playing with for some time: to move back to her old neighborhood in Flatbush. She and Yudy were nicely settled now. Shaking the dust of the move off her hands, Adela took stock of herself. She had her work, and her family, and her circle of friends. But the yearning in her would not be stilled; she needed more.

Unfortunately, no interesting prospects had come along in quite a while. Binyomin Hirsch was the first man she'd agreed to meet in her new home, under these new emotional conditions. She was aware that her heart beat in a different way tonight than it had through the long years of halfhearted *shidduchim* that had gone before. The difference was not Binyomin: she did not even know him yet. The difference was in her.

But even as she paused at the door to compose herself, the memory of Yudy's darkened room roiled inside her like the germ of some vague and frightening disease. At his signal, she'd laid aside her old protectiveness. She'd stepped back from pure motherhood and begun to think of herself. Now her son seemed to need her again. His mysterious pain called to her...

Adela stood still for a moment, caught by the competing pulls of the door in front of her and the one behind.

Then, taking a deep breath, she turned the knob and let the stranger in.

SEVEN

1

Y ou're not his mother, you know," Avi said mildly. "You don't have to
wait up."

Malka stopped — not without some difficulty — midway through a
face-splitting yawn. "How can I sleep when I'm dying of curiosity?" Her
fingers tapped an impatient tatoo on the sofa arm. "I wonder how the date is
going."

"You've been wondering all evening. Why not just wait till he comes
back and hear for yourself?"

"Oh, Avi. Admit it, you're curious, too."

"Sure I am. I'm also patient."

"You're just perfect." She made a face.

He grinned. "You said it, not me."

Abandoning the book she was pretending to read, Malka twisted around
to stare at the clock on the piano, which gazed blandly back. She was bundled
in her warmest robe and slippers; although the night was mercifully calm,
it was still very cold. "Nearly midnight already. Four-and-a-half hours. They
must have clicked!"

"We'll find out soon enough." Avi turned back to the dining-room table
and his papers. "Sammy Mirsky is showing excellent results already. R & N
Plumbing...Davidson Windows... All new names. Very generous donations, too." His face glowed in the yellow lamplight. "At this rate, we'll

be ready to bid on that lot much earlier than I expected. Maybe even as early as Pesach."

Malka forgot her absorption in the *shidduch* she'd concocted. "Avi, that's terrific! Who would've thought he'd manage all that so soon?"

"Yes. A hard-working kid — an enterprising one. Yankel Bruin may have found him a bit *too* enterprising for his business, but he's doing the job for the shul, all right."

"Bruin? What do you mean?"

Avi was startled out of his musing. He'd been thinking aloud — a dangerous practice. Shaking his head, he said, "Never mind," smiling to remove the words' sting. He'd nearly forgotten his cardinal rule: never to betray a word of what went on inside the four walls of his office. The people who came to see him for advice deserved the safeguard of absolute privacy. Not even Malka was privy to those secrets.

At the lingering curiosity in his wife's face, Avi adroitly changed the subject. "We haven't heard from Mutty in a while."

The ploy worked. Malka sat up and half-turned away, tossing back over her shoulder, "It's only been a week or so since the last letter. You don't honestly expect him to spend all his time writing, do you?" Light words, with a current of yearning behind them.

Mischievously, Avi asked, "Sure there isn't a letter hiding under all that junk on the counter?" In an unguarded moment, Malka had let slip the tale of his sister's long-buried letter. For some reason, her husband found the story amusing rather than exasperating. The reaction stymied Malka. She always expected her husband to be as critical of her slipshod habits as she was of them herself. He constantly surprised her.

Malka had only the vaguest notion of how precious Avi held the relaxed environment of his home. The lack of formality seemed to unlock reserves of spontaneity in the rabbi, granting him leave to set down the burden of his public persona and be himself. If the price of such peace included the occasional burnt dinner or missing letter, he was well prepared to pay.

Tossing her head, she answered, "Don't worry, I've learned my lesson."

She paused. "He sounds happy, though."

"Yes. Israel seems to agree with Mutty."

And just as agreeable, Avi thought, was this slice out of time — this chance for Mutty to ignore the exigency of the future in the more leisurely impressions and achievements of the present. For now, the calendar was frozen. Mutty had simply up and escaped.

It was childish, of course, and immature, and Avi would have preferred a son of his to have his feet planted much more firmly on solid ground. And yet, for an instant, he frankly envied the younger man the freedom he still enjoyed. Almost lost in the grand orchestra of the father's disapproval sang a tiny voice of admiration. Though old enough to know better, Mutty had managed to slip free, for the time being, of the handcuffs of responsibility.

He had put his future on hold in a way Avi had never managed to do. On the contrary, Avi *lived* the future, sometimes more fully than the present. For the rabbi, tomorrow's aim had always a greater allure than anything today had to offer. Mutty was different; he allowed himself the luxury of being caught up in the moment. Right now, undistracted by the need to earn a living and still unfettered by dependents, Mutty could sink into the sea of Torah and splash there to his heart's content, emerging from time to time, invigorated, to the ever-unfolding wonders of the Land of Israel.

Avi himself had not enjoyed such a pleasant hiatus. As a young man he'd been too busy plowing toward his self-imposed goals, making a name for himself. It struck him now, with all the force of a brand-new realization, that he would probably never have the opportunity again. In choosing public service over personal gratification, he had turned a key in a lock. Now he was too tightly chained to contemplate escape, even for so short a time as Mutty was now doing. Like the Biblical ram in the bush, Avi was caught fast.

The image made him frown. He had done the correct thing, of course. The only thing an Avi Weisner, with the talents HaKadosh Baruch Hu had given him, could have chosen to do. And something in him insisted that his *bechor* do the same. When a son follows in his father's footsteps, he does more than ensure that the father's chosen path endures. He also serves to vindicate those choices.

A cabinet-maker — ridiculous!

Malka was still speaking of their distant son, but Avi wasn't paying attention. His eyes strayed irresistibly back to the lists of figures spread out on the table before him. They had been prepared by Sammy Mirsky and typed neatly — if unenthusiastically — by Mrs. Gerber. As soon as the donations hit the fifty-thousand mark, he'd put in a bid on that lot. A mortgage would have to be taken out and a string of contractors hired. Why, it was conceivable that the foundation could be poured by the summer! If he closed his eyes, he could see the site, sitting in its square of pale city sun between two modest storefronts. He heard the racket of bulldozers as they chewed up the waiting earth and saw the monstrous cement mixers, like giant gray centipedes, whirring and rumbling and then spitting out the stuff of which buildings — and dreams — are made...

There was a tentative tap on the door.

Binyomin had a key, but had seen through the curtained window that the lights still burned in the living room. Malka was on her feet before the second knock.

"Come in, Binyomin! Quick now, don't let the cold in with you."

"Malka...Avi." He swung the door shut behind him. "Don't tell me you were waiting up for me."

"Waiting up?" Malka gazed at him in great innocence. Her glance strayed casually to the clock. "One o'clock! Is it that late already? I was so caught up in this great book, I completely lost track of the time. But," she smiled happily and flopped down into an armchair, "since we're all up anyway, you can report in full. How'd it go?"

Binyomin exchanged a quizzical look with Avi, who shrugged. Taking off his coat, Binyomin said slowly, "Well, she's a very nice woman, your friend. Intelligent. Forthright. Sense of humor, too."

"Okay, all that I know," Malka said eagerly. "So?"

"So...I think it went well."

"Will you see her again?" Malka held her breath.

"Yes." A pause. "Actually, I've already asked her."

"Whee!" The *rebbetzin*'s eyes shone. This was even better than she'd dared hope. "When?"

He looked embarrassed. "Day after tomorrow?"

"Are you asking me or telling me?"

"I guess I'm telling you." Binyomin shook his head as if he didn't quite believe it himself.

Avi squared off his papers and rose to his feet. Though he wore a broad smile, his tone was deliberately brisk. "I'm glad it worked out, Binyomin. I'm sure you must be wiped out. Why don't you get some sleep? There's a late minyan in the morning."

Malka stared from one man to the other in mounting exasperation. Here she was, every nerve ending tingling for further details of this marvelous, incredible first date, and Avi was talking about sleep! And what was worse, Binyomin was obeying. Yawning, he told her with an apologetic smile, "Guess I will turn in. Not as young as I used to be, I guess."

Malka smiled benignly. "Are any of us?"

She waited until the men were halfway up the stairs before fixing hungry eyes on the telephone. Avi turned back to ask if she was coming up.

"In a few minutes," she called. "I want to tidy up a few little things here first."

"Don't overdo it," he said dryly. And at the top of the stores, he called down again, sotto voce, "She'll be feeling tired, too, you know."

Malka didn't dignify this with a reply.

Avi and Binyomin parted in the upstairs hall with muted "good nights." As soon as the men were out of sight, Malka pounced on the phone and dialed Adela's number. She waited through four interminable rings for her friend to answer.

Adela's "hello" was, Malka had often thought, the only visible crack in her armor. It was the "hello" of one who has known loneliness, who lives with it: wary, eager, a little distrustful, containing in two short syllables the whole story of disappointment and tragedy and hope.

"Hi, Adela," she returned in an urgent undertone. "It's me. It's not too late, is it? I just couldn't bear to wait for tomorrow." Malka held her breath. Would she have to ask?

"Oh." Adela audibly smothered an enormous yawn. "I don't mind. I just got in, actually."

"What do you think I'm calling about, silly?"

"Oh?"

Belatedly, Malka realized that Adela was teasing. "Come on, out with it! How'd it go?"

"What does Binyomin say?" Cautious.

"That the two of you have agreed to meet again day after tomorrow."

"That's right."

"Well?"

"Well? We're meeting. What else is there to say?"

"How much you liked him, for one thing. How you hit it off from the very first second. How you can't wait to see him again."

There was a long pause. Then, softly, Adela said, "I have only one thing to say, Malka."

"*Nu*? Tell me already!"

Even more softly, "Thank you."

2

He'd forgotten what it was like — the dazed feeling, as if he were sleepwalking and yet more awake than he could remember ever feeling before. How long had it been since he'd met someone who made him feel this way?

That she belonged to him he knew, irrevocably and without question.

There were other things he instinctively understood. This would be no short and snappy courtship. For one thing, there was the question of Adela's son. Even as they had spoken together this evening — each delighting in the other's every word, secretly and then not-so-secretly astonished at their own delight — he had sensed her distraction.

Some quiet probing had induced her to open her heart. At first, she said, she'd thought Yudy was ill. Now she suspected some sort of depression — something preying on the boy's mind. She was too devoted a mother not to let that mysterious *something* prey on her own as well. Until the mystery was cleared up, he doubted whether she would be able to make any sort of commitment.

But now that he'd found her, he was content to wait.

Honesty bade him see that there were other factors — more longstanding and so, over the long term, more significant — standing in the way of a quick end to his suspense. Both he and Adela had lived too long alone. He had his work; she, her son. But each, in an essential way, was detached. Isolation had become the norm, had settled in as a permanent background to their lives; and even loneliness could turn into an old friend with time. Winning Adela would mean battling the force of habit, overcoming a certain inertia. They were neither of them youngsters anymore. The fight would be a real one — though he had high hopes of winning it. The prize for victory was too great.

He sat down at the edge of his bed, gazing without seeing at the parade of grinning Donald Ducks on the wallpaper opposite. His expression was sober as he tried to calculate the odds of reaching the wedding canopy with this newly met woman. He soon gave up. There were too many variables, too many factors still unknown. In fact, if truth be told, she herself was still very much an unknown. Though his soul had sent him an unmistakable message — though his destiny *must* wind together with hers — he had to admit that he hardly knew her. They needed time, both of them.

He tasted the name that had become, in a mere five hours, so important to him. Adela Moses. What was Adela thinking right now? When he'd said he'd like to see her again, she'd promptly agreed — a hopeful sign. She had enjoyed the evening, she said, and his inner social barometer told him she wasn't lying. He could usually tell when someone was feigning an interest in him, in his conversation. Heaven knew he'd learned to read the signs often enough during his marriage. Not that Pessie had made much of an effort to pretend, or to hide her dissatisfaction with just about everything he was. Binyomin had, frankly, bored her. Not a very sweet pill for a man's ego to swallow...

He shook his head in the dark, dispelling the image of his former wife. If he was to launch a courtship worthy of Adela, he would need every ounce of confidence he could muster. He had to remember the painfully won lessons of his marriage: he was a *good* person, one who deserved happiness as much as the next fellow. He'd made a mistake. So had Pessie. The mistake had grown to encompass their whole marriage, but it had ended ten years ago. He was free now — free to try again, free to make himself whole, with, please God, Adela beside him.

They would certainly need all the help He sent their way. The road, emotionally speaking, was tortuous and strewn with hidden obstacles. Adela was a widow. Knowing as she did, intimately, the pain of sudden bereavement, it would be no light matter for her to plunge into another serious relationship. Fear would guide her away from such a commitment, even as her own heart urged her onward.

And Binyomin's own fears were no less real, if differently based. If she was afraid of another loss — of being, however unwillingly, abandoned again — he lived in mortal fear of a second failure.

They both said they wanted to find another life partner, but how *driven* were they, really, to find one? In the passage of the years had she not forgotten, just as he had, what it was like to make a joint project out of a life together — to drop half your own load and take on half of another's and feel both burdens lighter for the sharing? Bitter reality had, for both of them, cast a pall of disillusionment over the early dreams of "happy ever after." Time brought forgetfulness in its train, but that had its own pitfalls: As the ache of loss faded, so, too, did the memory of shared sweetness.

Sweetness? Binyomin sighed. He had to take it on faith that wedded bliss was even really possible.

Somehow, Adela needed to be reminded — and Binyomin taught — about how it could be. The lesson would require great patience, gentleness, and dogged persistence. Binyomin wondered uneasily whether, and how much, he would hurt her in his stumbling efforts to connect.

But on one question he had no doubt at all. Adela Moses had been made for him.

Questions assailed him, and worries, but the earth seemed suddenly a brighter place than it had been a mere five hours before — because Adela walked it.

With a deep sigh, Binyomin turned over and closed his eyes. He felt immeasurably tired but filled with a sense of quiet, joyous purpose. He had his work cut out for him. And he couldn't wait.

3

He couldn't wait, Gedalia thought glumly as he plodded home from school under a pale sun, for his brother to come home. Life seemed flat and dull without him. Though Fish had spent most of his time in Lakewood during the past few years, his sporadic visits home had been like bursts of swift, golden light in Gedalia's humdrum life. He missed his brother sorely.

The big gray house sat regally in its square of winter-withered lawn, the square hedges and faded grass brittle as paper in the cold air. The whole had a dull, washed-out look, all browns and grays. There would be more color in the spring. In the spring, tulips would peek out of the warmed soil, and the rosebushes would bloom. In the spring, there'd be pink and yellow and red again. In the spring, Fish would be back.

Gedalia let himself in. The house was quiet, but not empty-quiet. If he strained, he could faintly make out the distant sounds of dinner-making from the kitchen. Leila, the live-in, would be there and probably his mother, too, issuing contradictory instructions and masses of friendly advice and generally getting in the way. Gedalia knew that Leila preferred having the kitchen to herself when she cooked. Rochel Mann's helpfulness made Leila nervous, and nervousness made her cooking uneven. But Leila liked sweet little Mrs. Mann too much to ever so much as drop a hint that her presence in the kitchen was superfluous. If Gedalia wanted to do Leila — and their dinner — a favor, he could go into the kitchen and draw his mother out of there. He stood in the big front hall by the mirrored coat closet, vaguely considering the possibilities.

A sound from the living room startled him. A small, rustling noise, as of paper. He dumped his schoolbag and coat in the closet, shut it halfway with his foot, and poked his head through the living-room doorway to see who was there.

"Dad! How come you're home so early?"

His father's answering smile was thin. Yechezkel Mann was seated in his favorite armchair before the vast, fake fireplace, unshod feet sunk into the thick pile carpeting and a partially unfolded newspaper on his lap.

"Things were going smoothly at work," he said. "Thought I'd take a little time off, get home in time for dinner for a change."

"Great." Gedalia studied his father uncertainly. Mann had a large head to fit a large physique. The head was gray-haired at the sides, balding at the top. He had always seemed removed to the young boy and hugely authoritative, like the principal of his school or the head of surgery at some top-flight hospital. Or maybe the general of an army. Someone to respect and obey, not necessarily someone you could sit down and talk to. Fish had filled that role for him.

But now, to his surprise, the father gestured at the velvet sofa near his right hand. "Come. Sit. Tell me about yeshivah."

Cautiously, Gedalia went over to the sofa and lowered himself into its yielding depths. He struggled upright, hating the sinking feeling. "Uh, what do you want to know?"

"Well, how's school? How's your rebbe this year?"

Nice of you to ask. It was only the end of February, six whole months into the school year... Still, Gedalia felt an unaccustomed flush of gratitude. The question at least denoted interest. "Fine," he answered. "So's my English teacher. Fine." He fixed his eyes on his father expectantly, like a puppy awaiting instructions.

"Do you understand the Gemara? I really should find the time to learn more with you..."

"We learn on Shabbos." Something in his father's tone was making Gedalia uncomfortable. He wished he were sitting in a straight-backed chair instead of this quicksand sofa — or, better yet, standing. He felt himself at a disadvantage.

"Yes, we do," Mann agreed. "But not enough."

"I'm doing okay in Gemara, Dad."

"That's good. I should call your rebbe one of these days, just to hear from him..." The voice trailed off. Gedalia's father half-raised his newspaper, then dropped it again. It fell over his knees. One page dangled nearly to his ankle, but he made no move to pick it up. Gedalia stared at the newspaper, then, uncertainly, up at his father.

Mann's face had turned a very strange color. He brought a hand to his chest. "Gedalia," he croaked.

"Dad?" The boy rose slowly to his feet. "Dad, what's wrong?"

His father made an urgent waving motion with his free arm, the one that wasn't clutching his chest. He was pointing at the lamp table behind him. "Drawer," he gasped. "Pills!"

Half-paralyzed with a sudden terror, the boy made a mighty effort. He leaped convulsively at the small, polished table; he had never even noticed that it had a drawer. He yanked it open, groped inside. With immense relief, he located a small vial. "This?" He held it up.

Mann nodded his head, a series of tiny jerks that would have been excruciatingly funny if Gedalia hadn't been so scared. He thrust the bottle into his father's hand.

"No..." Mr. Mann's head-jerking became a sideways motion. With an effort, he gasped, "Give me..."

It wasn't easy for his shaking fingers to find the right purchase on the bottle cap. After three despairing tries, Gedalia finally managed to haul it off. He tried to tap a single pill neatly into his palm, but in his desperation a clumsy stream came pouring out. A few of the pills rolled onto the carpet. Gedalia grabbed one from the lip of the bottle and handed it to his father. Big, trembling fingers seized on the pill and brought it to his mouth. Mann swallowed and closed his eyes.

Gedalia waited. And waited. "Dad?" he whispered. "Are you all right?"

The eyes opened. After a long moment, his father managed a sickly smile. "All...right. Now." The smile turned into a sigh. "Thanks."

"What was it, Dad? Did...did you have a heart attack?"

A violent shake of the head. "No. Just...angina. Chest pains." Mann drew in his breath. There was more strength in his next words. "I'm fine now. I get these slight attacks from time to time. Nothing to worry about." He paused for more breath. "Don't tell Mommy."

"But she'll want you to go to the doctor. I think you should, too. You looked pretty awful just now, Dad. Sort of blue in the face. Don't you think — "

"*No!* Gedalia, you are not to worry your mother. I'm fine. See?" He positioned himself more comfortably, retrieved the newspaper, and deliberately opened it. "I'm fine, really. It's nothing. I don't want you — or Mommy — to make a big deal out of nothing." The grizzled brows lowered forbiddingly.

Nothing? Gedalia wondered. It sure had looked like something to him. But, pathetically grateful to have his father looking and behaving more like himself again, he nodded quickly. "I won't tell."

"Good boy." Mann stopped frowning and glanced at the newspaper. "So how're you doing in math this year?"

"We're learning algebra, Dad. I got a ninety on my last test."

"A ninety? What's wrong with a hundred?"

Gedalia's heart sank in a rapid, familiar motion, but this time, there was relief in the feeling. Dad sure *was* himself again. It was just like his father had said: nothing to worry about.

Five minutes later, Yechezkel Mann was perusing his newspaper in peace, while his son climbed the stairs to his bedroom, the incident all but forgotten.

With the defense mechanism of youth, Gedalia had willed himself to forget.

4

W hat do you hear from home?" Mutty idly asked Fish.

The two were enjoying a bit of winter sun on the yeshivah roof. It was two o'clock, that dead time of the afternoon when many Israelis close their shutters and turn away from the world in determined sleep. Now that he'd finished reading his letter, Fish seemed poised at the edge of slumber himself. His eyes were closed, the black hat tipped over them to induce the illusion of night. Fish could sleep anywhere.

"Mm? Oh, everything as usual. Mom's going to chair some new committee or other. Gedalia's fine. Dad's working hard, also as usual. They miss me, etcetera, etcetera. Nothing new."

Mutty nodded, closing his own eyes against the glare. It was not yet spring — Purim was still two weeks off — but even in wintertime the sun had an insistent presence unique to this part of the world. It lent a hard shimmer to the air, an intense white light that was merciless on eyes and skin but unequaled for clarity. Artist's light, he'd heard it called. No wonder painters flocked to these parts from all over the globe to capture what the Mediterranean sun had to offer.

Moments later, he opened his eyes again. Sleep eluded him, though his companion had been more favored: Mutty noted Fish's soft, regular breathing. The hat had slipped down almost to the bridge of Fish's nose. Mutty adjusted it gently, then let his gaze wander over the view.

It was impossible to tear his eyes away, or to keep them shut for long against the beauty of this place. The white stones of Jerusalem doubled and trebled the already radiant light: Mutty, and everything his vision encompassed, seemed to be dancing on the edge of a halo. Right now, from his vantage point on the roof, he could see squat, old villas surmounted by red shingle roofs and modern hotels that soared upward to penetrate the blue. Vivid pink splotches were the roses that never stopped blooming, summer or winter. He saw bougainvillea spread its purple fantasy over the warm, white stones and crawling fingers of ivy. And above — ah, above, the stunning and unrepeatable cloud formations of Jerusalem. They were massed now in great snowy heaps, so pure and soft against the sky's azure that Mutty found himself blinking back tears. *How wondrous are Thy works, O Lord!*

These last days, he felt as if he'd been sleeping all his life and had only just wakened to something richer by far than any dream. He'd never realized just how much his soul had hungered for what he found here in such abundance: age and wisdom, truth and beauty. There was history here — *his* history. Every breath he drew, every detail to catch his devouring eye, seemed imbued with a stunning, almost mystical meaning. In comparison, the dingy, brick fastness of New York seemed appalling, though he'd never particularly minded it before. There was wealth untold to be mined here, and it was his for the asking — provided he had the right sort of shovel.

And he knew he had. All that was really needed was a willing heart, a rocklike devotion, and — most precious of all — time. Time to seek, to savor, to hold the bright jewels of experience in the palm of a hand and let them spill lightly through the fingers...

I just might stay here forever, he thought dreamily, as the sun forced his lids down once more. The warmth of this late-winter day was really astonishing. It soothed him and took away his ability to more closely examine this last, highly interesting thought — or even to think at all. Abruptly, he fell asleep.

In his dream, he was carving the most beautiful scene in the world on a block of pale wood.

The wood was polished to a high gloss, so that it shone with an almost unearthly glow. It lay flat and quiescent, waiting. Under Mutty's nimble hand, nicking and scraping and smoothing, the wood sprang to life.

Slowly, the scene grew under his fingers. It represented a medley of stone and sky, of flower and tree and dwelling place, all woven together with exquisite grace — a frozen wood dance. When it was completed, the dream-Mutty held the carving reverently, drinking in with the tips of his fingers the contours he had molded. Then he raised his arms to lift the picture and hang it on the wall opposite: a surface of pure white, waiting to be filled with the work of his hand and his heart.

The carving glowed like the gold that glances off the rooftops of Jerusalem at sunset. Gazing at it, a feeling grew inside the dreaming young man, swelling until he could scarcely breathe for sheer joy. The feeling was, simply, love — for the thing he'd created and for the city that had inspired it.

Fish, too, was dreaming.

The contours of his dream were less clearly delineated than Mutty's. He was standing somewhere, he knew not where; vistas far and near shared the same blurred quality. The dream's salient impression did not derive from a sense of time or place — both were equally vague — but rather from a strong and specific emotion that filled him inside. It was a feeling that Fish rarely experienced in his waking life: peace of mind.

His wandering footsteps had brought him to the place where he stood, and though he knew not where it was, precisely, he did know with absolute conviction that it was *his* place. There was not so much joy in the knowledge as there was certainty, and a sense of rightness. And what is peace of mind, after all, but the vibrant offspring of duty? Of choosing right — of doing right — of *being* right?

The friends snored gently in the sun. Two refugees from reality, their fathers might have dubbed them; and yet, reality was here, all around them, in the burgeoning awareness that sprouted in Mutty's heart and the inchoate longings that besieged Fish's.

The shadows sharpened on the roof, and still Mutty slept on, and his friend beside him.

In sleep they looked younger than their years and more vulnerable. The city wound protective arms around them. Above was spread the azure canopy and a mammoth cushion of cloud. Soon they would wake, to all the aches and pleasures, to the demands and stresses that the world made on them. But for now, they were safe.

5

Safe. The dark made him feel safe, Yudy had said in an unguarded moment. Why, Adela wondered with the peculiar stabbing anxiety that had ridden everywhere with her for the past two weeks, should her strapping teenager worry about *safety*? What in the world could have happened to make him curl up into a ball like this, day after day, snug as a bug in his darkened room? How to make him listen to her entreaties — to confide in her — and to let her help?

It was with the utmost reluctance that Yudy left the house for yeshivah each morning. He had skipped a few days, back when all this had begun and would have stayed home indefinitely if his mother had let him. Adela had originally diagnosed the disturbing new behavior as symptomatic of some sort of physical ailment and prepared to take appropriate steps. Under notice that a doctor's office loomed in his immediate future, Yudy had grudgingly consented to rejoin the ranks of the educated.

His routine had changed, though. Sometimes he left ridiculously early in the morning — right after the earliest minyan, in fact — and at others, very late. He took to wearing strange clothes, too: an old parka he dug up from the unremembered recesses of the hall closet or a belted raincoat two sizes too small on him. The shoulders that had stood so square and straight were hunched now as he slunk out the front door. They had become the shoulders of a coward. Adela's big, strong boy had turned, before her dismayed eyes, into a shrinking violet. And she hadn't an earthly clue why!

"Yudy?" Adela said softly, tapping on the door.

When no answer came, she opened it. At the threshold she halted and caught her breath. The room had undergone a transformation.

He had sent away to NASA for some outsize astronomical posters. She remembered when the tall, mysterious cylinders had arrived, but he had not unrolled them for his mother to see. She saw them now. From bed to ceiling they rose, with scarcely any space between them, flanking the window and sprouting like some alien outgrowth from the desk.

Everywhere were stars. Planets stared fixedly from the inky depths of space amid swirling stellar clusters and nebulae. By the closet, a huge comet reared its fiery head, trailing a gaseous tail that stretched far along the wall before flaring to extinction almost at the very door where Adela stood, frozen. Fathomless galaxies revolved before her befuddled vision. Slowly she turned her head, taking in the room from corner to corner. It was like stepping into a planetarium in mid-show or subsisting in the drugged slow-motion of outer space. The effect was eerie — frightening. All sense of normalcy was obliterated. An otherworldliness completely engulfed what had once been an ordinary boy's room.

"Yudy?" Adela squeaked. She willed him to turn and face her.

He did so, smiling faintly. "Hi, Mom. Well, what do you think?" He waved a languid arm at the decor.

"It's...unusual." Adela cleared her throat. There was something about the room that made it difficult to speak naturally. "What's the matter, don't you like living on earth anymore?"

Instantly, the smile vanished from Yudy's face. A look of intense anxiety replaced it. His mother took an impulsive step forward, hand outstretched. Impetuously she cried, "Yudy, what is it? What's wrong?"

He shook his head. "Nothing, Mom. It's okay." He resumed his favorite stance, flat on his back with his eyes riveted upward. The planets Jupiter and Saturn, Adela saw, were now fixed on the ceiling above the bed, to reign among the lesser luminaries there.

She gathered her wits. With an effort, the words came out calmly enough. "Yudy, I got a call from Malka Weisner before. She and her husband want us to come to their house for the Purim *se'udah*. That's in just over a week from now. I...I told them we'd come." The unspoken question — plea, really — hung in the air of the darkened room.

"Rabbi Weisner?" For the first time since the onset of his painful slide two endless weeks ago, Yudy evinced interest in her words. He propped himself up on one elbow and looked across at his mother. "At his house?"

"Yes."

He seemed to consider. "Purim... There'll be lots of people out on the street then. Kids... Adults, too."

"That's right." Adela tried to keep the puzzlement out of her voice. Yudy appeared to be talking aloud to himself.

"It's not far," he murmured. "Rabbi Weisner's house..." Abruptly, he declared, "I'll go!"

The decision seemed to sap him of strength. He fell back on the bed and resumed his silent communion with Saturn. Adela hesitated, then walked to the door. She watched her son for another painful moment. Then — with a last, shuddering glance that swept the starry reaches of the former bedroom — she gently closed the door.

"Malka?" she breathed into the mouthpiece of the phone a moment later. "He's agreed to come."

"Good!" The *rebbetzin*'s satisfaction was unmistakable. She smothered a yawn.

"Are you sure it won't be too much for you?" she asked with compunction.

"Too much? Are you kidding? I've been known to seat thirty people around my dining-room table — and, on Purim, a couple more *bachurim* sleeping it off underneath! You and Yudy will be more than welcome."

"Thank you." Malka's yawn was infectious; now Adela's face was hideously stretched in one of her own. She sagged on her feet in a sudden rush of weariness. These two weeks had taken their toll. She was one big tangle of nerves. Even Binyomin had noticed. He'd said — but she wouldn't think of Binyomin. Not yet. Not until she'd dealt with the malaise that had stricken her son and thereby earned the leisure she so desperately needed to sort out her feelings. Four dates in just over a week: surely that was rushing things? With Yudy so unsettled, she couldn't afford the luxury of happiness. She needed time!

She straightened up, saying briskly, "And thank your husband, too. I mean it."

"Never mind that. Our pleasure."

"Is there anything I can bring?"

"Just yourselves. Hindy's going to help with the cooking this year — she's gone all domestic suddenly."

"That's something to look forward to," Adela smiled. "At least, I think it is?"

"Sure. Hindy's got the makings of a first-class cook. She takes after her father. Competent." Malka laughed off the self-disparagement implicit in her own remark. "And speaking of Avi," she added in a conspiratorial undertone, "maybe he'll be able to drag Yudy's secret out of him."

"That," Adela said fervently, "is exactly what I'm hoping for."

If Yudy hadn't accepted the Purim invitation, her next step would have been to ask the rabbi to pay a house call. But this way was better — much better. Yudy had often spoken with admiration and youthful fervor of Malka's charismatic husband. If anyone could tunnel his way into Yudy's confidence, it ought to be Avi Weisner.

Adela was pinning her hopes on it.

EIGHT

1

Yudy's disguise that Thursday morning was simple enough: he merely pulled the hood of his parka very low down on his forehead and tightly around his head. Except for a few inches of his face showing in the middle, you wouldn't know him from a hundred other teenagers walking the frigid streets of Brooklyn on their way to school.

The parka belonged to last year (his present winter coat sported no hood) and made him look and feel like one of the seven dwarves, with the shiny material straining across his back, and red wrists, chapped from the wind, poking grotesquely out of too-short sleeves. But Yudy didn't mind any of that. Let the other kids tease. Let his mother give him those anxious, speculating glances when she thought he didn't see. It didn't matter, any of it, as long as he felt safe.

Of course, it was impossible to really feel safe, even for a moment. He wondered bleakly if he'd ever feel secure again, if he'd ever be able to drop the nervous habit of darting frightened looks over his shoulder, of stepping clear of dark alleys, of shying like an unbroken horse when a car came too near.

One block to go. His pace quickened, as did his heartbeat. He tried to keep his eyes riveted to the sidewalk, as if that could protect him. *See no evil, hear no evil...* The last part of the daily walk was always the worst. He never knew when that hated figure would step suddenly out of some shadowy niche, like a rattlesnake darting with deadly menace into his path. There was no predicting the hiss of that terrifying voice, of the flicker of metal — almost more imagined than seen — that reminded him of his promise. As if he'd ever forget!

The bile of fear rose into his throat, sickeningly familiar. Without realizing it, he'd begun to run. He pictured the solid bulk of the yeshivah, just around the corner now — four walls to shelter him for hours and hours. As he sped through the last agonizing yards to his destination, Yudy answered his own question. No, he wouldn't feel safe. He'd never feel safe again — not until it was possible to expunge from shuddering memory what had taken place that awful night.

It had happened only a couple of weeks before, but to the boy it felt much, much longer. Looking back on the time before he'd taken that doomed shortcut through the park, he was like an archeologist studying the remains of a bygone era. As a scientist will pick up a shard of stone or a fragment of broken ewer and dispassionately recite facts and figures to place them in their historical context, so Yudy thought wistfully and often of the time before ugliness and terror had invaded his innocent life. Only, in doing so, he was neither calm nor dispassionate — because the facts and figures belonged to his own life.

Except that right now, it sure didn't feel like his own. Whoever's life he was leading these days, it had nothing to do with the carefree Yudy Moses who'd inhabited his body for fifteen years. That Yudy was somewhere else — hiding in his bed like a little child, with the blanket over his head and the bleak comfort of endless frozen space all around him.

He was turning the corner when a sudden movement startled him. Gasping, Yudy jumped two feet in the air. Adrenalin racing through his system in time to the furious pounding of his heart, he turned...and saw that the danger was nothing more malevolent than a big orange tomcat.

"*Baruch Hashem*," he whispered weakly, resisting the temptation to lean for a moment against the wall of a butcher shop. His knees seemed to have turned to rubber. "Thank God."

He raised his eyes and saw the reassuring shape of the school building just ahead. Scuttling like a timid rabbit, he entered the yeshivah's portals and sighed gratefully as they closed behind him. Another morning walk safely gotten through. But his relief was tinged with a sharpened apprehension: each uneventful day only drew closer the next horrible encounter. The evil was there, fixed and inevitable as the moon that winked through the slats in his window blinds at home. If it had retreated for a morning, or a day, he knew it would be back.

He had *mishmar* tonight, which meant that he'd stay late. It would be thirteen hours before he had to face the outside world again. Maybe, if he was lucky, he could hitch a ride with someone so he didn't have to face the walk home alone. The mornings were bad enough; the nights were a thousand times worse.

Shrugging out of the tight parka, he walked toward his classroom and the well-known faces and routines that awaited him there. His Gemara, too, was waiting. Yudy's heart lifted slightly at the prospect of sitting before its open pages, of losing himself in the heady crosscurrents of the Talmud.

These days, the strong arm of the Torah was the only thing that held him above the abyss.

2

Adela locked her front door and slipped the key into the slim, velvet evening bag that — though feeling somewhat ridiculous — she persisted in carrying with her on dates. It made quite a change from the briefcase-sized monstrosity without which she was lost during the course of her normal day. Perhaps the velvet bag was her way, along with the high heels and the bit of extra makeup, of shedding her workaday self on these special evenings.

But tonight, even with all these reminders, it took her a long time to unwind, to slow the spinning wheel of her mind on its endless round of work, shop, cook, laundry, Yudy, work, shop, cook... These days, the wheel tended to drift to a halt, more and more often, on that most anxious entry of all. *Yudy...*

She followed Binyomin to the car. Behind her, the house was shrouded in darkness. Yudy had not yet returned. That wasn't unusual; this was his late night at yeshivah. Nothing to worry about... Still, if only she'd seen him, even just a glimpse, before leaving.

I'll make an excuse to call later, Adela planned. "I'm in the city, and I just had a horrible thought: could I have left the oven on?" A light tone, mildly worried, but not about *him*. "Could you just check it for me, Yudy?" While all along, it would be his voice that she was checking and his manner that she was assessing. Perhaps, with that little extra bit of reassurance to take with her, she might even have a good time this evening...

"It's a little warmer tonight," Binyomin remarked, politely opening the passenger door for her.

Absently, she murmured, "Hmm." Then, with a slight shake of her head, she tried again more brightly, with a smile this time, "Yes, it is, isn't it?" Binyomin smiled back and slipped into the driver's seat.

She realized with a vague sense of surprise that it *was* warmer. There was a general mugginess in the air that had nothing to do with snow. Maybe rain. Adela glanced up through the windshield. The sky was stuffed with a thick padding of orangey-gray cloud. Yes, definitely rain later.

In fact, the drizzle began before they were halfway to Manhattan. It fell lightly, monotonously, the mist settling like a gentle cloak round the shoulders of the night. For a while, the occupants of the car were silent, listening to the song of the wipers and the staccato drumbeat of the rain. It was a peaceful silence; for Adela, a thankfully mindless one. Presently, however, her own contentment made her wonder, guiltily, if she was neglecting her companion. She stirred and glanced at him. "Did you have any place special in mind to go tonight?"

Binyomin's expression was rueful in the passing headlamps. "Actually, I had thought of the Empire State Building...to see the view."

She joined in his laughter. "Why don't we just go somewhere warm and dry? Like the Rainbow Room."

"Suits me."

He kept the talk as light as his tone. If Adela could have known it, he'd enjoyed the relaxed quality of the silence as much as she. This was — what? Their fourth date? Or maybe the fifth. It all depended on how seriously you took the exchange they'd had, somewhere in the middle of last week. It had been the second time they'd met.

"I hate second dates," Adela had announced, some ten minutes into the meeting. They had been strained minutes, as each groped to recapture the miraculous sense of ease they'd shared at their first encounter, two nights before. There was a touch of melancholy in Adela's voice as she asked, "Know what I mean?"

"Second dates," he mused, unconsciously using his lawyer's trick of repeating the remark to gain time to think. "Especially second dates that follow perfect first dates. I guess I do know what you mean."

"Was it perfect?"

"Just about. Didn't you think so?"

She nodded. "Mm. Which makes it a hard act to follow. Here we are, both expecting the evening to go just as well this time around — "

"While secretly afraid that it won't," he finished for her.

Again she nodded.

"Second dates..." He sat up straight and snapped his fingers. "The solution's simple. Let's abolish them!"

"What?"

He smiled at her. "Good night, Adela. I had a very nice time."

"Binyomin — "

"There. End of second date." He grinned and continued imperturbably, "Beginning of third."

Slowly, she relaxed and smiled, too. "This is our third date?"

"You got it."

❧❦

So — depending on how you counted — they were seeing each other for either the fourth or the fifth time tonight. In any case, less than two weeks had elapsed since he'd heard the name Adela Moses. And he was more determined than ever to change that name, as speedily as possible, to Mrs. Binyomin Hirsch.

He knew her well enough by now to see that she was troubled. Yudy again. He had not met the boy but was beginning to share Adela's unease. The behavior she'd described — unwillingly and only after the most persistent prodding on his part — certainly sounded far from normal. And yet, she claimed he'd been perfectly healthy and eminently sane up until a couple of weeks before. Something must have happened to trigger this uncharacteristic behavior. Whatever it was, it would bear investigation. There were steps that could — should — be taken. Passive anxiety would get them nowhere.

Tonight, he thought with sudden determination. Tonight we'll have it out. I'll try to get her to let me help formulate some sort of plan. There's been enough pointless worrying. What we need here is a course of action.

His thoughts were interrupted. "Binyomin, when will you be moving into the apartment?" He'd finally found a decent place, with Malka's help, not far from the Weisners.

"Monday or Tuesday, I think. Why?"

She smiled. "I was just wondering if you'd be at the Weisners' Purim se'udah next week. Yudy and I are invited."

"Well, even if I hadn't been planning on it, I certainly intend to be there now." It would be, apart from its other pleasures, a chance to finally meet Yudy.

"I'm glad." The words were spoken softly and almost lost in the sudden strengthening of the rain. But Binyomin caught them. He smiled to himself and concentrated on the road. Tonight, a plan for dealing with Yudy. And Sunday — Purim — a shared meal at his closest friend's house. Things were going to be all right. Very much all right.

He was whistling under his breath as he pulled into a parking space only

half a block from the Rainbow Room. "An auspicious beginning," he told
Adela, "to a memorable evening."

"Are you trying to impress me with all those big words?"

"Who, me?" He switched off the ignition. "On the contrary. I'm just
trying to keep up."

She was laughing as he handed her an umbrella and pulled his own hat
lower over his eyes. Still smiling, they made the short dash through the
drizzly nighttime glitter of Manhattan.

The smile was nowhere in evidence some ten minutes later, as she
clutched the receiver with damp palms. "Yudy? Talk to me! What
happened?"

She heard her son take a long, shuddering breath — like the quivery
gasp of a child trying to control his tears. "I'm — It's okay, Ma. I'm fine. I'm
sorry I sounded funny just now. I guess I...fell asleep or something." He
stared at his hands. There was a spot of blood that hadn't washed off.

She gripped the phone more tightly. "I want the truth, Yudy. Has
something happened? Is it connected to all the rest of it — these crazy two
weeks? Tell me!"

"I'm fine, Ma. You didn't have to call." The living room window — had
he drawn the shades? He'd have to get up and check. And make sure —
again — that the door was double-locked. " 'Bye, Ma. Have a good time."

"Yudy," she said firmly. "Take it easy. I'm coming home."

"Ma! You don't have to do — "

She hung up on him.

Warmth and opulence surrounded Binyomin as he sat patiently at the
little table, awaiting her return. Other couples filled the dimness around him,
talking in undertones, their figures reflected in the rain-washed windows.
Occasionally, a tinkle of laughter interrupted the hush. The atmosphere was
one calculated to soothe, and Binyomin found himself responding to it. He'd
been perusing the drinks menu while she was gone and looked up at the
sound of her approach, smiling. "So what'll you have, Adela?"

She sat down. As the light fell on her face, he saw her expression. Slowly he put down the menu. "What's the matter?"

"It's Yudy." Her voice was toneless. "He was crying when he picked up the phone just now. I'm sure of it." She shook her head, meeting his eyes with her anguished ones. "I can't take this anymore, Binyomin. I'm terribly sorry, but I have to go home."

"Now?"

"Now. I'm sorry."

With a resigned shrug, he stood. It would do no good to try to talk her out of it. Whatever was wrong with Yudy, it would take more than his own fumbling efforts to decipher the problem — or to solve it. Tomorrow, when she'd calmed down, he would suggest that she seek professional help for her son.

As if she'd read his thoughts, she said, hesitantly, "Binyomin, I...I asked Rabbi Weisner to talk to Yudy. On Purim."

Somberly, he nodded. "Good idea." He led the way to the cloakroom for their coats.

"Binyomin — " There was an odd, pathetic quality in her voice as she called him again from behind. He turned, one eyebrow raised in silent inquiry.

"I'm... It's just that..." She drew a breath. "I'm *really* sorry. I hate to do this to you."

What about what you're doing to yourself?

He didn't ask it. Instead, with a funny, crooked grin not untouched by its own pathos, he said, "That's okay. But I just want to know one thing."

"What's that?"

"I'm getting confused. Does this count as a date, or what?"

3

Purim took what little order Malka managed to impose on her domicile and gleefully threw it to the winds.

The madness began the moment the family returned from hearing the megillah. Even before they could wolf a hasty breakfast, the doorbell began to ring — and continued to ring, incessantly, all morning long. The Weisner dining-room table quickly became a clearinghouse for *mishlo'ach manos* baskets of every description, pulling in and departing all day long like trains at a popular station. Under the endless piles of candies and chocolates; smashed hamantaschen and crumbled cakes; smeared faces and stained tablecloths; glitter and crepe paper and bits of ribbon, the detritus of the children's ambitious Purim costumes; and feverish preparations for the enormous, winey, festive meal that soon overflowed the long-suffering kitchen, the Weisner house seemed simply to shrug its homely shoulders and give up.

The mess, in a word, was horrendous. Tomorrow Malka would mind. Right now it all seemed delightful, part of some terrific game to which the grand epithet "Anything goes" might suitably apply. But her satisfaction was based on more than just her sense of fun. The faces she encountered in the course of that day — no less than the clutter that accrued as far as the eye could see — were living testimony to all that she and Avi, individually and together, had built.

Shul members came in a steady stream on this special Sunday to drop off a basket and linger to drink a schnapps with the rabbi. Friends and neighbors poked their heads through the door every few minutes, some to leave almost immediately on the rest of their Purim routes, others to deposit themselves on the couch like some specie of overfriendly houseplant come to happily take root in the Weisner living room.

Sammy Mirsky put in an appearance, followed in close succession by the husbands of Avi's two secretaries, faithful Mrs. Gerber and young Naomi

Brody, the new office assistant. Gerber was as gray-haired as his wife, though he carried a considerably larger paunch. His habitual expression was rather ferocious, though his smile — when permitted to break through — was of a sweetness that rarely failed to disarm its surprised recipient. Asher Brody was a lively young *kollelnik*, who passed through the open front door with a very little boy riding piggyback on his shoulders and a miniature Queen Esther clinging to his pants leg. The rabbi greeted both men warmly, pressed cake and drink on them and lollipops on the children, and sent them on their way with brimming baskets and special good wishes to the hard-working women at home whom Avi persisted in regarding as the true backbone of the shul.

All morning long, neighborhood kids trooped in higgledy-piggledy, bewigged and bemasked out of all recognition, trailing sheets and sashes, and leaving in their wake clouds of good cheer and candy wrappers. Outside, the ice had melted, and the long heaped ridges of graying snow seemed nothing more now than part of an old, bad dream. Winter had been exiled today.

Distant strains of music drifted in through windows newly opened to the springlike air. Malka was heady with the sheer, lovely insanity of the day. She was *rebbetzin*, mother, and eager little girl, all at the same time. When she impulsively picked up her youngest — fierce Tzvi, the Indian brave — and pressed his grubby striped cheek to her own, the resemblance between the two was remarkable. One would have been hard put to say which was the more excited.

Sometime in the middle of the morning, she and Avi slipped away from the revellers and placed a call to his sister's family in Israel. It would be late in the day there, with the family preparing to leave to shul for the reading of the megillah. Zalman Markovich picked up, slightly more boisterous than usual, in anticipation, perhaps, of the festivities of his own Purim the next day, but otherwise his quietly amiable self. After Zalman, Mutty got on. He'd been awaiting his parents' call before rushing to hear the megillah with his yeshivah friends. He spoke of technical things: with his mother, of plane reservations — to her joy, he was due to return to the States in just two weeks, on Rosh Chodesh Nissan — and to his father, of his progress in learning. He sounded good, Malka thought wistfully. Quiet, but distinctly happy. His friend Fischel Mann, on the other hand, was definitely, pleasurably, inebriated. It seemed that he'd spent Purim day in Bnei Brak, revelling in the festivities there, and had just returned to Jerusalem in time for that city's Shushan Purim fun. He snatched the receiver out of Mutty's hand to bellow his own good wishes over the line to Mutty's parents in America.

"Two days of Purim," he said happily. "It's just wild!"

Scarcely had Avi mustered a reply, when a noticeably more sober voice came on: Esther's. She tried, without much success, to carry on a reasonable conversation with the brother she so rarely got to talk to. Her discourse was interrupted by strange crashings and exclamations in the background, and Esther's exasperated asides to her various children ("Put it *down*, Eli! Bracha, strap Yoni in, he's falling out of the high chair. Aryeh Leib, I said no. Careful, Shoshie, you're dripping soup on the tablecloth. *Aryeh, Leib, stop that!*") At length, Tzippy being dispatched to "keep an eye on the boys," Esther was finally able to redirect her attention to the far-off Weisners. "Sorry about all this," she apologized breathlessly. "We're just preparing the *mishlo'ach manos* baskets and feeding Yoni before we go to shul. I don't know what's gotten into everyone today."

"Just Purim," Avi said with a smile.

Malka, at his side, looked around at the disaster area that was her own kitchen and gave ear to the merriment raising the rafters in her living room, and was suddenly, fiercely glad she didn't give two hoots if someone dripped a little soup on *her* Purim tablecloth. How chagrined Esther had sounded as she voiced her apology — like an officer whose troops had failed to impress visiting V.I.P's after extensive drilling. General Esther! Malka grinned.

Today she minded not a bit that her sister-in-law's home habitually ticked along like a well-run ship under the command of the most efficient of captains. She couldn't care less if such an extraordinary upset of routine in the Markovich household was hardly much worse than humdrum existence in her own home. Today, she didn't have to care. This was Purim, when reverses were extolled and topsy-turvy ruled the day. *"Venahafoch hu"* — today, Malka was queen!

When Avi signed off and exited hurriedly to see whether any furniture was still left standing in the living room, Malka warmly took over the reins of conversation. She chatted with Esther and sent her love to each of her nieces and nephews. Just before they said goodbye, Malka remembered something she'd been meaning to ask.

"So, did Shoshie actually begin *shidduchim* yet? You mentioned that she was about to start, last time we spoke." There'd been a curious absence of mail from the Markoviches these last weeks.

An odd, strained silence met her words. Then Esther cleared her throat and said, too lightly, "Oh no, in the end, it was Bracha who went out with the boy. You know how these things are..."

Malka *didn't* know, but there was no chance to pursue the topic. Beyond a brief, "Well, how's it going? Is she still seeing him?" and Esther's terse, "Yes. We'll keep you posted," Malka hung up hardly more knowledgeable than she'd been before. But the doorbell was ringing again, and the noises from the other room growing more pronounced, with someone giving voice to *"Mi Shenichnas Adar"* at a bellow, while two others were attempting to harmonize with a lively, if decidedly off-key, version of *"Shoshanas Yaakov."* She hurried out to join the fun.

❧❧

Morning passed into hectic afternoon. Young Tzvi, glorious in buckskin, feathers, and garish war paint, got sick to his stomach from too many sweets; Chaim ate most of a thickly frosted chocolate cake and looked slightly green for the rest of the day; Shani, behind the protective veneer of a clown's mask, abandoned her shyness and could be heard from time to time punctuating the general gaiety with torrents of high-pitched giggles. Hindy, cook for the day, darted from pot to pot stirring things with a long, wooden spoon, while her brother Shmulie, home from yeshivah along with a couple of his pals, led the others to new heights of merrymaking and mayhem. Binyomin Hirsch passed from room to room like a cheerful genie, with a quip, a helping hand, and a listening ear where and when they were needed. And now, here was the doorbell and Adela and Yudy standing on the stoop, a bottle of wine in the boy's hand and a home-baked cake in the mother's.

"Welcome! Welcome!" Malka cried, a little drunk herself on the spirit of the day. "Come in, you guys. We're just about to wash. Avi, Binyomin, they're here! Shmulie, get the boys to the table, would you please? I'll see how Hindy's doing in the kitchen."

Hindy was doing fine in the kitchen. Flushed and overheated and filled with a sense of virtuous accomplishment, she proudly brought a succession of superlative dishes to the table. It was unfortunate that most of the menfolk present were too tipsy, and their palates too blunted by liquor, to appreciate Hindy's offerings as they deserved to be appreciated. They would, Malka thought complacently, do ample justice to the leftovers, though. She herself was lavish in her praise. Hindy blushed and dimpled and thoroughly enjoyed the meal, which was every bit as much as she deserved to do.

Malka, covertly studying Yudy Moses as he entered the house, had noticed with a pang that he looked disappointingly sober. Of the sense of fun that drove the other youngsters today there was no sign on his face. But as the meal progressed, he began to cover some of the ground he'd lost. If no spark of actual gaiety animated Yudy yet, at least he was doing his determined best to catch up with the others in the drinking department. A bottle of wine stood at his elbow, the level of its contents steadily depleting as he filled and refilled his glass.

Adela was looking particularly pretty, Malka thought. She'd had her dark wig combed into a flattering new style that brought out the contours of her face and set off the shine in her eyes. Still, Malka had grown close enough to her friend to recognize the signs of strain beneath the surface. Tiny lines had etched themselves at the corners of Adela's mouth, which even her lovely smile could not quite erase, and a tiny furrow seemed permanently etched between the glowing eyes. The lines grew more pronounced whenever she glanced at Yudy, which was virtually every few seconds. It was as though the mother could not rest unless assured that her son was happy.

Happy he clearly was not; but under the influence of the wine, Yudy did grow noticeably more relaxed. Avi engaged him in conversation and was gratified by the boy's responsiveness. Malka had been on and on at him about some problem besetting Yudy and Adela's almost frantic concern; but for his part, he saw nothing more worrisome than a likeable teenager in the throes, perhaps, of a difficult adolescence. Then again, he didn't know Yudy all that well. The rabbi continued to talk pleasantly with the boy as they ate and drank, being careful not to direct too much overt attention Yudy's way and privately totting up his impressions.

Binyomin, too, was studying Yudy. Adela had introduced the two immediately upon their arrival. Yudy shook hands politely but evinced no particular interest in the man who had been seeing his mother steadily for the past three weeks. This in itself was unusual enough to trigger Adela's alarm bells. But Binyomin seemed content with the boy's reaction. Maybe it was a kind of male ritual, Adela thought as she toyed with Hindy's superb roast, a sort of sizing-up period before committing oneself to definite liking. The thought of Binyomin and Yudy liking each other seemed suddenly very important to her.

Twilight was falling by the time the meal drew to a close. Shani was good about clearing the table and bringing in the dessert — a fantastic creation featuring mounds of whipped cream over a mysterious but delicious-looking chocolatey center. By this time, the younger children had drifted away, Tzvi to snore placidly on the couch — the war-paint lipstick mingling gruesomely with a slightly different shade of ketchup on his chubby cheeks — and Chaim to retreat to a quiet corner to play by himself, his invariable habit when overtired. Shmulie and his friends were hard put to keep their own eyes open, but Yudy seemed exceptionally wide awake. It took Avi some moments to notice the extreme and unusual clarity of the boy's enunciation and the unfocused glitter in the big brown eyes. Yudy was, if not completely drunk, bordering on a state of genuine intoxication.

"That," the rabbi said, leaning back in his seat with a smile at Hindy, "was scrumptious. A top-notch *balebusta*, our daughter. Don't you think, Malka?"

Malka was vociferous in her agreement, and Hindy was wreathed in smiles. Shmulie came awake long enough to hoot with good-natured derision. "Hindy, a *balebusta*? Don't tell me you don't remember the time she accidentally put pepper in the — "

"Why don't we *bentch* now?" Avi interrupted smoothly. "Then we can all get comfortable." To Yudy he said, "You're welcome to step into my study for a little chat, Yudy, if you want."

"That's right, I once asked you for that," Yudy said, nodding owlishly and blinking his overbright eyes. "That's right, I did. Well, okay by me. O-*kay*. Fine."

Adela bit her lip and looked at Binyomin, who looked back, his glance carefully noncommittal.

"*Bentch*," Malka ordered her son. Shmulie was again showing signs of dropping into a serious sleep. He started awake, nudged his friends into a state resembling alertness, and, at a nod from his father, led the *bentching*. If Yudy's voice was a little higher and a little louder than the others', it was hardly noticeable except to someone listening with an especially attentive ear. His mother noticed. So did Binyomin...and Malka and Avi. Yudy's final crescendo attracted the attention even of the somnolent Shmulie, who turned with immense expansiveness to the younger boy and pumped his hand. "*Yasher koi'ach*, Moses. You're okay, kid. '*Shkoiach!*'"

"Thanksh," Yudy replied with dignity. "You're okay, too. We're all o-kay. Uh-huh. We are." He picked up his glass, held it up to examine the inch or so of sparkling liquid there, then tossed it back in one neat gulp.

Avi rose to his feet, the walls around him slightly less solid than usual. Slowly — each according to his current level of coordination — the others either followed suit or slept on peacefully, heads pillowed on their forearms right there on the table.

With a nod at his wife and guests, the rabbi bore a remarkably unsteady Yudy off to his study.

4

Mrs. Gerber was having a troubled Purim.

She knew the day was earmarked for gaiety, and each year she made a heroic attempt to transcend her own dour nature to celebrate it properly. This year, however, certain very specific worries made a mockery of her efforts. The worries did not revolve around herself or even her family — those she might have managed to subdue with her customary discipline. No, her anxieties today were all for her boss and spiritual mentor. Where Rabbi Weisner was concerned, had she any right to skimp on worrying?

Again and again she fretted about the way things had fallen out. Had the series of odd phone calls come to her attention only a few days earlier, she might have mentioned them to the rabbi in the course of their working day. Had she learned of them, in fact, any time but yesterday, on the Fast of Esther, she would have had no hesitation in knocking on his study door and demanding an audience. Busy as he always was, he would not have refused to give her a hearing — not when she so obviously had his own best interests at heart!

But the calls had come yesterday, when the rabbi had been fasting and preparing for the evening's megillah reading. Or, rather, she had learned about them yesterday, from young Naomi Brody, and personally taken a last call just as the rabbi was hurrying away in the car to fetch his wife and children back to shul for the megillah. There had been no time to think it through, and it had certainly not been the right time to say a word.

Well, she'd thought it through now. Moodily she scraped the remains of the Purim feast from a china plate into her daughter's garbage pail. Malya was resting with her feet up — she hadn't been feeling well lately — while her mother did the dishes and Zeidy Gerber entertained the other children. Why, oh, why, hadn't Naomi Brody told her about those calls earlier? Hadn't she the sense to recognize something suspicious when it was happening right under her nose? But no, these young women were all the same: flighty and uncaring, counting the minutes until they could escape the drudgery of office work — however worthy — and get back to their own cozy homes and families.

She wasn't being fair. She knew it, even as she stewed in anxious resentment. In her frustration, she twisted the tap too violently. Hot water gushed out of the faucet, nearly scalding Mrs. Gerber's hands until she adjusted the temperature by adding a little cold. Under the soothing stream, hands moving mechanically among the dishes, she mentally absolved Naomi.

Dozens of calls came into the office each day, and many more recently, with the building campaign in full swing. "That Mirsky" was presented with stacks of messages every time he walked into the office, most of them reading, "Returned your call." How was young Naomi to notice a pattern to some of those calls or be expected to pay close attention when the messages became more specific? She was trusting, as she should be. It was Mrs. Gerber's domain to take the hostile road, to pounce on suspicion where it reared its sly head. Ironically — she saw it clearly now — it was that very tendency in her that had made Rabbi Weisner deaf to her mutinous mutterings. She had started in on Mirsky from the start and kept on going ever since. The rabbi had learned to simply tune her out.

Well, she had a feeling he'd listen now. She felt no triumph in the thought; it was a sad sort of vindication. What would this do to the building fund — to the shul — to Rabbi Weisner? Glumly, she scrubbed and wondered.

Sammy Mirsky was leaving on a week's vacation, she remembered suddenly. Skiing, he'd said, somewhere up in New England. There was hardly a speck of snow left on the New York streets by this time, but she imagined it probably took longer to melt up there. Still, there was no point in waiting until he got back. The rabbi must hear about this — and soon, Mrs. Gerber decided, if she grasped anything of the situation. Maybe it was a blessing in disguise, Mirsky being out of the picture this week. Rabbi Weisner would be able to assess the situation without the distraction of that super-salesman's glib explanations.

But how to disturb the rabbi on Purim? She glanced through the low kitchen window to where the last light was draining out of the day. The sky was a flat, empty, the color of pewter. Officially the festival was just about over, but the fun — like the snow in cold New England — would doubtless linger far longer in the rabbi's household than here, at her tired daughter's.

No, it would be a while yet before she could justify disturbing his peace. She consulted the clock above the table to determine when she might reasonably make her call. A couple of hours, at the least. Or might she put it off till the morning?

She shook her head. She had a feeling, based on her long years of experience, that this was important enough to warrant immediate attention. The sooner Rabbi Weisner confronted Mirsky with the facts, the better off they'd all be.

Yes, she decided, reaching for another greasy plate and feeling better for having made her decision. In two hours, she'd call.

5

Have a seat, Yudy."

Avi sat behind his square, mahogany desk and gestured at a well-padded leather chair facing him, the stuffing beginning to escape at the seams. The chair was of a piece with the rest of the furniture in the study: perched on the vague border between comfortably old and downright shabby. Backing into it, Yudy misjudged the distance, staggered, and nearly ended up on the floor. Only the most adroit footwork at the last second spared him that ignonimy. Avi watched the boy's brief, awkward dance and final safe landing with dreamy detachment. He raised the glass that he found he had unwittingly carried in from the dining room. "*L'chaim!*" He drank.

Yudy mumbled, "*L'chaim*," and looked around as if wondering where his own drink had gotten to. The rabbi didn't give him a chance to wonder long. He set down the drained glass and leaned forward, hands clasped in front of him on the desk. "So, Yudy. What's new? How's life? How's it going in yeshivah?" The alcohol had loosened his tongue to the point where he felt uncertain of being understood unless he repeated himself in triplicate.

" 'Salright. Yeshivah, I mean." Yudy paused significantly. "Otherwise? Total loss."

Avi looked shocked. "Don't say that, boy! Life is wonderful. A true gift from the *Ribbono shel olam.*" He peered more closely at the teenager. "What makes you say that?"

"I say it," Yudy said sullenly, "because it's true. Rotten things happen in this world, Rabbi. You can't deny that. No, *sir.*" The tousled head shook vehemently. "No one could deny that."

"I won't deny it," the rabbi assured him solemnly. "But Hashem has His reasons for why those things happen. You can't deny *that!*" He was proud of having scored a point in this wine-soaked, theological debate.

Slowly, Yudy shook his head again. "I'm not denying it. The truth is, life is okay — for some people. Only not for others. No, *sir!*"

"Is it okay for you?" Avi asked shrewdly.

"Nope. I told you — total, complete, absolute loss."

Avi was nonplussed. What call had a strapping fifteen-year-old to be spouting such pessimism? At his age, he ought to be vibrant with the possibilities of life. Through his pleasant fog, Avi remembered what Malka had been telling him. Something was wrong with Yudy — some malady, mysterious and unnamed. It was worrying his mother, Adela Moses. It was worrying Malka, Avi's wife. For a moment, Avi considered the merits of worrying, too, and then decided it was much better to just find out what all the fuss was about.

He fixed the boy with a gimlet eye.

"Tell me, Yudy," he said, forthright as one can only be when the usual restraints are down, "what's on your mind? Why have you been acting so strange? Your mother wants to know. My wife wants to know. Matter of fact," he confided, with a sincere smile, "*I* want to know!"

Yudy was silent for a long time. Eyes closed, he leaned his head against the high back of the leather chair and remained in that position so long that Avi suspected he'd dropped off to sleep. He cleared his throat. Yudy's eyes flew open. Abruptly, he said, "Wha's on my mind? You really want to know? Well, I'll tell you, Rabbi. Or, rather, I won't tell you. I can't. He made me promise not to tell a soul." Suddenly, the boy's eyes were brimming with tears. "I promised..."

"What do you mean? Who made you promise?" Avi was more alert now, straining to understand.

"*He* did. *Or else.*" Yudy's voice had dropped to a whisper. The tears spilled over onto his cheeks, running in silent misery to his chin, his open collar.

"Who? *Who?* And why, Yudy?"

"He has a knife." Yudy was shaking so hard now that the words could hardly be distinguished. "He said if I ever told a soul...he would do something bad..."

"Something bad? To you?"

Yudy's eyes squeezed shut. "No," came the whisper. "To my mother."

Then, as if to prove that the threat was genuine, he tugged at the buttons on his left shirt cuff. When he'd gotten it open, he yanked the sleeve up to expose his arm. "Look, Rabbi. You don't believe me? You think he was joking? Look!"

Tears fell unchecked as he raised the sleeve higher, nearly to the shoulder. Avi gasped, all at once cold, stone sober.

On Yudy's upper arm, etched redly into the pale skin like a bolt of miniature lightning, was a long, raw, jagged scar.

NINE

1

M acramé," Malka was saying to Adela and Binyomin as they waited for
Avi and Yudy to join them. "That's where you tie long strings into
these interesting shapes. Now *that's* something I'd like to learn."

The three were seated in the center of the disordered living room, their
backs to the royal mess of china, cutlery, and half-consumed eatables
waiting in supreme indifference on the dining-room table. One of Shmulie's
friends was snoring raucously at the table. Hindy and Shani dealt
lackadaisically with the debris after their own fashion, which consisted of a
trip to and from the kitchen every ten minutes, with time out for nibbling
leftovers in between. Little Tzvi slept on a corner of the couch, while Chaim
played a solitary game behind it. Upstairs, Shmulie and his friends happily
finished the last drops at the bottom of the bottle.

"Macramé," Malka repeated with satisfaction. "I think I'll do it."

"Itching to tie yourself up in knots?" Adela murmured.

Malka made a face. "No, thanks. That much I can manage without
lessons. But haven't you ever seen those adorable plant holders? All sorts of
different shapes, and all made out of just a few strings. It looks incredibly
complicated, but I shouldn't think it would be too hard to learn."

"What's all this?" Binyomin asked from the depths of the room's biggest
armchair. "Have you embarked on a self-improvement program or
something? The other week you were talking about taking advanced

Chumash classes, and a few days ago, I think it was piano lessons. What's the story?"

Malka looked embarrassed. "Have I been overdoing it? Now why doesn't that surprise me? But yes, I do want to improve myself — to expand my horizons — to fly a little! After all," an expressive wave and a grimace took in the whole of her surroundings, "domesticity doesn't exactly seem to be my thing."

"Nonsense," Adela said robustly. "You're a terrific cook, and the house is always...cozy and comfortable. That's saying a lot, Malka. I mean it."

"A terrific cook — sometimes," Malka argued. "Uneven, that's the word for it. As for 'cozy and comfortable'..." The words trailed off in a disbelieving snort.

Binyomin said mildly, "Come on, you can't judge the house by the way it looks on Purim. We're none of us exactly at our most impressive then."

"You're very nice, you two. Thanks for the vote of confidence. But I'm really determined to start something different and exciting. Some new project." Then, remembering, the *rebbetzin* sighed. "*After* Pesach, of course."

"Pesach," Adela repeated. She gave a delicate shudder. "Don't remind me. I'm too comfortable right now. Even thinking about it makes me feel tired."

"I'm sure you handle Pesach-cleaning as efficiently as you run your business," Binyomin told her.

"My business doesn't collect dust kittens everywhere you look. But thanks." Adela smiled and forgot for a whole minute to glance at the closed door of the study, behind which her son had been immured with the rabbi for half an hour. "I've been lucky."

"You've been *good*." Binyomin, in his early research on the subject of "Adela Moses, prospective *shidduch*," had heard many an accolade about the way she conducted her one-woman enterprise. "Not everyone combines computer expertise with sound business sense. You've managed to do both."

"Thus speaketh the lawyer."

"Thus speaketh anybody!"

Malka listened to the interchange with a complacent sense of *nachas*. This little idea of hers, this match that Heaven had so obviously ordained and had channeled through her own puny efforts, looked like it was coming off very nicely. If only this business with Yudy could be cleared up soon.

Unwillingly, her gaze travelled after Adela's to the closed study door. At that precise moment, it opened. Avi stepped out, alone.

Adela had seen, too. She half-rose from her chair. "Yudy?" she asked in a voice suddenly too high-pitched.

He raised a finger to his lips as he crossed to them. "Sleeping it off. He should be all right in an hour or two, though his head won't be feeling very pleasant for a while."

Adela relaxed. "He's not used to strong drink."

"I should hope not!" Malka declared with a smile. She leaned forward urgently. "Avi, did you have a talk with him? Did he explain what's been going on?"

The rabbi found an empty chair and carefully lowered himself into it. His own head was still swimming, though whether from the effects of too much alcohol or from Yudy's shocking revelation he wasn't sure. "He talked a little," Avi admitted. Or had it been the drink talking? He frowned.

Malka persisted, "What? What did he say? You look upset."

"Please, rabbi. Tell us what he said," Adela pleaded.

There was compassion in his look. "I will. It wasn't much, though. What he told me was garbled — unclear — and not just from the drink. It was as though he was afraid of saying too much."

"Too much about *what?*" Malka almost screamed.

Avi gathered his thoughts, then repeated the boy's words as accurately as he could. His audience listened in frozen silence until he was done.

"A scar?" Adela whispered. "On his arm? But who did it? And why?" She had turned ashen.

"Adela," Binyomin said, very calmly, "this is going to be taken care of. We're going to take care of Yudy."

She took a deep breath. How many years had she lived without this simple reassurance, the knowledge that there was someone in her life who would be there to help when she needed it? She'd been without a protector for so long that she'd forgotten what other women took for granted. Adela would have felt less grateful, less comforted, if Binyomin had been more vehement in his declaration. The very quietness of his manner calmed her more than anything else could. It was so good to have someone to lean on...

Abruptly, she shook her head. *She mustn't give way.* It was too early to revel in the peace Binyomin offered her. *She* was Yudy's mother. She bore the responsibility for his welfare. For a last, lingering moment, her heart played with the notion of relaxing its guard, of accepting the hand outstretched to support her — and then, firmly, she pushed it away.

"I'm fine," she said, willing the words to be strong and steady. "But I'm absolutely determined to get to the bottom of this. I'll go to the police if necessary."

Avi passed a hand over his face and beard. "Yudy seemed particularly anxious that we leave the police out of this. He seems worried that this person — whoever he is — might want to harm you, *chas v'shalom.*"

"Harm *me?*"

"It's not so hard to be brave when it's only your own health at stake," Binyomin said quietly. "What better way of controlling someone than by threatening his loved ones?"

Avi nodded. "I suggest we think the situation through very carefully before making any sort of move." Whatever the reality behind Yudy's story, it was clear that something fragile and innocent in the boy had been cruelly shattered. His youth had been betrayed. He remembered the last time he'd had any sort of talk with Yudy — back on Yudy's father's *yahrtzeit*, in shul, when they'd made plans for the Shabbos lunch that had never materialized. How open the boy's face had been then, how candid his glance, how shy and eager the smile! That memory stood in heartbreakingly sharp contrast to the boy's demeanor today. Avi wondered bleakly at the source of the change. What was the nature of the damage that had been done, and how deep did it go? And — most crucial of all — what could be done to repair it?

The rabbi hesitated before adding gently to Adela, "We have to remember that he was considerably befuddled by all the alcohol in his system when he spoke to me. How much of his story is genuine is impossible to tell at this point. Part of his fear might be based on imagination."

Binyomin silently acquiesced; that fact had not escaped him. It was also significant, he thought — but didn't tell the already overanxious mother — that Yudy had retained enough presence of mind, even in the spilling of part of his story, to hold back the really vital secrets. He'd given out no names, facts, or places. His terror must be very powerful indeed to place such a lock on a tongue loosened by drink.

"Genuine! The scar was genuine enough, wasn't it?" Adela's words trembled with suppressed tears.

"Yes. But I think it's important that I speak with him again when he's...well, sober."

This was something the agonized mother could cling to. "Yes! Speak to him, Rabbi, please! If only we can get to the bottom of this..." She broke off, staring pop-eyed at Avi. "A scar on his arm! When did he get it? *And who gave it to him?*"

"We're going to find out," Binyomin said. There was steel in his voice. He sounded, Malka thought, more like a high-powered lawyer than at any time since she'd known him.

She nodded vigorously. "That's right."

Avi remembered something else Yudy had said. "He did mention that he got the scar one night on the way home from yeshivah. You and Binyomin were out together, he said."

"I *knew* it! Binyomin, remember?"

Binyomin certainly did remember the aborted evening. He nodded thoughtfully. Adela was frantic. "Yudy sounded like he was crying on the phone. He denied it, of course, but — " She buried her face in her hands. "Oh, what are we going to do?"

"With Hashem's help," Avi said firmly, "we'll catch that guy — "

"And put him behind bars," Binyomin finished.

Adela looked from one to the other, then turned away before they could see the tears that had finally, irresistibly, sprung to her eyes. There was a struggle for control. Then, in a subdued voice, she said, "Thank you. All of you."

"Ta-a!" Shani's musical summons came from the kitchen. "It's for you! Mrs. Gerber."

"Excuse me?" Avi asked absently, his mind still on Yudy and on the best step to be taken next. "What was that, Shani?"

"The phone. It's for you, Ta."

"I didn't even hear it ring," Malka exclaimed.

Avi stood up and, for the first time, noticed that the windows framed full darkness. Outside, the streets were quiet. Purim was over.

He felt all at once unutterably weary. "I'm coming, Shani."

Adela got up, too. "I'll go check on Yudy." Binyomin rose to go with her. With a sigh, Malka struggled to her own feet and made a halfhearted stab at some of the clutter that had accumulated on the couch. Tzvi murmured in his sleep, and behind the couch Chaim's voice droned on in subdued play.

At the kitchen door, Avi stopped to ask Shani, "Mrs. Gerber, you said?"

"Uh-huh. She said she's sorry to disturb you right now, but it's important."

Wondering, he took the receiver from his daughter and spoke into it. "Mrs. Gerber? Is everything all right?"

Her answer roused a faint, inexplicable dread in his heart.

"I'm not sure, Rabbi," the secretary said slowly. "That's the whole problem. I'm just not sure..."

2

Mrs. Gerber puttered nervously around her house, straightening a sofa cushion here, adjusting a window blind there. Passing her husband where he sat at his ease in the big leather recliner, as was his custom of an evening, it was all she could do not to adjust *him*. It wasn't often that her boss came to visit, and she wanted everything to look just right.

"Relax, Breina," came advice from the recliner. "What do you want to go and make such a fuss for?"

"I'm not making a fuss," she returned automatically. "Do you mind picking up that newspaper from the floor? If you're not reading it, I'll put it where it belongs."

"Fine." He yawned. "I could sleep like a log right now."

"Nochum! Don't you dare! You said you'd be here when I talk to the rabbi."

Nochum Gerber scratched his gray head, shifted his considerable bulk in the chair, and yawned again. "It's probably nothing. You're always suspicious about nothing, Breina."

"I just hope it's nothing," she said ominously. She was stooping for a stray bit of fluff on the carpet, when the front doorbell rang. Abandoning the fluff with a lurch, she marched across the carpet like a general to his doom and flung open the door.

The rabbi looked awful. His skin was pasty above the beard, and his eyes were bloodshot. Noticing her look, he raised a hand with a rueful grin to forestall the inevitable comment.

"I know, I know. I look like something the cat dragged in. There's a simple, one-word explanation that covers the situation nicely: hangover. *Shalom aleichem*, Reb Nochum. How are you?" He had followed Mrs. Gerber into the living room and now extended a friendly hand to her husband.

"*Baruch Hashem.*" With a grunt and a mighty effort, Nochum Gerber climbed out of the recliner — despite Avi's protests — to shake the rabbi's hand from an upright position. "Had a nice Purim, Rabbi Weisner? It certainly looked *leibedik* when I was there this morning."

"Purim was fine. Now my wife and daughters are left to clean up the aftermath. Why do you think I escaped?"

The other chuckled dutifully, while Mrs. Gerber essayed a strained smile. She was relieved when the rabbi — no hint of amusement in his face now — turned to her. "Shall we sit down, Mrs. Gerber?"

She nodded jerkily and led the way to the dining-room table. Rabbi Weisner and Gerber followed. On the table was an array of cakes and a hot-water urn flanked by the fixings of hot drinks. "A cup of tea, rabbi? Or maybe some coffee? They say black coffee's good for — er — after..."

"After indulging too freely? You're right, as usual. Black coffee it'll be. Thank you."

Preparing the coffee afforded Mrs. Gerber a little time to collect her thoughts. She was ready when Rabbi Weisner, after taking a sip, set down his cup and asked seriously, "What is it that's worrying you, Mrs. Gerber? You said it was about the building fund, and you said it was important."

She clasped her hands together tightly on the table. "Yes. First of all, Rabbi, I want you to know that I don't have anything personal against that — against Mirsky. I'll admit I don't go in for these brash, young types — I've made no secret of that — "

He nodded, a glint of humor in his eye that quickly faded as she continued.

"But I believed he was doing his job for us, for the shul, as best he could. That he was doing it *honestly*." She shook her iron-gray head and repeated the words that had given Avi such a sinking feeling when he first heard them over the telephone wire. "Now I'm not so sure."

Gerber cleared his throat. Avi glanced at him questioningly, but it seemed the sound was a prelude, not to speech, but to taking a deep drink from the glass of tea his wife had set before him. The rabbi sipped his own coffee. There was a dull pounding starting up behind his eyes. He said, "This is a very serious accusation, Mrs. Gerber. What exactly are you implying?"

"Tell it the way it happened," Gerber urged his wife. "The way you told it to me."

"All right." She drew a breath. "It was Naomi, Rabbi. Naomi Brody. She picked up a few strange phone calls over the last couple of weeks. It wasn't until yesterday that she thought of telling me about them. I myself answered the last one yesterday afternoon."

"What kind of calls? Threatening ones?"

She gaped. "Oh no! Nothing like that, Rabbi. What made you think I meant *that?*"

"I don't know." He sat back tiredly. "I'm sorry. Go on, please. Tell me in your own way. I won't interrupt again."

"The calls were from men — contractors — who wanted to know when we would be ready to start building. A plumbing supply company, an electrical firm, a window place. All of them asked for Mirsky, and when told he wasn't in, asked more or less the same thing. When do we expect to lay the foundation? When will we be ready to meet with them — to talk about the plumbing, or the shul's electrical needs, or whatever." She locked her eyes on the rabbi's, imploring.

He took the story to its conclusion, the way she'd hoped he would. "You think Mirsky made promises to these men? In return for — "

"Donations." She nodded vehemently. "I looked up the lists when Mirsky was out of the office one day. Each one of those firms has pledged sums — *big* sums — for the new shul building." She twisted up her face knowingly. "Tax deductible."

Avi Weisner drummed his fingers on the well-polished table. His expression was thoughtful and intensely unhappy. The silence stretched until Mrs. Gerber was ready to scream. Her husband took it calmly, occupying himself with his tea and a piece of rather dry chocolate cake. Finally, turning to his secretary, the rabbi said, "There is no way I can look into this — not even to check the lists — until I first hear what Sammy has to say. I must give him the benefit of the doubt. Do you understand, Mrs. Gerber?"

Dumbly, she nodded. "Yes. But I still think you could call up — "

"No. This is the way it has to be. I will not phone these men and find out what Sammy told them — yet. I'm going to wait to discuss it with Sammy himself tomorrow morning. Only then, and depending on what he has to say, will I decide on the proper course of action."

Mrs. Gerber blurted, "But Mirsky's out of town till next week!"

"Oh? That's right, I'd forgotten. He went skiing or something, didn't he?" The fingers resumed their drumming. "All right, then. We wait until next week."

Mrs. Gerber caught her lip between her teeth as if to bite back her reply. Nochum Gerber grunted his approval. "There's no fire," he rumbled, reaching for another piece of cake. "Nothing that won't wait a week."

"And until I do confront Sammy," Avi went on, "I'd like you to refrain from talking about this to anybody, Mrs. Gerber."

"Not even to Naomi?"

"Not even to Naomi. The less anyone knows of these...these suspicions, the better. They may well prove unfounded after doing irreparable damage to Sammy's good name." He was aware that he sounded pedantic but could think of no other way to impress his secretary with the gravity of the situation.

Mrs. Gerber muttered something rebellious under her breath, then said aloud, "And the phone calls? What do I do about them?"

Avi thought for a moment. "Instruct her to pass all of Mirsky's calls to you this week. Give her any reason you like. And meanwhile, *say and do nothing.*"

"All right." The middle-aged woman crossed her arms like a disgruntled warrior. Deprived, temporarily, of her ability to fight the foe, she felt unexpectedly vulnerable. "I'll do as you say, Rabbi. But I don't like it."

"Fair enough." He smiled — a smile that held neither joy nor humor — and rose from the chair. As his exhaustion struck him, it was all he could do not to sway visibly on his feet. "Thank you very much for coming to me with this, Mrs. Gerber. I trust your discretion, and your good sense, implicitly. We'll see this thing — whatever it is — through, together."

This parting shot left Mrs. Gerber in a mollified frame of mind, if not exactly a happier one. After she saw the rabbi to the door, she tried to engage Nochum in conversation about the just-ended meeting, but he would have none of it.

"I'm going to bed," he stated, and proceeded to do just that, carrying his paunch with tired dignity up the stairs.

At the Weisners, a few minutes later, Avi Weisner told his wife the same thing.

"I'll tell you about it another time, Malka. You would not believe how wiped out I am. I'm going up to bed."

Two women were left, then, to stew in silent frustration. For the first, the frustration came from the prospect of a week's enforced inactivity, a week in which to juggle her suspicions and bite her restless tongue.

For the second, it was the exquisite agony of curiosity balked.

It promised to be a very long week.

3

In her small Jerusalem bedroom, Shoshie Markovich was getting ready for her first date. Again.

There was something dreamlike about her preparations, as if she were reliving a movie she'd watched once before. These nervous flutterings of the heart, this indecision in front of her closet, that growing heap of discarded dresses and cast-off shoes — she'd felt and seen them all before. But where was the joy that had been such an intrinsic part then, that had colored the whole experience with a rosy hue of anticipation? Joy was conspicuously lacking tonight. No, she told herself honestly in the mirror. She couldn't say she particularly looked forward to this meeting tonight.

What made it even more difficult was the simmering resentment that could flare, unpredictably, into a full-blown blaze at the thought of her sister's good fortune. Bracha and Benzy were also out tonight. Shoshie had lost count of the number of dates they'd had. It didn't matter, really: Everyone knew they were fast heading toward an announcement. By Pesach at the very latest, Shoshie calculated, their engagement would be official.

Her anger had dulled into a generalized sadness of late, with stormy Beethoven giving way to melancholy Chopin beneath her questing fingers. But it lit up again now, full and red and as strong as ever.

It could have been me, she thought, heart hammering in sudden rage. It *should* have been me!

Then, just as quickly as it had come, the anger departed. In its wake was the flat, dull feeling she'd been carrying around for weeks. Desolation had become her boon companion. A miasma enveloped her now — a fog that blotted out the light of what should have been a happy occasion for any young girl. Tonight she would actually (barring unforseen disaster) have her first *shidduch* date. Somebody or other was coming to meet her in a very short while. And she couldn't care less.

She greeted the fog as the old friend it was fast becoming, and reached out an indifferent arm to pick up the first dress she touched. It didn't matter what she wore tonight. Nothing mattered.

കൈ

Tzippy Markovich was sitting at the tiny desk in the cramped room she shared with Batya and the baby, struggling with her math homework. She'd have loved to ask Shoshie for help, but her big sister was getting ready for a date tonight. Anyway, Shoshie had been out of sorts for a long time now. Ever since Bracha had stolen Benzy away from her.

The twelve-year-old caught herself with a gasp. That wasn't right. Bracha hadn't *stolen* Benzy. She'd explained it all to Tzippy one night, after Shoshie had staged a very unpleasant scene at dinner, full of accusations and tears. Shoshie had *asked* her twin to take her place that evening when she hurt herself falling down the stairs. Could Bracha help it if she and Benzy had liked each other right from the start? She felt sorry for Shoshie — they all did — but how would it help Shoshie if she, Bracha, refused to go on seeing Benzy?

It made sense, Tzippy admitted, chewing her pencil as she mused. But still, her soft heart twisted with pity for the rejected sister — for Shoshie, who never smiled anymore. The house reverberated with the harsh chords and dissonances she dragged protesting from the piano each evening. Bracha might be right, but Shoshie was *suffering*.

With a sigh, she bent her head over the detested math book. The ends of her braids brushed the page like a couple of soft, red-blond brooms. Tzippy wished they could whisk away those stupid numbers — along with the heartache that had become a permanent visitor in their home since Benzy had appeared at their door.

∾∾∾

Esther Markovich explained carefully to her mother-in-law, "Bracha left already. She went with Benzy. You know, the young man she's been seeing... And Shoshie has a date tonight, too." She raised her voice slightly. "A *shidduch* for Shoshie, Ima."

"Shoshie? Shoshie?" The old woman tugged querulously at the crocheted blanket that covered her knees. "She has a *shidduch* already?"

"Yes, Ima. His name is Mendel Baum. He's learning in..."

Her mother-in-law's head had fallen forward, eyes glazing over as they tended to do more and more often. A moment later she was breathing heavily, asleep. Esther gently lifted the slipping blanket to the old woman's knees. There was a new frailty about the blue-veined arms that rested on the blanket. Savta was nearing her ninetieth year, and, just now, defenseless in sleep, she looked every year her age.

Quietly, Esther rose and left the small room her mother-in-law called home. It was time to get dressed. Zalman should be up from his workroom at any moment to help her get the kids and the house in order before this Mendel's arrival. A memory assailed her of that other first date, of the nerves and laughter and anticipation that had charged every room of their apartment then. She wondered where all that energy had gone. She certainly didn't have it, and from the look on her husband's face as she greeted him a few minutes later, he was feeling just as drained. Shoshie was at the piano bench, already dressed: she looked beautiful but lifeless. As Zalman dealt with the boys' bedtime rituals and Esther, with Tzippy's help, tended Batya and the baby, the soft strains of a melody filled the house. The chords were blue, muted, with single piping notes speaking of yearning and loss. Though every light in the flat blazed brightly, the mood was definitely twilight.

Some three hours later, Esther sat up with a jerk on the couch, where she'd been dozing. A key had turned in the lock of the front door. Before she could gather her wits to move, Zalman had risen from the dining-room table and his Gemara. He met Shoshie coming in.

The girl returned her father's smile, a sight that heartened Esther and dispelled the mists of sleep. She rose with alacrity and crossed the room to them, also smiling.

"Nu? How did it go?"

Shoshie shrugged. "Okay, I guess. Nothing spectacular."

Zalman asked, "Do you think you want to meet him again?"

Her answer was another shrug. "Whatever."

The parents exchanged a glance. This was not, to say the least, very promising. Disappointment, even, would have been better than this gray, neutral reaction. "Do you want to sleep on it?" Esther suggested helpfully.

"Yes. I want to sleep."

Like an actress walking into the wings, Shoshie went to her room to erase the signs of tonight's performance. She was in bed, scrubbed clean and drifting toward slumber, when the sound of the opening front door startled her into wakefulness. Tonight's second act burst through the door, fresh-faced and laughing. Shoshie heard her parents greet Bracha and Benzy, heard the low friendly murmurings between the older and younger couples, before Benzy said "good night" and left.

When her twin tiptoed into their room, Shoshie's eyes were closed. But her straining ears heard clearly the humming that accompanied her sister's movements around the dark room. It lasted for quite some time.

The humming, in fact, did not stop until her sister at last crawled into her bed. There was a very brief pause. Then Bracha called softly, in a hesitant voice, "Shoshie? Are you awake?"

When no answer came, she hesitated once more, as if deciding whether to try again; then she turned over and composed herself for sleep.

On the other side of the small room, Shoshie stared in darkness at the wall, shaking with great, silent sobs for the thing that had come between her and her sister, which gagged her mouth and stoppered her heart against the one who had once been closest to her on earth.

4

It was the night before their departure from Israel. Mutty wanted to spend it aimlessly walking the beloved streets he had come to know so well, but Fish had other ideas.

"For an antisocial guy, you sure made a lot of friends here," Mutty grumbled, as Fish dragged him from one yeshivah to another, from one apartment to the next, in an endless round of farewells.

"Who says I'm antisocial?" Fish countered. "The opposite: I'm a friend to all the world."

But true friend to only a select few, Mutty acknowledged privately. As if in direct ratio to the smallness of his inner circle, Fish seemed to accrue light acquaintance in abundance — in Jerusalem just as in Lakewood. Good-naturedly Mutty went along, drinking in the atmosphere of the city he loved with a secret greed, while joining Fish in saying goodbye to a host of semi-strangers who laughed with them and wished them well and would scarcely remember their names when they'd gone.

As if to chide them for wanting to leave, the night was exceptionally beautiful. Spring had come early — it was still two weeks to Pesach — and had lavished her colors and scents on Jerusalem with special abandon. In the dark the fragrances of the flowers in the gardens they passed seemed to Mutty to vibrate with an intensity that was almost visual. He could *smell* the reds, the yellows, the exotic purples, and the tender green of young grass.

The night sky was softer than velvet, the stars brighter than diamonds, the air clearer and more uplifting than wine. Resolutely — almost desperately — Mutty pushed away the reality of tomorrow's flight. But the pleasure for him in this perfect evening was pricked with an ache he couldn't ignore. Time was a vulture, swooping with evil intent on the source of his newfound joy. Why, it felt as though he'd just arrived! Hardly had he begun to absorb the essence of this wonderful city, this amazing land — *his* land — than it was time to leave it. Like cloth caught on the spikes of thorns, a part of him, the skin of his very soul, refused to be torn away. Something must be left behind, even if it was only a piece of his heart.

It was too soon. He didn't want to go!

The last stop was the Markovich flat. As Mutty raised a finger to press the doorbell, Fish stopped him, suddenly nervous. "It's kind of late. Maybe we should have called first."

"Too late to think of that now," Mutty shrugged. "Besides, I'm *mishpachah*."

"Problem is, I'm not."

"Come on, Fish. You're a *ben bayis* here by this time — a regular." Mutty peered at him curiously in the gloom of the landing. "Boy, you really are nervous, aren't you? Take it easy, kid."

His friend took a deep breath. "If you're sure we won't catch them all in their pajamas or something — "

"It's barely after ten. Relax." Mutty rang the bell.

The door was opened by Esther who, far from being dressed for bed, looked like she was about to step out to a party. Behind her the house was tidy and very quiet. There was no sign of Zalman.

"Aunt Esther? Are you on your way out or something?"

Esther glanced down wryly at her attire. "No. Uncle Zalman and I saw Shoshie out on a *shidduch* a couple of hours ago, and neither one of us bothered to change afterwards. Hello, Fish. Come in."

"A *shidduch?*" Mutty asked interestedly as he followed her inside, trailed by Fish. "*Nu?* Anyone interesting?"

Esther sighed. "I wish Shoshie would find him more interesting. This is their second date, but for all the enthusiasm she's been showing he might as well not have bothered." Mutty's normally reticent aunt had gradually fallen into the habit of using her nephew as a sounding board. She'd found him extraordinarily sympathetic — a real comfort.

Mutty asked, "What's the matter? Anything wrong with the guy?"

"Nothing at all — with *him*," his aunt replied with meaning. Mutty's eyes widened above the new dark-blond beard he'd begun growing. "Oh, that old problem?" A few weeks before, in a moment of special stress, she had unburdened herself to her nephew. Mutty now understood the silent tension that lent a strained aura to any room that contained the twins.

Esther nodded. With practiced hands she reached into the freezer for a foil-wrapped hunk of cake. Fish tried to object, but she waved him off. "Sit down, boys. Tea? Coffee?"

The young men opted for coffee, which Esther prepared while the cake began to thaw on a plate.

"Yes," she answered at length. "That old problem. Mutty, it looks like we'll be getting a *mazel tov* soon. Bracha and Benzy are about ready to get engaged — "

"Wow! Terrific, Aunt Esther! *Mazel tov!*"

The expression on her face stopped his effusions very effectively. "Not yet. Not that it's much of a surprise. From what I understand, Benzy was ready to sign on the dotted line weeks ago. Bracha's held him off."

"Why?" It was Fish who asked. Apparently, in his absorption in the tale, he'd forgotten that he wasn't "*mishpachah*."

Esther, apparently, had also forgotten, or else chose to ignore the technicality. In the two months since Fish had enjoyed his first meal at the Markovich table, he'd been a frequent visitor, and one whom both Esther and Zalman liked very much. "She feels guilty because of the way she met Benzy. You know."

Fish nodded solemnly; Mutty had filled him in. "Has Shoshie actually objected to the engagement?"

"No, she wouldn't do that. She's just treating Bracha like a total stranger, that's all. Happy as Bracha is — as she should be these days — she's just heartbroken about it." She slashed almost savagely at an unopened bag of sugar, cutting it open and pouring some into the shaker. "It's all such a pity!"

Absent-mindedly, Fish took a piece of nearly frozen cake and bit into it. Stung by the cold and the extreme hardness, he put it down again just as absently and asked, "Isn't there anything anyone can do? Can't someone talk to her?"

"I've tried. Zalman's tried." Esther spread her hands in a very uncharacteristic gesture of despair. "What can we say? This is their *mazel*, the way Hashem wants it to be. Shoshie just has to accept it. Her *bashert* will come along at the right time, too." She made a face. "If she ever unbends enough to care about anyone, that is. She's made of ice, it seems."

Fish thought about the music he'd heard, not once, but many times in his visits to the apartment, coaxed from the piano by Shoshie's talented fingers. The storm-tossed emotions were there for anyone to read: anger and pain and an overwhelming sadness. He looked up, met Esther's eye. "I don't think ice, exactly," he said slowly. "I think...maybe...she's just given up. Lost hope."

"Lost hope!" Esther stared at him, uncomprehending. "Lost hope? But why should an eighteen-year-old girl, a girl who has everything going for her, lose hope? It's ridiculous!"

"I don't know," Fish said quietly. "But it seems to me she has. Maybe — " he paused to think about it, to relate the girl's experience with his own — "maybe she thinks she's being punished." His pleasant, homely face screwed up with embarrassment. "I'm sorry, this is none of my business — "

"Punished?" Mutty broke in. It seemed to be Fish's night for having his words echoed back to him in stupefaction. "But what for?"

"Not punished, exactly..." Fish was growing increasingly uncomfortable under the scrutiny of the other two. "Judged undeserving, maybe — which really comes out to the same thing. Think about it," he urged, throwing caution to the winds. "*She* was supposed to have the first *shidduch* in the family. *She* was supposed to meet Benzy, to have the chance to marry him. And it all went to her sister instead. She must be wondering why."

"Fish, I never knew you were such a psychologist," Esther said.

"Still waters run *very* deep," Mutty said, fixing his friend with a curious stare.

"I'm no psychologist. But I do think someone should talk to Shoshie, shake these thoughts out of her before she wrecks her life, *chas v'shalom.*" Fish paused. "And I think that someone should be Bracha herself."

"What should be me?" a new voice asked at the kitchen door. Three heads turned. Bracha stood there, smiling. "Sorry to eavesdrop. Didn't you hear me come in?"

"Apparently not," Mutty told his cousin. "Sit down, have some cake." He studied her. "Back from a big date?"

She laughed. "In these clothes? No, I was studying with a friend. Big Tanach test tomorrow. Last one before the Pesach break."

"How do you have a head for studying?"

Blushing, she said, "Life goes on, you know. Maybe after — uh, later on — my teachers will understand. But right now..." She stopped in confusion.

"Fischel here," her mother announced, "thinks you should have a talk with Shoshie."

Confusion changed to mortification. "Don't you think I've tried? She won't talk to me."

"Write her a letter, then," Fish suggested.

The others turned simultaneously to gaze at him. Esther said, in a considering way, "You know, that might not be such a bad idea."

"A letter," Bracha repeated. She hung her head. "I don't even know what to say anymore. It's all so complicated."

"Fish will tell you what to say," Mutty said. "He's got it all figured out."

Fish turned an even brighter crimson than Bracha had a moment before. In vain, he tried to squirm out of the necessary explanation, but Esther was adamant. "Tell her, Fischel. It makes sense. At least it's a beginning."

Bracha listened to Fish's halting recital in intense silence. She turned the idea over in her mind. "I thought she was just mad at me. Could she really be punishing herself? Thinking maybe there's something wrong with her, because of the way all this has turned out?"

"That," her mother said firmly, "is up to you to find out. Go on, Bracha, before Shoshie gets back. Write the letter. Leave it on her pillow or something." She pointed a finger at her daughter. "It's time you enjoyed your own *simchah*, Bracha. Let's get this thing cleared up, once and for all!"

Slowly, Bracha nodded. Then, at a noise from the front door, she shot to her feet. She was scarcely out of the room when the door opened and Shoshie put her head through the kitchen entrance. "I'm back, everyone. Oh, hi, Mutty. Did you come to say goodbye?" To Fish, a little shy as she always was with him, she merely said, "Hi."

"Yes. We leave tomorrow." Misery was in her cousin's voice and in the sudden droop of his shoulders. The drama at the Markovich's had nudged his own ache aside for a while, but it was back now in strength.

"You don't sound very happy about it."

"I'm not. I wish I could stay."

"Why don't you?" Esther asked, refilling his cup.

"I promised my mother I'd be home for Pesach."

"It's still two weeks to Pesach," Shoshie pointed out, taking a slice of cake.

Mutty grinned valiantly and said, "I figured I'd be a nice guy and pitch in a little around the house. My mother could use the help, I'm sure."

"What about you, Fish?" Esther asked politely. "Do you help your mother with Pesach-cleaning?"

"Who me? Mom won't even let me near her broom closet. We've got a full-time maid, and she gets extra help before Pesach. I'm sorry to say, I expect to sit around for the next couple of weeks with folded hands."

"A full-time maid," Shoshie mused in a tone of wonder. Then, becoming aware that she'd spoken aloud, she colored and leaped to her feet. "It's still early enough to get in some practice." She started purposefully for the dining room and her cherished piano.

Esther called, "Shoshie, wait."

But Shoshie didn't hear. A moment later, a melody of haunting beauty pierced the quiet of the apartment and reached the ears of the listeners in the kitchen.

"She's really good," Mutty said, picking up his jacket and slinging it over one shoulder.

"Yes," Fish said quietly. He looked at Esther. "I hope the letter does the trick. But whatever happens, please don't let her keep on hurting herself like this. It's such a waste..."

Rapidly, he blurted his goodbye, grabbed his own jacket and hat, and started for the door.

Mutty's leavetaking was more prolonged. Esther gave him a long list of messages and regards for the family back home, which Mutty promised faithfully to deliver. Waiting for him at the door, Fish listened to the lovely strains of music. He wondered if Bracha had finished her letter, and how Shoshie would react when she read it. With a strange sense of unreality, he realized that by this time tomorrow he'd be back in New York, immersed in his own life and his own affairs, and the joys and sorrows of the Markoviches would be as remote to him as those of mythical moon creatures. Right now, it was New York and his own house that seemed devoid of substance.

Abruptly, as if sensing his presence, Shoshie turned. The music stopped.

"Well, goodbye," he said awkwardly, bobbing his head in its black hat. "And the best of luck."

"You, too," she said in a rush. She half-turned self-consciously to the piano. Before she'd struck more than the first note, however, Mutty came out, adding his own farewell to his friend's. With a brief, cousinly goodbye, Shoshie gave her attention firmly back to the keyboard. For the last time, the two young men departed on the wings of her melody.

Mutty was soon sunk in his own thoughts, but Fish continued to heed the music for as long as he could hear it. Once again, as it had on his very first evening here, the sound of her playing accompanied him down the steps and out into the street, where it lingered on the silken air of his last night in the city.

It seemed to him that the music of the piano would forever carry for him a particular meaning whenever he heard it, or even thought of it. But what that meaning was, he couldn't fathom.

TEN

1

There wasn't much room for pacing in the shul's minuscule inner office, but Avi Weisner made a game attempt. The need to dodge jutting desk corners and ill-placed chairs and piles of *sefarim* roused him now and then from the bondage of his thoughts — a welcome relief. They were not pleasant thoughts.

Sammy Mirsky was due back this morning, and the rabbi had not yet determined how best to approach him. It was a sticky business. True to his word, he had refused to either answer or place a single call this week to the various new contributors, whose names Mrs. Gerber had brought to his attention, or even to discuss the matter with that worthy woman. This last, he knew had been a sore trial for the faithful secretary. She'd been fretful and worried all week. But even her anxious speculation paled, he believed, beside the agony of his own foreboding.

Schoenbrunner had called just the other day and made a point of asking about the progress of the building fund. Avi had been able to answer truthfully that — with Mirsky on vacation — things had come to a temporary standstill. Now the respite was over. The way he chose to deal with Sammy this morning would set the tone for the rest of their working relationship together; other, much more serious consequences, he refused to think about until he knew more.

He glanced at his watch, then through the window, where the

early-morning sun was making a valiant effort to flood his little room with light. Heaven knew he could use some now. Fervently, he murmured a brief prayer: *"Master of the Universe, Who in your infinite mercy grants sight to the blind — open my eyes, that I may see clearly..."*

There was still an hour and a half to put in before his confrontation with Sammy Mirsky. Resolutely, Avi returned to his desk and took his seat, though it would be nothing short of marvelous if he managed to get any real work done this morning. Such had been the case all week, ever since his Purim night meeting with the Gerbers. His concentration was shot, his train of thought tending always toward a single direction; this past Thursday's *shiur* had been as full of holes as a piece of Swiss cheese.

But it wasn't in Rabbi Weisner to waste time that might be put to good use. He had a job to do. He'd tend to that now and decide how to deal with Sammy when the time came.

The time came sooner than he expected.

To his surprise, he'd managed to lose himself in his scholarly work, roving from one holy text to the next in pursuit of an elusive source for his next *shiur*. In his absorption, he hardly noticed the sounds of life from the adjoining room. The feeble sun strengthened, without his becoming aware, into golden prominence. Lances of light lay across his threadbare rug. Trucks rumbled by his window in bass cadence, and soprano schoolchildren ran, jumped, and skipped off to school. At nine o'clock precisely there was a tap on his door. Mrs. Gerber entered, announcing in a voice of doom that Mirsky was in the outer office.

Avi set down his pen and rubbed his eyes. He felt reluctant as a child shaken from cocooned sleep to the reality of a gray winter's morning. A cup of hot coffee was what he wanted. A difficult scene was what he was going to get.

By sheer force of will, he straightened his back, sent up a silent, fleeting plea for wisdom, and told his secretary, "Send him in."

The door swung shut, then quickly opened again to disclose Mirsky's figure in place of Mrs. Gerber's.

"G'morning, Rabbi. Well, here I am, ready to get back to the grind." The young man grinned engagingly. In a sports jacket and pale-blue shirt, he looked tanned and fit.

"Have a seat, Sammy. There are one or two things I want to talk over with you."

"That's right," Mirsky said, skimming across the room to alight on one of the visitor's chairs opposite the rabbi's desk. "It's time for another update on the fund. Have you had a chance to look at the printout I prepared for you before I left? We're doing pretty well, I think." He assumed a modest air, awaiting the expected compliment.

Avi nodded. "Yes, the figures are mounting nicely." He paused. "I see that you canvassed some companies that were not on our initial contributor's list."

"Sure. In this business, you've gotta stay on your toes, dig up new names all the time. I must say, we struck it pretty rich with some of the new people."

"Davidson Windows, R & N Plumbing..."

Mirsky looked surprised. "That's right. Nice fellows. We might look into giving them a bit of business when it's time to put up the building."

"Is that what you had in mind when you asked them for a donation, Sammy?" Avi leaned forward intently.

"Well, you know what they say," Mirsky replied easily. "One hand washes the other."

The sun had begun to shift. Already half the carpet had bid farewell to its morning portion of light. Dust motes drifted idly by the window. From the outer office, utter silence reigned. For one hysterical moment, Avi imagined Mrs. Gerber and young Naomi Brody hunched at the other side of the door, ears pressed to the keyhole. Sternly, he pulled himself together. These were just silly mental tricks to divert himself from the gravity of this moment, in *this* room. Avi banished them, and every other extraneous thought. Fixing his eyes on Mirsky, he said bluntly, "Tell me just what you mean by that, Sammy."

For the first time, the young man looked slightly discomfited. He waved an airy hand. "Oh, you know how these things work. Or, rather, why should you? That's what you hired me for, to take the job off your shoulders. Don't worry about a thing, Rabbi. You'll get your new shul in record time, I promise you that."

"And who," Avi asked softly, "will put it up?"

"I thought Richman's was a good building firm. They work closely with Perlowitz and Sons, architects... What's the matter?"

"I seem to recall seeing all those names on the printout." Along with an electrical supply company, plumbers, and the window people. The list of top contributors read like name tags at a contractor's convention.

"Yes, they came through nicely. Not," Mirsky added, "that it didn't take some doing. I stuck to some of those guys like a burr until they coughed up."

"Gave you a hard time, did they?"

Mirsky shrugged. "Some of them. These people know how to drive a hard bargain."

"I wasn't aware that giving *tzedakah* came under the heading of bargaining." They were getting closer to the heart of things now. Avi's pulse began a quick, jerky dance beneath his collar.

"Uh, with all due respect, Rabbi..."

"Yes? Go on, Sammy."

"Well, I was just going to say, let's not be naive here. There are dozens of institutions knocking on these people's doors, all of them asking for money. Businessmen have to choose the ones that make the most sense for them, for their companies."

"Meaning — what, exactly?"

"Meaning that they want to know what — well, what they'll get out of it."

"Sammy." The rabbi placed his hands flat out on the desktop and riveted the other with eyes grown suddenly hard as steel. "The truth. Did you promise any of those companies anything in my — in the shul's — name?"

There was enough time, before Mirsky answered, for various small street sounds to penetrate and fill the small quiet room: an impatient car horn, an indecipherable bawl by a truck driver to some invisible crony, a sudden high shriek of childish laughter. Neither man seemed to hear.

"Actually," Mirsky said, picking industriously at a sliver of hangnail, "I thought it was a great way of killing two birds with one stone. Get a good contractor all lined up and ready to go — *and* a hefty donation in the kitty." He looked up, tried the engaging smile again. "What could be wrong?"

"What could be wrong? You've got it the wrong way around, that's what's wrong! You don't hire a good contractor and *then* ask for a donation, but just the opposite. That's irresponsible!"

A sullen obstinacy crept into Mirsky's features. The rabbi continued, "Sammy, don't you think we owe it to those who support the shul to consider long and carefully before we give our business away? To get the best prices available, along with a certain standard of workmanship. That has to be carefully checked, too."

"But Rabbi — "

"But the worst part," Avi continued doggedly, "is the fact that you made these promises without consulting me in any way. You made them *in my name!*"

Even now, had Mirsky shown contrition — some real understanding of the wrong he'd done, a glimmer of remorse, a hope of atonement — all might have been forgiven. But the salesman, chin set mulishly, flashed an unrepentant eye at the man behind the desk.

"Everybody in the business does it," Mirsky argued. "With all due respect, Rabbi — "

"All due respect," Avi said heavily, "is just what seems to be lacking here." He drew a long breath. His fingers tapped a little tatoo on the desktop. They looked like the fingers of a man deep in thought, but in truth, he had no need to think. His suspicions had been amply confirmed. The conclusion was a foregone thing.

He stopped his tapping and said finally, "I'm afraid, Sammy, that what you did was inexcusable. It's going to be very hard for me to tell our core of supporters — people who have stood behind the shul ever since it opened its doors."

"But suppose those guys — those builders, architects, plumbers, or whatever — are *good?* Why not at least check it out?" Mirsky sounded exasperated as a teacher lecturing a slow-witted child.

"That is beside the point."

Mirsky crossed his arms across his blue-shirted front. "I don't see why."

"No." Avi sounded sad. "I don't suppose you do." Abruptly, palms pressed down on the desktop, he levered himself to his feet. "I'm sorry, Sammy. You've put me in a very difficult position. There is a great deal I have to do now to rectify the situation you've created — none of it pleasant."

"I'll do it, Rabbi. Though I don't — "

"No, I will take care of it. From this moment, your connection with this shul is severed."

Mirsky gaped. "You mean, I'm *fired?*"

The rabbi nodded somberly.

That wasn't the end of it. More words were exchanged, some of them heated, while the last of the sun crawled away to illuminate happier scenes and the street sounds settled into a steady, muted background muttering. As young Naomi Brody told her husband over a late dinner that night, "Mr. Mirsky looked absolutely white when he came out of the rabbi's office. And Rabbi Weisner — well, his face was sort of greenish. He — "

"Colorful office you've got there." Asher Brody was interested in his supper, but not so much that he couldn't lend a genial ear to his wife's story. "Don't tell me. You and Mrs. Gerber were pink and red, respectively."

"Don't laugh," Naomi said solemnly. "It was an awful scene."

Asher looked suitably sympathetic. "I can imagine. Well, I don't blame Rabbi Weisner for chucking the guy out. Sounds like that Mirsky badly overstepped himself."

" 'That Mirsky' — that's what Mrs. Gerber always calls him. She also said Mr. Mirsky overstepped himself, though she put it much more strongly. She makes him sound like some character from the underworld."

"I don't think what he did is exactly criminal, Naomi, though it sure isn't very savory. Seems to me he was keeping his eye on the ends without caring much about the means. And it's the rabbi who's left holding the bag."

"Well, it sounds unethical to me — making promises in the rabbi's name."

"Unethical it certainly is. Why aren't you eating?"

Naomi picked up her fork, then put it down. "What I want to know is, what's going to happen to the building fund now?"

"Oh, I wouldn't worry about that," her husband said soothingly. "Rabbi Weisner's a smart man. I'm sure he'll think of something. Pass the ketchup?"

2

The return flight was, for Mutty, a very different proposition to the one that had carried him off to Israel some two and a half months earlier. For one thing, it was considerably more crowded.

The seats were crammed with homebound yeshivah students, as well as numerous young couples taking gracious advantage of parent-paid tickets to revisit the ancestral home and give those same parents the pleasure of seeing their faces again. Not a few of these were encumbered with the strollers, bulging diaper bags, and plethora of little plastic toys that went with the younger generation, also en route to gladden the hearts of doting *bubbies* and *zeidies*.

Nowhere in those murmurous aisles was there a sign of the stress and strain that attack so many householders in the hectic days before Pesach. This happy elite was in a holiday mood, secure in the comfortable knowledge that hard-working mothers back home were seeing to all that for them. They looked forward to the shopping, to reunions with relatives and friends, to the royal reception that awaited them simply by virtue of having been away. There was the seder to be enjoyed, new clothes to be worn, babies' cunning antics to be shown off. In a few weeks, sated with the pleasures of America and the pampering of wistful parents, they would be back in Israel, to resume the lives they'd chosen — some for only a year or two, others indefinitely — in that holy land.

The spirit before and behind, to the left and the right of Mutty, was one of anticipation — of rejoicing, even. All this was in stark contrast to his own careworn expression.

"See anything interesting down there?" Fish asked at his shoulder. Mutty had had his nose pressed to the square of window ever since takeoff.

"Only the Mediterranean." Soon those sparkling blue waters, too, would be obscured by cloud. As his popping ears attested, the plane was climbing steadily. Mutty half-turned. "Got any gum?"

Fish proffered a pack. Absently, Mutty took a slice, his face again in communion with the window as he unwrapped it. Only when a mass of snowy peaks proclaimed that they'd soared to cloud level did he turn reluctantly and completely to face his friend.

Fish paused in the act of making funny faces at a round-eyed baby across the aisle. "Back with the living? Good. I was beginning to think I'd have no one but one-year-olds to talk to on this trip." He wiggled his ears at his new little friend. "If you can call it talking."

"Sorry. I just hate to leave."

"So I noticed. What's the matter, Mutty? Afraid to go home and face reality?"

"It's not that. It's exactly what I said: I hate to leave Israel. There's something about Yerushalayim that speaks to me, Fish. This may sound corny, but...well, it feels like home."

Fish whistled softly. "Boy, you've got it bad, don't you?"

"Didn't it affect you that way?"

After a moment of consideration — during which Fish screwed his face into a terrifying mask of horror, to the baby's apparent delight — he answered, "Not so strongly, I guess. I mean, I love the place and wouldn't have minded staying on longer. But I've still got deep roots back home. They're calling to me."

"So you're happy to be going back?" Mutty sounded half-envious, half-incredulous. "You're just delighted?"

"Calm down, kid. I didn't say delighted, did I? I've got big headaches waiting for me back there. I promised my folks I'd give them a decision by the summer — whether I'll stay in learning or join the family business — and I know what kind of answer they're expecting." Heartlessly abandoning his infantile friend, Fish frowned in sudden, frank distress. "I just don't know what to do, Mutty."

Mutty was instantly contrite. "I'm sorry."

"What for?"

"You know. I didn't mean to belittle your *tzaros* or anything, Fish. It's just hard for me to understand how anyone can leave Eretz Yisrael without a pang."

"Pangs I've got — plenty of them. But only some of them are because of leaving Israel. I'm being honest." Fish looked at Mutty curiously. "You've got things to decide, too, don't you?"

"Yes." Mutty nodded. "Maybe this pain I'm feeling is just a coverup for the real thing, for the real-life stuff I'm avoiding. I don't know."

"Well" — Fish tilted his seat as luxuriously far back as its cramped dimensions allowed — "let's not analyze it now. In fact, let's not worry about anything for the next ten hours or so. This flight's our last respite."

For a moment, Mutty seemed disposed to argue. Then, with a shrug, he leaned back, too. "All right. But let's make that nine hours. I reserve the last hour for analyzing, discussing..."

"And worrying?"

Mutty sighed deeply. "And worrying."

The plane reached its summit and leveled out. Presently, the stewardesses began doling out breakfast trays. Though Fish attacked his food with relish, Mutty was not surprised to find that he'd lost his appetite.

❧❦

The promised hour of analysis, discussion, and worry proved vastly insufficient, but then, Mutty hadn't really expected to solve his life in that fragment of time. Very soon, his ears were popping again. The plane made a neat landing at J.F.K., to a scattering of applause, and then he and Fish became embroiled in helping a huge, straggling family deal with the intricacies of debarkation.

In the well-lit terminal, throngs of people eagerly craned their necks for a first glimpse of beloved arrivals. Malka and Avi Weisner were in the front row, the former frantically waving, while the latter waited with stoic calm. There was hardly time to exchange a hasty, "I'll be in touch!" with Fish, before Mutty was caught up in his mother's hug and his father's handclasp. Out of the corner of his eye he saw Fish submitting to a similar welcome by a short woman armored in sleek, dark fur against the chill of the late-March afternoon, with a gray-haired man and very excited young boy standing by, waiting their turns. Then his own parents' voices claimed his attention, and their smiles. He was home.

They stepped out of the terminal into a cold, sullen afternoon. The cars seemed overly long to Mutty after the compact vehicles of Jerusalem, and the very expanse of gray sky stretched too far for his comfort. He would have liked a little time to acclimatize himself. With his heart still anchored firmly in a distant city of white stone and antiquity, New York seemed too large. The noise, the size, the sheer impact of massed humanity was, to the newcomer, a little ferocious.

But time was something New York was not prepared to give him.

"Bet you can't wait to see the house and the kids," Malka burbled from the front seat of the old station wagon, twisting again and again in her seat to rest loving eyes on her firstborn son. "You wouldn't believe the kind of winter we've had, but it seems to be over now, *baruch Hashem*. Was it very cold in Yerushalayim?"

Before he could answer, she was rushing on, oblivious in her own happiness and the car's dim interior to the pale, sober cast of his face. "I hope you had enough blankets. Did they give you enough blankets, Mutty?"

"Sure. Everything was fine, Ma. Israel was great. But anyway, I'm" — he swallowed hard, then continued valiantly — "I'm glad to be home."

"We're glad to have you back," Avi Weisner said quietly, peering straight ahead at the unwinding road. These were almost the first words he'd addressed to Mutty since that first handshake in the terminal. To the son's ear, the rabbi sounded strained and tired. There was something in the way his mother glanced at his father — quick, anxious, aiming for nonchalance but not quite succeeding — that made Mutty uneasy.

"So what's been going on while I was away?" he asked. He found that he really wanted to know. Israel receded a little.

Again, the darting look, which Avi pretended not to see. The answer came on the heels of an awkward pause, and in a stilted fashion that clashed sharply with Malka's earlier impetuous chatter. Cautiously, she said, "Let's wait for all that till we get home, Mutty. Things," she added, rather obscurely, "have been happening."

She turned the talk to neutral channels. In the back seat, Mutty closed his eyes, reeling all at once from a mighty slap of fatigue. Vague visions of a steaming shower played at the edges of his consciousness, and a good, welcome-home dinner. It was easy to slip back into the comfort of the familiar. The smell of the car, slightly musty, had been long ago imprinted on his senses, and the rise and fall of his mother's speech was something he knew in the very marrow of his bones. He listened to the soothing wash of words without concentrating much on their meaning. His thoughts were busy — moving backward, to the place he'd just left, and forward, to the impending revelation of the "things" his mother had so mysteriously referred to.

At the wheel, Avi brooded in silence.

3

The promised revelation was a long time coming. First there was Mutty's luggage to unload and drag into the house and his sisters and brothers to greet. In honor of his brother's arrival, Shmulie had obtained permission to come home from yeshivah early for Shabbos this week, on Thursday night instead of on Friday. He was there on the front porch, beside Hindy and Shani, hand extended a little shyly for Mutty to shake. Little Tzvi — with Chaim's enthusiastic backing — demanded immediate distribution of the presents Mutty had brought back with him. Smiling, his exhaustion momentarily forgotten, Mutty complied. While he was about it, he presented his mother and father with their gifts, too: For Malka, a beautiful, hand-embroidered shawl, made in Tzefas; for Avi, a set of imposing jade bookends from Eilat.

While the others were exclaiming over their presents and hurling a barrage of questions at Mutty, Malka slipped into the kitchen to see to dinner. She had left potatoes, divested of their peels, soaking in water, and these she now — with a definite sense of triumph — put up to cook. The coating for her famous oven-fried chicken was lying ready, too: it would go nicely with the mashed potatoes. A whirl of the food processor supplied all the chopped onions she needed, to add perk to the potatoes. In less time than she'd have believed possible, things were busily baking, cooking, and sautéeing in her aromatic and for-once-efficient kitchen. Malka sniffed blissfully. Barring unforseen disasters (and she wouldn't do that until the filled platters had actually reached the table at journey's end), this meal looked like it would be one of her victorious ones.

It was, and full of the happy murmur and bustle of a family reunited. Mutty, blinking back the burning grit behind his eyelids, supplied the anecdotes, as suited his status as world traveler. Hindy was on tenterhooks until the time came to produce the special dessert she'd made for the occasion. When the last drumstick had been consumed and the last morsel of mashed potatoes scraped from the last plate, she bounded up from her seat. Some frantic scoopings and swirlings in the kitchen were followed by her regal re-entry into the dining room, bearing a laden tray.

"Yum! Pareve ice cream with chocolate fudge crunch!" Tzvi was beside himself with excitement. When, on an ordinary weekday, did they end a meal in such scrumptious style?

The dessert went over well, which pleased Hindy. What came next, however, met with a very different reaction.

"Okay, guys, why don't you help clear off, and then clear out?" Malka said, getting up and reaching for the empty chicken platter. "Tatty and I want to talk to Mutty a little."

The little boys were already out of earshot, being occupied with their new toys behind the living-room couch. Shani began collecting dinner plates. Rather less assiduously, Shmulie followed her example. Hindy frowned mightily.

"Again! Again I get excluded from everything around here. What am I, some sort of maid? When it comes to making dessert, it's 'Hurray for Hindy!' But for serious talk, it's 'Bye-bye, Hindy!' You call that fair?"

"You offered to make the dessert," Malka said equably. "No one forced you."

"What's the big deal?" Shmulie asked. For his part, he was glad to avoid what he privately thought of as "scenes." From his father's demeanor tonight, something was obviously brewing. Shmulie wasn't sure he wanted to find out what it was. "What's not fair? I'm not invited, either."

Hindy made a face that might have been interpreted as, "Oh, you! What do you know?" She directed her continuing tirade at her mother. "I'm serious, Ma! Why is it that I'm considered a baby around here? Do you realize that I'm nearly sixteen already? When are you going to start treating me like an adult?"

"When you act like one," her father admonished. "That's enough, Hindy."

The color rushed up into her cheeks. Hindy bit her lip, then whirled away from the table to seek refuge in her room. Anxiously, Shani watched her go. She, too, hated scenes like this. If only Hindy could just accept things. Why was she in such a hurry to grow up, anyhow?

❧❧

"So," Mutty said when he and his parents were comfortably ensconced in Avi's study, "tell me. What's been happening?"

Avi regarded his son in silence. Something had changed — something besides the new growth of blond beard on Mutty's chin. The former diffident youth was still present, but there was a suggestion of some other, stronger presence underneath. Mutty's eye was steadier in meeting his father's than it had been of old, though at the same time he seemed to be aware, as always, of being found wanting.

Avi mustered a smile and said, "You first. You've told us lots of stories, but what were your impressions of Israel, seriously? Of the learning, the land, the people?"

Mutty began speaking, and as the words tumbled off his tongue, his parents saw with a certain sense of wonder that their son had fallen in love with the place. He was positively lyrical in his descriptions of the trips he had taken in his free time, of the joy of being surrounded by Jews in a Jewish state, of the way the very earth and hills had seemed soaked in his own, his people's, history.

"Boy, you've got it bad," Malka teased, though there was a wary look in her eye. "So when are you making aliyah?"

To her surprise, and more to her dismay, Mutty didn't smile back. Neither did he answer. Instead, he turned to his father and said, "But that's enough of me now. Ta, I'm dying to know what's been going on. Does it have anything to do with the shul?"

"Yes." A mask seemed to settle on the rabbi's face, leaving it cold and still, as though nothing could touch it, or him. "You remember the fellow I hired to run the building fund? Sammy Mirsky?"

Mutty nodded. "Yankel Bruin's nephew, right?"

"That's right. I...took him on without checking thoroughly into his background and working practices. I should have checked." Malka stirred uneasily; she recognized the monotone that was her husband's signature way of talking when turbulent emotion wracked him from within. "Yes, I should have checked more carefully. I was remiss."

Mutty refrained from reminding his father that he'd questioned the choice at the time. "But can you trust him?" he'd asked. And, "Trust my judgment," Avi had shot back. It embarrassed the young man to remember that exchange, as though he, and not his father, had erred. Quickly, he asked, "Why? Did he mess up or something?"

"You could say that." Avi avoided his wife's eye, though Malka was beaming sympathetic glances at him, full strength. "It seems he induced various contractors to give generous donations, by promising them a part to play in putting up the new building."

Mutty frowned. "Is that legal?"

"I don't know. But it's certainly not ethical. We have an obligation to make the best use of the monies that people have contributed to us in good faith. We have to find the best men for the job, at the best price." For the first time, Avi's face was suffused with real anger, brick red in color. "*Not* hand out contracts on the buddy system."

"Buddy system?" Malka asked.

"Yes — you be my buddy, and I'll be yours. Or, as Mirsky so colorfully put it, one hand washes the other."

Contempt dripped from the rabbi's voice, but whether it was directed at the hapless Mirsky or at himself, Mutty didn't know. He asked, "Well, what's to be done?"

"I fired Mirsky, of course." His father's color had returned to normal, but the monotone remained. "Belatedly, I had a talk with Bruin. It seems his nephew makes a habit of these less-than-savory practices when out on the job. He considers it par for the salesman's course. All in a day's work."

"The ends," Mutty supplied, "justifying the means." The gritty feeling behind his eyelids had intensified. He had to fight to keep them propped open.

"Exactly." Avi sighed. "Now comes the hard part. Later on tonight, I'll be meeting with some of the men on the shul board." At Mutty's questioning look, he added, "Oh, it's not a formal board of directors, in the sense of a corporation. I just call it that. Some of the founding members — Schoenbrunner, Dickstein, Manny Gordon, and a few others — have been so active on the shul's behalf that they've constituted themselves a sort of deciding committee."

"You're meeting them tonight?"

"Yes." Avi's voice hardened in self-flagellation. "I'm going to put the facts before them. The donations Mirsky received from those contractors will have to be returned, explanations and apologies made all around. By me." The prospect, Mutty saw, was acutely painful to his father — and no wonder. Accustomed as he was to veneration and admiration on every side, to his opinion asked at every juncture, to hundreds of rapt listeners at every *shiur*, how would he bear telling the tale of his own misjudgment? Even worse, how to bear the setback to his long-cherished dream?

"Will this set the shul back a lot, Ta?" Mutty asked softly.

Avi nodded, an ungraceful jerk of the head, as if his neck had grown suddenly stiff. "I still have to go over the figures, but yes. We won't be able to put in a bid on that lot now. The worst part, though," he added, though the effort cost him visible agony, "is the loss of credibility. Who'll want to give money to the shul once they hear what happened?"

"Oh, I'm sure you're exaggerating, Avi," Malka protested.

"Maybe. I don't think so. Loss of credibility," he repeated. The words sounded like a death knell. And for the rabbi, whose career rested on his reputation, in a way it might be.

The air in the room was thick was unspoken feelings. Shrill, happy cries penetrated from the other side of the study door: Chaim and Tzvi playing. Vaguely Malka heard the phone ring; just as vaguely, she realized that someone had picked up. Her gaze, like Mutty's, was riveted on her husband.

Where Avi's vision was focused was known only to himself: eyes closed, he was wandering in regions inward.

"What time is the meeting?" Mutty asked.

Avi's eyes sprang open. The words had yanked him from a deep well of thought, painful, confused, very much at variance with their normal, confident trend. It was an effort to dwell on such mundane details as time and place. Shaking his head to clear it, he said, "The meeting? Uh, eight-thirty. At the shul."

"I'm coming with you."

"What?" The word shot out simultaneously from Malka and Avi.

Mutty stammered, blushing a little behind the new beard, "I mean, if that's okay with you, Ta. I'd like to come. I...I just think I should be there with you."

Something seemed to break in his father's face. It was as if a thin skin of ice had cracked, revealing the raw, vulnerable man beneath. Mutty could hardly bear to witness it.

It was some minutes before Avi could speak. When he did, it was merely to croak, "Thank you, Mutty. I'd like to have you."

"A good boy," Malka said beatifically. "I've always said it, Avi. We've got one good boy here."

Mutty smiled at her, and at his father, and wondered how in the world he was going to stay awake until the meeting was over.

4

The phone rang again as soon as Avi and Mutty were gone. It was Adela. She sounded distraught, which didn't surprise Malka: it was the way she'd been sounding ever since Yudy's Purim revelation. The once fiercely independent woman had begun to wear a fearful air, as if perpetually cringing from some unknown foe. Which wasn't so far, actually, from the truth.

However frantically she might hammer at the sealed box that contained Yudy's secret, it refused to yield. Yudy was the key, but Yudy wasn't talking. He had only the vaguest recollection of his confidences in the rabbi's study on Purim — and the most urgent regrets.

"Nothing," he would mutter, when pressed repeatedly by his mother, or Avi, to open up further. "I have nothing to say. I don't even know what all this fuss is about."

Meanwhile, the boy grew paler and more hunched inside himself. He wore his outgrown parka even on warm days, earning more than a few curious glances and some incredulous snickers. Finally, as if he realized that this garb, rather than providing camouflage, made him stand out, he abandoned the coat. After that, clothes seemed not to matter much to him at all. He simply stopped paying attention to his appearance. Never a vain boy, now he became prone to downright sloppiness. It was all Adela could do to make sure his pants were pressed and his sweater free of holes when he left the house in the morning.

On many mornings, he simply refused to get out of bed. It was as though the effort of facing that hidden peril had become all at once too much for him. He was sick to death of hiding, of dissembling to those who cared about him. He was weary of his own life — of what it had become. Adela would let him stay, fighting back tears, weary, too, of the constant struggle against invisible enemies. In the two weeks after Purim, mother and son achieved a complicity — a stalemate — that was nothing more or less than a resigned obeisance to fear.

Malka picked up the phone with a pang of compassion that swept away, for the moment, her own anxieties for Avi. She had grown accustomed to the nightly call, when her friend would pour out the litany of her worries. It was all very troubling, but at least there had been no more untoward incidents that they knew of. The only real sign of panic in the boy had arisen at the mention of the police; Avi, Malka, Adela, and Binyomin had agreed to go along with his wishes for now. Yudy's scar was presumably healing. Whoever had inflicted it seemed — to all appearances, at any rate — to be keeping his distance.

It took Malka all of two seconds to realize that this call was different.

For one thing, Adela's voice was shaking. Not faintly aquiver, not alive with a slight tremor, but honest-to-goodness shaking.

"What happened?" Malka demanded. "Adela, tell me."

"Yudy came home before all shaken up. That man — whoever he is — that *fiend* — must have spoken to him, or attacked him, or something. Yudy wouldn't tell me..."

"Okay, let's stay calm now." Malka's mind was racing. If only Avi were here! He would know what to do. "Do you want to call the police?"

"More than anything." Over the wire, Adela's ragged breathing sounded harsh as a chainsaw. "But I promised Yudy I wouldn't. Not without his permission. He trusts me, Malka. I can't go back on my word!"

"But won't he even tell you what's going on?"

"No. He went straight to his room." To the dark, interplanetary spaces, Adela thought in rising hysteria. "And he won't even speak to me."

"Okay." Malka gripped the receiver. "Stay put. I'll be right over."

"Oh, Malka." The words came out in a great rush of relief. "Can you? What about the children?"

"That's what I've got big girls for, don't I? And Shmulie's home tonight, too."

"That's right — Mutty's back! I'm so sorry, it slipped right out of my mind — "

"And I don't blame you a bit. Mutty went out with Avi, but the others'll keep an eye on the boys. Can I bring you anything?"

"Just yourself." Just your sweet, sane self, Adela added silently. Her heart pumped in gratitude. A true friend, Malka.

Irresistibly, her thoughts strayed to Binyomin. Never, in all the long years since her Reuven died, had Adela felt so in need of someone — someone loyal and true and capable — to share her life, ease her burdens.

And never had she been so determined to deny herself that very thing.

❧❦

Two days passed. Yudy got over his newest brush with whatever it was that stalked him and tiredly resumed his wary routine. After her compassionate evening at Adela's — in which a great many cups of tea were consumed and most of a box of chocolate chip cookies — Malka sank back into her own cares. The meeting, from what she could glean (from Mutty — Avi had been highly uncommunicative), had been as uncomfortable as her husband had predicted. Though the informal "board" had ended by expressing their confidence in their rabbi, there still remained the painful task of confronting each of the contributing contractors. Mutty had announced his intention of going along with Avi on these meetings, too. Malka would have been gratified to see such touching solidarity, if not for the iron lines around her husband's mouth that, effectively as any bars of steel, locked her out.

Adela, meanwhile, had been doing a lot of thinking. She felt limp and helpless, as though life, while she'd been looking the other way, had slipped nimbly out of her control. To be more exact, it had been Binyomin she'd been looking at — Binyomin, and the life she'd begun to hope they could have together. Instead, she should have been a better mother, more alert to the dangers that threatened her son. She'd been guilty of negligence of the most culpable sort! Her rational mind might protest that there was nothing she could have done to prevent whatever it was that had begun to haunt Yudy; her anxiety-ridden heart told her otherwise. There was no room in that heart now for anything or anyone but Yudy. Her business she couldn't abandon, not unless she and her child could subsist on air. Already several of her clients had commented on her strange preoccupation. It had taken every ounce of willpower to provide her usual service, albeit without her characteristic calm.

She could not afford any further distraction. Binyomin *was* such a distraction, she was forced to admit to herself, a very compelling one. And as such, he represented, just now, her greatest danger. Until she saw her son safe and happy, bright visions of her own possible happiness were off-limits.

There was only one thing she could do, and she was sadly determined to do it. So what if it felt like she was about to chop off her own arm?

For a few timid moments she played with the idea of asking the Weisners to tell him. Then she steeled herself. They had come to know each other well enough by now to warrant a more graceful gesture. If it took courage of a peculiar kind — one that seemed almost as hard to dredge up as the kind she needed for contending with Yudy's bogeyman — well, she'd find it somehow. If the pain of what she was planning almost overthrew her resolution again and again, especially in the black and lonely night reaches, it was no more than she deserved. Through some lack in herself, some inattention at a crucial moment, her son was suffering. Not precisely her fault, perhaps, but neither was she absolved. She was responsible for his life. He *was* her life!

"Yudy," she murmured, to give herself strength. She pictured him as a curly-haired toddler, two pudgy arms held aloft to her. She saw him as a schoolboy, frowning over his homework, clapping his hands in delight at a lucky spin in a dreidel game, presiding tall and solemn at his bar mitzvah.

Then she sat back in her living room, lit tonight only by a pair of softly glowing yellow lamps, to await Binyomin's call.

He did not take it well.

"Adela, I don't think you've thought this through carefully. You're feeling overwhelmed by your fears for Yudy. Don't worry. Sooner or later we'll get him to open up, and then we'll dispense with this problem. All we need is a little patience."

"I *have* thought it through," she said stubbornly. "I know what I'm doing. I'm sorry, Binyomin. I'm really sorry. But this is the right thing for me to do. I...I can't afford any distractions now. I have to concentrate."

"On what? On a boy who lies around in a dark room and won't even tell you what's bothering him?" His tone changed, became persuasive. "Don't lock me out, Adela. Let me help."

"I'm sorry," she said again, dully. "I'm sorry." It seemed to be all she was able to say.

He waited. His head was reeling as though he had crashed into something very hard. Deep down, below the level of consciousness, something in him still refused to believe what she was saying. He refused to accept that this was — the end. Surely she was joking? This was the future Mrs. Hirsch speaking, wasn't it? It just wasn't possible that she was really saying —

"Goodbye," whispered Adela.

Part III
NEW MOON

ELEVEN

1

Pesach was hurtling toward them all with the force of a speeding locomotive. There was no time to think; they must hurry and purchase their tickets, then shove themselves and their sparkling homes aboard for the eight-day journey. Workaday concerns were perforce pushed to the side, to be picked up at the other end of the trip.

Malka Weisner leaped aboard — pulling her three-story residence behind her — at the last moment, as usual. Up to the very last day, she was scrubbing and shopping, while Hindy made veiled references to Rebbetzin So-and-So and Mrs. Such-and-Such, who had not only started, but also fully completed, their Pesach-baking "ages" before.

The girl did shoulder her share of the labor, for which Malka had to be grateful. But Shani, her twelve-year-old, proved the real treasure. Once she could be induced to put down her book, Shani worked with a will and a smile — the latter a real bonus, as smiles were notably absent in the Weisner house these days.

Avi had rarely felt less like smiling. As he'd promised, one by one he paid his calls on the builders, plumbers, electrical firms and others who had poured their largesse, at Mirsky's behest, into the shul's coffers. And, one by one, he returned those hefty checks, to the tune of many apologetic words.

Their recipients were, understandably, taken aback. Some were puzzled, and not a few of them outraged. As Rabbi Weisner's personal representative, they had invested Sammy Mirsky with an authority he had not, after all, possessed. They had viewed Mirsky's promises as tantamount to the rabbi's own. For Avi to confess otherwise — to make a bald admission of his own failure to either competently judge or adequately control his hireling — was a taste of bitterest gall.

To a man of his temperament — a proud man — the humiliation of the affair was unbearable. The sympathetic cluckings of his longtime secretary (with the building fund on hold, young Naomi Brody had been sent home) rang in his ears like the harshest invective. The unthinking, if well-meant, comments of veteran shul supporters such as Dickstein and Schoenbrunner were as lashes from a punishing whip. Avi Weisner was forced to stand up and admit that he'd been wrong — that he'd been fooled — that, in a word, he'd fallen far short of his much-vaunted brilliance. Was it any wonder he wasn't smiling?

With his oldest son beside him he made his rounds and, with each visit, grew more taciturn, more withdrawn. Mutty, understanding his own role to be that of a comforting prop, didn't mind the silence. He was glad to be useful. Maybe that would make up, just a little, for his father's past disappointment in him and the disappointments he was bound to suffer in the future.

Malka was not so understanding. Her Avi had fallen on hard times and seemed bent on enduring them alone! Had there ever been anything so stupid? Warmhearted to a fault, she perceived hard days as precisely the time when families — and especially husbands and wives — draw closer to one another. She resented Avi's growing detachment. More, she was afraid of it.

To others, friends and strangers, she dispensed sympathy with a lavish hand, and yet understood if they responded by turning away and crawling off into a hole of personal preoccupation. With her own husband, she could not understand. She was simply not able to muster the objectivity not to let it hurt. The reasons were deeply imbedded in her own personality — in the way she perceived herself. When it came to her Avi, Malka was perennially insecure.

This insecurity was heightened now, in the face of his withdrawal. Her vision of herself as unworthy of being *rebbetzin* to such a man rose up to play her false. It convinced her that here, in Avi's silence, was the proof she'd been dreading — evidence that her husband didn't really respect her, or even need her very much.

And so, instead of standing stoic and compassionate, she fluttered in restless, agitated wrath. Rather than wait for him to emerge from the burrow he'd dug and come back to her, she filled herself with a righteous indignation that was really a substitute for sorrow and self-condemnation.

Malka Weisner scoured and vacuumed and rubbed raw the walls of her home, while the walls of her soul sadly quivered.

Avi Weisner roiled in the grip of his own private torment.

Add this seething, emotional undercurrent to the already frenzied and fast-bubbling pre-Pesach pot, and we have a household from which it is kindest to avert our eyes for the moment.

On to Jerusalem.

2

E sther Markovich had her own modest apartment well under control. Ever assiduous when it came to attacking dirt and disorder, she was particularly energetic this season. And this year there was an additional spur to lend a special keenness to her work: the spur of her own happiness. This year, joy lent wings to feet already super-quick and a new nimbleness to her busy fingers.

One week after Bracha wrote her letter to Shoshie, her mother and father had been handed the green light to sit down with Benzy's parents at last. The meeting had taken place around the Markovich dining-room table, with the younger children firmly banished into the apartment's back recesses under Shoshie's watchful eye. The greetings had been cautiously friendly; the financial part of the discussion sharp, pointed, and — thank God —

quickly settled. Benzy's father and Zalman, in an excess of relief, then subsided into an animated Talmudic argument, while the women sipped tea and complimented each other on their children. And, finally, in a spirit of great joy and celebration, on a *motza'ei Shabbos* just a ten days before the seder, a hearty toast was drunk — *l'chaim!* — to the newly engaged couple.

"What took you so long, eh?" asked a middle-aged uncle who, together with his wife, sister of Benzy's mother, had travelled in from Bnei Brak for the *vort*. "We hear you two were running around for two and a half months! Why'd it take so long to make up your minds, eh? Someone got cold feet?"

Bracha smiled dutifully. Inwardly, she admitted: yes. Someone had had cold feet, and the someone had been her. With a pang, she remembered her own hedging, time after time, as Benzy urged her to take the plunge. It was not her will that was lacking; she'd been as eager as he to bind their lots together. It was Shoshie's pain that had stopped her.

Her sister's fury had been like a dagger in the sand, drawing an invisible line that announced, "This far, and no farther." Until she could, somehow, placate her twin, Bracha was paralyzed. While Shoshie suffered, Bracha could not move another step toward the fulfillment of her own happiness.

She recalled, too, with special clarity, the look on Shoshie's face on that last night — the night of the letter. For many long minutes Bracha had dawdled, mouth dry with the fear that this move, too, would lead up just another blind alley. Finally, she'd found the courage to step into the room she shared with her sister. Shoshie had looked up at her entrance. The letter was in her hand.

"Did...did you read it?" Bracha asked with a timidity toward her injured sister that was new to her, or at least as old as her first meeting with Benzy Koenig.

"Yes." Shoshie cast her eyes down, as though uncertain of her own reaction.

Sensitive as ever to the fine nuance of expression on her twin's face, Bracha asked softly, "Do you want some time to yourself?"

The question seemed to help Shoshie make up her mind. She looked up and met Bracha's eyes. Her own were swimming.

"No. I know how I feel about this letter. How I *have* to feel. I guess it's time to forgive and forget, Bracha."

"You don't sound very happy about it."

"What's to be happy about?" A flash of bitterness. "Should I be singing and dancing because *you've* found your *bashert*? But I guess," she added, answering her own question with a start of surprise, "that's just what I should be doing." She softened, no sign remaining now of the rage that had torn her from her twin all these long weeks. "I'm the one who should be apologizing, Bracha. Not," she held up the letter with a hangdog air, "you."

Bracha sat on her bed, facing her sister, and said, "I guess we're both a little responsible. We probably shouldn't have done what we did that night. Fooling Benzy and putting Ima and Abba on the spot like that."

"But if we hadn't," Shoshie smiled impishly, "you wouldn't have met Benzy. Except maybe as your future brother-in-law!"

Bracha laughed, but she was thoughtful. "I wonder..."

"What?"

"If the two of you would have hit it off."

"Who knows?" Shoshie shrugged. "Obviously, he was meant for you. 'Forty days before a baby is born, a voice calls out from Heaven, decreeing who will marry whom.' So it was meant to happen. See?"

"Yes. *I* see. Do you, Shoshie — really?"

There was no hesitation in Shoshie's reply. "I do *now*. It was just hard being the one left out. To see the two of you together, so happy, and know that none of that happiness was for me." Already she had fallen back into the old habit of sharing confidences with her twin. There didn't seem to be anything that she could not tell Bracha and that Bracha would not understand. How had she survived without her all these weeks?

"You'll meet your own *bashert* one of these days," Bracha promised solemnly. "And then you'll wonder what you were making such a fuss about." She paused, then added with a twinkle, "I reserve the right to say, 'I told you so!' "

"Oh, you'll forget. You'll be too busy with babies and things."

"No, I won't. You'll see."

"Okay, we'll see."

The sisters smiled at each other, revelling in the peace, the rapport, the fine, beautiful *wholeness* of the moment. Shoshie settled herself comfortably against her pillow and asked, "Where'd you get the idea of writing a letter from, anyway? You never used to like to write. Did Benzy suggest it?"

"Um, no. Actually, it was Fish."

"*Fish?*"

"Yes. You know, Mutty's —"

"I know who Fish is! But where does he come into this?"

Embarrassed, Bracha told her about the conversation earlier in the evening, when Mutty and his friend had come to say goodbye. "He didn't want to poke his nose in where it didn't belong, he said. But he seemed to know what was going on inside your head, Shosh, better than any of us. I guess we're all too close to you or something."

"Interesting." Shoshie ruminated a bit, then turned to her sister with a smile. "So, Bracha. When do I get to wish you *mazel tov?*"

"Oh, Shoshie!" In one bound, Bracha switched to the other bed. Then the twins had their heads together, whispering and wondering and laughing about the miracle called Benzy Koenig. It was very late before they finally separated, each to fall onto her own pillow in utter exhaustion. But it was a joyous exhaustion. They had a lot to time to make up for, but they'd made a very good start tonight.

So, in song and speeches and words of Torah, Bracha was betrothed to her Benzy, while her twin looked on in approval. A great many good wishes fell on Shoshie's own head, too: "*Im yirtzeh Hashem* by you, my dear! You should be next!" The words fell from the lips of her mother's friends, from Shoshie's teachers and her neighbors. The classmates in their Shabbos finery who clustered in little groups across the breadth of the bright, noisy, overheated room seemed to be saying nothing else tonight, to Shoshie or to

one another — always with a little simper and a glance at the radiant Bracha
which was half envy and three-quarters wonder. *They* would return to school
tomorrow, the same, plain high-school seniors, while *her* life had taken a
quantum leap into the unknown.

Shoshie, as the *kallah*'s sister, was subject to many sly winks and jokes at
her own expense, especially from the jovial Bnei Brak uncle and one
particularly obnoxious neighbor. She didn't mind. This was how it should
be. If it were she getting engaged, Bracha would have served as the butt of
the humor and the high hopes. A fleeting remembrance of her own brief,
unsuccessful forays in the world of *shidduchim* cast her down — but only
for a minute. Resolutely, she cranked up her spirits. Her turn would come.
Maybe sooner, maybe later, but come it would. Tonight, it was easy to be
optimistic.

Her eyes followed members of her family as they moved about the room,
focal points for the gaiety that permeated it. Esther, in her black dress and
the special-occasion pearl necklace, was in her element tonight: glowing
with excitement, *nachas*, and a bit of unaccustomed makeup. Zalman's was
a quieter joy that spoke out of his soft brown eyes and in the warmth of his
clasp as he shook the hands of guest after guest. Moshe Dovid was trying to
emulate his father's dignity but forgot it now and again in a display of boyish
high spirits with a couple of the *chasan*'s brothers. Eli was stiff and smiling
in his white shirt and Shabbos sweater, Batya prattling unabashedly with
everyone in sight. Little Yoni, passed from arm to arm through the crowded
room — though he'd much rather have been crawling — stole the show with
his smart sailor suit and sudden crows of delighted laughter.

Shoshie finished her visual tour with a smile at her grandmother, seated in
lavender splendor on one of the high-backed dining-room chairs, cane at her
elbow. The old woman was so thin as to seem almost translucent. The blue veins
showed clearly at her wrists and throat. "Are you feeling all right, Savta?"

"*Baruch Hashem.*" The rheumy eyes were full of light as they rested on
the *kallah*, then on Shoshie. "*Im yirtzeh Hashem* by you, Shoshaleh. I should
live to see it."

Swooping like a bird, Shoshie bent down to peck her grandmother's cheek. "Oh, Savta. Of course you will!"

☙◆❧

Esther flew through the apartment, humming as she cleaned, much less ascorbic than usual for this time of year. Things were going well. Moshe Dovid, home from yeshivah for the holiday, proved surprisingly helpful. The girls — even Bracha — pitched in, as did Tzippy, with an earnestness that surpassed that of everyone else. The usually undemonstrative mother was moved, on seeing Tzippy bundle up little Yoni for yet another long walk, to pat her on the head and murmur, "You're a good girl, Tzippaleh." The girl's face turned brighter than the reddish-gold glow of her hair.

The younger boys, Eli and Aryeh Leib, were more of a hindrance than a help. Esther tended — after seeing them through a token job or two for "training" purposes — to send them outdoors to play. In this practice she was far from alone. The cries and shouts of the neighborhood boys reverberated in the quiet street and reached the ears of their many mothers, toiling stories above. If those good women thought about it at all, in the midst of all the hot water and bleach, it was to thank Hashem that their youngsters were safely out of the way. Some of them, perhaps, added a guilty postscript: "Tomorrow I'll make them stay home to help some more. Tomorrow I'll put them to work."

But "tomorrow" would see the boys just as eagerly shooed out of their various doors. Dirt these women were prepared to contend with, and cooking up whole mountains of Pesachdik food; but the rambunctious energy of small boys in small apartments was just too much.

3

Esther was very much on Avi's mind these days. How would his big sister react if she knew of the debacle her dear brother had perpetrated?

Not that he planned to tell her. She'd always been the kind of older sister who modeled good behavior, rather than invited confidences. Weakness and error elicited, not her compassion, but her censure. When, as a boy, he'd done just as he ought, there had been no warmer approbationer in his life than Esther. On the other hand, should he let his guard slip and fall into some childish misdemeanor, she could, with a single look from those direct gray eyes, reduce him to squirming shame.

"Why don't you ever say anything to Yossi?" Avi sometimes demanded, referring to their feckless younger brother (now working as a *mashgiach* on a Canadian dairy farm). "Yossi always gets in trouble, but him you don't scold. Why me?"

"Because you," Esther would respond, bestowing oblique praise, "are different. You know better."

"Why?" Avi continued, a shade less aggressively. Her approval meant a lot to him. "Just because I'm older?"

Her smile held a secret which the youngster had no trouble interpreting. "No. Only smarter."

You're special, Esther was telling him then, as she told him over and over again through the years. *Avi Weisner is a cut above the rest. You're smart — and you're good.*

As Avi prepared to leave to shul on a blustery March morning, it occurred to him for the first time that his sister might not have actually done him a favor by encouraging this lavish self-image. Maybe — he frowned in concentration, a hand frozen on the knob of the coat closet — maybe he ought to have concentrated a little less on his own "smartness" and "goodness," and more on the qualities that go into making up those things. He felt poised on the edge of a startling discovery. What had been lacking

in that promising boy, that dazzling young man — this accomplished rabbi?
The answer eluded him.

He reached for his coat and hat. Esther's good opinion notwithstanding,
his behavior in the Mirsky affair had been neither very smart nor very good.
And, ironically — ludicrously, almost — one of his first concerns was to
keep that fact hidden from his sister. On the evening after his confrontation
with Sammy, he sought out his wife to request, low-voiced, "I'd appreciate
it, Malka, if you didn't mention this shul business when you write to Esther.
About Mirsky, I mean."

"I *know* what you mean," Malka had replied, speaking coldly. "I won't
say a word. She owes me a letter, anyway."

Then, some three days later, the phone had rung with the happy news
of Bracha's engagement. For a little time, Avi had lost sight of his own
troubles in the greater illumination of his sister's *simchah* before the
breakers of gloom rolled back over him again. Self-disgust choked him,
making it difficult to address with his usual coherence the hordes who
continued faithfully to pack the rented shul for his Thursday night *shiur*.

The *shiurim* had to go on, but he'd drastically cut down on his counseling
schedule. Ostensibly, the cut was due to pre-Pesach pressures; but the true
reason was that he couldn't conceive of advising others when he'd done such
a very poor job of guiding himself. He'd let himself down, and — what was
infinitely worse — he'd let down the shul.

There would be no new foundation poured this year, no joyous ceremony
marking the laying of the cornerstone. Sometime, when all this had receded
a little into the liveable past, he would think about the next step. Somehow,
the dream might be revived. Just now he had no heart for it.

"It's embarrassing, of course," Malka had said impatiently, early in the
grim business, "but I honestly don't see why you're *so* upset, Avi. It isn't as
though Mirsky embezzled shul funds or anything."

"No, and thank God for that."

"So why are you tearing your hair out?"

"Who's tearing hair?"

"You are! Don't try and deny it. So you'll return the donations from those contractors. So the shul will take a little longer to be built. Is that such a tragedy?"

Avi had sighed. "You don't understand."

"So make me understand. Explain what this means to you." There had been a note of pleading in Malka's voice, which Avi, in the depths of his own distress, did not catch. He just shook his head, mute. Malka pressed her own lips tightly together. Two patches of white stood out on either side of her nose — danger signals her husband had long since learned to recognize. But he, turning away, never even saw them.

Yes, Esther had been on his mind lately — and Binyomin.

"Talk about arrogance," Binyomin had said that night in the car on the way home from the airport. It seemed a long time ago, though no more than a couple of months had actually passed since his old friend had moved back to New York. Rapidly and inextricably, Binyomin had rewoven himself into the pattern of Avi's life. The Purim *se'udah* had found him at the Weisner table, and the Pesach seder would do the same. Who knew him better than Binyomin?

Binyomin knew him, and he had never said a truer mouthful than that comment of his in the car. *Arrogance.*

Avi buttoned his overcoat against the sharp wind and stepped out into an early morning of scudding cloud and peekaboo sun. The words beat time with the rhythm of his footsteps.

Arrogant. Prideful.

Guilty as charged.

And *blind.* His pride had made him so. As surely as if he'd tied a bandanna around his eyes, he had blindfolded his inner vision. Preening self-confidence had veiled the light of intuition every rabbi must rely on.

He'd been introduced to Mirsky in the first place as a problem, a man whose basic trustworthiness was called into question by his own uncle, but had that been enough to start the alarm bells ringing? In anyone else it would have done so; but not in Rabbi Weisner. Even his own son, his Mutty, had raised a doubt about the former salesman, but Avi had not chosen to listen. Mrs. Gerber had distrusted Mirsky from the start; her instincts, it seemed, were surer than his own. Or perhaps his instincts were sound enough, only he'd never given them a proper hearing. Impregnable (so he'd thought) inside the fortress of his own intelligence, it had been beneath the great rabbi to heed his son's warning, or his secretary's, or even the whisper of his own inner doubts.

The wind freshened, sending a shower of pods swirling to the sidewalk at his feet. Looking down, he saw that the pavement was already littered with a thousand such packages, each representing a new tree, a new life. Moodily he stepped through them, hearing the pods crunch underfoot with a sound that seemed to him to underline the basic futility of life. Visions, dreams — what were they but so many hopeful seeds, fated to end in sad anonymity beneath some careless heel?

Oh, come on. Enough of the gloom and doom!

The thought burst into his consciousness like a gust of fresh air. Distressed as he was, he could still spot the pitfalls of overdramatization and mock that tendency in himself. Why, as Malka had asked, take it so much to heart? It was just a shul, after all. He heaved a mighty sigh. Just a shul. *His* shul...

As he neared his destination, the buildings, the trees, even the very cracks in the much-traversed sidewalk, began to take on an acute familiarity. He began to remember: the very first time he'd pulled out the key to unlock the door of his shul; the first time he'd led the *shacharis* service there; his first *daf yomi* class, leading a half-dozen yawning householders through the intricacies of the Talmud. Though it was only rented, though it rubbed modest shoulders on either side with the humblest of brick-and-mortar neighbors — though his congregation was then still scarcely larger than a couple of *minyanim* — it had been *his.*

He vividly recalled his feelings as he'd stepped up to the bimah on that first Shabbos to deliver his first words of Torah. That speech, and those feelings, had been the culmination of the long-cherished ambition that had guided him into the rabbinate.

He hadn't always held that particular ambition. In fact, if asked what he wanted to be when he grew up, the very young Avi Weisner had been wont to say, "A fireman." A little later, it was, "A teacher." And finally, "Rabbi of a shul." The same motive had informed all three goals, he realized now: the urge to serve and the desire to educate.

Well, he'd done it. With God's help, he'd realized the dream. His *kehillah* had been his baby, just as surely as Mutty or Hindy or little Tzvi. Doting as any father, he'd rocked that shul in the cradle of his arms, guiding its first tentative steps and taking pride in its slow but steady growth. How he'd cared for them, that first loyal core of worshippers!

And how he still cared. That was what hurt the most. The rabbi thrust his hands deep into his coat pockets and quickened his pace. He'd let them down. He'd been weak in an area where a rabbi must not be weak: in correctly judging his fellowman, in judging himself. With a little more awareness, he would have discerned the seeds of weakness in Mirsky, and in his own nature.

Trust my judgment, he'd demanded. And they had. They all had. And look where it had taken them! The famous Weisner judgment had landed them all squarely in the soup. The great leader had led his people right into a towering sea of shame.

His only consolation was the knowledge that, of all those who would be affected by the shul's changing fortunes, it was he himself who would suffer most — who had suffered most already.

Not that the shul wouldn't feel it, too. His faithful congregants would continue to crowd into a space too small for them. The shul would keep paying rent for the larger space to accommodate his public *shiurim*. Yes, the congregation would assuredly suffer. But worst of all, to Avi, was the dent this affair had made — must make — in his own reputation.

At best, he'd come out looking silly. At worst... But that wouldn't bear thinking of at all.

4

Binyomin came home from work tired and hungry. The furnished apartment met him with its bleak, impersonal welcome, like that afforded by motel rooms around the world. Determined to leave the Weisners after weeks of enjoying their hospitality, this had been the first place he'd found that had seemed halfway acceptable — though, on closer acquaintance, he now had his doubts about that. He'd been too busy with his new job — and first heady meetings with Adela — to bother searching further. Anyway, at the back of his mind this place had been a temporary stop. Even as he plunked down the deposit for the first month, his inner eye had been picturing the fine house he'd be buying soon. He and Adela.

The first few days he'd recoiled, each time he entered the place, with a kind of loathing. By now he'd grown inured to it. What did it matter, anyway, where he lived? Even a luxury mansion would seem bare and sterile without anyone to share it with.

The thought of Adela was a black hole around which he tiptoed with agonizing care. He hadn't believed her when she'd said goodbye. He'd thought she would relent, would come to see, as he had, that they were meant for one another. He'd waited in vain for the phone to ring — Avi or Malka Weisner calling, perhaps, or even Adela herself. But the silence remained inviolate. It was as though Adela Moses had never stepped into his life, to brighten it for a few minutes or a few hours. He was back to that state decreed for him, it seemed, at his very inception: alone.

Throwing his briefcase on a chair, he walked to the kitchen while loosening the noose of his tie around his neck. He found an unopened can of tuna in a nearly bare pantry and, in the bread box, an opened package of bread. He sniffed the latter suspiciously and decided it was still edible; no sign of mold yet, anyway.

The illustrious New York attorney prepares to dine, he thought, as he set about mashing the tuna with a remnant of mayonnaise found lurking at the back of the fridge. There was no lettuce. *The well-known courtroom personality sits down to an exquisite experience in dining elegance*, he added as he washed his hands and sat down to take his first bite of the meager sandwich.

The phone chose this moment to ring.

Or rather, he thought wryly, *not just yet*. The phone shrilled again, insistent. Swallowing hastily, he went to get it.

"Binyomin?"

"Avi, is that you?"

"Yes. How are you?"

"Can't complain. How's Malka, the kids?"

"*Baruch Hashem*. The little ones can't understand why you're not still upstairs in 'your' room."

"I miss 'en too. Tell them I'll have a new story for them next time I come over."

"All right." The rabbi was obviously eager to move on. "Binyomin, am I catching you in the middle of something?"

Binyomin thought of the stale sandwich and looked at the stained cushions on the fraying couch and the broken slat on the window blind. *The famous trial lawyer spends an evening of refinement and grace...* He caught himself with a grin. "Nothing that won't wait. What's up?"

"I'll tell you. Adela just called."

For an instant, Binyomin's heart lurched in a mad upwelling of excitement. Then Avi hurried on, "About Yudy."

The fast-pumping heart sank again, more forlorn now for the instant's relinquishing of its careful control. Binyomin forced himself to say calmly, "Yes? Has anything new happened?"

"Not recently. But Yudy seems as disturbed as ever. Adela has just about convinced herself that her best recourse is to go to the police."

Slowly, Binyomin said, "She may be right, you know."

"Binyomin, I'll tell you frankly — I'm worried. We seem to be dealing with a very unbalanced individual. Bringing in the police may be just the thing to push this guy over the edge. Unless the authorities can guarantee Yudy's safety every minute of the day and night — which I'm afraid they can't do — we'll be playing with fire."

"And Adela's life." It hurt to say her name.

"Yes. He threatened her, too, Yudy said. If he should get wind of police involvement, I'm afraid she may be putting herself at risk."

"What do you suggest, then?"

He could hear the intake of Avi's breath. "Binyomin, please tell me if I'm overstepping myself here. Are you — have you and Adela broken off for good?"

"It seems that way," Binyomin said briefly. "Her choice, not mine."

"I'm sorry. But...are you willing to help me anyway? Or, rather, to help Yudy?"

"What do you have in mind, Avi?"

"I thought maybe the two of us could try a little behind-the-scenes guard duty. If we could just get a glimpse of this guy, something we can bring to the police, we may be able to do some good."

Binyomin was quiet a moment, considering. "My contacts with the D.A.'s office should be useful, if I can just get a whiff of who we're dealing with. But you're right in thinking that we'd have to bring in something more concrete than a tipsy teenager's Purim story."

"Don't forget the scar."

"I haven't forgotten. Avi, are we supposed to shadow Yudy to and from school, or what?"

Stammering a little, Avi said, "W...well, why not? I thought just on the way home, and only for a few days. Maybe we'll be lucky and actually be on the spot at the right time."

"And if we aren't lucky?"

"Then we'll have to reassess our options."

"You sound very lawyer-like."

"That's your department." Avi was clearly glad of that. "Well, what do you say?"

"I'll bet you've been waiting for this all your life," Binyomin teased. "Your big chance to play detective. Or is it cops and robbers?"

"I'm not sure what it is," Avi answered, suddenly very serious. "All I know is, I want to do something to help that kid. And I...well, I need your help."

Binyomin waited a beat, as if to underscore the extent of the commitment. Then he said, "I guess I'm with you, then."

Avi exhaled. "Thanks. I knew I could count on you. Now, can you swing it with your job? What are your hours like?"

"Flexible. I can swing it. Starting tomorrow night?"

"Fine. There's only a few more days of school left before the Pesach break." Avi refrained, as did Binyomin, from wondering aloud how long their protective measures would be necessary. Would they be out on the streets again with Yudy after Pesach as well? Warmly he added, "Thanks again, Binyomin. Uh, consider your hand shaken."

"Likewise. 'Bye, now."

"Good night."

For a few moments after they'd hung up, Binyomin stood by the scarred, stumpy telephone table in the unappealing living room, lost in thought. He admitted to himself, with painful honesty, that at least part of his motivation in agreeing to Avi's scheme was the desire to be of use to Adela. Even if she never knew about it, even if the distance between them never lessened, he would have been a part of her life for a little while longer. And maybe — who knew? — fortune would smile on them, and he and Avi would actually be instrumental in restoring her son to her again.

Even if the distance between them never lessened.

Without warning, a geyser of pain shot up, decimating the carefully schooled calm with which he'd been functioning — or, more accurately, sleepwalking — ever since Adela had said goodbye. The reality struck him now, vicious and cruel, with the force of a well-aimed bullet. She would not, for all his bright dreams, belong to him after all. The home he had pictured, the Shabbos table he'd lingered over in delighted imagination — all gone now, spiralling to oblivion like a wisp from a smoking gun.

His anguish translated into a soundless wail: *Hashem! All I wanted was to build a Jewish home — for You! To bring children into the world, to fulfill my obligations as a man and as a Jew, and to raise those children in the light of Your Torah. For You, Ribbono shel olam! You are the one who laid these obligations on me. Why are You making it so hard for me to fulfill them?*

Then came the rage. With short, hard steps he began to measure a staccato path round the dismal living room. And why had Adela turned her back on so promising a beginning? Because some street punk, some dark, hooded figure from the slimy underside of New York, had decided to turn her son's life into a living nightmare. Binyomin's initial consent to Avi's proposal had been no more than lukewarm; now the flame of his anger lit a new heat in him, an iron resolve. If Avi had suggested the mission, Binyomin now adopted it as his own. Be it the last thing he accomplished on earth, he would track down that sadistic fiend and see him clapped behind bars. Without stopping his frenetic progress through the room, he directed another plea Heavenward, for success in his burning mission.

Murderers, he thought, should be caught and punished. This monster — whoever he was — had effectively destroyed three lives: Yudy's, Adela's, and his, Binyomin's own. He could only hope and pray that the destruction was ultimately reversible.

His pacing led him back to the telephone. On impulse, he picked it up and dialled a long-distance number from memory. After five rings, it was answered by an elderly woman.

"Yes?"

"Rebbetzin? It's Binyomin — Binyomin Hirsch. I'm calling from New York. How have you been, and the Rav?" It seemed marvelous to him that he could sound so normal, even commonplace.

"Binyomin! How nice to hear from you! We're doing well, *baruch Hashem*. But we miss having you at our Shabbos table."

"I miss that, too, believe me. Is the Rav feeling okay these days? And yourself?"

The *rebbetzin* obliged him with a short litany of the complaints that plagued her and her aged husband. There was nothing new in the story; Binyomin had personally driven both of them, on numerous occasions, to doctor's offices and hospital outpatient facilities near their small California community. He listened courteously, sent along a heartfelt wish for their continued good health, then asked if the Rav was available to speak to him.

"Binyomin? *Vi machst du?* How are you?"

It was wonderful hearing that beloved voice again. If Binyomin closed his eyes he could imagine himself back in the old, book-lined study, as they'd sat together so many a time, he and the Rav: struggling humanity, face to face with the pure light of goodness. He had been the ambitious modern American; the other, a white-bearded, prewar-European scholar. With the sense of respectful ease that had long characterized their relations, Binyomin found himself pouring out the tale of the sorrow that consumed him. His success at his new job, his temporary lodgings, the renewed ties with old friends — all of these he touched upon only as they related to the central fact in his life: Adela Moses, and her willful absence from it.

Afterwards, he found it hard to replay the Rav's exact answer in his memory. The words themselves had been forgettable, perhaps, but not their message. Ultimately, what the Rav had done — apart from commiserating with his pain — was to urge Binyomin to live gallantly.

" '*Kaveh el Hashem*,' " the soft voice intoned with peculiar power. " 'Strengthen your heart, and trust in Hashem.' "

It was no more than Binyomin had been telling himself for days, or perhaps even years. But from the Rav's lips the message rang with new meaning. The Rav did not offer any promises. The future — Binyomin's and Adela's — was just as much a sealed book as before. Yet, unaccountably, by the time Binyomin hung up the phone his spirits were lighter.

He became aware that he was, physically, very tired. Moving slowly, as if his legs had suddenly sprouted steel weights, he returned to the tiny kitchen and his unappetizing sandwich. There was one more brief to go through this evening and a long-overdue call to his other Californian friend,

Danny. (Did those three precious *yingelach* remember him anymore? Did the youngest ever ask, at the shining Shabbos table, where 'Uncle Binyomin' had gone?)

After that, he'd opt for an early night. He was bone-weary, and with the prospect of shadowing Yudy on top of a full day's work, it looked like it would be a long day tomorrow.

❦

For some minutes after he hung up, Avi sat at his study desk, flexing his fingers and gazing, without seeing, at the framed *semichah* on the wall. For the first time since the Mirsky affair had come to light, he felt the return of something that resembled, if not actual peace, then the tentative conviction that peace might — with time and the right effort — be possible again.

Arrogance, he'd decided in the course of intense introspection, was self-absorption in its most virulent form. Why, this very morning, even as he'd bemoaned the effects of this Mirsky debacle on his own *kehillah*, he'd still been, at heart, more concerned about its inroads into his own good name. He had, he painfully admitted, his work cut out for him.

Sitting in his little shul office after *shacharis*, the rabbi did not take down his *sefarim* and plunge into his usual work. He'd taken no calls, given no thought to his commitments, his ambitions, or his future. Instead, for the first time in much too long, he'd looked inward.

For the space of a morning, Avi Weisner deeply, honestly, examined the recesses of his own nature. Nothing was too black, or too petty, to escape his scrutiny. Every character trait was placed under the laser beam of his rebuking eye. His most hidden motives came under the scalpel. And when the operation was over, he was left with what he hoped was a cure for what afflicted him.

He knew now what it was that had tantalized the edges of his consciousness on his walk to shul.

Humility was the answer. A true humbleness of spirit, which would place the needs of his congregants above any consideration of his own desires or carefully nourished reputation. And the road to humility, he'd decided, must pass through the garden of giving.

Because the lion's share of his energy had been focused for so long on *people*, in the plural, he would begin his corrective course in a small way: with a single individual. Heart and soul he would devote himself — beyond any thought for his own comfort or well-being — to one person who truly needed him.

He would dedicate himself and all his resources to relieving Yudy Moses of whatever terrible burden he was carrying.

Humbly, frankly, he beseeched Heaven to smooth his way. Maybe, with the *Aibeshter's* help, he'd be able to solve Yudy's problem, and his own, at the same time.

5

"Well, Fischel," said Yechezkel Mann.

Fish's heart sank. It was a purely reflexive reaction. That "well, Fischel," spoken in just that intonation, had been the precursor to many a stern lecture in his younger days. Right here in the living room he'd stood on those memorable occasions, in front of his father's big easy chair, often with his mother on the couch, as she was now, plying her needle in one of her never-ending tapestries. Time rolled back with an almost irresistible insistence. It was hard to hold on to the knowledge that he was fast approaching his twenty-third birthday, and that the worst his father could do now — the worst he had ever done, really — was send him to his room.

He clasped his hands behind his back, as he'd often done back then, and restrained the desire to shift from foot to foot. Standing very straight, he mustered an engaging grin to counter the other's commanding eye. There was no answering smile.

Fish cleared his throat, nervous in spite of the bravado of the grin. "Yes, Dad? Has my rebbe called to complain again?"

If he'd expected his father to find that funny, he was disappointed. Yechezkel Mann prided himself on his single-mindedness. When he set himself to a purpose, nothing short of cannon fire could dissuade him from his course. His purpose now became very clear to the increasingly uneasy son: he was about to deliver the ultimate lecture. Fish wanted it over with. He tried again: "What's wrong, Dad?"

"Nothing wrong," Mann said gruffly. "But nothing's right, either. Yet." He imbued the last word with a significance that Fish couldn't miss.

His mother chose this moment to look up brightly from her needlepoint and say, "Oh, let's not have any unpleasantness, Yechezkel. Fischel just came home. Give him a chance."

"He came home a week ago," Mann stated. "And I don't want any 'unpleasantness' either. I just want to know if he's decided to grow up and face his responsibilities."

"Oh, Yechezkel," Rochel Mann sighed. She bent her head again to her tapestry. Fish, however, could not so easily escape.

"Well, Fischel?"

Those words again.

"Dad, I've given it some serious thought. I'm really into my learning. It's going pretty well, and...and I always thought I'd like to learn in a *kollel* for a couple of years after I married. What's the rush with going into the business anyway?"

"You've been learning how many years already? Five? Five years since you finished high school, Fischel. Isn't it time to move on? Besides," his father ended on a note of sour triumph, "I don't see you rushing to get married."

"There's a lovely girl who came to shul last Shabbos," Rochel Mann murmured eagerly. "Adler's granddaughter. Just beautiful. And the way she davened, you could tell she's a real pearl. I could find out more about her if you're interested, Fischel."

"Uh, I don't know, Ma. Maybe in a while..."

"See? I told you, he's not interested! All he can think of is how to *kvetch the benk* a little longer." Mann was breathing heavily. The magnificent gray head shook from side to side in genuine bafflement. "I just don't understand it. When I was your age, I couldn't wait to get out into the world, to make something of myself. What's with these boys nowadays?"

It was a rhetorical question, but Fish — had he not known his father better — would not have minded entering into a serious discussion to answer it. The past couple of decades had seen a tremendous upswing in the number of young people immersed in the study of Torah. Where once the yeshivah had been considered — by people like his father — as the domain of the uniquely gifted scholar, now it was the natural habitat of any and every piously inclined youth. It was nothing short of wonderful, Fish often thought, that even a notoriously unaccomplished student like himself had found entry into the best yeshivos and even, of late, a measure of success there.

The love for learning for its own sake seemed to have bypassed his father, who had come of age in the fifties, when the urge toward material security had been paramount. Why couldn't he understand that a different motor drove today's young Jews?

"Fischel, I'm not going to live forever, you know," Mann said, leaning forward in his chair, broad hands on broad knees. "Who'll run the place if you don't learn the ropes? Gedalia?"

"Why not? He'll grow up sooner or later, won't he? Besides" — Fish produced the engaging grin again, with the same results as before — "you're strong as a horse, Dad. You'll be around forever."

What his father would have replied to this sally Fish was not to know. Before he could say a word, his mother broke in. "Yechezkel, look at you! You're getting all red in the face. Remember your blood pressure."

"Rochel —"

"I'm serious. Enough for now. You're both getting upset. Take it easy. Nothing has to be settled in one night."

With a glowering look at his firstborn, Mann subsided and groped with his right hand for the newspaper that was never very far away. When his father's glare had been fully transferred to the *Wall Street Journal*, Fish sidled from the room. As he went, he castigated himself for his own surge of guilt. What was he doing that was so wrong? How was he behaving differently from so many other *yungerleit* in Lakewood and other places? Why couldn't he have been blessed with a parent who appreciated his commitment to Torah instead of deploring it?

"It's a *nisayon*," he said aloud as he entered his bedroom. "It's meant to test me."

"What's a *nisayon*?" his kid brother asked from the bed. Gedalia was propped against the headboard, a book dangling unread from his fingers.

"Have you moved in?" Fish asked equably. "I was under the impression — correct me if I'm wrong — that this was my room."

"You're not wrong. But I knew Dad was ranking you out down there. I figured I might as well wait for you here and get the lowdown."

Fish sank into the desk chair. "There's nothing to say. Just the same old ground, covered and recovered."

"The business again? Or getting married?"

"A little of both, I guess."

A lovely girl in shul...

See? I told you he's not interested!

He roused himself just as Gedalia was framing another question. "Play you a game of chess?"

As a distraction, the ploy was effective. Gedalia's face lit up, and the pointed questions ceased as the chessboard was whipped into place on the desk.

"Black or white?" Gedalia asked eagerly.

"Your choice."

Fish regarded his younger brother. Gedalia's features were remarkably like their father's, except for a certain sweet quality about the eyes that was reminiscent of their mother.

"Gedalia?"

"Yeah?" The boy had picked up a black piece and a white, and was scrutinizing them as if trying to determine which would bring him the most luck.

"Hurry and grow up already, would you?"

TWELVE

1

Chol Hamo'ed Pesach. Another night, another date.

It was becoming familiar to her, this painful frenzy of preparation, the wondering, the imagining...the disappointment. Shoshie paused in the act of zipping up her pocketbook, struck by a thought. Would she feel the same way — this resigned, almost doomed feeling — before her first date with her future husband? Or would some warning, some intimation of things to come, send a signal shooting up from her very soul?

With a shrug, she finished zipping the bag and slung it over her shoulder. If her mood this evening was anything to go by, either her soul was asleep on the job, or this one was not, after all, her *bashert*. The next few hours would tell.

They did tell — just what she had expected.

"No," she sighed to her waiting mother as she walked through the door a few hours later. The sigh was part blissful relief as she kicked off her shoes — they'd walked miles, it seemed, to the accompaniment of some of the most uninspiring conversation it had ever been her misfortune to endure — and part frustration. A very large part frustration. Esther's echoing sigh sounded very much the same.

Shoshie bade her mother "good night" and went to her room to see if Bracha was awake. Shoshie found herself, in these last precious weeks before the wedding, longing just to be near her sister. She wanted to soak up the last remaining moments of togetherness before the habits of a lifetime must be irrevocably broken.

Also (though she smiled to admit it), she couldn't help having the childish feeling that — if only she hung around her twin long enough — maybe some of Bracha's marvelous luck would rub off on her.

She had not yet reached her own room when a sound from the little niche off the balcony gave her pause. The door was slightly ajar; tentatively, Shoshie tapped on it and then pushed it open.

"Savta, you're still awake? It's very late!"

Her grandmother was seated in the rocking chair that, apart from the single bed and narrow chest of drawers, made up all of the room's furniture. She smiled a toothless smile — her teeth were in a glass by the bed — and said, rather indistinctly, "I slept too much in the afternoon. I'm not so tired now."

"Can I get you something? A drink of water or maybe some tea?"

"No, no. I don't need anything." The grandmother gave her a shrewd look. "So, you just came home?"

"Uh, yes. I was...out."

"A nice boy?"

Impossible to keep anything from Savta. With her daughter-in-law she could be a quavering dependent; to her grandchildren she sometimes, privately, showed another, stronger face.

Shoshie, in no mood to discuss the state of her *shidduchim*, answered with what she hoped was discouraging brevity. "He's okay. Not for me, though."

Esther would have been astonished at her mother-in-law's robust reply. "*Mamaleh*, don't worry. You're a baby yet. At the right time, he will come."

Shoshie forced a smile and a playful, "Who is he? Do I get a name?"

"Not from me. From Him, maybe." Savta pointed at the ceiling of her tiny domain.

A rush of love swept through Shoshie then for this spent, old woman with a faith as mighty as ten emperors. There was nothing ahead of her in this world, the girl thought, but the black abyss of death. She was a skeleton with

a bit of flesh tacked on; her teeth were gone, and most of her hair. And yet
— Shoshie realized this at a level that leap-frogged the need for words —
when they stood in this little space together, it was Savta who seemed to fill
it and not herself at all.

She didn't understand it, but she was willing to revel in it — to let the
inexplicable something that was her grandmother's essence warm her and
give her strength. This dried-up bundle of bones for whom Shoshie had often,
unthinkingly, felt such a vast pity seemed all at once infinitely dear to her.
Gently, as if afraid of bruising a tender flower, she reached down to hug the
old woman.

Savta accepted the hug calmly. Whether she had grasped the nature of
Shoshie's feelings it was impossible to say. When the girl had released her
finally and stood regarding her with overbright eyes, Savta merely said, "I
think I'll sleep now. You go, too, Shoshaleh. Go to sleep now."

Quietly, Shoshie turned to obey.

She overslept the next morning. Her first thought, upon fixing bleary
eyes on the bedside clock, was, *Late again. I'll need a note for the teacher.*
She closed her eyes for an extra minute of delicious rest.

Then Bracha was shaking her, with a peculiar, urgent note in her voice.
"Wake up, Shoshie. Wake up!"

"I'm up," Shoshie mumbled.

"Well, *get* up! Something happened. There's something wrong with
Savta. Ima and Abba have taken her to the hospital in an ambulance, and
we have to stay home to take care of Yoni and everyone. *And* start cooking
for the last day of *yom tov*. Ima has no idea when she'll be back."

As her twin stared at her in mounting horror and dismay — indubitably
wide awake now — Bracha sat abruptly on the bed and continued in a
breathless rush, "It looks like a stroke, Abba said. They think she's had a
stroke." She leaped up as if the blanket had bit her. "I'm going to call
Benzy."

"What can he do?"

But Bracha was already out of the room. *She* knew, if no one else did, that her *chasan* was the only one who could give her what she so sorely needed at this moment: a healthy dose of tender reassurance.

Shoshie would have to find some from another source, or make do without.

2

"S ssh. Here they come."

Avi heard Binyomin's hiss at the same moment he saw the doors of the yeshivah open to disgorge an amorphous mass of students. In the dark, they were nothing to the watchers but tangled silhouettes, etched sharply against the light pouring through the doors. Taking cover under the sudden swell of noise from many young voices, Avi started his car. "Keep your eyes on them, Binyomin. Don't lose him."

"I won't — if I can *find* him. How in the world are we supposed to make Yudy out in that crowd, and in this dark?" This was Binyomin's standard complaint. Patiently, Avi provided his stock reply.

"He's bound to walk in this direction. The guy" — their name for Yudy's mysterious assailant — "would wait to catch up with him when he's alone. That won't be until he gets a lot closer to home."

"*If* he catches up with him tonight." This was the first time since the Pesach break that they had resumed their vigil. On the four evenings they'd trailed Yudy home before Pesach, nothing untoward had happened on the walk between the boy's yeshivah and his home. Once they'd even lost sight of Yudy altogether. For the would-be protectors, it was downright discouraging.

Had it been up to Binyomin alone, he would have abandoned the project before this. The underlying logic was faulty: The unknown bogeyman might wait weeks to approach Yudy again, and when he did, it might just as easily happen at a time when they weren't around to witness it. Binyomin was carrying a full load at his job, which was still new enough to bear the additional stress of unfamiliarity. Any lawyer worth his salt must be prepared, when necessary, to brood over his briefs even into the wee hours. On the last day before Pesach — knowing that he was going to be taking a couple of days off for the holiday — his partners had expected him to stay overtime to clear his desk. Binyomin was hard-pressed to explain his need to rush away yet again. The partners had not been pleased.

It was Avi's example, even more than his concern for Yudy, that kept him going. The intensity with which the rabbi had begun "playing detective," as they liked to call it, had not left him. He seemed fueled by some inexplicable inner fire that only shrugged off their lack of success. Binyomin, watching him and hearing the way he talked, was frankly shamed into continuing the strange partnership.

Strange it certainly was. A rabbi and a lawyer — the first sporting a most respectable beard and hat; the second in a three-piece business suit, a calfskin attaché case tossed carelessly into the back seat — made a highly doubtful pair of bodyguards.

But Avi, it was clear, had no doubts.

"If not tonight, then tomorrow night. He's bound to make another move, sooner or later. Unless," Avi smiled at a new and happier thought, "the guy's given up. Left town or something."

"We should be so lucky." Binyomin peered intently through the windshield, trying to make out the figure he wanted. To his satisfaction — and, also, somewhat to his consternation — he suddenly saw Yudy detach himself from the group and begin hurrying homeward on his own. Perhaps the respite he'd enjoyed over Pesach — not surprising, considering that he'd scarcely left home — had injected the boy with a new courage. In any case, Yudy seemed to have decided that the loss of protection provided by walking home part of the way with the other boys would be well compensated by getting there faster. He started off at a rapid clip, quickly leaving the others behind.

The moment Yudy was well ahead of them, Avi put his foot on the accelerator. The car began rolling silently in his wake.

The streets grew progressively more deserted as first his classmates, and then the smattering of shops, fell back. Yudy trotted steadily forward, willing himself not to think. There were no stores now, just single-family homes behind their squares of garden or hedge. Just another three blocks...two now. He pictured his room and the silent swirling constellations that gave him the illusion of being untouched by the world and its threats. Concentrate on that, he encouraged himself. Almost there.

The last block was completely empty. In the windows of the houses he passed, curtains were drawn against the cool of the spring night. Behind them, oblongs of golden light told Yudy that families were sitting safe and secure. He thought of his own living room, doubtless equally well lit, and his mother waiting for him. Or, no — he frowned as he remembered — she had said she'd be out tonight. Some appointment about a job. His mother's computer work sometimes took her into people's businesses, at others into their homes — usually in the evenings.

Yudy would have liked to see her when he came in, her eyes lighting up in love and relief at the sight of him. But no matter. He was nearly there. He would double-lock the door and wait for her to come home instead. Maybe he would even put up some coffee in anticipation of her return. She would like that.

These pleasant thoughts kept him company on the last long stretch and carried him, almost forgetting to be afraid, to the very gate of his house. As he put a hand on the latch to open it, another hand snaked out suddenly from behind and stopped him.

A jolt of physical pain slammed through Yudy's chest. Breathing became impossible. He couldn't think. He couldn't move. He could not do a thing except clench his fists and wait for the inevitable.

It came. A steely blade caught the light of the quarter-moon and flashed ominously before his eyes.

"Not so fast, kiddo." The knife did a grotesque little dance in the air. "What's your rush?"

"I —" Yudy's voice came out raspy as old pebbles. He cleared it and ran his tongue over his parched lips, feeling as he did the salt tears running freely down his cheeks to his chin. The tears came automatically now, each time he heard that voice. He was three years old again and crying at the shadows. He fell silent.

"That's what I like." Sneering approval. "A boy who knows how to keep his mouth shut. Remember that." The knife bobbed closer. "Remember it good, kid."

"I remember." The words came out like the mewl of a frightened cat.

"Maybe I should help you remember," the horrible voice continued, musingly. "Maybe it's time for another little reminder. Just to make sure, like, that you stay away from the cops." The knife slashed suddenly through the air, half an inch from his arm.

Yudy flinched violently. "I stayed away!" In a sudden panic, he almost shouted the words. The figure stirred angrily. "I'm sorry," Yudy whispered, passing a hand over his face to dash away the tears that blinded him. "I didn't mean it to come out so loud. But I didn't tell the police. Honest! Please..."

The knife danced. "Beg pretty now," the other laughed.

That laugh was the stuff of Yudy's nightmares. He said softly, as though to placate a raging beast, "I didn't tell. I won't tell. Please. I...I have to get home."

Out of the corner of his eye, Yudy saw a car turn the corner at the far end of the block. Making sure to keep his head carefully averted from the figure behind him — he'd learned, to his sorrow, that his tormentor didn't take well to being looked at full in the face — he watched its progress with a mixture of terror and hope. He was panic-stricken lest it was his mother's car. When was she due home from her meeting? *Please, don't let it be her!*

But if it wasn't her, he prayed that the car would continue moving his way. He knew from experience that nothing but the fear of exposure could rid him of his tormentor.

It kept moving.

"Hey, there's someone talking to him!" Binyomin practically leaped through the window in his attempt to see more clearly. "Avi, step on it!"

The car had been crawling along well behind the boy, careful not to alert him to the fact that he was being shadowed. Now Avi put on a burst of speed. Four, six, eight houses passed in a blur. With a screech of brakes, they pulled up in front of the house. Yudy whirled around. The second figure broke into a run — but not before Binyomin got a good look at his face in the light of the street lamp.

"Follow him?" gasped Avi. "Or take care of Yudy?"

"No use by car," Binyomin shot back. "He'll just slip into an alley somewhere." He gripped the inside handle of the passenger door as, for one wild moment, he considered taking off in pursuit on foot. Then calmer reason prevailed. By the time he'd be halfway out of the car, the guy would have melted into the shadows. He and Avi watched helplessly as the figure pounded around the near corner and out of sight.

The whole episode had lasted some ten seconds, no more. Yudy stood transfixed, also watching. Then, darting a nervous glance at the car, he began fumbling at the latch.

"Yudy! Wait!"

For a moment it seemed that the boy would run away from them, into the shelter of his own four walls. Avi called out again, "*Yudy!*"

For the first time, it seemed to penetrate Yudy's fear-numbed mind that his rescuers knew him. He turned, leaving one hand on the gate: an escape route at the ready. "R...Rabbi Weisner?"

"Yes, it's me." Avi came forward into the halo of the street lamp, followed by Binyomin. Yudy looked at him in surprise, then broke into a small, shy smile. Binyomin nodded somberly.

"Was that him, Yudy?" Avi asked. "The one who gave you the scar?"

As the boy hesitated, the rabbi added forcefully, "Don't try to hide it now! *Tell us.* We want to help!"

"Yes," Yudy whispered.

Binyomin said, "I got a look at him as he turned to run. Tomorrow I go to the D.A.'s office. Wheels are going to start turning very soon."

"Don't!" Yudy clutched at Binyomin's sleeve. He was a sturdily built youth, but beside the tall lawyer he seemed small and vulnerable. "Please don't tell the police. He'll hurt my mother!"

"Not," Avi said firmly, "if we have anything to do with it." He seemed to reach a decision. "You're coming to our house tonight. Both of you."

"But my mother... She's not home."

"Where is she?" Binyomin asked sharply.

"Out. About a job."

Something in Binyomin's chest eased. "Well, here's what I suggest. Avi, why don't I take Yudy over to your place, while you wait here to tell A — Mrs. Moses what's going on."

Avi agreed to this plan and climbed back into his car to await the mother's arrival. Yudy had some idea of remaining to greet her himself, but both men overrode that. Reluctantly — though harboring a vast, secret relief — he allowed himself to be led away by the attorney with the calm manner and rock-steady voice.

He could not know that inside Binyomin was at a fever pitch, every nerve alert, like a high-wire artist about to step out in front of a record crowd. He was living through the next morning's agenda.

While the man's face was fresh in his mind, he would arrange to see some mug shots. He would speak to the police inspector and to his contact at the D.A.'s office. Things, as he had promised, were going to start moving quickly now.

As they skimmed down the block — two wraiths bent on achieving their destination in the shortest possible time — he spared a thought for Adela, soon to return to the sight of the rabbi, waiting in front of her empty house, and his explanations. Quite apart from his own forlorn ambition to marry

Yudy's mother, Binyomin felt a powerful sense of responsibility for both of them now.

Tomorrow morning, he hoped, the wheels of justice would begin to turn — but there was no telling how long it would be until they succeeded in spinning that still-unidentified assailant into the arms of the law. Until that happened, it remained for Avi and him to keep mother and son safe.

He mouthed a silent prayer for help from Above. From the single glimpse he'd had in the glow of the street light, they would need every bit they could get.

3

H e was middle-*aged*, for goodness' sake." Binyomin shook his head, disgusted. "You'd think he'd be a young punk, at least. But the guy had — I'm sure of it — gray hair!"

The police officer shrugged. "An aging punk. The worst kind." He watched Binyomin turn the pages of the thick book, each filled with a rogue's gallery of scowling mug shots. "Any luck yet?"

"No." Another page flipped. "But he's here somewhere, I'm sure of it." Again, as he had a thousand times through the long hours of a troubled night, he reviewed his memory of the attacker. The man had been no novice at his nefarious trade; Binyomin would have testified to that, even apart from the signs of age. His had not been the manner of a new thug on the block. He had been too slick, too practiced in the ways of the city's night walks. This kind of work was very, very familiar to him. Binyomin would have staked his reputation on it.

He turned another page, fighting down a stab of anxiety. The guy had to be here somewhere. He had to be!

It was twenty minutes and some thirty pages later when he stopped short.

"Here," he said, stabbing a finger down on a picture two-thirds of the way down. He struggled to keep the excitement from his expression. "That's him."

The officer bent closer to see. "Sure?"

"Yes." Binyomin took another moment to study the pasty, coarse-grained skin, the hint of a sneer about the lips, the dark hair just beginning to frost around the edges. "He's a little grayer now, but I'm sure."

"Okay." The officer picked up the book and motioned for Binyomin to follow him. Drawing a long breath, the lawyer found his feet.

The wheels had begun to turn.

"His name's Andy Malone," Binyomin said into the phone. He was at his desk in his legal office in the twilight of that same day. "A two-time loser. The first time, breaking and entering. The second time — assault."

"Binyomin, this is terrific!" There was no mistaking Avi's jubilation. "I — we — can't thank you enough." He fell silent.

At his desk, Binyomin swiveled around to face the window. Outside, the darkness was nearly complete. The outer office, and the corridors, rang with the hollow silence of after-hours. "Avi? You still there?"

"I'm here. Just thinking." He roused himself. "Listen, Binyomin, I want you to come over. Now that the police have been pulled in, Yudy seems to have resigned himself to the fact that there's no more need for secrecy. He's promised to tell us the whole story this evening. I've got a class at seven-thirty. Is nine all right for you?"

"I don't think so," Binyomin said slowly.

"Too early? Too late? We could —"

"I mean, I don't think I'd better come at all. I'll handle things at this end, but I don't think...I don't think Yudy's mother would appreciate having me there."

"Nonsense." Avi's voice was warm over the phone. "She'll want to thank you. And you deserve to hear what Yudy has to say, if anyone does."

I don't want her gratitude. He would not insinuate himself back into her life in the guise of friend and protector. It had to be the real thing — or nothing.

"You can tell me tomorrow," he said gently. "I have a ton of work to get through here, Avi. Let's talk in the morning."

The line was charged with unspoken words — both Avi's and his own. But all the rabbi said was, "All right. I'll call you."

"Fine."

"Binyomin..."

"Yes?"

"Any message for Yudy?"

Binyomin considered a moment, then said, "Yes. Tell him he's been one brave kid. He should be proud of himself."

"I'll tell him. Though I think he's been feeling rather the opposite of brave lately."

"I know. That's why I want you to tell him."

4

As it turned out, Benzy Koenig served a more practical role for the Markoviches than simply that of provider of moral support to his *kallah*. Within hours of hearing the news about her grandmother's stroke and the subsequent domestic upheaval, he caught a bus to Jerusalem, where he moved in with a cousin for the remainder of Pesach. If the situation did not stabilize by the time the new *zeman* began, he intended to transfer temporarily to a local yeshivah.

"He's going to borrow his cousin's car whenever he can," Bracha said happily, "and help us with the shopping, and getting to and from the hospital — whatever we need. Isn't that wonderful?"

What she meant was, *Isn't he wonderful?* Shoshie smiled. "That'll certainly be a big help." She thought of something. "We were supposed to have the Kleins over for a meal on the last day. Should we put them off, do you think?"

"That's two days from now. Chances are Ima or Abba, or even both, will still have to be at the hospital. Better put them off."

With the passage of the next couple of days, it became clear that "chances were" Esther and Zalman would be haunting the hospital for considerably longer than the twins had feared. It was an anxious time, a time for quiet prayer and brooding thought, as their beloved *savta* clung precariously to life. The festive meals passed quietly, with Benzy presiding in his future father-in-law's place; Zalman, after a brief trip home the night before to change his clothes, had returned to the hospital until after the holiday.

Shoshie had caught hardly more than a glimpse of her father before he'd rushed away again, but that glimpse had been enough to shock her. Zalman had looked ravaged. There was no other word for it. There was a new hollowness to his deep brown eyes that came from more than sleepless nights. He had been the only son of an aging couple: the much-beloved "miracle child" who had become more than ever the prop and mainstay of his mother's life after the death of his elderly father. Much as it must pain him to witness her condition, it was made much harder because he had to bear it without the support of siblings. His wife was an angel; she did all she could. But Zalman was the son. The greatest share of the burden must be his.

Esther returned home just before sundown to shower hastily in honor of the holiday and to greet her children. "I can't wait to sit down and have a normal meal with my family. I really missed you guys." But she fell asleep before the boys returned from shul, and nobody had the heart to wake her for the meal.

"Let her sleep," Shoshie insisted, though Yoni was whimpering for his mother, and even young Batya kept casting longing looks toward the bedroom door. "She's exhausted from being with Savta day and night. Ima'll be a wreck if we don't let her rest a little."

Shoshie had, over the past few months, become the family's unofficial expert on suffering. Her opinion was accepted as authoritative. Esther slept on.

She tried to make up for it the next day, cuddling Yoni, reading stories to Batya and Eli, remaining patient with Aryeh Leib, and sometimes remembering to smile at Tzippy, ever hovering at her shoulder to see if she could be of use. It was Tzippy who took Yoni out for a walk in the afternoon so her mother could lie down, and Tzippy, again, who played endless games of marbles with Eli and Aryeh Leib just to keep them quiet.

An hour or two before dark, Benzy walked in from his cousin's house, where he'd eaten lunch, to take Bracha out for a walk. He recited the Havdalah for all of them when night fell. Then he, the twins, and Moshe Dovid began the labor of transforming the Pesach kitchen back into its everyday guise.

Cartons had to be hauled up from the *machsan*; dishes scrubbed, dried, and packed away; and the everyday dishes returned to their year-long places. It was a job of many hours. They had barely begun when Esther phoned for a taxi to take her back to the hospital.

"I'm going to send Abba back to sleep here tonight," she told the girls. "He needs a night in his own bed." Her tone foretold the expected opposition and also the determination with which she planned to counter her husband's objections.

She phoned for a cab, then threw her coat over her shoulders, her gaze sweeping the disorderly kitchen and the many signs of eager activity. Eyeing the boxes waiting to be filled, she felt a pang: this special chore had always been her own. "No one packs like Ima," Zalman had told the kids on so many post-Pesach occasions. "You kids can help with the washing and the shlepping, but Ima packs."

"Thanks again," she told her older children. "You, too, Benzy. I don't know how we would have managed without you."

"Benzy's taking me to the supermarket tomorrow," Bracha announced. "We'll stock up on *chametzdik* food — everything in sight, the way I'm feeling right now." She and her *chasan* exchanged a smile.

Aryeh Leib apparently felt the same. "Ima, can we have pizza?" he shouted from the living room.

"No, not tonight. The pizza shops aren't even open yet."

"So what about a Danish?"

"The bakeries," Shoshie told him, "are only just starting to bake. And they'll be concentrating on making bread, not Danishes."

"My friend Dani says he *always* has pizza on *motza'ei Pesach!* Why can't we?" Aryeh Leib was beginning to work himself up into a tantrum. These last few days had strained, not only the parents, but also the children. The strain had been showing in these sudden emotional storms; in spurts of pointless, nervous bickering; in tiny fusses that rose and fell over nothing. Esther knit her brow, wondering how to proceed. Bracha was about to step in with the offer of a *Pesachdik* macaroon — though it took little guess work to know how her brother would react to *that* — when, providentially, a honk sounded from below. Esther seized her bag.

"Whoops! There's my taxi. Be good, kids. See you tomorrow..." Under her breath, she added, "I hope." Blowing a kiss in the direction of the baby, she dashed out the door. Yoni began to cry.

Aryeh Leib watched his mother go. When the door closed behind her, he reached for his soccer ball and, scowling furiously, began kicking it around the living room.

Instantly, Tzippy was there, scolding, "You know Ima doesn't let you do that! Aryeh Leib, is this what you do the minute Ima's gone? Don't you know that Savta's very sick in the hospital? Don't you even *care?*"

His response was an even blacker scowl and a heftier kick. His toe made contact with the ball as though he wished it were the hospital that had swallowed up not only his grandmother, but his Ima and Abba, too. The ball bounced off the big, clay planter in the corner, tipping it and a big, leafy plant onto its side with a crash. Leaves and dirt mixed with gravel spilled across the floor.

"Aryeh Leib!"

The boy glanced shamefaced at Tzippy, then shrugged and turned away. "Eli, wanna play cards?"

In the kitchen, activity — suspended during this little drama — resumed.

"He's upset about Ima," Bracha told Benzy, sotto voce.

"He'll be more upset when I give him a good *potch*," Moshe Dovid remarked mildly. "Shosh, pass me that pareve stuff, will you?"

It was Tzippy who got the broom and cleaned up the mess.

The phone became their lifeline over the next days, bringing periodic transfusions of their mother's voice, or, occasionally, their father's, with updated reports on Savta's condition. She was "holding her own" but still very weak. The left side of her face and body had been paralyzed, though the doctors were hopeful that — if she pulled through — she might regain some sensation there eventually.

Shoshie and Bracha stopped attending school. These were the days when Bracha had been expecting to prepare for her wedding. Instead, she spent them shopping for food, cleaning a little, cooking a meal now and then, and tending sporadically to her younger brothers and sisters. Shoshie carried by far the greater share of the burden: Moshe Dovid had returned to yeshivah, and Bracha's shopping excursions with Benzy tended to lasted much longer than strictly necessary.

Shoshie understood her sister's need to get out of the house, to escape the atmosphere of anxiety and stress and forget domestic drudgery for a few hours — to simply enjoy being with her betrothed on these lovely spring days. In a spirit of noble self-sacrifice, Shoshie encouraged her twin to go, chaining herself in Bracha's place to do double duty at stove and laundry hamper.

Between worrying about her grandmother and the very real job of running a large household virtually single-handed, Shoshie grew paler and thinner. She fell into the habit of reaching for the same old blue skirt and worn, comfortable blouse, morning after morning. She fixed nutritious meals for the family that she hardly tasted; washed, ironed, sewed, swept, and was on hand to greet her parents' calls and rare appearances with the calm assurance that everything was going smoothly. At night, as soon as the younger children were asleep, she fell into her own bed and slept like a stone for a few hours. The remainder of the night passed in fitful, restless dazing.

Things would have been even harder, if not for her sister. Tzippy was Shoshie's right hand. As soon as the twelve-year-old returned from school each afternoon, she undertook the complete care of Yoni and Batya. She also kept an eagle eye on her other brothers. She was especially assiduous about making sure that Aryeh Leib didn't, as she put it, "turn over the whole house" while their mother was gone. Tzippy dreamed of the day her mother would return home, and Abba — and, of course, Savta. She was determined to hand the apartment back to Esther, on that blessed day, in perfect shape.

જ્જ્જ્

It was on an afternoon some two weeks after Pesach that Savta turned the corner. Her prognosis became definitely positive. Savta was on the mend.

There would be a lengthy period of rehabilitation before she regained any sort of use of her left arm and leg, and her face would remain frozen in its abnormal, twisted position for a good while longer — maybe forever. But she was getting better and would, sooner rather than later, be coming home.

Esther phoned the good news to Shoshie at noon, and Shoshie greeted the others with it, one by one, as they came home. Their parents' shifts at the hospital bedside would ease a little in the next week or two before the old woman's homecoming. Shoshie and Bracha would be able to take up a more normal schedule again and join their classmates in savoring the last golden weeks of high school. Bracha could begin thinking about her June wedding. Tzippy breathed a great sigh of relief; Batya danced Yoni around the living room; and Eli and Aryeh Leib, in high spirits, ran out to play ball with their friends.

"Remember, supper's at six!" Tzippy yelled after them down the stairwell. There was no answer.

At five to six, with good smells filtering through the kitchen door and out to the rest of the house, Tzippy looked up from her book. Yoni was playing on the floor at her feet. She gave him a smile. "Getting hungry, Yoni-pony?

Me, too." She glanced at her watch. "The boys aren't back yet, as usual. I'd better go down and get them."

She put Batya in charge of the baby and tripped lightly down the stairs to the street. With the clock put ahead an hour, bright daylight still reigned, spilling over the yellow-white buildings and the gardens, the mothers chatting together over their baby strollers, and the heads of the boys running and shouting with their ball. Tzippy squinted into the sun.

"Eli! Aryeh Le-e-ib! Supper!"

The boys, if they heard, ignored the summons. She called again. Again, they played deaf.

With an exasperated sniff, she started into the street after them. The mother's chatted. The baby's babbled and cried. The boys shouted. The sun was still in Tzippy's eyes, so she never noticed that her brothers and their friends had scattered to the sides of the road. Their well-attuned ears had told them what her own had not: there was a vehicle bearing down on the spot where they'd been playing.

"Eli! Aryeh Le-e-eiiib!"

Her voice was lost in the general tumult. There was a little thud, too quiet to frighten anyone. Even the squeal of the minivan's brakes hardly dented the noise level in the busy street. A few heads turned. Eli's was one of them.

He clutched his brother's arm.

"Aryeh Leib? Look. *Look*, Aryeh Leib — there, in the middle of the street. Why is Tzippy lying down like that?"

5

It was just as well that Binyomin had declined to come over to the Weisners to hear Yudy's story. The way the evening turned out, no one else got to hear it, either. That was the night the call came from Yerushalayim.

A steady hum in the trees spoke of a rising wind, as a sullen April day faded into a cloud-choked evening. There had been a hint of rain in the air all afternoon; Avi brought it with him on his arrival, just in time for the dinner hour.

The rain thundered down all during dinner. The meal was a strained affair, with Adela sitting white-faced and silent, picking at her food, and Yudy only marginally more animated. Avi spoke to them in a gentle way calculated to reassure, but, though they nodded dutifully at intervals, neither seemed really to hear. Malka — harboring some vague idea of comforting the refugees under her roof — maintained a steady stream of falsely cheerful and largely pointless chatter that soon had Adela's nerves wired to the screaming point...or would have, had she not seen the genuine concern that prompted it.

To the younger children, it was dinner as usual. Hindy knew better. Though not permitted into the confidence of the adults, her quick wits and open ears had caught enough to tell her that something highly unusual had been happening. Malka, to explain the unexpected presence of their two house guests, had referred vaguely to "some trouble at their house." Hindy cast suspicious looks around the table now, as though trying to glean the secrets they insisted on keeping from her. Normally, she would have made her disgruntlement known. Tonight, with guests at the table, her mouth was closed in a thin, unhappy line.

Mutty was somber. His parents had told him Yudy's story, or as much of it as they themselves possessed. He knew that Binyomin had been to the police and that Yudy had not set foot out of the house since. His assailant, it seemed, had threatened harm to both the boy and his mother if the police were called in. The die had been cast: there was no going back. The question was, what to do now?

"Your rebbe called today," Adela told Yudy. She'd been home briefly, with Mutty acting as escort, to retrieve the messages from her answering machine. "He wondered why you haven't been going to school and hoped you're not sick."

"Nice of him," Yudy mumbled. His rebbe belonged to that other world, that place of safety and normalcy from which he'd been so rudely torn. From his banishment, he could not bear to contemplate that world, or to imagine his classmates pursuing studies and pleasures in which he now had no part.

With Yudy's remark, conversation dragged to a halt. Even Malka fell into a brooding silence, spearing the last morsel on her plate and then putting it down again. Hindy rose to get the dessert, pushing back her chair with a little more force than strictly necessary. Under cover of her drinking glass, Adela cast yet another covert glance at her son.

Yudy seemed calmer since they moved into the Weisner house two nights before, though she herself, unaccountably, had been feeling, if anything, even more jittery. With clarity, she hoped, would come the serenity she craved. She was grateful for his promise to reveal the whole of his long-drawn tale tonight. Surely it was a good thing, this laying of cards out on the table so that they could see the hand they'd been dealt? Only by openness could they assess the odds they faced and what bid they might make to win through (would it ever be possible again?) to peace of mind.

The promise had been extracted with reluctance, as though the boy clung to his old reticence from sheer habit. He'd resisted at first and then, suddenly, capitulated. After all, as Yudy had said, with a twisted smile that drove a dagger into his mother's heart, what did it matter now?

Secrecy had lost whatever protection it offered, the moment he'd given the rabbi a glimpse, that Purim evening, of the agony he'd been suffering. Revealing the scar, he'd signalled the onset of a process that had reached its culmination now: the gradual handing-over of his private burden.

The decisions were no longer in his own hands. For that, he felt an overwhelming relief — and also the fear that comes when control slips out of our grasp. What would happen next? Shuddering, Yudy pictured *his* face, and the anger that would leap into it once he became aware — as he surely would — that the police had his number. The boy was convulsed with a frantic anxiety, all the stronger for being well-hidden. How to keep his mother safe?

Dessert over, the younger children were dismissed from the table. Hindy rose and began pointedly collecting plates for transfer to the kitchen, leaving the adults to speak openly if they wished. Avi cleared his throat and glanced at Yudy. Adela was gripping her spoon until the knuckles were white. Without warning, she found herself wishing Binyomin were there. She found she missed his strength and the reassuring calm he could bring to the most difficult situation. She couldn't do it all herself. This was just too much for her to handle alone...

She caught herself angrily. She was *not* alone — to say so was the height of ingratitude! Hadn't Malka and her husband taken them in without question, to roost in their home like a couple of frightened hens? She glanced at the rabbi, at his son, and at his wife, her friend. They were with her and Yudy in this crisis — with them all the way... With a stern effort of will she dismissed Binyomin from her mind. There was no place for personal gratification while her son remained in danger.

Catching sight of the lines of anxiety on her boy's face — lines that, such a short time ago, had not been there — her expression tightened with a fierce, glowing determination. Nothing came before Yudy. Nothing!

"Well!" Avi said. "Shall we adjourn to the study?" He tried for a light note, but fell clearly short of the mark. Heads nodded quickly, unevenly, like marionettes in the hands of a nervous amateur. As they rose from their seats, Adela threw an uncertain glance at the table.

"Leave it alone," Malka ordered. "Hindy and Shani'll take care of it." Obediently, Adela followed the others to the study. They had just reached the door when the phone rang.

"I'll get it," Malka said. "Avi, if it's for you...?"

"Just say I'm not available."

Malka watched her husband usher the others into the study and close the door. She chewed her lip as she hurried to the phone. There was so much he kept inside, her Avi. So much he carried on his own shoulders. He refused to make it easier on himself by sharing the load — or not with her, anyway. She just didn't seem to have the right combination to open the closely guarded vault of his nature.

And why, after all, should he confide in her? What did she have — in terms of brain power, dynamism, or practical sense — that he couldn't find in a dozen or more of his cronies? She'd harbored the illusion, through the peaceful, rising years, that they were a partnership. But the first sign of trouble had taken him from her as surely as if he'd taken sail to a distant shore. With a sigh, she picked up the phone on its sixth ring.

"Hello?" Still distracted by her thoughts, it took her a moment to orient herself to the speaker. The call had that long-distance quality she recognized immediately. The voice at the other end was also familiar — disturbingly so.

"Is that Aunt Malka?"

"Who — Shoshie? Bracha? Is that you? And which?"

"Yes, it's me! Shoshie. Oh, *Aunt Malka!*" The befuddled *rebbetzin* was subjected to a plaintive outpouring, tears and sobs mingling in her niece's voice in the violent release of some long-dammed emotion. Once, twice, Malka tried to interrupt the flow, to stem her own rising fear with a plea for coherence. At last, she got through.

"Shoshie, stop it! Stop it, do you hear? How can I understand a word you're saying when you're crying like that? This is a long-distance call. NOW TELL ME WHAT'S GOING ON!"

At the other end, Shoshie drew a long, quivering breath. "I'm sorry, Aunt Malka."

"Forget sorry. Just tell me, why did you call? What's wrong?"

Her own words raised a ghost, the memory of a midnight conversation with Israel in which she'd been at the receiving end of the same reaction. Only let the long-distance phone ring, and the question springs instantly to mind: *What's wrong?*

That time, Malka had laughingly assured her far-off relatives that all was well. Shoshie, now, did not do the same. With a sinking heart, Malka heard her say, "There's been... an accident, Aunt Malka."

"An accident? Who?"

"Tz...Tzippy." The voice dissolved as tears rose up again. Malka was about to remonstrate — sharply, out of her rising anxiety — when Shoshie regained her grip on herself. "S...sorry." Another long breath. "Tzippy was hit by a car yesterday evening, Aunt Malka."

"How is she?" The question came rapid-fire, before Malka could lose her nerve to ask it.

"Bad. Oh, Aunt Malka, it's very bad. She was thrown by the car and hit her head when she fell. There's been a concussion. She's still unconscious..."

"What? Still? How long?"

"A whole day so far. The doctors say..." The voice faded now, as Shoshie fought for control. Malka, straining, caught the word "coma."

She closed her eyes. Little Tzippy — though surely not as little, now, as Malka remembered her from her last visit — with the red-gold braids and the ever-willing spirit. Esther had referred to her as "my reliable one" — though never, if Malka recalled correctly, in the girl's presence. Either she didn't believe in overpraising her children, or it had simply not occurred to her that her "good" daughter might yearn for a word, a sign, of motherly approval. On the contrary, it was this same Tzippy who often came in for the sharp edge of Esther's tongue, as fatigue and the many burdens of raising a large family sometimes exhausted the mother's store of patience.

Tzippy always took it stoically, without rancor — which was precisely why, perhaps, Esther used her as her verbal whipping post. Tzippy never minded. It was as though the girl understood her mother better than Esther, even, understood herself.

Malka shook herself alert. Shoshie was talking, and here she was, six thousand expensive miles away, woolgathering.

"Ima and Abba don't know I'm calling you," Shoshie said. "I'll pay them back, if they want, out of my babysitting money. I just...I just couldn't stand it anymore, all alone..."

"Why alone? Where's Bracha?" Esther and Zalman, she knew, would be mounting an endless vigil at Tzippy's bedside.

"She's here. But so is Benzy. Most of the time. And I..." The words faltered, trailed away. But Malka understood. Bracha and Benzy were a pair, sufficient unto themselves. Any emotion, shared, becomes by definition easier to bear. Distress, anxiety, and comfort would revolve between the engaged couple in a closed circle, while Shoshie was left to contend with her own battered heart all alone.

Doubtless she bore the lion's share of the responsibility for the little ones, too. Malka asked, "How are the boys? And the baby?"

"*Baruch Hashem*." Shoshie spoke dully now, as though worn out by the violence of her own emotion. "We're all fine. The kids were already used to Ima and Abba being away at the hospital, so they're not complaining too —"

"What do you mean?"

"Oh! I didn't realize that you don't know. Savta — my grandmother — had a stroke two weeks ago. She's still in the hospital, though the doctors say she's going to recover, *baruch Hashem*. Now Ima and Abba are tearing themselves in half, running from one to the other."

Aunt and niece conversed for another few minutes. When she hung up — after adjuring Shoshie to call again the next day with an update, reversing the charges — Malka was pale and thoughtful. As she turned away from the phone, she became vaguely aware that the wind had risen sharply. A stray branch, somewhere, was tapping persistently on one of the upstairs windows. Around the corner of the house, gusts of violent air tore and whistled: a strange, hollow sound. A sudden shiver went through her.

She went to the study and abstractedly pushed open the door.

Avi broke off in mid-sentence. "Ah, Malka. We've been waiting for you. Have a seat and —"

"That was Shoshie." She might almost not have heard her husband speak. "From Israel."

"What happened? What's wrong?" Avi half-rose from his chair.

At the question, Malka smiled faintly. Her words, however, were anything but amused. "It's Tzippy. She's had an accident. She's in the hospital — in a coma." She stopped.

Exclamations, questions, a babble of reactions. Malka waited, eyes on her husband. Hoarsely, Avi asked, "What's the prognosis?"

"The doctors say it's too early to tell...how long she'll remain unconscious, or what damage there'll be when she wakes." For the first time since she'd heard Shoshie's voice, her own broke. "Poor girl..."

"And her poor parents!" Adela exclaimed. "They must be going out of their minds."

Malka looked at Adela, briefly, as though she'd forgotten why her friend was there. Then her gaze returned to her husband. "Avi, I told her I'm coming to help."

"You're what?" Avi sounded dazed. He'd come in here to hear one tale of woe and had been afflicted suddenly with another.

"Going to Israel," Malka repeated patiently. "Esther needs someone. You know that Zalman's an only child, and his mother's been hospitalized, too, and Esther has no other family in Israel. With your permission, I'm going out there."

"Of course," Avi said slowly. "Of course."

"Hindy's old enough to keep things going here. Shani will help."

"So will I," Mutty said. He'd been planning — hoping — to break the news of his own intended return to Israel, as soon as this business with Yudy was cleared up. Now, with a stifled sigh of regret, he put those dreams aside. Jerusalem would have to wait. He was needed here.

From both his parents he'd received a healthy sense of responsibility; he was constitutionally unable to evade that responsibility now. As he'd gone with his father on his "journey of atonement" (Mutty's private name for the rabbi's post-Mirsky rounds), so he now offered himself for his mother's service.

Malka smiled at him. "Thanks, Mutty. But aren't you going back to Lakewood?"

"That can wait. I'll learn somewhere close by in the meantime." Without knowing it, he was duplicating Benzy Koenig's move. Learning was learning, wherever you did it. He had his preferences, of course — and just wait till his parents found out just where they really lay! — but in a pinch he could open his Gemara anywhere.

"I want to go as soon as possible," Malka told her husband. "I have a feeling Shoshie's about at the end of her tether. First her grandmother's stroke, and now this. She needs someone, Avi. She needs *me*."

"Of course," Avi said again. He rose and started for the door. "I'll call the travel agent right away."

"Wait. Please."

It was Adela, standing by the couch where she'd been, until a moment ago, perched beside her son. Her gaze travelled from Avi to his wife. "Malka, if you don't mind, I'd like to come, too. With Yudy."

A stunned silence met her announcement. Yudy broke it.

"To Israel, Mom? You think that's a good idea?"

"Yes. Let's leave the men to handle the police end of things. We can go away, far away, where it's safe."

An earnest discussion ensued, during which Avi, Malka, Adela, Yudy, and Mutty each voiced an opinion — sometimes several times over — on the startling notion of the Moseses, mother and son, debunking to Israel. In the end, Avi gave the decisive vote.

"It's a good idea. I was thinking that it would be best to get you out of the city. Though I have to admit, I hadn't thought quite along the line of six thousand miles."

"It's far enough, anyway." Yudy's face shone, for the first time, without a trace of fear. "Mom, it's a super idea. When should we leave?" Already he'd returned to his youthful habit of confidence in his mother, of expecting her to know best, to be equal to any problem. With a few simple words he had handed over to her the adult weight he'd been carrying these last months. With it, he cast off the mein of weary age. He was a boy again.

Seeing him so, Adela felt a lurch of emotion — joy and pain, intermingled. She wondered whether she was fitted anymore to the responsibility he'd so abruptly thrust back on her. It was no easy job, raising a son in this city. She'd thought him secure in his protected environment, moving safely from the sheltering arms of the yeshivah to those of home. Exactly how wrong she'd been she was only just beginning to learn.

She smiled. "Like Mrs. Weisner said, as soon as we can get ready, Yudy. You agree?"

Smiling back, so that the light rose in his eyes and filled his face, Yudy answered with all the earnest warmth his young heart could muster: "The sooner the better!"

THIRTEEN

1

After that, all thought and emotion was buried beneath an avalanche of practical detail. There were plane reservations to be obtained — no easy matter at such short notice — and myriad domestic affairs to be arranged. Yudy's yeshivah must be called and a bewildered rebbe informed of his student's imminent departure for Israel, return date unknown.

Avi undertook to make the travel arrangements. Adela would contact Yudy's school, with backup support from Rabbi Weisner, if necessary. As for Malka, in a rush of unprecedented adrenalin, she threw herself into a frenzy of activity unequaled except in the immediate prelude to Pesach. There was no time to do all the things she'd set her heart on to ease her absence for her family — it would have taken her several days just to prepare and freeze their meals for the next weeks — but she could, and did, delegate.

First, however, came the hard part: telling the children. She broke the news to the older ones first. Shmulie she phoned at his yeshivah; her plans affected him least of all. His father would be there when he returned home for Shabbos, and his room, and his bed. There was nothing to worry about where Shmulie was concerned. With a sense of one tiny hurdle crossed, Malka crossed the first name off her mental list.

Shani was next. She was, by turns, surprised, woebegone, and, finally, accepting.

"Don't worry, Ma," she said, drawing from her kindly heart a gift of reassurance for her mother, though she craved it sorely herself. "We'll take care of everything." She chewed her lip. "Poor Tzippy!"

The cousin that lay in a coma in Jerusalem was almost exactly Shani's age, Malka reflected — and similar in temperament, too. Both were the "good girls" of their families, more willing than the rest to lend a hand when needed. The difference was that Shani, the perennial bookworm, had to be asked. Tzippy, on the other hand, was always on the alert to the things that needed doing, taking on her own thin shoulders, sometimes, even more than her mother would have wished.

Impulsively, Malka hugged her young daughter. What if it had been Shani lying in that hospital bed instead of Tzippy? The hug tightened to a near-stranglehold. The thought was appalling — unthinkable! And yet, should it be any less appalling that it was Tzippy? The question, and the vague, guilty feeling it engendered, impelled Malka to even more prodigious efforts at organizing herself for the trip ahead. She must waste no time in flying to the aid of the stricken family.

She released Shani. "Send Hindy in, please."

Waiting for the summons to be answered, she thought about packing. Too bad there was no time to buy presents for all the children; then again, this wasn't that kind of trip. Still, there must be some things she could take along — convenience items. She began rummaging through her kitchen cabinets. What to bring to ease their lives in small ways?

She threw a jumbo package of paper plates into a carton, and extra-absorbent paper towels, and a couple of rolls of aluminum foil. Paper cups. Disposable tablecloths. The carton slowly filled. Later she would ask Mutty to carry it upstairs, where it would make its way into her suitcase. Tucking in a package of plastic straws — guaranteed to make any youngster's morning milk taste twice as good — she was filled with a glow of virtue. Her rummaging grew more creative. American tuna. Lollipops.

Hindy entered the kitchen, wearing a faint but definite scowl. Malka's heart sank. Adolescent fury was exactly what she didn't need at this particular moment.

In the end, though, the interview went better than she'd expected. When Hindy threatened to become difficult, Malka made a quick decision. Her surest course to winning Hindy's favor was to take the girl fully into her confidence. It was what Hindy desired most of all. And why, after all, shouldn't she?

For the first time, after weeks of absorption in her distress over Avi, in the juggling of her ever-erratic Pesach schedule, and the sheltering of Yudy and Adela, Malka took a good, hard look at her eldest daughter. Hindy was a young woman now — sixteen next month. She had wit and capability far beyond what Malka remembered having herself at that age. She had no qualms about leaving Hindy in charge for a few weeks. Hindy would do what was required of her. She would manage the house and the younger children, a capable mother-substitute. But Malka wanted her to do it with a willing spirit.

The girl, she saw, had been brooding and unhappy ever since the Moseses had come beneath their roof — and, in subtler ways, for far longer than that. She longed to be part of things. She craved new status as one of the grown-ups, a person "in the know." Was it fair to ask her to take on the running of the household — surely a formidable task for any adult — while leaving her, childlike, in the dark?

The decision made, the rest followed with surprising ease. Elbows on the kitchen table, Malka in a few succinct sentences filled Hindy in on the broad outlines of Yudy's predicament. "The details I don't know myself yet," she ended. "He was supposed to tell us all about it tonight — before the call came about Tzippy." She looked her daughter squarely in the eye. "Hindy, I need your help. I need you to be strong now. Just like Shoshie is being the strong one in her house. She's only a year or two older than you are, you know."

"Okay, Ma." Hindy was visibly shaken by what she'd heard. "I...I'm sorry I acted like such a baby. I didn't mean to make things harder for everybody."

"You've been wonderful," her mother said robustly. "The way you've been taking over some of the cooking has been the biggest help. But this will be harder, Hindaleh. Tatty will be as busy as always with the shul and his *shiurim*. It'll be up to you to keep the house going. Shani will help, but" — she switched to a comic drawl, halfway between cowboy and sailor — "you're the captain of this here ship. Think you can do it?"

Hindy squared her shoulders and smiled — a real smile. It lit up her face and gave Malka back the daughter she remembered. There was nothing Hindy loved more than a challenge. Chip off the old block, Malka thought wryly. Like father, like daughter.

"I can do it, Ma. You don't worry about a thing."

"I won't have time to freeze lots of meals — "

"Who needs them? I can cook. You just said so." Already — as clearly as though she'd been handed a picture — Malka could see the girl's mind beginning to spin with plans: menus, schedules, tactics to heighten the efficiency of this, to her young mind, woefully inadequate household. Hindy beamed on her mother with a new benevolence, the sparkle of battle in her eye. She would straighten out what was wrong with this place. She would show 'en — meaning, her mother — just how it ought to be done.

Malka smiled back. *Just try it for a few weeks, mamaleh*, she thought but didn't say aloud. *Then we'll talk.*

Chaim and Tzvi took it the hardest.

"Why can't you take us along?" Chaim wailed. "We'll be good!"

"Cousin Tzippy is very sick," Malka explained gently. "We need to daven that she should have a *refuah sheleimah*. And I have to go help take care of Tzippy's brothers and sisters so her mommy and *tatty* can be with her in the hospital. Understand?"

She might as well not have bothered. Chaim's eyes had filled, and only partly in pity for Tzippy. By far the largest part of his sorrow was reserved for his own small self. "It's n...not fair," he quavered. "Tzippy gets her mommy *and* mine — and I get n...nothing!"

Melting with love and shared anguish, she put her arms around him. Her own eyes were bright with unshed tears. Why was the right thing sometimes so hard to do? Did lovingkindness to one have to mean dispensing heartache to another? Chaim, as though wishing to give his mother a taste of his own pain, was stiff and unyielding to his mother's embrace at first. In the end, though, he slumped against her and enjoyed a hearty cry.

Sturdy Tzvi, of the angelic curls and the obstinate mouth, crossed his pudgy arms across his little chest and declared, "You're *not* going!"

"No?" Malka asked, looking at him tenderly over Chaim's bowed head. "Why not, sweetie?"

" 'Cause I don't let!"

She held her tongue. Time, and the promise of a generous present at the end of it, would, she devoutly hoped, reconcile both her little ones to her going. She stroked the small head on her shoulder and smiled sadly at her furious Tzvi, all the while stifling her own sighs. It was hard to go, and it was bound to get harder as the time drew nearer.

There wasn't an awful lot of time left. A series of phone consultations ended in firm reservations — sooner than she'd expected. They were to leave the following evening.

❧

Adela reeled through the hours of the next day in a daze.

The list of things that must be done before the trip was endless. Inform her clients. Call Yudy's school. Cancel the newspaper subscription. Arrange about the mail. Ask a neighbor to water the plants...*and* keep an eye on the house. (Check for lurking strangers in the shadows?) Clothes to the laundry and the one-day dry cleaner's. Suitcases up from the basement. Pack.

There the list stopped cold. The thought of being in her house, packing their suitcases, sent a chill up her spine. Her own home had become enemy territory. What had once represented the epitome of safety — the security of her four sweet walls — had been transformed, by the actions of a man she'd never even laid eyes on, into a shivering quicksand, a place of sinister possibility. Her own front door was a black moat she dared not traverse.

What if *he* was still prowling around out there, at the perimeters of her life and Yudy's, waiting for his chance to pounce? He mustn't get an inkling that they were contemplating flight. The whole point of the exercise was to slip Yudy out of the country while that maniac's back, so to speak, was turned. (Which reminded her: she'd better pack up her valuables, too, and take them over to the Weisners for safekeeping. No telling who might decide to break in once it sank in that the Moseses were well and truly gone.)

She needn't have worried about packing alone. Both Avi and Malka Weisner were adamant in their opposition to any thought of it.

"Mutty and I will drive you and Yudy home right after *shacharis*. I get a feeling our 'friend' is not exactly a morning person. We should have a couple of clear hours, at the very least, before he might roll around." Avi spoke humorously, as though the man who had engraved his mark — literally — on Yudy, were no more than a passing irritation, a clown, a buffoon. Adela was grateful for his humor, and for his unshakable devotion to their safety. For form's sake, she did essay a protest — and was lightheaded with thankfulness when he firmly squelched it. "After breakfast," he promised.

The meal duly dispatched, Avi took the wheel, with Mutty beside him and Yudy and Adela seated behind.

"I hate to sound melodramatic," the rabbi said — actually sounding, if anything, more than a little nervous — "but it might be a good idea if the two of you would sort of scrunch down in that back seat a bit. Yes," he glanced into the rearview mirror, nodding, "that's it. No need to attract undue attention." Not for the first time, he wished Binyomin were with them. He thought with nostalgia of their good old cops-and-robbers days. He could use a partner now.

In the back seat, crouched absurdly behind the driver's seat with cramped legs and pounding heart, Adela was thinking the same thing.

"Your *sheitel's* showing, Mom," Yudy giggled. "Bend a little lower."

"If I bend any lower," she gasped, "I'll fold in two."

"We're almost there," Mutty called back softly.

"Thank goodness," Adela said. Yudy laughed.

He was still laughing as he sprinted into the house and went for the suitcases. Neither the dim, dank basement nor the memory of his tormentor could dampen his spirits. Soon, tonight, he would board that plane and take off into a limitless expanse of indigo sky. He would swarm weightless among the stars, brother to the unshackled moon. Away, away... Free!

He pulled the set of matched luggage away from the wall they'd been propping up since their last real vacation — how many years ago now? (He didn't count summer camp, strictly a duffel-bag affair.) The suitcases weighed nothing in his arms as he carried them swiftly up the stairs to the kitchen, through the living room, then up another flight to his mother's room. "Heah you ah, Modom," he announced, depositing one of the cases on her bed. "I'll just take the other one over to my suite." Hefting the remaining piece of luggage over his shoulder, he turned to go.

"Yudy."

He stopped, turned back. "You rang?"

"Yudy, stop it." Her voice shook. "Stop clowning around. I can't bear it. The...the danger's not past yet. Not till we're out of here."

"We will be, soon, Mom. Don't worry."

He was the strong one now. He was too happy, or too young, to care about anything now that a plan had been made and was being set in motion. She felt ashamed.

"I'm sorry. Oh, what's wrong with me? I don't know why I'm biting your head off just for being lighthearted." Hadn't she been praying for just that, week after week? "Forgive me, Yudy."

"Come on, Mom. There's no reason for sorries." He hesitated awkwardly in the doorway. "Uh, I'll go pack now." He made it a question.

"Wait. Please." Adela sat at the edge of her bed, ignoring the armful of clothing she'd just taken from her bureau and which she still held. "You never got to tell us last night what actually happened with...that man. Why he's been after you. Why...the scar."

"Oh. Yeah, right, I never did, did I?" Slowly, he set down the suitcase. "Mom, why don't we go downstairs for a few minutes, so Rabbi Weisner and

Mutty can hear it, too? I think they deserve it, after all they've been doing for us."

"An excellent idea." She smiled and cast aside the clothes. "Who feels like packing anyway?"

"We'll pack soon," he said gravely, leading the way from the room. "This won't take very long."

2

"The thing is," Yudy told the small audience assembled around the living room, "I think I may have witnessed a murder."

The drapes had been drawn, shutting out a watery spring sun. Inside, the room was cool and swam in an eerie semi-dusk. Adela brought a fist to her mouth.

Avi nodded slowly. "Yes," he murmured, half to himself. "It had to be something like that." He would have the police check their records for a possible local manslaughter. Of course, the body — if there *had* been a murder — might have been removed, hidden, never to be discovered. Alternatively, what Yudy had thought was a killing may have been nothing more than an injury inflicted, with the victim either carried, or carrying himself, out of the area as soon as he was able.

"Where?" asked Mutty. "When?"

"And how?" Avi added.

Yudy smiled faintly at this litany. "It was the day after my father's *yahrtzeit*. You remember, Rabbi Weisner? We talked a little after davening."

"We agreed to spend some time together that Shabbos," Avi agreed. "In the end, you never came." He sat up, alert. "Was that why? Did this thing happen between that day — a Thursday, wasn't it? — and Shabbos?"

"That same night. I was still pretty new in the neighborhood and decided to walk home from school a different way after *mishmar*. I guess I hoped I'd get home quicker that way." He shivered.

"Which way did you go?" Mutty asked.

"Through the playground." He mentioned a street. Mutty knew the place: a modest, fairly rundown, concrete jungle, with a couple of basketball hoops and a few swings that still worked well enough to delight the children who ventured there. It had been years since he'd set foot in the place himself.

Yudy went on. "The minute I went in, I was ready to turn around and head back. Talk about spooky. It was dark, and it was empty. Or, at least, I thought it was." He swallowed. He was coming to the hard part — the stuff of dreams so vivid they still had the power to wake him with the force of his own weeping. "I remembered noticing, once, a second gate on the other side. I thought it would bring me a full block closer to home than if I went all the way around, so I kept walking. I heard a noise — a scuffling. There was a little moonlight. Over by the seesaws, two guys were fighting. Then one of them suddenly gave a sort of grunt and slipped down to the ground. He lay there, not moving." Yudy closed his eyes. His breathing had become rapid and shallow.

"Sssh," Adela said, laying a protective hand on his sleeve. "You don't have to tell us. Sssh."

Yudy opened his eyes and attempted a weak smile. A sheen of sweat stood out on his forehead. "I'm okay, Mom. I think it's a good thing to get it all out. You know — therapeutic."

My brave boy. Adela's eyes were swimming. The mother in her longed to shield him, to bid him stop reliving the nightmare and put it behind him. But another, wiser Adela knew enough to hold her tongue. Yudy would choose his telling or not-telling. He had earned that right.

Avi leaned forward. "Yudy, did you actually see a weapon in the other man's hand?"

"No." The boy thought for a moment, then said, "But from the way the other guy fell, so suddenly, he must have been knifed in the stomach or something. That's the only thing I can think of. Unless it was a gun with a silencer. But I would've heard at least a little pop then, wouldn't I?"

"Must we go into the gory details?" Adela asked faintly.

Avi gave Yudy a look that said, "Later." Now he merely said, "What did you do then?"

"What do you think?" Yudy offered the ghost of a smile. "I ran. I ran so hard I thought my heart would jump right out of my chest and into the street! And he ran after me."

"No," gasped his mother.

"Yes. He caught up with me, too." Yudy shook his head again, violently now, as if to dislodge the memory. "Luckily, I was back on the street by then, and people were still passing. He grabbed my arm and made me listen to him, but there wasn't much he could do in public."

"If he really had just killed someone," Mutty observed, "he might have been scared to get in any deeper. Knocking off some fellow hoodlum — I assume that's what the victim was? — is one thing. Messing with a neighborhood kid is something else." He tilted his head curiously. "Well, what did he do?"

"First he asked me what I'd seen. I kept saying, 'Nothing. Honest, I didn't see a thing!' I could tell he wasn't sure whether or not to believe me."

Avi nodded approvingly and said, "You were smart. If you'd admitted you'd actually witnessed the crime, I'm afraid your life would have been in a lot more danger than it already was."

"I guess so. He pretended not to believe me, though. Kept threatening me. Said he'd follow me around, make sure I didn't talk to the police. I told him I wouldn't. He said I'd better not, or he'd know how to settle the score."

"You said he threatened your mother, too," Avi remembered. "When was that?"

"That was later on. After he started haunting me." Yudy grinned sheepishly. "That's the way I thought of it. Haunting. I never knew when he would pop up. Once in a while, it was early in the morning, on my way home from shul or on the way to yeshivah. He'd be real bleary-eyed then, like he hadn't been to bed at all."

"Like I said, a night bird," Avi murmured.

"Right. Most times, though, it was in the evening, on my way home. Especially on Thursday nights, when we stayed late for *mishmar*. But he wasn't as predictable as it might sound. That," he said plaintively, "was the hardest part. Not knowing when he'd come up behind me suddenly...with the knife..."

"How many times, all together?" Mutty wanted to know.

Yudy considered. "Maybe six or seven in all." He shuddered. "It was enough."

"Do you think he actually followed you?" Adela had regained some of her color but was looking far from her usual self. Poor baby. No wonder he'd wanted to do nothing but curl up beneath his blankets all day. Instead, she'd made him get up, go to school, face that monster again and again. How had he stood it?

"He must have. Or else he waited around for me. That wasn't hard to do once he knew my routine."

"Why," asked Mutty, "didn't you change your route? Go a different way?"

Yudy's answer was a look of profound distress. How to explain the paralysis that had set in after the first encounter or two — the sense of being under the control of a stronger power, a malevolent force against which it was useless to struggle? He had been like a fly caught in a web, with the spider gloating in superiority above him. And then, there was the knife...

"The scar," Avi said, as though reading his thoughts. "When did that happen?"

"It must have been the third time he jumped me, or maybe the fourth. It was on my way home from school — on the last block, where the other guys turn in and I have to walk by myself. He went into his usual line: What had I seen? What had I told anyone? What did I plan on saying? He acted very weird this time — weirder than usual, that is." He paused. "Drugs, maybe."

Mutty said shortly, "The whole scene in the park was probably about drugs."

"Maybe. He talked sort of crazy. Then he pulled out the knife and played around with it — you know, to scare me. He did that lots of times. Only this time, he did more than just play. Before I knew what was happening, I was bleeding all over the place." Yudy looked at his mother. "Mom, that was the night you called from Manhattan, remember? When you'd gone out with Binyomin."

Slowly, she nodded as the memory flooded back. "You were crying."

At the clear signs of her son's embarrassment, she regretted the words the instant they were out of her mouth. But he twisted his lips into a smile and said, shrugging, "I guess I was. I was pretty shook up."

"I don't blame you!" Avi said. "I'd have been blubbering myself. How'd you treat the cut?"

"Iodine and a couple of bandaids. Once I cleaned it up, it wasn't as bad as I'd thought. Hurt like anything, though, for a couple of days."

"You could probably have done with a few stitches," the rabbi said. "You may find you'll carry that scar around for the rest of your life."

"I know it."

Echoes of the rabbi's words seemed to pass through the room, resonating there. The four kept their vigil in the dim, cool shadows, watching the long hand of the past stretch into the future.

Abruptly, Avi sat upright. In a voice calculated to banish shadows and demons, he said, "Thank you, Yudy. It's out of your hands now. Tonight you'll fly out of here, leaving the matter to the police. Believe me, they'll be delighted to lay their hands on your friend."

"Don't call him that." Yudy looked sick. "Please."

"Do they know who he is?" Adela asked the rabbi eagerly. "Does he have a record?"

"He certainly does. No convictions yet, but there's always a first time!" Avi rose. "I suggest that the two of you go upstairs and get on with the packing. Mutty and I will guard the ranch."

Adela got up with a grateful smile for both of them. "We'll try to be as fast as possible. Coming, Yudy?"

"Sure." Yudy jumped up with alacrity. "I'll be through in — oh, fifteen minutes, give or take a minute or two. How much do I need to pack, anyhow?"

"Better be conservative. We don't know how long we'll be gone."

"That's true." Nodding thoughtfully, Yudy started for the stairs and his gaping suitcase. He felt curiously cleansed. It had been a good idea of his mother's, this spilling of his tale. It was out of his system now — almost as though it had happened to someone else and not to him at all.

Entering his room, he thought suddenly, as he hadn't in years, of a game they used to play at birthday parties when he was very young. Hot Potato, they'd called it. You passed the potato from hand to hand while the music played; when it stopped, whoever was holding the potato was the loser. He was out of the game.

For too long now, Yudy had been "out." Life had passed on its way all around him, while he held on unwilling to that hot potato until it scorched his fingers and seared his very soul.

He laughed softly to himself at the analogy. Well, the hot potato was out of his hands now.

His room welcomed him, his haven and refuge during all those long weeks of terror. The astronomy posters made him remember the real stars that would welcome him into their midst tonight. Elation washed over him, rendering him light and bubbly as the best champagne. He felt as though he'd be soaring into the great, dark sky tonight on the power of his own wings and not a set of engines at all.

With a single yank, he pulled the entire top drawer of his bureau out and dumped its contents onto his bed. Packing would be a cinch. Everything was going to be easier now. With a creak and a groan, the wheel of life had begun to turn for him again.

Free!

3

S he'd been away too long.

That was Malka's first thought on setting foot in Jerusalem and inhaling the combination of scents so particular to that place, and still so well-remembered. The brief, sweet Mediterranean spring had splashed the country with fragrance and color. Yellow, green, crimson, and violet shimmered in every hedge and garden. Soon the burning summer sun would dry the grass and cast a hard, white sheen over pavement and building and every living thing; but for these few heady weeks, just to see, simply to breathe, was paradise.

Not that she had the leisure to savor either activity. Arriving as she did late in the afternoon, she found the Markovich apartment — and Shoshie's hands — full. They were, at the moment Malka walked through the door, literally full of a sad-eyed Yoni. The bigger boys had abandoned their perpetual soccer game in the street below for the security of their own living room. Batya prowled the place, forlorn as a ghost without her Tzippy. Moshe Dovid had come home from yeshivah at this new crisis in the family, ostensibly to lend support. He seemed to Malka to be merely taking up a great deal of space that might have been put to better use in the cramped apartment. Of Bracha there was no sign.

"Aunt Malka! I'm so glad you came." Shoshie gazed at her wonderingly. "You actually picked up and came..."

"Of course!" the aunt replied, with a robustness she was far from feeling. She smiled at the many faces turned to stare at her. Moshe Dovid stammered a bashful hello. Malka's smile broadened.

"Hi, gang. It's great to see you again. We can all get reacquainted later. But right now," she turned back to Shoshie, "if you'll just show me where to dump by bag, I'll start supper."

Shoshie looked acutely embarrassed. "Oh! You must be hungry after that whole long trip. Just sit down" — setting Yoni abruptly on the floor, she made an awkward dash for the couch, which she attempted to sweep clear of books, toys, and Moshe Dovid — "and have a little rest. I'm making supper."

Malka ignored this injunction. Following her niece into the kitchen, she asked, "What were you planning to make?"

"Uh, there's not much in the house at the moment. Bracha and Benzy are going to do some shopping a little later, right after they finish checking out a hall. They wished they could have been here to greet you, but the caterer said — "

"No problem. There's plenty of time. Now go take care of that adorable little brother of yours." (Yoni, who had not budged from the spot where Shoshie had dumped him in such unceremonious haste, was making his discontent very plainly known.) "I'll take care of the cooking. Scrambled eggs all right with everybody?"

All the protests Shoshie had marshalled — Aunt Malka had just stepped off the plane; she must be exhausted; it was her first night here — deserted her. "Thanks," she said gratefully, and she hurried off to get Yoni; "hurry" seemed to be the only pace she moved at these days. As she reentered the kitchen, lugging the child, she passed a hand quickly over her tired eyes. Malka peered at her more closely.

The girl was clearly worn to the bone. Her skin had an unhealthy pallor, and there were gray smudges under her eyes, which spoke of restless nights. Whether it had been the baby keeping her up or her own worries, Malka didn't know. Shoshie, she also saw, was sniffling almost continuously. It couldn't be easy to shake off a cold while living in a pressure cooker.

Malka set down the eggs she'd just fetched from the fridge and led Shoshie firmly over to a kitchen chair. "You sit here, and don't move a muscle. Just talk to me. How's Tzippy? And how has everything been going around this place?"

"Tzippy's the same," Shoshie answered slowly, while her aunt moved about the small kitchen, gathering her utensils from neatly marked drawers and cupboards. "Unconscious. They did something — some sort of procedure — to ease the pressure on her brain or something. I'm not sure exactly. But she still hasn't woken up. The pan's in the bottom cabinet, Aunt Malka."

"Thanks. Got it. Ima and Abba are there at night, too?"

"Yes. One of them with Tzippy, the other with Savta. She — Savta, I'm talking about — isn't able to feed herself yet, and she'd rather eat from Ima or Abba than the nurses. Also, she can't sleep so well at night. She needs someone there with her." She paused, then added wistfully, "I wish I could say the same thing about Tzippy. She doesn't seem to be in a lot of pain or anything, Aunt Malka. She just sleeps and sleeps!"

Malka nodded. "I'll go see her tomorrow, if you'll take me." She looked around. "And the situation here?"

"We're doing okay. The boys have been angels, for them." Shoshie smiled weakly. "So has Batya. Poor Yoni's suffering the most, I think. He's still such a little baby." She hugged "poor Yoni," at which the child whimpered and stuck his thumb into his mouth. "Bracha does a lot, of course, and Benzy's usually around, too. They can't help it if they have to keep running around getting things ready for the wedding. Benzy's mother is doing all she can, but she's in Bnei Brak, so it's hard. Poor Bracha. We're all hoping the wedding won't have to be postponed."

"And what about 'poor Shoshie?' " Malka said softly.

Suddenly, Shoshie's eyes filled. She dashed the back of her hand over them and let out a tiny sigh, reminiscent of Yoni's whimper. Malka stopped whipping eggs and was at her niece's side in two swift strides. As she gathered Shoshie into her arms, she gave a passing thought to her sister-in-law. If Shoshie was worn this ragged, what must Esther be feeling?

"Sssh," she murmured. "It's all right. I'm here now. I'm going to do everything. You can finally get some rest. My brave girl, you deserve it."

The tension seemed to flow out of Shoshie as she leaned gratefully into her aunt. "Oh, Aunt Malka." She cried quietly into a shoulder growing rapidly damp, indeed. "I can't tell you how glad I am that you came."

"So am I," Malka said. "I'd nearly forgotten how gorgeous Israel is. I may not get to do much touring this trip — beyond the local supermarket, that is — but I'm going to be the most enthusiastic fan this country has ever seen."

Shoshie smiled through her tears. The smile turned into a king-sized yawn.

"And as soon as we're finished eating," Malka continued, "I'm putting you to bed." She chucked the baby under the chin. "You and Yoni, both."

"Oh, Aunt Malka," Shoshie said again, her voice cracking in the wonder, the amazing luxury, of passing over a burden that was just too heavy for her. "That sounds like *gan eden*."

Malka was as good as her word. In less than an hour, she had the modest supper cooked, served, and cleared away. The table talk was all of Tzippy. She urged Eli and Aryeh Leib to recite some *tehillim* — it could only help their sister and would occupy them while she busied herself with putting the little ones to bed. Then she scooped up a protesting Yoni, took Batya by the hand, and led the two of them and Shoshie off to their respective rooms.

"He'll cry," Shoshie warned at her door, casting longing looks at her bed. "I'd better put him in."

"He'll have to get used to me sooner or later," Malka said cheerfully. She freed a hand to give Shoshie a playful shove. "Go on. To bed."

Shoshie obeyed gratefully. Some little while later, both index fingers stuffed into her ears to block out Yoni's indignant wails, she fell into the closest thing to a tranquil sleep that she'd had since her grandmother had taken sick.

4

Adela, meanwhile, had not been idle. After checking into a hotel, and even before she began unpacking their bags, she began making calls — networking, as her computer-trained mind liked to think of it. Yudy had asked her, on the interminable flight, where they were going to live in Jerusalem. "We can't stay at the hotel forever," he worried. "It costs too much."

"Don't you fret," Adela had answered with a new calm born the moment she'd led her son onto the plane and away from the city that had so terrorized him. "Somehow, things will work out. Hashem has brought us this far. He won't let us down now."

One call led to another: old friends, friends of friends, neighbors and relatives of friends' friends. And, by the end of their first evening in Israel, Adela's faith was rewarded.

"It is not very large," a Mrs. Kunslinger told her over the line, her English slow and careful. "Only two bedrooms. My own flat, across the street, is bigger. But the furniture is good, though pretty old. My sister and brother-in-law are renting it out for about six years now — or rather, I am renting it out for them, and it gives me a big headache sometimes. But don't worry, it is in pretty good shape. No problem."

"Does it have appliances? Washer, dryer, fridge, stove?"

"No dryer. Everything else, yes. The refrigerator is a little — how do you say? — cranky? But it works. Usually." A pause. "There are two balconies. Neither one big enough to turn around in, but good for hanging the laundry, no problem. Let me see, what else? Oh yes — closets. There are two. Not the best wood, only *sandwich*, but they are still standing."

Rather uncertainly, Adela said, "Oh, good." She had forgotten about the absence of walk-in closets in Israeli flats. "What kind of furniture?"

"Kitchen table and chairs — small, but okay. Dining-room set, so-so; living-room couch and chair — nothing to look at, but it's a place to sit; youth beds in one bedroom, regular beds in the other, no problem. Oh, and kitchen cabinets above and below, and dishes, *chalavi* and *besari* — cheap stuff, but plastic breaks less than china. There are pots and pans, too. Does it sound all right for you?"

Adela nearly answered, "No problem." Her head was spinning from the woman's excruciating honesty. "It certainly sounds, er, adequate." She tried to think. "How is the water heated? Some sort of boiler?"

"There's a *dud shemesh* — solar panel — on the roof. In these warm months, you won't have to turn on the boiler at all!" Mrs. Kunslinger sounded inordinately proud of the fact. Suspiciously, she added, "Unless you and your family like to take long baths every day?" Just what might be expected, her tone implied, from pampered Americans.

"Oh — er, no. There's just two of us. My son and me."

"Only two? That's good. The last family had five little ones. You should see the walls. But the marks are mostly low down where you hardly notice them. No problem."

"Terrific," Adela said drily. "The rent is what?"

Mrs. Kunslinger named a figure. Adela calculated rapidly. "That sounds reasonable. Can we — "

"Plus the *va'ad habayit* payments, of course. That's for keeping up the building. You know, taking care of the garden — if you could call it that — and the elevator (I told them they should switch elevator companies, the way it keeps breaking down, but do they listen to me?), and cleaning the lobby once a week (they should clean it once a *day*, with those children, *sheyihiyu bri'im*, always playing there and eating all over the place!). The last tenant tried to get out of it, but everybody pays. It's the law. Don't worry, it's not too much. I pay more in my building."

"Oh, sure. Fine." Adela was hardly listening. Who cared what the place looked like? A roof over their heads and a couple of basic amenities was all she needed. Lifting a corner of the thick, drab drape covering the window, she smiled out at the yellow lights of Jerusalem. Her spirits soared. "Can we come see it in the morning?"

"No problem. I'm here all day. Just call first to make sure I'm home. How long did you say you wanted the apartment for?"

"I didn't say." Some of Adela's ebullience drained away. She glanced at her son, absorbed in a book he'd started on the plane. He looked strangely forlorn in the impersonal room, a storybook waif in search of a home. Had she done the right thing in uprooting him from all that was familiar? Would she make a success of this transplantation — find him a place to learn, people to befriend?

She turned away, resolutely battling the shadows. "To tell you the truth, Mrs. Kunslinger, I'm just not sure at the moment," she said with forced heartiness. "But I'm sure things will be a little clearer in the morning."

In a way, they were. Seeing the little apartment, adequately if not at all lavishly furnished and — most important — a few minutes' walk from the Markovich flat where Malka was staying, Adela knew she had found what they needed. Behind Mrs. Kunslinger's broad back and elaborate turban, Yudy winked his satisfaction with the place.

"We'll take it," Adela said. "Is a three-month lease okay?"

Three months would bring them to midsummer; by then, she hoped, the outlines of their immediate future would be a little more definable. Either that madman would be behind bars, and they could return to New York in preparation for the new school year; or else, he would still be roaming the streets, a menace to the innocent, and especially to her son — in which case, their path would have to take a different turning.

"With an option to renew," she added. Yudy glanced at her sharply. As though reading her reasons in her face, he slowly nodded.

"No problem." They could move in the day after next, their new landlady told them as, with a firm tread, she led them out of the rental apartment. "We can sign the contract in my flat, right across the street," she said, with the air of one conferring a vast treat. Today and tomorrow she would see to it that their place got a thorough cleaning.

"The last people, they didn't know how to do a good *sponja* at all. You have to use a lot of water, not a bunch of wet strings. A mop, she called it. A mop!" The good woman snorted. "If you want, I will show you how to do *sponja* — the real way."

Adela thanked her absently for the offer. The floors could sprout mushrooms for all she cared. They had a place to live now, she and Yudy. They had a foothold in Jerusalem — but that was only the first step. *Sponja* was the least of her concerns now. She had more important things on her mind.

One of the foremost of her concerns was to find a suitable school for Yudy. As things turned out, it was Malka who helped find it for him.

They had been in daily telephone contact since the landing in Ben Gurion Airport. While Malka cooked and cleaned and mothered Esther's desolate children, Adela and Yudy visited the Western Wall and the Old City, whirled through the newer parts of Jerusalem seeing what they could, and then made the move to their temporary flat. Malka dispatched a few of the Markovich children to help them get settled. This step reaped an unexpected bonus: Aryeh Leib conceived an instant adoration for Yudy Moses. From the moment the teenager moved in, the younger boy could be found dogging his footsteps virtually everywhere.

"I don't mind," Yudy confided a little sheepishly when he and his mother came for supper on their first night in the neighborhood. "This is a good kind of haunting."

The women smiled and watched — Malka with satisfaction, Adela with unabashed *nachas* — as Yudy delighted Aryeh Leib with the sort of nonchalant attentions boys thrive on. It was good to see Aryeh Leib's truculence melt away as Yudy chatted with him of this and that, as the two flicked around some marbles on the floor and competed in a hotly contested match of Kugelach. Best still, the American agreed to go downstairs and kick around a ball with the Markovich boys and their pals. Having grown up on stickball rather than soccer, Yudy was in a perfect position to be outshone by Aryeh Leib: the beautiful, rosy cherry on top of the cake.

"So how's it going, Malka?" Adela asked over coffee when the boys had gone. Batya was playing at puzzles, with Yoni beside her on the living-room rug, while Shoshie, at the kitchen sink, disposed of the dishes.

"I saw Tzippy today," Malka sighed. "Still in a coma, poor thing. Esther looks like a rag, Zalman like a ghost — did I tell you his mother's in the hospital, too? Recovering from a stroke."

Both women fell into a respectful silence in the face of this double dollop of ill fortune. Malka took a sip of coffee, making a face as it scalded her tongue. "Bracha — that's Shoshie's twin sister — is hardly ever around. She's frantic with wedding preparations, and I don't blame her a bit. She's got it all on her shoulders now, and only eighteen years old. Why, she hasn't even graduated from high school yet! There's still a few weeks left to the school year. I insisted that Shoshie go back tomorrow. She deserves a chance to lead something of a normal life, poor thing. And I sent Moshe Dovid back to his yeshivah. He was moping around here, getting in everyone's way and not doing himself or anyone else a bit of good."

"Sounds like you've got things under control. Do you think maybe Moshe Dovid or Bracha's *chasan*, what's-his-name, can come up with a suitable yeshivah for Yudy? I figure we'll stay at least till the summer...depending on how things develop."

Malka sat up straight. "I can do better than that. There's a marvelous couple downstairs. The wife's been cooking up something for the family practically every day since all this began, not to mention babysitting for Yoni when Shoshie needed her. And all this on top of ten kids of her own! I've put a stop to all that, but she's been so supportive in every way, you wouldn't believe it if I told you. The whole neighborhood looks up to her — as well they should. She's apparently a brilliant woman, too. Shoshie says Rebbetzin Kahn gives a popular *shiur* for women; maybe I'll even get a chance to slip out for an hour this Shabbos afternoon... But that's besides the point."

Adela was trying, not very successfully, to follow her friend's train of thought. "What *is* the point?"

"Her husband. Shoshie tells me he helps run a *ba'al teshuvah* yeshivah. You've heard of Rabbi Hoffman, I'm sure? Well, he's getting on in years, and this Rabbi Kahn's his right-hand man. I hear he's done lots of wonderful work with teenagers, too. I'm going down right now to ask him to help find the right place for Yudy." She was on her feet and heading purposefully for the door before Adela could react.

"Malka, wait!" Adela hastily set down her cup and rushed after her. "Shouldn't you call first to see if they're home?"

"Someone's always home," Malka tossed over her shoulder. She was already at the door. "I told you, ten kids... Batyaleh, keep on eye on Yoni. I'm just going down to the Kahns. Shoshie's in the kitchen."

"Okay, Aunt Malka," Batya looked up to smile abstractedly, then frowned at a piece of jigsaw puzzle in her hand.

The baby, seeing Malka about to leave, stretched out his arms. "Bye-bye?"

"See, Aunt Malka?" Batya beamed. "He's learning how to talk!"

"I can see that." And Esther was missing it. "Not now, honey pie. It's nearly your bedtime. We'll take a walk tomorrow, okay?"

"I see you've made a hit with the nieces and nephews," Adela remarked as they waited for the elevator.

"And why shouldn't I? I only bribed them with the entire contents of the Paskesz candy store. Here it is. Let's go." They stepped into the elevator and rode the three flights down in silence.

Adela hung back as the door opened to them, but Malka strode right in with a smiling, "Hi, there — Rivky, isn't it? Is your Ima home?"

The bashful, dark-braided girl answered softly, "Ima's in the kitchen. She's on the phone, I think." Her English was faintly accented.

"Don't bother her. We'll wait."

Malka, with Adela following, sidestepped an assortment of children — all dark-haired, dark-eyed, and displaying a shy but avid interest in the newcomers — to the dining-room table. As they took seats, another figure emerged from the rear of the apartment.

"Abba!" squealed a younger version of Rivky, running to him. She peeked at Malka and Adela from between the flaps of her father's suit jacket. "Batya's *dodah* is here," she stage-whispered. "And also another lady."

"So I see." The man moved into the room, smiling politely. Adela saw where the children got their coloring from and the unusual hue of their eyes: a gold-flecked brown. There was a good deal of silver in the dark beard, and the eyes belonged to someone who had known suffering and the wisdom that comes from it.

He came to a stop in front of the women. "Mrs. Weisner, is there anything I can do for you? How's the little girl, Tzippy?"

"The same," Malka replied. "We're all davening hard for her, Rabbi Kahn. Please have your boys continue saying *tehillim*. It can only help. But I've come for a different reason." Quickly, she introduced Adela. "She and her son, Yudy, are here for a short time — maybe two, three months. Basically, they're escaping from America. Remind me to tell you the details another time. He needs a place to learn, Rabbi. Can you help us?"

There was a rustle at the kitchen door. Turning, Adela found herself looking into a face that was warm, grave, quiet, and alive all at the same time. The owner of the face looked quite a bit younger than the rabbi. There was a baby in her arms.

"Sharona," the rabbi said, "Mrs. Weisner's here, and her friend, Mrs. Moses."

Sharona Kahn bent her head to say a few quick words to Rivky. Instantly, the girl disappeared into the kitchen, to reappear a few minutes later bearing a platter of cake. "The tea will be ready soon," she announced as she set it down on the table.

Malka protested, "Oh, there was no need to go to all that — "

"No trouble," Sharona Kahn said, smiling. Adela was fascinated by the woman's English, which was soft, fluid, and clearly not her native tongue. The rabbi, on the other hand, had a distinctive Midwestern accent. Sharona murmured to her husband, "Levi, maybe you should help Rivky with the hot water."

He nodded at the women and went into the kitchen. Adela marvelled at the way the children continued what they were doing — playing, reading, one or two in a corner halfheartedly bickering — while their parents sat down to an impromptu tea party with unexpected guests. From their behavior, this might be the sort of thing that happened in their household any day of the week — as perhaps it did. She was beginning to see what Malka had meant when she'd called the Kahns a most unusual couple.

When the rabbi returned with four cups of steaming tea and Rivky in tow, who seemed to have forgotten her shyness, he asked, "What kind of school are you looking for exactly, Mrs. Moses?"

"Well, the circumstances are a little unusual, Rabbi. In short, my son, who's fifteen, has just gone through a horrifying experience back in New York. He was learning very nicely before that, but the past couple of months have been pretty much of a washout as far as his learning's concerned."

"I understand." Levi Kahn leaned back, cradling his mug of tea thoughtfully. "I'd like to meet the boy. I have one or two ideas, though the language could be a problem."

He raised an inquisitive brow at Adela, who shook her head ruefully. "His Hebrew's no better than that of any other New York kid, I'm afraid."

"Then this is what I think. There are two possibilities right here in the neighborhood. I can speak to the *roshei yeshivah*, if you like. And in the evenings, a few times a week, I'd be happy to learn with Yudy — in English. Would that be helpful?"

Adela stared. "Rabbi! You must be incredibly busy. How could I even —"

"I have to learn in any case," he broke in imperturbably. "And, as it happens, my own evening *chavrusa* just left to the States." He held up a warning hand. "Please don't say anything to your son yet. I want him to feel comfortable. Let us meet first. Let's see if we click."

"All right. And thank you, Rabbi."

"Where are you living?" Sharona Kahn wanted to know. In short order, she elicited the information that Adela had never been in Israel before.

"I'll take you to the supermarket tomorrow," she promised. "And on Thursdays I usually go to the *shuk* for fruits and vegetables. You're welcome to come along, if it interests you."

"It does. Oh, I don't even know what to say!" Clasping her hands like a young girl, Adela gazed at them, at the gold-flecked eyes of the rabbi, at his wife's quiet smile, and the children of varying ages talking, playing, jumping, reading all over the apartment, while their parents dropped everything to help her, a total stranger. In fact — she realized this with a start and the beginnings of laughter — Malka, who had entered their home blithe as an old friend and introduced them, had known the Kahns all of three days herself!

Adela was overwhelmed suddenly with gratitude, proportional (she understood) to the stress and loneliness of her position. Malka would be leaving in two or three weeks. Adela had been facing the prospect of learning to live in a totally new environment, with full responsibility for a growing, and recently emotionally scarred, adolescent. At a single, easy stroke — or, at any rate, they'd made it look easy — she'd had her worries cut in half, transferred into the capable hands of these two special people.

To cover her emotion, she drank deeply of her tea, though she wasn't thirsty. Looking up, she found the Kahns and Malka regarding her, the former with benevolent calm, the latter a little anxiously. She gave them all a radiant smile. "I'll bring Yudy down later, Rabbi Kahn, if I may."

He nodded. "That'll be fine. I have to give a *shiur* at eight, though, so don't make it too late, all right? I'd like to have a few minutes to spend with him."

"Sure. As soon as I can dislodge him from the soccer game Aryeh Leib roped him into."

They stood up shortly after that. Adela was strangely reluctant to leave the apartment, the way she might dread stepping out of her own warm house on a frigid, wintry morning. Her mind raced with plans, anticipation. She would find Yudy, tell him about the rabbi, this wonderful Rabbi Kahn, and introduce them. The rest was in God's hands — and in Levi Kahn's.

She was no prophetess, but in the matter of Yudy and the rabbi "clicking," Adela had a very strong feeling. As the good Mrs. Kunslinger might have put it: "No problem."

"Goodbye," Sharona told her at the door, the brown eyes smiling and serious and intent. "I'll get your number from Malka and call you tomorrow."

Adela sighed like a contented child as she stepped out to the elevator after her friend.

No problem at all.

5

It wasn't until that Shabbos that Malka and Esther had their first real chance to talk.

In the four days since Malka's arrival, they had met briefly over Tzippy's hospital bed and once in the apartment as Esther made a lightning dash back home for a change of clothes. Tzippy was still unconscious, lost in a deep, silent world of her own. Beyond the concussion that had led to coma, there had been no internal injuries of a lasting nature; those she had sustained were already healing. The doctors had no real idea as to the reason for the continuing unconsciousness; she might wake at any moment, they informed the girl's parents gravely, or else linger on this way for months...

Savta, due to be released from the hospital in a week or so, was particularly fractious these days, as she fretted in her enforced bed rest. She hated the hospital, the nurses, and, most of all, her own helplessness. She missed the grandchildren and her little room. If she had to submit to the indignities of age and illness, let her own walls and her loved ones be the witnesses and not a pack of strangers.

After a fierce, brief battle of wills, Zalman — by dint of simple, dogged persistence — persuaded his exhausted wife to go home for Shabbos. Esther had perforce to make her way to the apartment late on Friday, to shower and dress and worry about those she'd left behind in the hospital.

Malka, though outwardly cheerful, was secretly horrified by the change in her sister-in-law. Esther had dropped a great deal of weight that she could ill afford to lose. Great dark circles, racoonlike, outlined her eyes. She moved slowly and, at the same time, with a ragged, nervy grace that made the children wary of her. When she took Yoni into her arms for the first time, she hugged him too hard, making him cry. Esther looked ready to cry herself.

"I'm sorry, *matek*," she whispered into the fragrant hair of the freshly bathed baby. "I'm sorry for everything."

Malka took charge. She had cooked most of the Shabbos menu, fighting a belated wave of jet-lag fatigue that kept her at the coffeepot far more often than was good for her. That Friday, seeing the state her sister-in-law was in, she mentally swore off caffeine. One of them had to inject this Shabbos with some measure of serenity, and it didn't look like it was going to be Esther.

When Avi phoned, just before candlelighting, Malka found herself oddly constrained. Flatbush, even her own home, seemed absurdly removed from the concerns that consumed her here. Busy as she had been this week just helping the Markoviches survive, the world outside seemed to fall away, a discarded husk. *This* was reality: this never-ending worry over a comatose girl, this baby who missed his mother, these boys who needed to be kept active and out of trouble, this exhausted niece with the cough that wouldn't go away. The other life had no substance for her, not now.

Also, she hadn't forgotten her husband's remoteness these past weeks. Though the intensity of the last days — as they'd succored the Moseses and prepared for the flight — had erased a little of the tension, she was still off balance with him and uneasy. Their conversation was brief and to the point, a mere exchange of information. Then Esther got on. With his sister, Avi seemed to expand. At any rate, their talk lasted longer and, from what Malka couldn't help overhearing as she bustled about the kitchen with tea kettle and hot tray, plumbed far greater emotional depths.

Resolutely, she tore her thoughts away from the ache that had sprouted, weedlike, in her heart. She had neither the time, nor the mental leisure, for the indulgence of personal worry. There was too much on her plate already right here and now.

Moshe Dovid had returned again from yeshivah. Benzy, having decided to grant his parents' long-standing wish that he and Bracha spend Shabbos with his family in Bnei Brak, Moshe Dovid became, this Shabbos, the man of the house. In his dark suit and air of half-scared solemnity, he recited Kiddush for the family and sliced the huge, braided challah with a surgeon's precision. Batya created a difficult moment when, seeing her oldest brother pour small goblets cups of wine for those seated around the table, she exclaimed, "What about Tzippy? You didn't pour wine for Tzippy!" The feisty first-grader reverted all at once to babyhood, crying and kicking and refusing to be comforted. Watching her flailing in her mother's sad arms, Malka wished that she — just once, just for a moment — could do the same. Just to kick and scream and shout, "Look, everyone, I'm in pain! Somebody, *do* something!"

All Esther could do, in the end, was put her little girl to bed and sit with her until she cried herself to sleep.

The meal picked up a bit after that, though it was far from a merry affair. Malka, as was her custom in tense situations, kept up a determined stream of talk; and Shoshie, following her lead, got the younger children to share what they knew about the weekly Torah portion. Moshe Dovid and his mother were mostly silent, he picking morosely at his food, she in a struggle to keep her eyes — heavy with weariness and sorrow — open till the end of the meal.

She succeeded — barely. Before Malka and Shoshie were halfway through with clearing the table, Esther, mumbling vague, thick-tongued excuses, had stumbled off to her bed. She tried to offer an apology the next morning, but Malka waved it away.

"You need sleep more than anything, Esther. It won't help anyone if you collapse, *chas v'shalom*. You just spend the rest of today in bed, if you want."

Esther yawned. "That sounds wonderful."

The apartment was quiet. Moshe Dovid and the boys had borne a now quiescent Batya off to shul, while Shoshie had taken Yoni along for as long as he would behave. The table had already been set for lunch. A definite peacefulness filled the empty rooms, despite the anxiety that never quite left them. Esther moved uneasily in her armchair. "I keep thinking about poor Zalman, sleeping as best he can on those hard, skinny hospital cots. I wonder how Savta is, and if there's been any change in Tzippy."

As she uttered her daughter's name, Esther's face grew even longer and paler than before. Before Malka's eyes she seemed to shrink into herself. There was a lost air about her, as though something — some wellspring of courage and stamina — had shriveled and died. There was more here than a mother's frantic concern for her child's health.

"Esther," Malka said, twisting on the couch the better to see her sister-in-law, "what is it? I really think it's best that you...well, that you get things off your chest. You'll explode otherwise. I know I'm not the world's best *balebusta*, but I do know how to listen. Try me."

"You're a fine person, Malka." Esther spoke dully, without inflection. "A fine mother. What's the difference if your house doesn't run with tip-top efficiency? You put people before the house. Before *things*. I see it in the way you treat my kids right here. That's the right way."

Malka sat forward, puzzled. "Of course efficiency is important. You want to guess how often I've wished I could manage my house the way you do yours? Why, if I was able to step in and take over here so easily, it's only because you've kept it in such perfect condition that a child could keep it going. You're the best *balebusta* I know."

"A lot of good it does me, being a good *balebusta*," Esther said bitterly. "It got me a child in the hospital!"

"What do you mean?"

"Oh, Malka..." Esther's eyes filled. "I'm such a rotten mother. So rotten... Terrible..."

"Stop it! Esther, are you out of your mind? What are you talking about? You're a terrific mother!"

Slowly, mournfully, Esther shook her head. "No. Not to my Tzippy." She raised her head, as though seeking a reflection of her self-condemnation in the other's eyes. "She was the best daughter a mother could ask for. Always helping, always obedient — a pleasure to have in the house, pure and simple. But did I appreciate her? Did I ever tell her how much she meant to me? Did I ever smile at her and tell her how wonderful she was?" The words came faster now, brutal as slaps to the face. "She got hit by a car because she wanted to call her brothers in for dinner, because *I* was away at the hospital with my mother-in-law and she wanted things to run smoothly — for me. Always for me." She leaned her cheek on her hand, suddenly listless. Her last energy went into a sarcastic, "A fine mother, yes?"

"Yes! You *are* a good mother. We all have times when we take people in our family for granted — and it's usually the good ones that it happens to most. Esther, you've got to get hold of yourself! The other children are depending on you. Tzippy's depending on you!"

A racking laugh was Esther's answer, and a gush of tears she made no attempt to check, and the hollow words "If Tzippy's depending on *me*, then all I can say is, Heaven help her."

Tiredly, silently weeping, she rose from her armchair and wove past couch and table and chairs, drunk with stress, intoxicated with shame, to her room.

Watching her go, Malka bleakly wondered how many tears it took to flood one small apartment.

ﻪﻮﻮﻪ

In distant Flatbush, a flood of a different order had taken place.

That Thursday night, Avi decided to dash home in between the early *ma'ariv* and his *shiur*, to supervise bathtime for his two youngest children. Of what prompted him to such an extraordinary action he had no inkling; Hindy and Shani were more than capable of seeing that the little boys were well-scrubbed. In fact, he'd been avoiding the emptiness of his wifeless home these past few days, burying himself instead in the shul and his classes and his learning. On this Thursday, however, some unexamined urge had him stepping briskly homeward — his car was at the garage undergoing one of its periodic patch-up jobs — through the balmy spring evening.

"Girls, you take care of making Shabbos. I'll see to the baths!" Ignoring his older daughter's dubious look and the younger's startled giggle, he proceeded up the stairs to corral Chaim and Tzvi. He dumped the boys into the tub, turned on the taps ("Not so hot, Tatty!"), and went off to collect the mass of equipment without which, his sons assured him, baths were impossible.

By the time he'd finished gathering the toys and sponges and water blocks and deposited them strategically all around the boys, he was sagging on his feet. Did Malka really do this every other night? When the phone rang he leaped for it with alacrity, glad of the reprieve.

It was Binyomin, phoning to offer him a ride to the *shiur*. Avi gladly accepted; slyly, he invited his friend to come right over, although it was early. The instant the lawyer set foot in the door, he was roped into bath duty.

With the two of them coping together, it wasn't so bad. The problem arose when they stepped out of the damp, misty cubicle to lean against the upstairs balustrade and talk for a minute. The minute stretched to two, until Avi noticed a slow-seeping puddle moving toward them from the direction of the bathroom.

"Flood!" he shouted, running for the door. Binyomin, right behind him, slipped in the water and barely managed, by grabbing hold of the newel post at the last second, to avoid a sound dunking in his wool business suit.

"Chaim, Tzvi, what do you think you're doing?" Avi bellowed.

"Turning on the water, Ta," Chaim said innocently. "We didn't have enough in here."

"Why not? The tub was nearly full just a minute ago."

"Yes, but that was before some spilled out."

"And *why*," the father growled, "did it spill out?"

It was Tzvi who answered. "We were swimming, Ta. Don't you know you have to splash when you swim? Look." He proceeded to demonstrate. Another inch or so joined the lake on the bathroom floor.

Binyomin was laughing so hard he nearly slipped again. With a resigned sigh, and a muttered, "Remind me never to do this again," Avi went for the mop.

But he was laughing, too, by the time they got into Binyomin's car. "Those kids," he said, shaking his head. "They're too much."

"They're sweet. So what do you hear from Malka?"

"Not enough." He'd been startled and a little astonished to find how much he missed her. The house was actually neater these days with Hindy's firm hand on the tiller, but something seemed to have gone out of the place. Its heart was missing.

The rabbi glanced sideways at his friend with sudden new understanding. Was this how Binyomin felt all the time — spinning rudderless in circles, like a ship asea without a hope of safe harbor?

The thought was disturbing; the more so, because there was no way Avi could express it without sounding pitying. So he asked instead, "Any word from the police?"

"They've got their eye on Andy Malone. Just one false move, that's all they need. They haven't turned up any unexplained corpses yet, though in New York that's not so surprising." Binyomin hesitated, eyes on the road. "If Yudy would agree to testify, they could indict him on the harassment charge and pursue the manslaughter thing. As it is — "

"His mother will never agree to that." Avi spoke from knowledge; he'd already discussed the option with Adela before her flight to Israel. "She won't expose him to publicity and possible revenge-taking later, and I can't say I blame her there."

"Me, neither." Binyomin was silent, seemingly intent on maintaining the proper distance between his own front fender and the rear bumper of the car in front. In reality, he was completely absorbed in tamping down the upsurge of pain that the reminder of Adela had brought with it. It was nothing new, the pain, and yet it had the power to hurt afresh every time. "Anyway," he continued firmly, "they're sure to nail him on some other charge, sooner or later. He's into all sorts of nefarious schemes, our Andy. It's simply a question of biding our time. The cat will get his mouse."

But how long could Adela and Yudy afford to wait, banished from their ordinary lives? From the short account Avi had had from Malka, in their single phone conversation the day after her arrival in Jerusalem, he knew that the Moseses had found an apartment in his sister's neighborhood. That was all. He'd call again tomorrow, before Shabbos. Maybe there was more news. It would be good to hear it — especially if it was Malka who was doing the telling.

Binyomin slowed down at a red light and asked, "How's your niece doing? Any change?"

Which brought him to Tzippy, and her long sleep, and the way the rest of his sister's family was coping — and so, right back around again to Malka.

It was only the need to divest himself of self as he began to deliver his *shiur* — to step into his rabbi persona even as he stepped up onto the shul dais and focus every particle of concentration on the subject matter at hand — that Avi managed to put his absent wife out of his mind for a while. To the audience, listening raptly to the words that flowed so freely from his lips, he was a perfect example of leadership, a teacher par excellence.

Only Avi himself knew that, above and beyond all else, tonight he was just a very lonely man.

6

Another Shabbos had come and gone. The Markovich household was running as smoothly as might be expected, given the circumstances. Malka rose each morning with the birds that greeted the dawn — in fact, it was the birds that woke her with their incessant chattering — and went about the business of keeping the place running for another day. Slowly she was learning to recognize the products she wanted in the local *makolet* and the faces of some of her neighbors. She could sniff the cholent from her bed on Shabbos mornings and tell by the texture of the aroma how well it had cooked overnight, just like at home.

Yoni seemed quite content in her care, and was daily adding new words to his vocabulary. He'd taken his first step just yesterday. Batya, if no happier than before, had had no more disturbing outbursts. With the natural resilience of children, Aryeh Leib and Eli had reverted almost to normal, which meant they'd stopped moping around the house and had returned wholeheartedly to the ongoing soccer game below.

All the children's schools were reciting *tehillim* for their sister, and Tzippy's family and classmates had prepared barrages of "get well soon" cards, which decked every available space in the patient's room — and which she never saw.

‹⁂›

Esther glanced at her watch as she once again boarded the bus for the hospital. Her life had become circumscribed by a medical routine, bounded by a particular bus line, the interior of a cab, and two hospital rooms. She could hardly remember a time when illness and disaster had not played a role in her life — more, had completely taken it over.

Dimly, she recalled Bracha's engagement party and the joy she'd felt then in contemplating the future. If she would have known of the two-fisted blow of fate lying in wait for her, would she still have smiled so happily that evening?

Riding the bus, Esther leaned her head on the window pane and half-dozed. Old scenes rose up in her mind's eye and some impossible ones. Everywhere, Tzippy intruded. In every memory she was there, looming much larger than life, for in reality she'd been self-effacing. The memories tortured Esther with tantalizing views of what could have been: she might have put her arms around her daughter *that* time, or offered a word or praise *then*. Her mind played the trick of double vision, reminding her of what was, and then showing what might have been.

It was a grim lesson for a woman to learn at any time, let alone when her daughter was lying still and cold in a coma. It was especially hard for Esther, so used to having things her way, to assessing herself so eminently right in all her judgments. Daily, desperately, she tried to recapture her sense of self-worth. It was a grueling struggle, and most of the time she lost. The mother grew daily grayer and more wasted with the effort.

She entered the hospital portals unseeing, so familiar had this journey become. Turn left for the elevators; ride up to the fifth floor to look in on

Savta, Zalman seated beside her with his *sefer* looking like a monument to patience itself. (His idle hands still looked strange to her. It had been weeks since her husband had picked up a quill — or earned a penny; when Malka had tucked a check from Avi into her hand, Esther was forced to swallow her pride and utter no word of protest.) Sometimes there were doctors to talk to. Savta's physician was thin, wiry, sallow, with a fierce intelligence shining from dark, dark eyes. Tzippy's doctor resembled nothing so much as a prosperous businessman, with plumpish jowls — very close-shaven — and large, well-tended white hands that stuck out of his spotless white coat. Both radiated competence and confidence; Esther felt really comfortable with neither of them. But then, these days she wasn't feeling very comfortable with herself.

Tzippy's bed was on the seventh floor. To reach it, Esther walked along a bustling corridor, past parents and children in various states of action and inaction. Instinctively, as she entered Tzippy's still, silent domain, she slowed her step; even the clicking of her heels sounded overloud here.

Nothing ever changed in this room. The flowers, perhaps, delivered dutifully from time to time by sad-eyed visitors, but that was all. Slowly, timidly almost, Esther approached the bed and looked down at her daughter.

They had shorn her head. All the lovely, red-gold hair was gone, except where it grew in tender new tufts around the bandages. Tzippy's eyes were closed, the lashes casting a faint shadow on her lightly freckled cheeks. A golden girl, thought Esther, feeling the old ache in her throat and fighting the tears it portended. An angel. She pulled a chair up to the bed, gently, as though Tzippy might be disturbed by the noise, and sat.

First she brought out the *tehillim*, so worn from constant use at hospital bedsides lately that the binding was beginning to come loose at the edges. Her pleas rose so accustomed to her lips as to be almost mechanical. There was a tinge of despair to her prayers now that had not been there before.

When she closed the little book at last and tucked it into her bag, the silence drew in again. *Talk to her*, the doctors had urged. *No one knows exactly what a patient in a coma hears or knows. Talk to her. Ask her questions. Tell her about your day.*

Esther took a deep breath and began.

She started, as always, self-consciously. She felt silly, the way one does when speaking into a tape recorder in an empty room. Soon, however, the strangeness wore off, and she was speaking more naturally.

"...and the wedding's been set for June twenty-third, Tzippy. That's about six weeks from now. Bracha and Benzy have taken a nice hall not too far away from our house. I'm sure you'll be there to see them get married, together with the rest of the family." She paused, then went on to tell of some new trick of Yoni's, as related to her by Malka, and to pass on Batya's command that she "get well quick and come home already. The room's so lonely without you!"

The plaintive message triggered a response in Esther that she couldn't ignore. And why should she? What was the point of fighting the despair, of holding the insistent tears at bay, when there was no one to see?

No one but a sleeping girl, just inches away from her, but as far away as it was possible to be. She scraped the chair a little closer to the bed and spoke in a softer voice, as though to confide in her daughter the way she'd never done in real life.

"I feel like crying again, Tzippaleh. These days, I feel like crying most of the time. It's because of you, my darling. Here you lie, day after day, and I feel like you never even knew how much I care about you. Years we had together, twelve long years, and I never found the time to tell you. Do you know, Tzippy? Have you any idea how you light up a room just by walking into it?

"I remember, when you were very small, Abba used to joke that your hair could take the place of any three light bulbs. He was right. Only it's not your beautiful hair that does it. Here's proof: they've cut off your hair, but the room is still full of that special light — Tzippy light. All it needs is one little smile from you, my dear, and the light would be too blinding to bear!"

The girl slept on, cool and unmoving. In sudden, overwhelming weariness Esther lowered her face into her hands. The next words came out muffled.

"I never told you any of this, Tzippy. I was always too busy. There was always something waiting to be done and not enough time to do it in. Now we have time. You have time to sleep — and I, to sit here watching you, day after day, and wonder why in the world I was always in such a tearing hurry...

"*Tzippy*. Did I ever tell you why I chose that name for you? Shoshie and Bracha were named for relatives, but yours I picked out myself. I was in the hospital — this very hospital, in fact. You'd just been born. I lay in my bed feeling very tired and very happy, and you lay beside me, sleeping. Sleeping... The sun was pouring through the window, falling on your head and making your hair look more red than gold, and a bird suddenly flew by, making a little shadow on the glass. Then it circled around and landed on the sill. And I smiled at it, a foolish smile, just because I had my baby girl by me and was happy, and I said, '*Shalom, tzipporah*.' That was when I knew I was going to call you that — Tzipporah. Tzippy."

She lifted her head, and her face was wet. A nurse wheeled a trolley briskly down the corridor and past the half-open door of the room. There was a burst of laughter from somewhere nearby, abruptly broken off. Bits of bright blue sky colored the window. The world outside was sealed away behind thick glass, mute and powerless. Inside, there was only silence and sleep.

Esther's eyes rested on her immobile daughter. In her stillness, Tzippy might have been carved from stone. Esther wished she could say the same of her own heart. It was too heavy — just too heavy to bear. How had she fallen so far and so fast, she who had always prided herself on being so utterly in control? Was that her sin, that she'd had the audacity, the hubris, to think control was possible? "Forgive me," she whispered to the One who wields the strings from afar. "I didn't know..."

The pain, the exhaustion, and the guilt joined in a mocking triumvirate. She felt herself defeated.

"Tzippy," she said in a low, uneven voice. "The warm one, the helping one, a girl in a million. I never told you, did I, how I hold you in my heart" — she placed a hand on her chest, heaving now with dry sobs — "here. You can sleep a thousand years, and you'll always be here, Tzippaleh. But I wish

— oh, how I wish you'd wake up already, so I can tell you myself! I wish you could hear me finally!" In a sudden agony of frustration, she cried, "Oh, Tzippy, do you have any idea how much I want you back?"

She subsided into quiet, face buried again in the black canyon of her fingers. Minutes passed, uncounted and unheeded. There was a strange comfort in the position. She was in a darkness of her own devising, swimming in a little pool of her own grief. How peaceful it was. She might never lift her face again.

But lift it she did at last, as she'd known she would. She was Esther Markovich, after all, and Esther Markovich was nothing if not responsible. It was time to get up and go back down to Savta, to give Zalman the chance to sit with his daughter. Wearily she rose to her feet, casting a last glance at Tzippy.

She stood transfixed.

The girl's eyes had opened. Tzippy looked at the wall by her bed in a puzzled, unfocused way, then turned her head and saw her mother. A smile, shy and radiant, crept into her face.

"Ima," she said, her voice hoarse from not speaking so long. "Ima, I had the most beautiful dream." A delicate blush suffused the pallor of her cheeks with soft rose. "You were in it. You said the most beautiful things to me."

Esther stood frozen for an eternity. Words were an impossibility. Action was out of the question. She had entered a dimension where she could be passive only, a mere vessel — recipient of a miracle.

"Ima?" Tzippy said again. She sounded a little frightened. "Are you all right? You look funny."

The spell was broken. "I'm fine, darling," Esther said, flinging herself down on her chair and seizing both of the girl's cold hands. "Oh, Tzippy — "

"What, Ima?"

"I...love you."

Tzippy smiled beatifically and heaved a sigh of utter contentment.

"Just like my dream," she said.

FOURTEEN

1

Malka brought a surprise back home with her from Israel.

The first inkling Avi had of it came together with his first sight of his wife, barreling a laden luggage cart to the arrivals' welcoming area. Something seemed not quite right to him. Through the glass partition he watched her uneven progress, subduing his gladness in mental effort. What was wrong with this picture?

Then he had it. There were too many suitcases on the cart.

"Avi!" Malka had seen him. Waving wildly, she nearly lost control of the cart, which veered to the left and was only just in time prevented from crashing into a blue-haired old woman to her left. The girl who had done the preventing looked familiar somehow. Avi's eyes widened.

Malka nodded jubilantly. "Yes!" she mouthed through the glass. Then she was passing through the door and following the mountain of luggage right to where he was standing.

"Is that Shoshie?" he managed to ask.

"Yes! Shoshie, come and say hello to Uncle Avi." Malka twinkled. "How'd you know it wasn't Bracha? You never could tell them apart before."

"Of course he knew, Aunt Malka," Shoshie said, overcoming her sudden shyness at meeting her uncle again. "Would Bracha leave Israel a month before her own wedding?"

"Oh, you're too logical, both of you." Malka dismissed the logic with a shrug. "Well, Avi? Aren't you surprised?"

"Flabbergasted."

"I've brought her to stay with us for three weeks or so. She'll get back just in time for the wedding. We're going shopping tomorrow for a gorgeous dress, aren't we, Shosh?"

Shoshie nodded, smiling in a dazed sort of way. She had been feeling exactly that — dazed — ever since her aunt had informed her and her parents that she intended to bring Shoshie back home with her. The announcement had been made on the day after Tzippy's recovery, in her hospital room, where she was staying a little longer for observation.

Malka had been determined. "I'm going to see if I can get a seat for her on my flight. How excited the kids will be to see her!"

Esther had protested, and Zalman had worried about the cost of a ticket. But Malka was adamant.

"Take a good look at her, both of you," she ordered. "Wasted away to nothing. She's a *kallah moid*, too, you know. Want to get her married off one of these days? Then let me take her back for a real vacation. A little time to relax, with no responsibilities. A chance to throw off this stupid cold and put the roses back in her cheeks. Don't you think she deserves it?"

"Of course she deserves it," Zalman had said warmly. "I don't know what we would have done without her. What with Bracha running around getting ready for the wedding, not to mention also going to Bnei Brak to look for an apartment, there was no one but Shoshie to see to the kids and the house. Deserve it? Is that a question?" He sighed. "But to accept the price of a plane ticket — that's too much, Malka."

But his sister-in-law insisted that it wasn't too much, and in the end she'd prevailed. There was no gainsaying the truth of her comments about Shoshie's indifferent health or lackluster looks. The girl obviously needed a change, and three weeks with her aunt and uncle in New York certainly qualified.

It was Tzippy, though, who tilted the balance. If the girl had asked for the moon, just then, her mother and father would gladly have undertaken to steal it out of the sky for her. When she said, lying back on her pillows with a smile for her big sister, "You do look kind of tired, Shoshie. I think you should go. I'll be all better by the time you get back, and we can dance together at Brachie's wedding," the matter was settled. Shoshie was going.

She gazed around the enormous airport now, excited and a little apprehensive. This was her first time away from home. The trip had meant that she would miss her high-school graduation, but all her friends had agreed that this was too good a chance to pass up. Having dropped out of the scene at school for such a long time by then, the old connection had already in large measure been broken. The thought of what she might miss caused her hardly a pang beside the enormity of the adventure awaiting her.

Malka gave her arm a squeeze. "We're going to have such fun, Shoshie! It's only three weeks, but we'll cram in as much as we can in that time. I promise you, this will be one vacation you'll never forget."

Prophetic words, though neither the woman nor the girl had any idea of that yet.

And then they were home, and sitting in the living room after a long, noisy, and satisfying dinner. Avi had canceled his classes for that night, and Malka decided she wasn't in the mood to unpack yet. The younger ones were allowed to stay up late, revelling in their mother's presence and getting acquainted with their cousin from Jerusalem.

There were also the Israeli toys to learn about, after they were dragged helter-skelter from Malka's suitcase. Hindy had carefully orchestrated the homecoming, slaving for days to bring the house up to her own scrupulous standards in time for her mother's arrival and to cook her a welcome-back dinner that ranked with the finest. The food was duly appreciated, but five minutes of Malka's gaping luggage and her little ones' boisterous welcome destroyed the neatness as if it had never been. Somewhat to her own surprise, Hindy found that she hardly cared. She was too happy having her mother home again.

She was also intrigued by her cousin. It was quickly decided that Shani would bunk with her two small brothers, so that Shoshie could have her bed. Hindy was thrilled with her new roommate, even when Shoshie — after a series of face-splitting yawns — admitted that she wanted nothing more that night than to sleep around the clock.

"Three weeks," Hindy gloated, watching her older cousin rummage in her suitcase for pajamas and a robe. For three glorious weeks, sixteen would have eighteen all to herself. Getting to know her would be a little like peeking into her own future — a tantalizing prospect. Let Shoshie sleep all she wanted now; Hindy planned to keep busy enough informing all her friends by phone of the wonderful surprise her mother had sprung on them. She could already imagine their reactions.

"Sounds just like your mother," her best friend would giggle. And Hindy would pretend to groan and roll her eyes, while privately agreeing, with a secret thrill of pride, that it did. For all her failings, Rebbetzin Weisner — Ma — was okay!

❧◦❧

"Let's take a walk," Malka said suddenly. Shani had led the boys off to bed at last, and the house had grown drowsy and quiet. The sounds of her own home hummed all around her with reassuring predictability, but Malka felt edgy, unable to enjoy them. Minutes before, the clock on the piano had chimed its ten strangled chimes. With the time difference between New York and Israel, she should have been dropping from exhaustion. Instead, she felt wired, tingly with the need for action.

"That's fine with me," Avi said. "But aren't you tired?"

"I need to stretch my legs. That flight was deadly."

"Crowded?" Avi asked, getting up and going for their coats.

"I'll say. And someone's baby, in the row behind us, didn't stop screaming the entire time. Ah," she said, breathing deeply of the soft spring air as she stepped outside. "Lovely, lovely pollution. Just what I've been dreaming of all these weeks."

Her husband, smiling, fell in beside her. Automatically, almost of their own accord, his feet turned in the direction of the shul. "How was it, really?" he asked, serious now.

"Awful, at first. I survived by simply making up my mind that my life was on hold for a while. When you don't expect to relax or enjoy yourself, you don't feel disappointed. I expected to work, and work I did."

"But not more than you do at home."

"Not more — but all different. Someone else's children, someone else's kvetches, different products, different appliances — different everything! On the surface of things, I was doing just what I do at home, but I was on alien territory." She paused. "And then, behind everything, was the worry about Tzippy."

"*Baruch Hashem*," he said fervently, and she quietly echoed his words. They walked on in silence.

There were few people out on the streets. Despite Malka's flippant remark, the air was remarkably clear for New York. Silver stars sparked the night sky over the sprawl of homes and trees. Nearer at hand, the breeze set up a sibilant rustle in the leaves that hung above their heads like a canopy.

"I missed you," Avi said.

She glanced at him, inscrutable in the darkness, and continued walking. "Did you?"

"You sound surprised."

"Well," she drew a breath, "you certainly weren't seeking out my company for a while before I left. You hardly talked to me at all — really talked to me, I mean."

There. The words that she'd wanted for so long to say were out. Now that she'd spoken them, she wondered why she'd lacked the courage before.

The answer was clear to her even before the question was fully articulated in her mind: it was Israel, and what she'd lived through there, that had changed things. Changed her. For three difficult weeks in Jerusalem, she had been the strong one, efficient beyond her wildest dreams, and the center of warmth around whom the Markoviches had clung in their need; and she had seen her formidable sister-in-law wracked by a sense of her own inadequacies. Long-cherished beliefs had fallen by the wayside, and a new conviction of her own worth crept in to replace them.

Black and white comparisons and seesaw superiority — "you're up and I'm down" — had given way to a more compassionate grasp of what it means to be human. Malka had flown out there to lend a helping hand and had flown back feeling that she'd helped herself most of all.

There was silence between them, but she refused to be the one to break it. It was his turn now.

"Malka," he said, with obvious difficulty, "I don't think you realize what that whole...Mirsky business...meant to me. How...painful it was."

"I guessed," she said. "But you never told me."

"I know. I couldn't talk about it." He stopped. "I still don't find it easy to talk about it."

They had reached the shul. Avi hesitated at the door, looking inquiringly at his wife. She took the cue. "Want to sit down for a few minutes?"

The place was empty. After the last *ma'ariv* service, the *gabbai* had locked up and gone home. Malka stood in the doorway as her husband fumbled for the light switch. She'd never seen the shul dark before. The absence of light made the place seem unfamiliar, investing it with the weight of the unknown. Then the light went on, flooding the pews and bookcases and the ark in a wash of gold. Someone had suggested once that fluorescent lighting would be cheaper, but the rabbi had always insisted on yellow lights. They were warmer, he'd said. At the time, Malka had been glad of his decision.

She was still glad now, following him inside. A mantle lay over the shul along with the light: echoes of the thousands of prayers that had been spoken within those walls. Here, in the hush left over after the worshippers had gone, was that which is balm to the tortured spirit. Some of the peace filtered through to the couple sitting on the hard benches, but not enough. Not nearly enough. Malka waited.

Groping for words, very far from his usual articulate self, Avi began to talk. Long and earnestly he spoke — of the Mirsky affair and the humiliation he'd suffered through it; of the painful shattering of his smug self-image; and then, haltingly, of the lesson in humility and humanity he'd culled from the wreckage. As he talked, it seemed to Malka that doors were opening up, and windows, letting in fresh winds of tender understanding so long denied entrance. The shul seemed redolent with a new fragrance, and a sweetness hung in the very air around them.

When he'd fallen still at last, she said simply, "Thank you."

He relaxed, but something of a frown lingered in his eyes. He didn't tell her about his resolution to rectify the flaw of pride by selflessly giving himself to Yudy Moses. For, somewhere in his recital, he had recognized — suddenly and with a jolt of dismay — that that very desire bespoke a concern with the ego he sought to diminish. What had he hoped for, in throwing himself into the crusade, but to salvage the remnants of his tattered pride — to find a way to live comfortably with himself again?

And still beyond that: what did his withdrawal from his wife tell, but the ongoing story of his need to nurse his bruised ego in solitude? Had he really thrown it to the winds, there would have been no hesitation in turning to her and accepting the gift of her compassion.

There was much work yet to be done, he saw, before he came to the end — if he ever did, if a person ever could — of his own deepest nature.

Malka was watching him, wondering at his continued absorption. Rousing himself, Avi asked with a twinkle, "Now do you believe me?"

"About what?"

"That I missed you. Who else could I have told all that to?"

She didn't smile back. Slowly, she said, "You hardly ever talked to me like this before. I felt like I was hardly more than a housekeeper to you." As he was moved to protest, she made an impatient gesture and said, "Oh, I know, I know. You're going to say I was a lot more. I know I was. Am. But on the emotional level, you'll have to admit that you've always locked me out. The more important a thing is to you, the more withdrawn you get."

He bowed his head in acknowledgement.

"It's all connected — the pride and the silence. I couldn't bear not to have you think well of me."

"Well, here's a lesson for you about women, Rabbi," the *rebbetzin* said spiritedly. "We can't bear not be let in. We want more than anything to be allowed up close — to give our husbands sympathy and to help them — even if they're not smelling their most savory at the moment!"

"I guess...I was smelling pretty bad right then." Here it was, the confession he'd refused her before — the plea, and the test.

Malka passed with flying colors. She may have been no mighty intellectual, but there were some things she knew without even trying. No gifted linguist, a call to the heart was something she always had the language to answer.

"Bad? Maybe," she told him. "But when it comes to the men we love, we women might as well not have noses."

There was more after that, but it was inconsequential stuff, mere idle murmurings to while away the stroll home. The important things had already been said, under a wash of golden light in the empty shul, with only the holy ark as witness.

Malka was happy on that walk home, as she had not been happy in a long time. So much so, that she hardly reacted at all — and certainly not with the dismay her husband had expected — when he stopped abruptly at their front door and said, "Oh, I nearly forgot to tell you! Malka, Mutty spoke to me last night. You're not going to like this. In fact, I'm not sure how much I like it myself."

"What?"

"It seems he was deeply impressed by his stay in Yerushalayim. For him, it was more than just a couple of months of learning in a different setting. The place seems to have spoken to him, somehow, in a way he didn't anticipate." He held her eyes, and there was compassion in his gaze. "He wants to go back there, Malka."

"Back? To Israel?"

"Yes."

"For how long this time?"

"Indefinitely."

2

It was never really clear who suggested the *shidduch*. For years afterwards, a lively controversy would rage between Malka and Mutty, as each claimed the honor. The only fact both agreed on was that the idea emerged from a conversation on the Weisner back porch, as Shoshie romped with Chaim and Tzvi on the swing set below.

"She's good with kids," Malka remarked to her son, who sat at the small wicker table on the back porch with his Gemara.

He looked up, eyes unfocused. "What?"

"Shoshie. Isn't she wonderful with the boys?"

"Oh? Uh — yes. Wonderful!" His eyes returned to the Gemara.

Malka was sitting in the sunny part of the porch with a basket of mending, the picture of wifely virtue. Actually, she'd done considerably more sunbathing than sewing in the ten minutes she'd been sitting there. "Comes from being part of a large family, I suppose."

Once again, Mutty tore his concentration away from his learning to attend to his mother. "What was that?"

"I said she's probably got all that experience from being part of a large family."

"*I* come from a large family, and I don't particularly care for fooling around with a pack of grubby kids."

"Those grubby kids," Malka reminded him, "happen to be your brothers. Aren't you going to miss them when you go?" A new element had crept into her voice.

He said with studied casualness, "Sure I will."

"Besides," Malka went on with determined bravery, "she's a girl."

"Who is? Shoshie?"

"Who else are we discussing? Now tell me, isn't she looking wonderful? Healthy, and so much more relaxed, and it's only been three days." She shook her head. "You should have seen her in Israel. A bundle of nerves."

"I can imagine." Idly, he began smoothing the pages of his Gemara. "She was pretty unhappy even before all the disaster struck. About Bracha, I mean, and Benzy."

"Oh?" Malka looked interested.

Briefly, he outlined the state of affairs between the Markovich twins in the era immediately preceding their grandmother's stroke. "It's a good thing they straightened it all out before the old lady got sick, and then Tzippy's accident. The way it turned out, Bracha was already engaged, and Benzy was there to support her. And she and Shoshie were on speaking terms again."

"How'd they finally straighten it out?"

"That was Fish, actually." He grinned, struck by the recollection.

Before she could ask where Fischel Mann came into the picture, he went on to explain about the letter. "Bracha took his advice. She wrote Shoshie a letter, and it seemed to do the trick. He seemed to understand Shoshie pretty well." He chuckled. "Never knew old Fish was a psychologist."

"You don't have to be a psychologist to understand people." Malka spoke absently, her unseeing eyes fixed on Shoshie at the swing. Her expression was thoughtful.

Sometime in the next few minutes, in a dialogue that took place in increasingly excited whispers and undertones, the idea was hatched — though who, exactly, hatched it remains hotly contested to this day. There's no disputing the fact, however, that Mutty was the one who went inside to phone Fish.

❧

"Shoshie? You mean your cousin from Israel? Shoshie *Markovich*?"

"Right on all three counts. Well, what do you think? I don't have to plug her. You already know what she's like. I guess you've seen her at her best and her worst, Fish."

"I'm...taken aback." This was a gross understatement. Mutty, lolling at his ease in his living room at home, had no idea of the look of utter bemusement that had reduced Fish's expression to something that gave him a close resemblance to his namesake. "I...I'll have to think about it, Mutty. Did she — " his vocal cords seemed to have developed engine trouble. He cleared his throat and tried again. "Did she agree?"

"I'm asking you first. My mother says that's the way to do these things. To save the girl the disappointment of being rejected, I guess."

What about the guy's disappointment?

"I've never gone out before. I have to think."

Mutty urged, "So think. But do it fast. She's only here for three weeks. More like two and a half by now."

"I'll talk to my parents and think it over. I'll get back to you as soon as I can." A pause. "Thanks, Mutty."

"Don't mention it. I just figured that here's your chance to spread a little sunshine. If you agree to see my cousin, you'll be making your parents happy, me happy, and my mother happy. Not to mention Shoshie, probably."

Not to mention me, Fish thought. But he didn't say it aloud.

⤲⤳

A flurry of phone calls between Avi Weisner — who'd been drafted by his wife in the good cause of matchmaking — and his sister and brother-in-law in Israel, ended by confirming the decision already tentatively reached by the two young people involved. Fish and Shoshie would meet. With Avi vouching for the boy and his family, her parents felt secure in approving the match.

"Have you said anything to Shoshie yet?"

"Yes, Malka has. The few times she saw Fish at your place, Shoshie seems to have been favorably impressed. She says she'd like to meet him again."

Esther, remembering her daughter's dismal record with *shidduchim* to date, was heartened. What with one thing and another, Shoshie had been laboring under a great deal of stress lately. If she was showing interest in a *shidduch* again, it could only be a favorable sign.

Their first date seemed inundated with favorable signs. The stars shone brilliantly in a sky that appeared to have grown blacker and clearer than Fish, driving to the Weisners in his father's gray Cadillac, ever remembered seeing it. Then, accepting a glass of juice from Malka while waiting for Shoshie to appear, it slipped from his fingers and crashed to splinters on the floor.

"*Mazel tov*," quipped Mutty.

"Ha, ha," Fish answered mechanically. He stuck a finger in his tie to loosen its stranglehold. "This feels weird. I mean, I must have been in this house a hundred times, and here I am all dressed up like a stuffed dummy — "

"You said it," Mutty grinned, "not me."

"— waiting for your cousin, who I've also seen a dozen times, to come downstairs all dressed up for a date." He shook his head. "Weird."

"Don't be nervous," Malka said comfortably. She held out another brimming glass of juice. "Here, drink up."

Shoshie came down then, dressed in a new, forest-green summer knit her aunt had helped her purchase only the day before.

She was unaccountably bashful, saying "hello" to her cousin's friend, who'd been in and out of her parent's apartment for two whole months that winter while she sulked over her sister's usurpation of her *shidduch*. Earlier, getting ready for the date in the room she shared with Hindy, she'd alternated between cringing embarrassment at the memory of the way she'd behaved then and mounting curiosity about the person who'd plumbed her motives so accurately in explaining that behavior to Bracha. Each time, the curiosity, and the respect, had proved the stronger. Fish was a question mark — an intriguing one. How had he understood her so well, before he even really knew her?

She would have to get to know him better, to find out.

They got to know each other, the two of them, through two whirlwind weeks in early June that took them across the length and breadth of New

York City and into the emotional recesses of their own and each other's natures. Malka and Avi were excited, and Fish's parents, and Hindy and Mutty — and most of all, Esther and Zalman, hanging over the phone in distant Jerusalem. Twice, four times, six times they met, and each time Shoshie returned with brighter eyes, Fish with a springier step.

When they weren't out together they were on the telephone, talking quietly into the small hours about everything in the world. At the end of two weeks, just days before Shoshie was due to fly back home, Fish made reservations at a good restaurant in the city. Shoshie dressed in her nicest lightweight outfit, the one that made her feel as though she were floating — though she didn't really need any help in *that* area these days. Bidding farewell to the Weisners, the couple slipped into the steel-gray Cadillac and sped off toward the twinkling lights of Manhattan.

Fish had planned to make his speech over dessert, but in the end it happened quite suddenly, in the eternity between placing their order and waiting for the waiter to crawl back with it. He looked at Shoshie over the single candle in the center of the table and said without preamble, "What are we waiting for?"

She smiled radiantly. "I accept."

By the time the waiter returned with a pitcher of water for their table, he found nothing there but a hefty tip and a note.

Sorry, Fish had scribbled on a scrap of paper. *I guess we weren't that hungry after all.*

3

There were phone calls to be put through, and Fish's family to be presented to, and plans — so many plans! — to be made. Shoshie felt like a sleepwalker. There was a dreamlike quality to her existence now, as though she were floating through some clear, fluid medium. The medium, she knew, was happiness.

It was sheer bliss breaking the news to her parents, accepting their *mazel tovs* and laughing with them, in wonder, at the suddenness, the speed, of her engagement. There was joy in discussing every angle of the incredible business with Malka and Hindy for hours on end. But the biggest happiness of all lay in being with Fish and in devising their plans for a lifetime. They had already developed, in this short time together, a vocabulary of their own, which they used to build a verbal model of their future. It was the dearest hope of both that that model would, someday soon, come to embody the material shape and form of reality.

She'd been nervous about meeting his parents, but Yechezkel Mann was at his most genial, and Rachel was bubbling with a welcoming warmth. If the father was disappointed to hear that the young couple planned to live in Israel for a few years so that Fish could continue his study of Torah, he gave no sign. It was enough, for the present at any rate, to see his son suitably and happily engaged. One could see him almost visibly restraining himself from weighing in with his opinions; see the wheels of his mind slowly churning out the words "one thing at a time."

The first and most practical necessity was, again, making travel arrangements. Malka, deep in consultation with her agent, marvelled at the sudden primacy of planes in their lives. The airport had become a second home to them, Israel as familiar as their own backyard.

The flight was booked. Shoshie was to fly on ahead, this Saturday night, to give her a chance to help prepare for Bracha's wedding; and also, it was understood, to personally fill her parents in on the details of her courtship and her betrothed.

Fish would follow her in another week, just in time to attend the wedding. He would remain ten days. It would be an opportunity for him and his future wife's family to get reacquainted from a whole new perspective. Before, he had been a hungry yeshivah *bachur* coming round in hope of a square meal. A future son-in-law was another thing entirely!

☙◦❧

Binyomin heard about the engagement peripherally, as it were. He happened to drop in on the Weisners on the day after it was announced. He found the house bustling with gaiety.

It was Shani who told him the news about her cousin and her brother's best friend and of the breathtaking rapidity with which the whole thing had come to fruition.

Binyomin nodded sagely and said from the peak of lonely experience, "Yes, that's the way it goes sometimes. Quick as lightning." Firmly, he squelched the flare of hurt inside. The pain was becoming a familiar thing now and more easily subdued.

Malka, emerging from the kitchen with floury hands, ecstatic smile, and phone to her ear, stopped long enough to say hello and impart the news that the *vort* was scheduled to take place the next night, a Thursday. "They have to squeeze it in before Shoshie flies back," she chuckled. "Fish's parents insisted. Let Shoshie's parents do what they want in Israel, they said; *they're* going to throw the party of the year right here."

"Not much notice," he said, smiling. "Is his mother up to it? There'll be a lot of organizing to do, I imagine."

"Oh, Rochel Mann's a whiz at that kind of thing. She'll be in her element." In a lowered voice, she added, "Isn't it wonderful the way things can work out? Here's Esther and Zalman with hardly two pennies to rub together, over their heads in debt just getting Bracha married — and Shoshie goes and gets herself engaged to the son of a wealthy man. There'll be no negotiations about who pays for the apartment in *this* match!"

"Yes," he agreed. "Things do work out sometimes."

"*Im yirtzeh Hashem* by you, Binyomin. Soon."

"Amen," he said lightly, and turned to go.

His secretary looked up from her word processor as he strode into the office very late on the following afternoon, after a drawn-out courthouse appointment.

"Still here?" he asked. "It's after five."

"I waited for you, Mr. Hirsch. The D.A.'s office called." She did not trouble to conceal her curiosity.

His reaction was merely a lifted brow, but his hands shook slightly as he picked up the phone in his own inner office and punched in the number. In short order, he was connected to his contact — one Jack Nelson, an assistant district attorney who'd befriended him after a recent grand-larceny trial, one of Binyomin's first cases in New York.

"I think you'd better come down here, Ben," Jack said. "Things are popping."

Binyomin resisted the urge to ask for more information over the phone. "Be there in twenty minutes."

The girl at the computer was startled to see him leave the office again so soon, raincoat flapping and still wet from the June shower that had caught him on his way into the building just minutes earlier. "Leaving already?" she asked, her voice rising to a surprised squeak.

"D.A.'s office," he said tersely. "I have a feeling they've made an arrest."

She nodded and bent her head to her monitor again with a sigh. Calls from the D.A.'s office...arrests... Just wait till she told her mother about this! Who would've guessed, when she got this job, that working for a staid, old legal firm would be so exciting?

∾∾∾

Jack greeted him with a firm handclasp. "Well, they brought him in."

"Malone?"

"Yes. Caught him with possession, about to hit the streets with a dozen or more packets of the stuff in his pockets."

"When was this?"

Nelson looked at his watch. "Oh, maybe an hour ago."

"A little early for a pusher to start doing business, isn't it?"

"Not if you're aiming for the high-school market."

"I see." Binyomin's lips tightened. He glanced around the tiny office, at the dusty bookcases and scarred, metal desk lamp and the window, streaming with rain. "What happens next?"

"We have enough to indict him on the possessions charge. Now, what about the kid? A conviction on manslaughter would put Malone away for a lot longer."

"The longer the better. But the boy's not going to testify. That's definite. In fact, he and his mother have left the country until all this clears up."

Thoughtfully, Nelson said, "Frankly, I don't blame them. If it were a kid of my own..." He shook his head. "I'd push harder, except that we haven't got our hands on the corpse yet — if there *is* a corpse."

"There's that slight problem," the lawyer agreed.

"I hate to see that scum get off scot-free, though, after sticking a knife in someone." Nelson sounded frustrated.

"That," said Binyomin, "is what makes you such a good D.A."

"Assistant D.A., as of present date. Well, we've got him, at least. It's a start. Old Andy'll be off the streets for a while."

"And afterwards?"

"Afterwards, I have a piece of advice for your friend and his mom. I'd suggest they look around for another place to live. No need to be where Malone can look them up when he gets out."

Filled with an enormous relief and a gladness for Adela that even his own personal disappointment could not dilute, Binyomin stood up and extended his hand for a parting shake. "I'll pass it on," he promised. "And Jack?"

"What?"

"Thanks. I owe you one."

As he stepped out into the start of a gray, wet twilight, his first instinct was to make for a phone. Avi would want to hear about this, and Malka.

Then, with a glance at his watch, he realized that the news would have to wait. The Weisners, he remembered, would be leaving to attend an engagement party right about now.

4

It would have been hard to imagine a greater contrast than that which lay between Bracha Markovich's *vort*, some two months earlier, and the party thrown by Yechezkel and Rochel Mann to celebrate their son's engagement to Bracha's sister.

Shoshie had known that Fish was well-off, but she'd never dreamed of the extent to which her betrothed was rolling in the stuff. Her eyes wore a look of perpetual astonishment from the moment she entered the well-appointed hall and got her first glimpse of the buffet. She had never heard of the word "smorgasbord," but it didn't take much imagination to know that here was only a slightly truncated version of actual wedding fare.

The massed variety of meats and drinks, the bewildering profusion of color, the band sawing away in their amplified corner, the jewelry, the perfume, the clothes! Where were her Bais Yaakov classmates in their demure Shabbos dresses, giggling in awe at the newly engaged pair? Never was Shoshie more acutely conscious of the difference between her own family's style of living and Fish's. She experienced a sharp stab of homesickness. She longed for her mother and father, for Bracha and the boys.

Aunt Malka, Uncle Avi, and her cousin Mutty were here tonight, which was a definite help; but they were not enough. Not on such a once-in-a-lifetime evening. To feel herself such a stranger at her own *vort* was a painful thing. It didn't have the power to dim her happiness — nothing could do that — but beneath the joy was something that might almost have been called (if it had not been such a ludicrous thing, with Fish right beside her) loneliness.

After a while, she stopped concentrating on the differences and began noting the things that were the same. The bearded rabbis who rose to speak a few words of Torah were not so very different from the ones who had risen to speak at Bracha's *vort*. The *mazel tovs* were offered in the same tone of sincere warmth; and the expression on the faces of Fish's parents were remarkably similar to the one her own parents had worn on that other occasion. Even young Gedalia reminded her of her own Aryeh Leib: he wore his stiff suit with the same air of resigned discomfort and broke into the same delighted smile when Fish found a few minutes to draw him into the hub of the celebration.

As the strangeness wore off, she found herself enjoying the proceedings immensely. Fish, who had been covertly watching her — reading her mood with the inbuilt antennae he'd seemed to possess ever since the first strains of Beethoven had followed him down a Jerusalem street one memorable evening — breathed a soundless sigh of relief. It was going to be all right.

Toward the end of the affair, when many of the guests had departed and only close friends and family remained along with the tiredly thumping band, Fish and Shoshie drifted together near a window. He was pink and shining from his exertions on the dance floor; her hair was disheveled and her face stretched in a nonstop smile. Her *chasan* smiled, too. "Having fun?"

"It's great. And so beautiful." She hesitated. "Your parents must have spent a fortune tonight, Fish."

He shrugged. "It gives them pleasure, making a big splash for their son. There's only Gedalia and me, you know. Who else should they spend their money on?"

Shoshie had no answer to this, and she could not find the words to frame the uneasiness that persisted whenever she thought of the Mann fortune. When she had accepted Fish as her future husband, she had not fully understood all the ramifications of sudden, dazzling wealth. She was not sure she liked it.

He changed the subject. "Looking forward to going home?"

"I can't wait. Everyone'll be so excited! And then there's Bracha's wedding. There'll be a million things to do."

"I'm sure they'll keep you hopping. First the *aufruf*, then the wedding and *sheva berachos*."

"Yes. Ever since Tzippy recovered, Ima's been flying! I don't know where she gets her energy."

"I hope she'll lend some of it to you. You'll have a lot to do in the next couple of months, Shosh." He looked troubled. "I wish I could be there, to help find an apartment and everything else. It's a lot for you do alone."

"I don't mind." She was still so caught up in the imminence of her twin's wedding that she'd hardly given a thought to her own, tentatively slated for a date in mid-September, some three months off.

"Sure you don't want to change your mind and opt for Lakewood instead?" he asked, only half-joking. "Then *I'd* have the headache of apartment-hunting."

She stared in dismay. "Fish, are you serious? I thought we agreed that Israel —"

"Take it easy — only kidding! You know me, I can adapt to any environment. I'm just used to Lakewood, that's all."

"I want you to tell me, *honestly*, if you really mind living in Israel for a while first. I...I just thought it'd make it easier..."

He was contrite. She was so young, just eighteen, and about to enter on a whole new life, a new set of responsibilities that were bound to weigh heavily on her inexperienced shoulders. The least he could do was stand by his commitment to begin their married life in the city she knew so well, near her parents and just a bus ride away from her twin sister in Bnei Brak. Mentally Fish kicked himself. This was absolutely the last time he would do this to her. Firmly and with finality, he put his private preferences behind him. If he was doing this, he would do it wholeheartedly.

"Honestly?" he repeated. "I liked Israel fine the last time I was there. I'm going to love it now, as long as we're together." There was nothing halfhearted in the smile he gave her. It served to melt away the last shreds of worry from her eyes.

"Okay, then," she said.

"So what're you doing tomorrow, Shosh?"

"First, sleep as late as I can. Then I guess I'll pack and help Aunt Malka get ready for Shabbos. What about you? What time are you leaving?"

"About noon." Some old friends had invited him down to Lakewood for

Shabbos to celebrate at their leisure. It would be their only chance to spend time together anytime soon; the following Saturday night Fish was due to leave for Israel. He peered at her. "Sure it's okay with you? I can still cancel."

"No, I think it's better this way. I ought to spend this last Shabbos with the family. Aunt Malka's been so wonderful, and who knows when I'll see her again?"

"At our wedding, please God. Or didn't you think I'd buy a plane ticket for our *shadchanit?*"

"Oh, Fish!" Her eyes were shining. "You never told me!"

"Your uncle says he intends to fly in for Bracha's wedding, so I don't know if he'll be up for ours. And Mutty's planning to be there anyway. He hopes to come to see Bracha married off, and then stay on. He'll be at the yeshivah for *Elul zeman* with me."

"Oh, I'm so happy! With Mutty and Aunt Malka there, it'll be just right. They'll be the link between my two lives — at home, and here."

He assumed a hurt expression. "I thought *I* was the missing link!"

They were laughing as Mutty strolled over. "What's the joke?"

"Fish says he's the missing link," Shoshie told him.

"Oh, is that it? I always wondered why he looked like that."

Shoshie clasped her hands as if to contain her joy within them. "Mutty, I'm so glad you'll be in Israel next year! You can come to us for Shabbos any time."

Her cousin looked faintly alarmed. "Maybe you'd better take a little time first. You know, to learn your way around the kitchen." He was remembering the disastrous dinner she'd cooked the first time he and Fish had come over to her parents' place.

Fish had called to mind that night, too. He looked around. "Wish we had a piano here. I could use a good dose of music tonight."

Mutty grinned. "There's plenty of music. Loud, too."

"Not Shoshie's music." He turned to his *kallah*. "If you had a piano here right now, what would you play?"

She smiled. "That's easy. It'd have to be something by Mozart — or maybe Haydn. Happy music."

Mutty tactfully wandered away. The young couple talked a while longer in desultory fashion. Then Fish said, "Your flight's at midnight, right?"

"Yes. Uncle Avi and Aunt Malka are taking me to the airport."

"I'll drive up from Lakewood on *motza'ei Shabbos* and meet you there."

"You don't have to, Fish. We could say goodbye tomorrow. And it's only for a week..." But she was smiling.

Plans, plans. They had so many of them, one piled on the other: short-term plans, and long-term, and plans for every minute in between.

Then came Friday afternoon, when all the plans were turned on their heads, like so many clowns in a circus ring.

5

Yechezkel Mann came home from work early that Friday. It was only two o'clock when his key scraped in the lock and the front door heaved slowly open. His wife, in the kitchen supervising the maid in the preparation of a perfect potato kugel, didn't hear a thing. It wasn't until she came out of the kitchen, flushed from the oven and humming, that she saw him in his big armchair.

"Yechezkel? You're home already?"

He was sitting quite still, not reading the paper or anything. With some difficulty, he said, "I wasn't feeling so well."

"What's the matter? Should I call the doctor?" In two swift strides she was at his side.

"No. Just...need to rest. I'll be fine."

But he wasn't fine. At two-fifteen, with Yechezkel gasping in his chair from pain and lack of breath, Rochel Mann dialed Hatzalah and asked, in a voice of rising hysteria, for an ambulance. The paramedics were at the house within minutes. They quickly confirmed what she had fearfully conjectured: her husband had just suffered a massive coronary.

಄ஓ

The most frightening thing for Fish, almost, was the way his mother looked. He had rarely seen her in anything approaching an unkempt state. Even after Gedalia's birth, when as a twelve-year-old he'd visited his mother in the hospital, she had been smiling and serene in an exquisite bed jacket. She'd even been wearing makeup then.

But in the aftermath of her husband's heart attack, there was no sign of either makeup or serenity. She clung to Fish's arm, her usual unflappable optimism a vanished thing.

"He's so sick, Fischel!" she wailed. "Intensive care... They had to inject a whole... And his blood pressure's dropped... They don't know if he'll... Oh, what will I do without him?"

"Sssh, Ma. Let's daven a little. He's got a good chance, the doctor said. He's basically a strong man. Here." He drew out a hastily snatched Tehillim. "Do you want it first?"

"You daven for me. I can't concentrate. Oh, why did he hide it from me? I would have taken such good care of him!"

Maybe, Fish reflected sadly, that was why. Independence was the keystone of his father's character. Nothing would have exasperated him more than a hovering, overprotective wife.

"He asked me for those pills," a white-faced Gedalia whispered to Fish, after the mother had been led weeping to a chair in the waiting area. "The ones in the drawer in the living room."

"When?"

"Once, when I came home from school. It was while you were still in Israel. Daddy looked funny — like he couldn't breathe. I was scared. But after he took one of the pills he felt better."

Fish nodded slowly. "Sit next to Mommy. I want to say some *tehillim*."

What words are enough to ask for a father's life? He was infinitely grateful to King David for having thought them up for him so long ago. Tenderly, sorrowfully, he recited the words and prayed that Heaven's gates would open wide to receive them.

As the Sabbath Queen made her regal entrance into the city, in all the pomp and finery of a crimson sunset, she found a moving trio huddled near the door to the Intensive Care room: a weeping woman, a prayerful young man, and one very frightened boy watching the other two with wide, dry eyes.

ॐ∘ॐ

"Cancel my reservation, Aunt Malka!" Shoshie cried when she heard the news. "There's still time, isn't there?"

"I'll call the travel agent and see." Malka tried to sound calm and failed abysmally. "Are you sure, Shoshie? There isn't much you can do here, and your parents —"

"My parents will understand! How can I leave Fish with his father...his father..." She broke down, sobbing.

Malka contacted the agent, who was able, in the last hours before Shabbos, to cancel the booking. "Do you want to put her down for another date? These planes fill up pretty fast, you know."

With a hasty glance at the calendar, Malka gave him another tentative booking. There was no question now of Shoshie's returning home in time to help with the wedding preparations. She'd be lucky if she made it to the wedding.

ॐ∘ॐ

Shabbos passed, a slow, damp, overcast day. Fish sent his mother home with Gedalia, while he kept a solitary vigil in the hospital, breaking his watch only long enough to join some neighboring acquaintances for the Shabbos meals. His father's doctor came to meet him as the day was drawing to a close. Behind the doctor's shoulders, in the huge, plate-glass windows that fronted the street, Fish saw the leaden sky lighten slightly toward dusk, as the sun did its best to make up for the slack job it had done that day.

"Well?" he asked, brusque in his anxiety.

"I think he's out of the woods," the doctor answered soberly. "For now. It was touch-and-go there for a few minutes."

"We've been praying hard." A faint smile touched Fish's eyes.

"So I understand. Well, don't stop praying now. He's still got a long way to go."

"How so?"

"I've scheduled him for bypass surgery tomorrow or the next day, as soon as he's got a little of his strength back. A triple bypass, I think; we performed an angiogram an hour ago to find out for sure. Your father's a very sick man, Mr. Mann."

"Fischel. Fish."

"Fish. He's going to have to make some drastic changes in his lifestyle. It's up to you and your mother to make sure he understands that."

Fish grinned, though not with amusement. "Anything else you want me to do — like pick up the Twin Towers in my bare hands? I've always believed in doing six impossible things before breakfast."

"Not so impossible." The doctor responded heavily to the other's wit. "At any rate, it's up to you to make sure it's not impossible. Your father won't survive another attack like this one, Fish."

"I understand."

"Good."

"When can I see him?"

"He's sleeping now. You can check with the nurse later." The doctor paused. "I don't want your mother here before tomorrow morning, though — and as calm as you can get her."

"Aye-aye, sir."

With a fleeting smile tinged with weariness, the doctor walked away.

Fish recited one more verse of *tehillim*, then closed the little book. He glanced through the window again. In this, the last moment of the day, the sun appeared in its full splendor, red and blazing as it dipped toward the horizon. His father had made it. He was going to live. The son sighed deeply, in gratitude and relief, and hurried off to find a minyan for *ma'ariv*.

He might as well not have closed his Tehillim quite so quickly. He was about to learn that a good deal more prayer was in order. His father's life might have been spared — for now — but his own was about to become a whole lot more complicated.

6

First came the talk with his mother, then the talk with Shoshie. Looking back much, much later, from the vantage point of greater age and — he hoped — greater wisdom, he would find it hard to decide which conversation had been the most difficult for him.

The first oppressed him with a terrible weight — the lonely burden of decision-making. In the second, he passed that weight on to the girl he loved — and, paradoxically, felt himself more bowed down than he'd been before.

He brought his mother to see his father on Sunday morning, as the doctor had ordered. Of the Rochel Mann of Friday afternoon there was no sign. She was in full control now: impeccably groomed, filled with a newfound strength. There was no sign of the sweet, rather complaisant woman her sons knew. She radiated a very positive energy and iron determination. They would survive this, all of them. If the line between her eyes and around her mouth had grown more pronounced overnight, that was a small price to pay for living a couple of days under the shadow of the greatest anxiety she had ever known. Her Yechezkel was better. He was, with her help, going to get well. That was all that mattered.

She spent a scant half-hour with him, in the company of various blinking, beeping aids to medical science. When she emerged, she looked very calm and very resolute.

"Fischel," she said, peremptory as any monarch. "Come here. I want to talk to you. Not you, Gedalia," she added, softening for the boy, who'd come to stand beside his brother. "You can slip in and see Daddy for a minute, if the nurse lets."

Gedalia obediently slipped away. Rochel led Fish to a couple of chairs. "Sit," she said. "We need to talk."

"What is it, Ma?"

"Fischel, you know what the doctor said. Your father is still a very sick man. He's not out of danger yet and won't be unless he starts taking better care of himself. He has to change the way he lives."

"I know that. I was the one who told you, remember?"

"I remember." She sounded grim. Fish felt a strange dread clutch at his chest as he waited for her to go on.

When she did, it was in a different tone, less autocratic and more heart-rending. "I also spoke to the doctor just now. He says that even after this bypass surgery, Daddy will have to be much less active. He has to stop going into the office — give up running the business."

Fish said quietly, "I figured as much. He's always driven himself too hard."

"He drove himself because he loves that business like a baby. He built it up from nothing. To leave it now — to hand it over to strangers — would kill him, Fischel." She eyed him solemnly. "Do you understand what I'm saying?"

He said nothing. He understood her only too well.

"You have to take over, Fish. That's the only way he can be comfortable, the only way for him to get well. You'll run the business for him, the way he always thought you would someday. Only, the day is now."

The day is now. Like the tolling of doom's bell, the words echoed in his consciousness. *The day is now.*

"I have to think it over, Ma."

"Think it over? What's there to think over? Did Daddy think it over when you needed braces? Did he spend time thinking when you broke your leg and needed to be driven everywhere?"

"It's not just me, Ma. There's Shoshie. She expects me to sit and learn. That was the basis of our engagement. It's not fair to her."

"If she doesn't want you because you're saving your father's life, then who needs her?" Rochel's face was white and set, fury just behind the careful facade. "You go over there today, Fischel, and talk to her. Tell her your father made this request. Tell her he's about to undergo open-heart surgery. Ask her what she wants to do."

"What's the rush?" he asked, despising himself for his weakness. "Daddy'll be in the hospital a while. There's no need to jump to any — "

"Yes — there — is." There was no arguing with the flat finality in his mother's voice. "Daddy is hanging by a thread. His heart is broken in more ways than one. It's broken because he thinks he's going to lose the one thing he spent his whole life building. He wouldn't ask you himself. *I'm* asking you. Don't do this to him!"

He stared at his hands.

"Fischel." She spoke softly, but there was no mistaking the steel behind the silk. "I want you to go in there before they wheel him into the operating room and tell him you'll be the kind of son he deserves. Will you do that?"

He finally raised his head, but he wouldn't meet her eye.

"I'll think about it, Ma," he mumbled, sidling dejectedly out of the hospital — and out of range of his mother's pleading, accusing stare.

His father's surgery was scheduled for three that afternoon. He had a few hours until then to come to a decision — and to impart that decision to Shoshie.

But once he'd driven himself down to Bensonhurst Bay and was leaning at the railing, looking seaward, he found that he didn't need that much time after all. Some decisions are made even before we understand the obligation to choose. If someone had asked young Fischel Mann, at any point during his youth, whether he would turn his back on his father as he lay broken and ill on his hospital bed — whether he would deny his father what he needed to be whole and content, even at the expense of his own deepest desire — the answer would have been clear enough to obviate the need for putting it into words. He knew where his duty lay. He was his father's son.

A gull cried nearby, swooping for crumbs. Fish watched its progress across the sky. For five years, ever since his graduation from high school, he'd deftly avoided the trap of his father's will. He'd danced adroitly out of

range, graceful as that gull, moving from one yeshivah to another and learning
to love learning both for its own sake and for the sake of the freedom it gave
him from his father's ambitions for him.

Today, that freedom had been snatched away. This was no longer a
choice of "having it my way" or "doing it his way." It was a question of
honoring his father in the only way that would have any meaning for
Yechezkel, of carrying on his father's lifework so that he might live to enjoy
a peaceful old age. As his mother had put it, what was there to think over?

He turned away from the railing and put the misty blue horizon behind
him.

Though he knew the peace of doing what was right, he felt frightened —
more frightened than he'd ever been in his life. He stood on the verge of
losing the precious prize he'd so recently won. All his dearly bought dreams
were poised on a precipice. One breath, a single "I'm sorry" from her lips,
and they would tumble to the immeasurable canyon of despair far below.

He forced his feet to carry him to the car. Ahead lay the indifferent road
and the drive back to Brooklyn — and Shoshie at the journey's end, waiting,
though she didn't know it, for her own heart to be broken.

❧

"I see."

Shoshie was immobile. One shock had supplanted another before she
could properly absorb them. She didn't know what to think, feel, or say. Right
now, she should have been approaching the Mediterranean coast of Israel.
The sun would be winking on the silver wings of the plane and the great
snowy clouds massed below. Her parents would have been waiting to meet
her at the airport with hugs and exclamations and an unfaltering love. She
needed that love now, as never before. She was so alone!

"So that's the story," Fish said. His voice was dry and emotionless as
the dust motes that swirled past Shoshie's vision in the clear, summery air.
They were sitting on the Weisner patio, overlooking the backyard.

"You agreed to marry me on the understanding that I'd sit and learn. That we'd be a *kollel* couple," Fish continued doggedly. "Well, that can't happen now. And we wouldn't be able to live in Israel, either. I have to stay here in New York and take control of the business." He swallowed a great lungful of air, but it made things no easier. "Of course, I intend to put in as much time learning Torah as I possibly can. I'll line up *chavrusas* every evening. You wouldn't get to see much of me, but that's the way it would have to be. A full day's work, maybe a quick bite of dinner together, and then a few hours of learning. I...I just want you to know what would be involved, Shoshie, if...if you decide to stick with me."

"I see." She seemed to know no other words.

"I'll be a businessman. Gemara will have to come second for a while, at least, until I learn the ropes and make sure things are running smoothly. Honestly, though, I may as well admit that I'll probably never get to learn full-time again. Maybe when I retire, I don't know. But not in the foreseeable future. It'll always be first in my heart, though. That much will never change." He gazed at her as a sailor might gaze upon the fast-receding shore of a beloved homeland. "Do you understand?"

"Yes."

He stood up. "That's all, then. I have to go back to the hospital. My father is having his surgery in a little while." He hesitated, forlorn and uncertain. "Should...should I call you later? Or maybe come by in person?"

"Call me." Her eyes were fixed rigidly on the swing set. "And *refuah sheleimah.*"

"Thank you."

With that, formal as any two strangers taking leave of each other in some crowded subway car, he left her staring sightlessly ahead in the sun.

Now it was Shoshie's turn to think; that is, when her mind had sufficiently unfrozen to make coherent thought possible. She didn't go anywhere. There was no foot on the accelerator to take her toward the sea or the mountains in the hope that clearer air would make for a clearer mind.

She remained seated exactly where Fish had left her, on the wooden patio behind the Weisner house, facing the red-painted swing that was beginning to rust and the blue one, beginning to come loose from its moorings.

Little Tzvi, cranky from a lingering cold, spotted his cousin from the door and was eager to run out and engage her in play. He found his progress impeded by the large, determined bulk of his mother.

"Not now, Tzviki. Shoshie's busy."

Tzvi, with some logic, protested, "But she's not doing anything. She's just sitting there!"

Malka sighed. "She's thinking, honey."

"Aw, that's stupid. What's she want to go and do that for?"

"She may not want to," Malka replied, more to herself than to the indignant youngster, "but I get the feeling she has to."

Oddly, Shoshie's thoughts took her away from her present dilemma. They carried her backwards, to the winter just past. She was in her tiny bedroom at home again, crying into her sodden pillow because — she thought — her only hope of happiness had been cruelly dashed to the ground. Once again, with sullen eyes, she was watching her twin sister grow daily more radiant in the knowledge that she'd met her *bashert*, the one fated to make her happy forever after in the happiest of marriages. The one whom Shoshie had been supposed to see first.

How young she'd been then — and how innocent, to waste a tear over a Benzy she'd never even met! She knew the real article now. She had known and savored the true joy of finding the one who'd been created for her from the beginning of time. And he'd just left her with such a strange, stern note in his voice and the words, "Think it over, Shoshie." Think it over!

Restlessly she arose and began walking the perimeter of the small yard. Round and round went her footsteps, and round and round went her thoughts. She'd always pictured herself a young *kollel* bride, chattering with the other new wives on the block as they waited for their husbands to finish their last *seder* and come home to them. Sometimes, in her imaginings, there'd been a baby stroller nearby; at others, she was alone, hurrying home at sunset to prepare a delicious dinner for her husband from one of the many delightful cookbooks she'd amassed at her marriage.

She could cook still, and the baby stroller was no more impossible now than it had been yesterday. But the camaraderie of the *kollel* — the knowledge that her own husband was one of the proud ranks of men devoting the energy of their youth to Torah, and only to Torah — that was no more. The prospect of a placid, familiar existence in the city she knew so intimately had melted into the warm, blue air. The very picture vanished as if it had never been. She must adjust to a different reality now.

Her choice was clear: to remain fixed in the preconceived notion of her own life, or to try for flexibility and change. Change had always frightened her — and the more so since two of the people she loved had come so near to being lost to her forever. She wanted everything to stay exactly the way it was, always. She wanted, really, to remain a child, with a child's security at her mother's knee.

Or did she? Hadn't she travelled too far in these last weeks — these last months, really — to ever be a child again? She might go home to bask in her parents' eternal love, but wouldn't she be forfeiting something else, something equally as precious?

Yes, she saw her choice clearly. To abandon Fish and return to Israel to pick up the threads of her life as though these three weeks in America had never been; to re-embark on the *shidduch* train, gazing mournfully out the window at the passing scenery. Or to become Mrs. Fischel Mann, Mrs. Businessman, Mrs. New York...and close the door on her native land, her young dreams, her childhood.

Something shone into her eyes, forcing her to close them for a moment. It was the diamond on her finger, picking up the sun. She watched the facets of the big stone glint and dance, changing color too quickly for the human eye to follow and certainly too quick for it to grasp. You couldn't grasp color — just as you couldn't seize too tightly onto anything that was really worth having. If you held on too tight, if you refused to relax your hold, the greatest treasures could slip right through your fingers.

Moving slowly, she got to her feet and went inside. Somehow, there were several hours to be endured before the call came. Malka, turning at her entrance and noting the expression on her face, said heartily, "Just the person I was looking for! Someone has to peel the potatoes for dinner, and someone else has to entertain Tzvi before he starts climbing the walls. Take your pick."

Shoshie chose Tzvi, guaranteed to prevent any further serious thought that afternoon. If she was lucky, he would keep her busy right up until the time the phone rang, bringing with it Fish's tidings from the hospital and the need to put her answer into words.

When the phone did ring, some two hours later, she was deeply immersed in a game of dominoes with her energetic young cousin. Tzvi was highly indignant at being left in mid-game.

"I'll finish later," she gasped, dashing out the door to the stairs. "Phone!"

"Stupid phone," he called after her. "Stupid Shoshie!"

Fish sounded tired but elated.

"He made it through okay, Shoshie. He's still sleeping — will probably keep sleeping at least till the morning — but the doctors are hopeful."

"That's wonderful, Fish. *Baruch Hashem.*"

"For sure." There was a pause, charged with a new and quivering tension. "Before the surgery, just before they put him under, I told him what I intended to do. I told him I was prepared leave the yeshivah and start learning the ropes at the firm. He — I could tell it eased his mind, Shoshie. Despite everything, I'm glad I told him." He sounded sadly defiant.

"So am I."

"What?"

"I'm glad you told him, poor man. And Fish?"

"Wh...what?"

"I guess the headache of finding a place to live will be all yours now. Good luck."

"What are you saying, Shoshie?"

"I'm saying," she smiled tearfully into the phone, "that you're going to be very busy for the next couple of months, getting us set up. Try to find some place that's near your parents and also not too far from Aunt Malka."

"Shoshie — "

"Of course," she went on, smiling more widely now, though he couldn't see it, "I won't be sitting on my hands. I'll be busy, too."

"Doing what?" He seemed to have recovered. In place of trepidation, his voice held only jubilation now.

"What do you think, silly? Getting ready for our wedding."

"SHOSHIE!" shouted Tzvi from the bottom of the stairs. "Come back. We're in the middle of a game!"

"Oops. Sorry, Fish, I have to run. My presence is wanted."

He was about to tell her that it would be wanted again later that evening and that he'd be coming by just as soon as he could safely leave the hospital. But she'd already hung up.

He replaced his own receiver on the cold public phone. Never mind. There'd be plenty of time later on to tell her how much her presence meant to him. A lifetime.

FIFTEEN

1

Mutty ran a hand lovingly along the molding that adorned the four corners of the bookcase. It had been some headache, that molding. Several sleepless nights and a bruised thumb had been the price he'd paid for its execution, but he was well satisfied with the result. At the customer's request, he'd tried something he'd never done before and succeeded even beyond his hopeful imaginings.

The wood had been a good choice, too. A deep red-brown, it glowed with its own innate luster, touched up by some judiciously applied pine oil. He was, by now, well versed in the various moods of the woods he employed in his building: the obedient oak; the mahogany, ever promising more than it could deliver; and the sweet, light pine. He wondered what sort of wood he'd have to work with in Israel. The durable stuff of the olive tree had always fascinated him. Well, there would be plenty of opportunity to investigate the age-old woods of antiquity there, in the land where they'd been tried and tested over centuries.

He bent to inspect a last detail around the handle of one of the cabinets, knowing as he did so that he was merely delaying the inevitable. There was nothing more to be done. The piece was finished.

Mutty experienced, as always, a touch of regret at the thought. Starting one of his carpentry projects was exhilarating, the labor arduous, and the finishing up always bittersweet. This particular beauty had given him a good deal of trouble, with tricky measurements and lavish glasswork. Maybe that was why he was especially loath to let it go.

With a smile at his own sentimentality, he went to phone his friend Leibish with the news that the bookcase was ready for delivery. Leibish's wife would be pleased with the way it had turned out. Too bad he was leaving: this piece would have been his best advertising vehicle yet. Already he'd had to turn away potential clients, eager for one of his custom-made, lovingly finished pieces.

But this had been his swan song: Mutty's last project in Lakewood. When the bookcase had been picked up he would pay the final month's rent on the modest basement-cum-workshop he leased from a householder in the yeshivah's vicinity and clear out his things. That, as much as the packing up of his Gemara, was his signal that his Lakewood days were really over.

The bookcase was still on his mind as he neatly dodged an overfull luggage compartment on the uncomfortably full plane. He wore a look of distaste as he strapped himself into his seat.

"Everything okay?" his father asked.

"Fine." Mutty shrugged. "Planes don't thrill me. Too plastic."

Avi looked intrigued. "What do you mean?"

"Look around. Is there anything here you'd want to keep, anything you'd enjoy looking at for five minutes more than you absolutely have to?" He snorted. "Plastic, all of it." Not a sign of rich, living wood anywhere in sight.

"Would you rather have had them build planes out of wood?" Avi asked, uncannily reading his mind.

"No, of course not." Mutty grinned. "Not that it wouldn't improve things by a whole lot."

They were distracted then by the business of buckling up and lifting off. When their ears had stopped popping and conversation resumed, it was of Israel they spoke — of Bracha's fast-approaching wedding and Mutty's plans. He was returning to the same yeshivah, essentially picking up the threads of his two-month winter sojourn in Jerusalem. Ironically, the prospect — though it took him half a world away from the place where he'd grown up — had all the hallmarks, for Mutty, of a homecoming.

"Do you want me to ask Aunt Esther to keep an eye open for any interesting prospects?" Avi asked. "Marriage-wise, I mean."

"I don't know, Ta. I'm young yet. Maybe when I turn twenty-two..."

"At twenty-one you thought you were ready."

The memory of the ill-fated birthday dinner rose to both of their minds at the same time. Mutty colored; Avi frowned.

"Maybe," Mutty said softly, "at twenty-one and a half, I know better."

His father's frown deepened at the apparent levity of the response. Seeing it, Mutty hastened to add, "I mean that seriously, Ta. Finding out how much I love Eretz Yisrael made me realize how many of my — well, call them values — are still unexplored. I don't think I'll be an old bachelor, don't worry. I just need a little time to sink my roots in and look around a little. To think things through."

It was a night flight. Around them, people were flipping open magazines and newspapers with tired, practiced gestures. A few, ignoring the imminent dinner service, had defiantly rolled themselves up in the airline blanket, courting sleep. Mutty felt unnaturally alert, but he knew that his tingling nerves were just the aftermath of the drive to the airport, the suspense over the weighing of his suitcases, the emotional parting with his mother. After dinner — more plastic! — he would become drowsy. Maybe he'd sleep.

"That's right," Avi nodded. "Think about things. Maybe the future will be a little clearer after a while."

The words struck a chord in Mutty's memory. "That's what you told me when I went away in January," he said slowly. "Ta, I hope..." He faltered, casting about for the right words.

"What? You hope what?"

"I hope you're not expecting me to change my mind about becoming a pulpit rabbi. Because that's never been up for review. I thought you understood that."

It occurred to Avi, watching the play of expressions on his son's face, that he had *not* understood. Not really. He remembered, cringing a little, his first outburst at Mutty's betrayal on that long-ago birthday night. That was what he had termed it in his own mind: a betrayal. The heir apparent to the Weisner dynasty had chosen to abdicate.

He'd been very sure, back then, that Mutty was wrong and he, Avi, absolutely in the right. But then, hadn't he felt exactly the same way about Mirsky?

More food for thought.

His disappointment with his son's decision still rankled, but it was a quieter emotion now than the hurt and rage that had held him in thrall six months before. If he couldn't agree with Mutty yet, at least he recognized the need for review. That was something.

"Mutty," he said, gravely and with sincerity, "I want you to know that I'm not going to fight you on this anymore. You're going to devote some more time to learning now, and that can only be good. Maybe you'll find that, in time, you'll change your mind of your own accord. But if not" — he paused, to lend emphasis to his declaration — "if building things out of wood is what you feel capable of doing with your life, then you have my blessing."

He didn't know how, exactly, he'd expected his son to react. With a certain thankfulness, maybe — an appreciation for a parent's blessing. To his surprise, that reaction was not forthcoming. Instead, Mutty stared at him, slowly shaking his head. "You don't understand, Ta."

"What don't I understand? I thought — "

"You thought — you *think* — that I've turned to carpentry because I don't feel up to anything more ambitious. You think it's a second-best choice with me. The way it would have been for you."

Avi met Mutty's eyes. The plane lurched a little in sudden turbulence, but neither one felt it. "Well?" he asked.

"What you don't get," Mutty said earnestly, "is why I do it. Why I take a piece of wood and conceive of the shape it could hold and the way it could look, and why I take down my tools to make it take that shape and that look." He clenched a fist. "I do it, Ta, for one reason only. Because I love it."

Seeing the incomprehension loom large in his father's eyes, he added with the desperate force of his desire, his need, to make his father *see*: "The way you feel when you step up on that dais to address the crowd, that's how I feel when I pick up my hammer, Ta. Now do you see?"

But he could tell, even before Avi shook his head and let his eyes slip away, that for all his effort, his father didn't see.

Bleakly, Mutty wondered if he ever would.

2

Adela painstakingly copied the letter onto a clean sheet of stationery. Before inserting it into its envelope she reread the single page.

It was, on the surface, a casual letter. But in this case, style camouflaged intent. The kernel of truth that lay at the heart of the missive had been cleverly concealed inside a tissue of trivialities. Would Malka have the eyes — the wisdom — to uncover it?

Adela might have trusted her friend a little more.

Not only did Malka, with the instinct of a well-trained homing pigeon, fly unerringly to the relevant paragraph; she hardly paid an iota of attention to anything else in the letter. A smile creased her face as she put down the page and sat back in her post-breakfast, pre-lunch kitchen to map out her next move.

If only Avi were here to share this delicious moment with her! But he was far away, getting ready to attend their niece's wedding this very night. Or was it already tonight over there? The time difference always got Malka in a muddle.

The outlines of her strategy came to her some ten minutes later, catching her elbow-deep in suds at the sink. She scarcely allowed herself time to dry off before snatching up the telephone receiver. She'd felt sad, initially, when family responsibilities had forced her to decline Fish's generous offer of a ticket to Israel for his and Shoshie's wedding; it was just too soon after her recent trip there. Now she was glad she hadn't gone with Avi. She was here, on the spot, where she could do the most good for two people she really cared about.

Binyomin's office number was pencilled beside his name in the big, haphazard address book that lived inside the kitchen drawer nearest the phone.

"Mr. Hirsch's office," a bored voice greeted her.

"Give me Bin — that is, Mr. Hirsch, please. It's Malka Weisner calling."

"I'm sorry, Mr. Hirsch is in a meeting." The voice didn't sound sorry at all. "Would you like to leave a message?"

"Yes! Tell your boss that I'm expecting him over here at our house this evening. For dinner, for dessert, whatever. Just tell him to make sure and show up. Do you have that?"

"Yes, Ms. Weisner." The voice was disapproving. Obviously, one was expected to treat the great lawyer with more deference.

To placate her, Malka smiled impishly and added, just before she hung up, "Tell him I said 'please.' "

Binyomin turned up too late for dinner and even for dessert, but in plenty of time to give Tzvi and Chaim piggyback rides up to their room and tuck them into bed. The youngsters loved big Uncle Binyomin and would have kept him there forever, listening to him retell favorite old stories and laughing at the hand shadows he was so proficient at forming on the wall of their room. All too soon, however, their mother came bustling in to retrieve her guest.

"Aw, Ma, can't he stay a little longer?"

"Not tonight, sweets. I need to talk to Uncle Binyomin."

"Can't you talk tomorrow?"

"Sorry." She motioned for Binyomin to precede her out of the room. "This won't wait."

"What won't wait?" Binyomin asked when they were seated over cups of tea at the dining-room table. Hindy passed by with an armful of notebooks and a school friend in tow, throwing them a curious glance as she went. Her mother looked serious; Binyomin, she saw, wore what Hindy privately thought of as his "lawyer look": neutral, giving away nothing. Malka waited until the girls were out of earshot before answering Binyomin's question.

"This." She produced Adela's letter. "This can't wait." Without another word, she handed it to him.

He glanced at the salutation, then at the signature, shying back as if the paper had scorched him. "It's addressed to you!"

"I know. I want you to read it."

"I'm not sure I — "

"Read it. Please."

Reluctantly, Binyomin scanned the letter. He had never seen Adela's handwriting before.

Dear Malka (it read),

> *It's hard to believe we've been here seven weeks already. A month or more has passed since you left, and I miss you, of course, but Esther Markovich and Sharona Kahn are taking good care of me. Not to mention Rabbi Kahn, who's worked wonders with Yudy. He (Yudy) practically lives for the minute when he can take off for the neighborhood shul, where he meets Rabbi Kahn to learn each night. I don't know what the man talks to him about, but it seems to be doing something terrific for my boy. It was worth the whole trip just for this exposure to such a wonderful person. I won't, however, go so far as to say the whole nightmare was worth it — nothing could ever be that.*

> *We've heard the good news through the grapevine: that monster has been put behind bars. Baruch Hashem! As I understand it, the chain of communications went something like this: the D.A. told Binyomin Hirsch, who told Avi, who passed the info on to Esther, who told me. Yudy was the last one to hear — but not the least of the revellers at the joyous news! Long may that madman rot in prison. As far as I'm concerned, I hope he never comes out again.*

> *I'm so terribly grateful to all of you for everything you've done for us. One lesson I've learned from the whole ordeal is that you can't go*

it alone. I thought I was so strong and independent, and then one evil person came along and was almost enough to destroy my world. Thank God he didn't succeed.

You know, there's one person I never got to express my thanks to, and that's Binyomin. Maybe you could pass it on? Yudy adds his own yasher ko'ach, *too. I didn't treat him awfully well, but he behaved just like a knight in shining armor.*

The weather here has been glorious: hot, sunny, dry, and deliciously cool at night. I'm writing this at midnight, with a million stars overhead (many more than back home, I'm convinced of it) and the sweet smell of some anonymous flower drifting up from the garden below. If it wasn't for some New York faces I'd miss, I could seriously think about staying here forever.

Love to all,
Adela

Malka watched carefully as Binyomin read through the letter, but his expression told her nothing. That, she felt, would not do at all. She had hoped to betray him into some sort of declaration — a revelation of some long-cherished and well-hidden feeling. But his face was a mask. Control was this lawyer's watchword.

"Very nice," he said noncommittally, putting the paper down.

"She says she wants to thank you."

"All right. Consider me thanked."

"She also says she misses you."

"Where does she say that?"

"Right here" — she handed him back the letter and pointed to the last sentence — "see?"

He sat back, smiling sardonically. "Interesting interpretation."

Malka decided on a frontal attack.

"Binyomin," she said, taking the letter back and placing it on the table between them, "enough of this nonsense. We have to talk."

"Okay," he said pleasantly. "So talk."

"I've made one *shidduch* already this year — Shoshie and Fish. I'm determined that my other one will end up just as well."

"Malka, don't you think you're a little late? All that was over...a long time ago."

She swept aside his words as if they'd never been spoken. The *rebbetzin*'s eyes sparkled with the light of battle. Gone was the old, insecure Malka Weisner who had once peered into the gleaming surface of her toaster and mocked her own image. She was a woman at the height of her powers now. She would, please God, use them wisely and well.

"No nonsense now, Binyomin," she said imperiously. "Now listen to me. Here's what I want you to do..."

രങ്ങൾ

Weddings, thought Adela, as she gazed around the modest hall with its throngs of happy celebrants, were made to remind you that life could be good.

Heaven knew, there were enough reminders of the other kind. Everywhere you looked, you could find poverty and illness and faces registering greater or lesser degrees of despair. Here, tonight, there was no despair — only the pure, uplifting joy that comes of knowing oneself blessed and overwhelmed with gratitude for that blessing. The only tears shed here tonight were Esther's, and they were tears of thanksgiving.

Adela, too, was grateful. Thank God, she thought, for weddings.

Once she'd found them difficult. Right after her husband's death, weddings had been cruel reminders of her own bereavement. The union of two happy people had underscored, as with a thick, black pen stroke, her own unwilling solitude. But that stage had passed long ago. Together with her acceptance of her widowhood had come the resumption of her ability to feel joy for others.

Why, then, the return of some of the old desolation tonight?

The answer made no attempt to hide from her. It jumped out, demanding to be seen in all its stark fullness. She was sad because she was no longer resigned. She wanted more, and the wanting was a constant ache. Right smack in the middle of her agreeable musings the gnawing question kept intruding: Would her letter find its mark? And what was going to happen next?

She managed to push the questions aside as the evening wore on, losing herself in the music, the dance, the food, and the company. Bracha was a delightful bride, the simple white tiara queenly on her auburn head. She danced with a lightness and a grace Adela admired. Shoshie danced well, too, although the constant lure of exchanging a few words with her *chasan*, standing at the edges of the hall near the door, broke seriously into her dancing time. Though not familiar with the newest dance steps, Adela made a game effort to join in. She was footsore, weary, and smiling hazily as she and Yudy reentered their small apartment very late that night, after it was all over.

"Whew, I'm pooped." Yudy collapsed onto the scratchy sofa. "I could fall asleep right here."

"You speak for both of us," his mother said. "But I suggest you try and make it to your own bed. It's a whole lot more comfortable. *Shacharis* is in just six hours."

"All right," he mock grumbled. "You talked me into it." Heaving himself to his feet with a groan, Yudy went off to his tiny bedroom.

The phone rang.

"Who could that be at this hour?" Adela wondered aloud. She half-considered not picking up. Probably a wrong number. There was something spooky about picking up a phone very late at night.

The shrill ring went on. "Okay, okay, I'm coming." Saying the words out loud did away with some of her uneasiness. She picked up the phone. "Hello?"

Even before a word was uttered, the distinctive humming silence told her it was a long-distance call. She had exactly one second to prepare herself before a familiar voice, a voice she'd never expected to hear again, answered, "Hello. Is that Adela?"

"Yes. Is that — Binyomin?"

"Good for you. I didn't know if you'd remember."

She pulled herself together, though she was clutching the receiver much too tightly. "That New York accent? How could I forget?"

He chuckled, and suddenly the tension was gone. "And I thought I sounded Californian by now. How've you been, Adela?"

"Fine. We're both fine. We're all settled in. Yudy's learning well and is happy here, though he gets these terrible cravings for Kosher Delight pastrami sandwiches. Yudy says falafel and shwarma just don't do it for him. Why don't they have decent fast food in this country?" What on earth was she babbling about?

"A good question. Maybe we can discuss it in person in a few days. I have some business in Israel, Adela. I'll be flying in on Thursday." Business — hah! If she only knew...

She suddenly found she had to sit down. Her knees had developed a strange weakness, doubtless from all that dancing. "Oh, are you? How nice. Yudy and I will be glad to see you. I hope you'll find some time for us."

"Oh, I think I'll be able to squeeze you in. My best to Yudy."

"I'll pass it on. *L'hitraot*, Binyomin. That means — "

"I know what it means. On Thursday."

"Thursday," she repeated faintly.

If high hopes had the power to burn, the telephone lines that snaked beneath the wide blue sea would have been up in flames that night.

❧

She and Yudy were at the airport to meet him.

It had taken only a single phone call to Malka to ascertain the flight he'd be on. Yudy hadn't needed much persuading; on the contrary, he was eager to meet his benefactor again. Taking a crumpled tissue from her pocket she dabbed at her forehead, damp with Tel Aviv humidity. She was ill at ease as she waited. What if she'd read him wrong, in that one transatlantic conversation, as she'd swayed on her feet from fatigue and a confused tangle of feelings? How horrible it would be if he registered dismay upon seeing them, if the gesture was taken as too great a presumption on her part!

The dread was almost enough to make her turn and flee. If Yudy hadn't been there, anchoring her, she might actually have done it. As things stood, it was too late to turn back. She glanced at her son as he craned his neck to see over the people lined up in the arrivals area. He was tanned and smiling — a far cry from the Yudy who'd scurried home through the sinister streets of nighttime Brooklyn with Binyomin and Avi following faithfully behind. How much she owed them. How much she owed *him*, especially. More than anything, she owed Binyomin the realization that she didn't want to continue carrying the load alone anymore.

It was not just a question of admitting her own weakness — something she'd always hated to do. What this was really about was her own humanness. She had come face to face, in these last, turbulent weeks, with her own mortal frailty. She couldn't do it alone. And was that really so surprising? Was there anyone, really, who wasn't the better off with a partner in this glorious, treacherous dance of life?

She had prayed for the thing Binyomin represented, time after innumerable time, all down the lonely years of her widowhood, though at times the prayer had been rote, scarcely meant. Well, she meant it now. If her plea was answered, she would know what to do next. It would not only be churlishly ungrateful to turn down a gift presented to her by Heaven itself, it would be the height of bad manners!

The passengers were beginning to stream through the glass portals. Now it remained to be seen just what Heaven — and Binyomin — had to offer.

He spotted them before they saw him. His eyes grew round in astonishment, then pleasure. Dusk was falling, making rapid inroads on the glare and the heat as he hurried toward them.

"Hello! This is a surprise!"

Adela started. Palely, she turned to face him. "Binyomin. Yudy and I thought... That is, we wanted to say 'thank you' in person. I know how lousy it feels not to be met at the airport. Anyway" — she spread her hands in a gesture that spoke, more loudly than any words, of her acute embarrassment — "here we are.""Terrific. Now come. First things first." He led them away, hefting his suitcase by one strong arm and declining Yudy's offer of help. "I need to rent a car. How did you two get here?"

"By bus."

"Fine. You can ride back with me."

"What's second?" Yudy asked when the suitcase had been deposited in the trunk of the small, white rental car and they themselves arranged comfortably inside.

"Eh?" Binyomin turned to face Yudy. "What's that?"

"You said 'first things first.' So what's second?"

Binyomin grinned widely. "Presents."

"Yippee!"

"Yudy," Adela admonished, trying to be stern but sounding only deliriously happy. "Where are your manners?"

"I left them in New York."

"So've I," Binyomin confided. He reached for a bag lying at Adela's feet and tossed it to Yudy, who made a neat catch. "Mustard and pickle okay?"

"Pastrami sandwiches!" Yudy yelped. "How'd you know?"

Adela burst out laughing. "Don't tell me — from Kosher Delight?"

"You got it. There's one for you there, too. But you'll have to save it for tomorrow. I'm taking you out to dinner tonight."

"This is what I call some present," Yudy said, ecstatically inhaling the fragrance that emanated from the paper bag. "Any more?"

"Yudy!"

"Aw, just kidding, Mom."

"As a matter of fact," said Binyomin, starting the car, "I do have another present. One more. But it'll have to wait."

"For what?" Yudy demanded.

"For the time to be ripe." He glanced at Adela. "I have a message from Rebbetzin Weisner, too."

"Oh? What does Malka have to say?"

"All will be revealed in good time."

"Mysterious, aren't we?" Adela murmured, smiling.

"You know us lawyers," Binyomin returned, eyes straight ahead on the road to Jerusalem, bluish under the shadows of encroaching evening. "We keep our counsel."

Adela fell into a contented silence. In the back seat, Yudy communed blissfully with his pastrami sandwich. Binyomin, at the wheel, used one hand to steer, while the other played with something in his jacket pocket.

It was a small, hard box, the kind the finest jewelers use for their wares. If he tried, Binyomin could see the diamond twinkling on its velvet bed, with all the fire and fervor of the stars at midnight.

And, with a little extra effort, it wasn't hard to imagine Adela's face when he presented it to her. He hoped — oh, how very much he hoped — that that would be glowing, too.

He would find out for himself, he hoped, in due course. At any rate, he didn't intend to leave Israel until he did. And he'd pass on Malka's message — a single, impatient *"Nu?"* — also.

When the time was ripe.

3

Esther Markovich was crying into the chicken soup.

She tried to stem the tide, but the tears kept coming, drip-drip-dripping as she stood over the huge, bubbling vat. "Oh, well," she thought philosophically. "A little more salt won't hurt it any."

The idea made her smile, and the smile was more effective than anything in banishing the tears. She was still red-eyed, though, and sniffling, when Tzippy wandered into the kitchen.

The girl stood stock-still in the doorway. "Ima? Are you *crying?*"

Denial quivered on Esther's lips. Then, shrugging, she said, "It's nothing. It just hit me that Bracha's gone, and Shoshie's on her way out. Tzippaleh, do you realize you're going to be the oldest girl around here now?"

Tzippy looked pleased at the prospect. The red-gold hair had begun to grow out and was clustered in soft curls around her face. There was, perhaps, a new gravity in her eyes now, but she still looked very much a child.

"What're you making?" she asked.

"Meat blintzes." This was for the Shabbos *sheva berachos* she was hosting for Bracha and Benzy in a couple of days: forty people for each of the three Shabbos meals. As ever, Esther had the culinary end of the operation well under control. It was the emotional aspect that was proving so unexpectedly daunting.

Yoni, her little man, chose that moment to stagger into the kitchen. "He's walking already," Esther marvelled, suddenly misty-eyed again. "So much has happened these past few weeks. I'm finding it hard to get used to it all." She blew her nose vigorously.

"I know. When I got out of the hospital, I couldn't believe I'd actually been out of things for so long. To me, it felt like the same day! But before I knew it, Bracha was getting married, Shoshie was engaged, Yoni was walking, and you — " She halted in confusion, blushing.

"What about me?" Esther asked, pausing with her hand on the handle of her chopping knife.

"You've changed too, Ima."

"Have I?" But Esther knew that she had. If she needed any proof of that, witness the extra flavoring she'd just inadvertently added to the soup. The old Esther had never cried.

"Me, too," Tzippy added quickly, as though to make her mother feel better. "I've also changed. I mean, my hair's shorter and everything."

"No," Esther said, reaching out with her free arm to give her daughter a quick hug. "You haven't changed a bit, Tzippy. You're still the same good girl you always were — and always will be, I hope."

She had the pleasure then, of seeing Tzippy's eyes light up with a brilliant, inner illumination. To cover her embarrassment, the girl stooped to tickle her little brother, who, in the throes of his glee, fell with a thud onto his well-padded bottom.

"Okay, that's enough, guys," Esther said briskly. "I can't turn around in here. Everyone out!"

Tzippy hustled Yoni out of the kitchen, secretly relieved. This sounded much more like the Ima she knew and loved.

❧

The festive meals passed amid much gaiety and song. Bracha, radiant in her new *sheva berachos* dress, watched adoringly as her husband rose on Friday night to say a few words of Torah to honor the occasion. In a few days, when the partying was all behind them, they would be moving to Bnei Brak, to an apartment near Benzy's yeshivah. Some sadness was attendant on this leave-taking — how could it not be, when it forced her to say goodbye to the town she'd grown up in and the parents who'd provided her with the only home she'd ever known?

But any tendency Bracha might have had to feel sorry for herself over this circumstance paled beside the enormity of Shoshie's future. Her twin sister would be leaving soon, too — and moving much, much farther away. New York, to Bracha's untravelled mind, was about as distant as the moon.

Shoshie wasn't feeling sorry for herself. In fact, with her devoted Fish dancing attendance, she was the picture of happiness. His return flight to New York was scheduled for the following night. After that, life would revert to normal — or as normal as it could ever be for a girl before her marriage. There would be halls to look at and decisions big and small to make, and all without Fish there to help her. But Shoshie didn't mind. The busier she was, the less time she'd have to moon over her *chasan* and think about how very great a distance lay between them.

He would be busy, too, taking over the reins of the business his father had built up over the course of his own adult lifetime, while also attempting, in every spare hour, to maintain a serious level of commitment to Torah study. In that way, Fish hoped to ensure the security — both financial and spiritual — of the girl who was entrusting her life to him. It was no mean undertaking, but he was determined to do it right.

Mutty, seated beside his father, watched first the newly married couple, and then the soon-to-be-married one, and felt anew the unique satisfaction of having had a hand in bringing the second pair together. Whether he or Malka had actually been the one to come up with the notion was, he realized, irrelevant; Hashem was the true matchmaker, and the rest of them nothing but His willing messengers. Through every doubt, each setback and cloud of uncertainty, the rock-steady thread in His guiding Hand had pulled them all, firmly and inexorably, toward His planned end. The thought was immensely comforting. As long as his own future lay between those divinely capable Hands, Mutty knew he need never waste a second on the profitless exercise of worry.

One decision lay behind him. He was here, in Jerusalem, enrolled in the yeshivah of his choice and hoping, slowly, at the right time, to begin earning a living with his beloved carpentry. First, though, he would like to meet the girl who'd become his wife and stand beside him for the rest of this long, complex, and ever-interesting trip. But that would come later. As Binyomin Hirsch, sitting across from him in his custom suit might have said, "All in good time..."

Binyomin, Adela, Yudy; Levi Kahn and his wife, Sharona; Avi and Mutty and Fish; Zalman Markovich beaming paternalistically at his daughter and new son-in-law: all wore expressions of joy and goodwill. But by far the most joyous face belonged to the woman who sat near the *kallah* in the regal splendor of a gleaming wheelchair — whose eyes, seamed and wrinkled all around like the parchment her son used to write his mezuzos on, was stamped with a maze of a thousand added lines from the slightly twisted smile she wore on her slightly drooping face.

There was no question about it: if the *kallah* was the princess, Savta, her grandmother, home from the hospital to enjoy whatever time was left to her on this earth in peace and *nachas*, was the queen of the day.

こめめ

Rabbi Weisner was asked to speak at the lunchtime *se'udah*. As the rhythm of his speech flowed over the hushed crowd, Mutty became aware of some new element in his father's manner. There was something different in his speaking style these days, though Mutty couldn't put his finger on the nature of the change.

The rabbi's words came like an arrow: straight from the heart and true.

"*B'nei Yisrael* passed through fire and water — the slavery of Egypt, ten plagues, the splitting of the Reed Sea and the tribulations of forty years in the desert — in order to finally attain the prize of all their labors: entrance into the Promised Land. So, too, has our young couple today come through difficult times and sore hardships to the joy of this, their fulfillment.

"Difficulty has brought out the best in both of them. Illness and suffering have only drawn from them a spirit of greater self-sacrifice. For most young people, the engagement period is an irresponsible time, a time to enjoy each other, to dream lightly of the future. Of course, there's the wedding to prepare for, but they can leave most of the tedious details safely in the hands of the older generation.

"Benzy and Bracha had no such leisure. They had to take the responsibility all on their own shoulders — along with the burden of helping keep Bracha's household going during many hard and fearful weeks. They did it all, and did it gallantly, without a whisper of complaint." He turned to the newlywed pair and raised a hand in an invisible toast. "Bracha. Benzy. We're proud of you."

Assembled family and friends burst into a thunderclap of song, the only possible way to give vent to the emotion the rabbi's speech had stirred in them. A rousing *bentching* followed, with the traditional cup of wine passed from hand to hand. Then the group disbanded, some to seek sleep in the various rented apartments Esther had found for them around the neighborhood, others to tend children or stack dishes or pursue conversations begun at the lunch table. Esther, having shooed both Yoni and her husband, Zalman, off to well-deserved naps, was denied entrance to her own kitchen by a trio of Kahn girls who insisted on having the pleasure of clearing the meal away all by themselves. Sighing with the luxury of acquiescence, Esther made for the living-room sofa. Her brother was already ensconced in an ample armchair, a *sefer* in hand.

Avi put the *sefer* aside at her approach. "What's this? Do we actually get a few minutes to chat uninterrupted?"

She smiled and said, "I don't how long we'll be uninterrupted. Let's make the most of it while it lasts."

To the background music of muted clinking of plates and cutlery in the kitchen, and periodic bouts of soft giggling from the same place, brother and sister wandered from the present *simchah* to *simchahs* long past, and from there to memories of the parents they'd sat *shivah* for years before. Mellowed by the experience of being in this special city, a part of this special occasion, Avi found himself presently confiding in his sister in a way he had not intended to do. He told her about the Mirsky debacle — it seemed so far away from where he sat — and a little of what it had taught him about himself.

Esther, with her own painful education so recently behind her, was more understanding than he'd had any right to anticipate.

"We're two of a kind, you and me," she said unexpectedly.

He nodded. "Proud. Ambitious."

"Perfectionists, both of us. Hard-driving and demanding the best of those around us. Determined to have things our way." She grinned wryly. "I wonder why they put up with us."

"You forget one thing," he said. "We're also good choosers. We picked the right people to marry — ones who not only put up with us, but maybe even help tone us down a little."

She eyed him speculatively. "I do believe Malka has managed to tone you down, as you put it. You've changed, Avrumi." She paused, smiling in sudden recollection. "As a matter of fact, so have I. At least, that's what Tzippy says."

"And about time — for me, I mean. When I think about how a perfectly intelligent person can go around with blinkers on for so long — years and years, even — until something comes along to bump him on the head and wake him up a little!"

"*Baruch Hashem* for those bumps on the head," his sister said softly.

"Yes." And thank God, too, for his Malka and Esther's Zalman. Where would they be without the support and gentle guidance of those two extraordinary souls?

Zalman: the other side of the no-nonsense coin that was Esther Markovich. He softened the sharp edges of her nature and provided the sane, steady drumbeat to her melody. Though Esther ran the home, and ran it superlatively, Zalman was in many ways its fixed, quiet center.

And Malka. His Malka, whose exuberance and warmheartedness had never faltered through the years, ever present to offset his own blind, thrusting drive for success. If his trajectory had been that of a shooting star, then his wife was the soft night sky that formed its background and its meaning.

He smiled at his sister. "The truth? We're a couple of lucky stiffs. And we don't even deserve it."

Yoni was calling for her from his crib. Esther rose with a last nod for Avi as she turned to obey the summons.

"You never spoke a truer word," she said.

EPILOGUE

On the day before Avi was due to fly back to New York, his sister entrusted him with a commission.

"You're going to Geulah? I have something for you to take along, if you don't mind."

"I don't mind. I'm only a tourist around here; my time is yours to command. What is it?"

"Here." She went to the breakfront and extracted a silver Kiddush cup. "There's a dent here, near the bottom. Somebody got too enthusiastic during the *sheva berachos*, I guess. There's a wonderful silversmith in town. Ask him if he can have it ready for me by Shabbos."

"Will do." Avi took the goblet and the address from her, then called to his son. "Ready, Mutty?"

Mutty hurried to his side, planting his hat on his head as he went. "Ready. Need anything from Geulah, Aunt Esther?"

"I've already asked your father to do me a favor there." She looked longingly out the window to the balcony, and beyond, to where the leaves of the shade trees were gently moving against the fierce blue sky. "It's such a beautiful day."

"Why don't you come with us?" Avi urged. "Take a little break, Esther."

"What?" She sounded horrified. "And leave this mess? It'll take me days to dig out from under it. I can't believe the *sheva berachos* was two days ago already. I haven't gotten anywhere, hardly! And then there's Shoshie to get ready. I'll be doing plenty of shopping, believe me. Only not today."

"Some things," Avi remarked to no one in particular, "never change." He winked at Mutty.

His sister gave him a very speaking look, which dissolved into a smile. "Oh, go, you two. Enjoy your day."

It was truly a day made for enjoyment. A day of bone-soaking warmth with the gentlest hint of a breeze to fan away any discomfort. The leaves, so stridently green just a few weeks ago, were already fading just a little in the summer heat. They formed a persistent swishing accompaniment to the men as they walked down the street to the bus stop.

The ride was not too long, nor was the address in Avi's pocket difficult to find. Father and son entered the silversmith's shop and looked around with some curiosity.

As a workshop, the place had no pretensions. There were no fragile glass shelves to proclaim it a gallery, no artistic sign over the door to lure the tourists. This was a place where a craftsman did his work, quietly and single-mindedly. On every side were odd-looking machines, some with brushes and rollers attached, and the instruments of the silversmith's trade. The floor was cluttered with silver artifacts of every description: candlesticks, goblets, incense boxes, menorahs. Avi moved politely into an unoccupied corner and waited for the man to take notice of him.

The smith was busy with a customer carrying a huge, badly tarnished silver tray.

"Leave it here. I call you when it's ready," the silversmith concluded in the brusque though not discourteous tone of one whose mind has already moved on. When the door had jangled shut behind the woman, he turned to Avi. "Yes? What do you need?"

He was tall, taller than Avi had imagined at first, and very thin. With his gangly limbs and the shock of straight brown hair falling over his forehead, he resembled nothing so much as an animated scarecrow. He wore a striped apron over a surprisingly clean shirt and pants.

"There's a dent here," Avi showed him. "My sister wants to know if you can straighten it out for her. If you can have it ready in time for Shabbos, she'd appreciate it."

The man assessed him shrewdly and relaxed into a smile. "You're from America?"

Startled, Avi agreed that he was.

"And this is your son?"

"Yes. Why? Can you see a resemblance?"

"In the face, yes. But not in the personality."

Mutty stepped forward, intrigued. "Really? How can you tell?"

Shrugging, the man grew abruptly uninterested in the topic. "Come, I have a few minutes of quiet. You want to see how I do it?"

"You mean you'll do the cup right now?" Avi asked.

"Yes. You watch me."

Mutty and Avi exchanged a glance. They had no pressing business, and this looked like it might be interesting. They moved closer to the silversmith as he took the goblet to the first of his worktables.

What followed was a half-hour of almost complete silence, as the smith paid the closest and most minute attention to the details of his craft. His two visitors followed him around, absorbed as children at a master performance.

First, with a hammer, he removed the dent in the Kiddush cup. He held it up to the light to check the accuracy of his work, then set it down, hammered a bit more, and moved on to the brushing machine. Here, a set of stiff, round bristles whirred across the surface of the goblet, polishing it to a high gloss.

Avi thought he was finished then, but the silversmith had only begun. The cup was deposited in a bucket of some liquid, where it remained soaking while the craftsman, oblivious to the two observers, worked on one or two other small jobs. When the requisite number of minutes had passed, he scooped the goblet out of its bath, dried it, and subjected it to the ministrations of another fast-humming machine. Then he beckoned them into his inner workroom. "I do the gold now," he said, breaking the long silence.

"The what?" Mutty was the first one in after him, face alight with interest.

"I put gold inside. It is worn away, see?" He showed them the inside surface of the cup, where the original gold plating had been eroded to a patchy dullness. "With electric I do it. Here is the switch." He went over and flipped it. With gloved hands he inserted an electrode into the goblet. Nothing happened.

Again he flipped the switch, but the results were the same: negative.

"Something is wrong with the electric. Wait. I fix." Before their eyes, the silversmith turned electrician. He fiddled with wires for a few minutes, moving back and forth across the little room on his long, loose-jointed legs. Finally, the electricity worked. With the electrode in place, he smeared some substance on the inside of the cup and left the current going. "It will take a few minutes. Come, we can wait outside." He led them back to the outer workshop.

Avi was quiet, thinking over the steps of the intricate process. He never realized there was so much involved in maintaining silver. Mutty, however, was full of questions. He wanted an explanation of the way each machine worked and of the various fluids and pastes the man had used. This time, the silversmith seemed not at all averse to talking. He demonstrated again the process they had seen, addressing his comments exclusively to Mutty.

A tinging from the next room alerted him. "We go back now. The gold is finished."

He removed the electrode and switched off the current. The goblet was presented for their inspection.

"It's all yellow again inside!" Mutty exclaimed, studying it.

"Yes," said the craftsman. "I told you. I put in new gold."

Avi took the cup from Mutty. It had looked all right to him when he'd taken it from his sister that morning, but that other version paled beside the object he held now. Inside, the goblet gleamed with a new, pure gold; the outside surface of silver shone near-white. It was a thing to grace a king's table.

"It's beautiful," he said quietly. He actually hesitated before reaching for his wallet. It seemed sacrilegious, almost, to offer payment for such workmanship.

Avi was quiet for some time after their encounter with the silversmith. Mutty shared in the silence. He wanted to think about what he'd just seen and relate it to his own work. He'd felt right at home in that workshop, redolent with the tools and smells so peculiar to the craft they served. It was not so very different from his own carpentry shop in Lakewood, though wood shavings had littered the floor there, and sections of exquisitely turned-out bookcases had filled the floor space, not pieces of silver.

He paused in his walking to ask his father, "Penny for your thoughts, Ta? You've been awfully quiet today."

Avi shook himself awake. "I was just thinking. About Mommy, mostly. Wondering if I should bring her a new set of *leichter*. I know she'd love to have one. Our old candelabra is twenty-two years old and has seen better days. What do you think?"

"That silversmith inspired you." Mutty grinned.

"Yes, he did. A real craftsman, eh?"

"That's for sure."

People passed them, jostling, chattering, intent on their destinations. The streets were too narrow to accommodate the vast swarm of humanity that passed through them on any given day, but that was all part of the picturesqueness, Avi felt. Absently, he straightened his hat where someone had pushed it askew in an over-hasty passage.

Still thinking of silver candelabra, a vision rose all at once before his mind's eye: a man in a striped apron over scrupulously clean clothes, laboring with intense concentration at the craft he loved. Only, the man in the apron was not scarecrow-thin and six feet tall. He was medium-sized and short-bearded, and he had Mutty's face.

Avi moved to the side, so that he could stand by the wall and avoid the oncoming rush of pedestrians. "Mutty?" There was a strange note in his voice.

"Yes, Ta?"

"You're like him, aren't you? The craftsman."

Mutty was quiet for a long moment. Then he looked his father in the eye and answered, "Yes."

"An artist, in a way. Not a common laborer."

"Both, Ta," the son said firmly. "An artist *and* a laborer. There's no way to do it without getting your hands dirty. But I wouldn't want it any other way." There was the life of the mind and life of the body — and building something, creating some solid work of beauty from the intangible fancies of his own brain, was the incredible thing that bridged the two.

"I owe you an apology." Avi spoke slowly, as though he were working out his thoughts at the same time. "I didn't understand what you meant. I thought you were throwing something precious away, only to take up something of lesser value. But I had it wrong. You don't have to be a pulpit rabbi to realize your potential." *You don't have to be me.* "You can give to people — contribute to their lives — in other ways."

"I hope so. I can't imagine a sweeter existence than learning Torah part of the time and building beautiful things with the rest. One day I'll have to earn a living, Ta. Why can't I do it the way I know best?"

"Why not, indeed?" Avi said it softly, but Mutty heard. They smiled at each other.

"Pizza?" Avi asked. "Suddenly I'm hungry."

"I'm starved." As they executed a complex 180-degree maneuver to bring them to the door of the local pizza shop, Mutty added, "Are you going to get the *leichter* in the end?"

"I think so. I want to surprise your mother. She's been through a lot lately."

Hadn't they all? Mutty suddenly remembered something.

"Ta, about the shul. If you're still interested in the building campaign, Fish said he'd like to contribute something. He'll come up with a nice fat check, probably. After giving him Shoshie, he can't do enough for the Weisners!"

"I have something to tell you about that, Mutty. But let's order first."

Presently, the slices of pizza folded in their hands to allow the oil to drip down, Mutty prompted, "About the building fund?"

Avi took a bite. "I never actually stopped to think about it, but my friend Binyomin Hirsch is a very wealthy man. Seems he's been earning a six-figure income for years now with no one but himself to support. He's also earned a name as a generous philanthropist, though naturally he's kept that hidden from his closest friends."

"Meaning you."

"Exactly." The Coke was fizzy and ice-cold. Avi drank deeply, enjoying the feel of the cool paper cup against his overheated skin. The air was steamy from the huge pizza ovens and some two dozen or so patrons who'd had the same idea as they about the most convenient spot to have lunch.

"So he offered you a nice fat check, too?" Mutty asked.

"More than that. He offered to pay for the empty lot. With the mortgage we could get, the shul would be able to start building by next month if we want."

Mutty had stopped eating and was staring at his father. "Of course you want! Or," he stopped, alerted by something in the rabbi's face, "don't you?"

Slowly, Avi shook his head. "I told him thanks, but no thanks. Not for now. Not for a while."

"But why?"

How to explain? It was no easy thing for a father to tell his son he'd been guilty of the sin of arrogance; that he'd built a following based on the force of his personality as much as on the fruit of his Torah; and that he would not erect a temple to that personality. Maybe someday, when he'd done the work of exorcising the seed of pride — maybe then he'd think again about a shul of his own. But by that time, he knew, it would mean something entirely different to him.

"I have my reasons," was all he said in the end, lightly. "No offence, but some things are a little hard to talk about. You know how it is."

Mutty knew. He nodded, eating his pizza and remembering Avi's last Thursday-night appearance. The rented shul had, as always, been packed for the popular *shiur*. Rows of men below, and women in the balcony, had filled the pews, minds and recorders ready at the push of a button to go into record mode.

But something had been different that night. The difference had not been in the shul or in the audience, Mutty thought, but in his father.

The Avi who spoke that night had been subdued, as though he'd decided to deliberately mute the power of his own personality. A gossamer veil had been thrown over the famous Weisner charisma, so that the *shiur*'s impact derived less from who he was and more from what he was saying. The lesson itself had carried the message home to the listeners and not the verbal pyrotechnics of the rabbi up on the podium.

Somehow — Mutty didn't know just how — this was all tied up with the rabbi's refusal of Binyomin's staggering offer. And did it matter, really? His father was willing to accept him, even without a full and logical spelling-out of his inner agenda. Mutty would just have to do the same for him.

He looked up to find his father smiling at him.

"I don't know when I'll have my own shul," the rabbi said. "But when I do, I know who I'm going to commission to build my *aron kodesh*." The smile widened. "Maybe you'd better start thinking about it already, Mutty. I want it to be the most stunning thing you've ever created."

There was something in Mutty's throat that made it hard for him to speak. He took a swig of Coke, set his cup down precisely opposite his father's, and said with quiet determination — as from one master craftsman to another — "You'll have it, Ta."